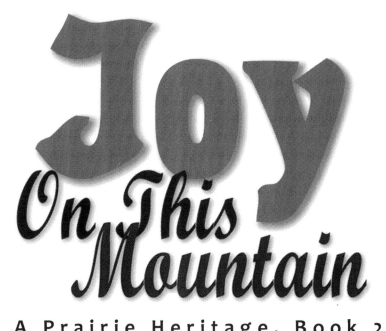

Joy On This Mountain

A Prairie Heritage, Book 2

by
Vikki Kestell

www.vikkikestell.com
www.facebook.com/TheWritingOfVikkiKestell

A Prairie Heritage

Book 1: *A Rose Blooms Twice*
Book 2: *Joy on This Mountain*

Scriptures quotations taken from
The King James Version (KJV), Public Domain.

New Living Translation (NLT) Holy Bible.
New Living Translation copyright© 1996, 2004, 2007
by Tyndale House Foundation.
Used by permission of Tyndale House Publishers Inc.,
Carol Stream, Illinois 60188. All rights reserved.

Joy on This Mountain
Vikki Kestell

Also Available in Kindle Format

The little town of Corinth, Colorado, lies in the gateway to the majestic Rocky Mountains just west of Denver . . . just far enough from the city to avoid close scrutiny, but close enough to be accessible. Few know of the wickedness hidden in the small town, so picturesquely set in the foothills of the mighty mountains.

Joy on This Mountain is the eagerly-awaited sequel to *A Rose Blooms Twice* and is Book 2 in the series, *A Prairie Heritage*. The legacy of Jan and Rose has far-reaching and unexpected consequences.

A Rose Blooms Twice
Vikki Kestell

Available in Kindle and Print Format

Rose Brownlee must choose whether she will bow to conventional wisdom or, like Abraham, follow where God leads her . . . even to a country she does not know.

Set in the American prairie of the late 1800s, this story of loss, disillusionment, rebirth, and love will inspire, challenge, and encourage you. *A Rose Blooms Twice* is Book 1 in the series, *A Prairie Heritage*.

Dedication

Dedicated to all those who give their lives to rescue and bring the healing of Jesus the Messiah to those who have been oppressed.

Acknowledgements

Many thanks to my esteemed proofreaders, Cheryl Adkins and Greg McCann. I could not have done this without you! The Lord reward and bless you.

To My Readers

This book is a work of fiction, what I term "faith-filled fiction." The town of Corinth, Colorado, and the events in this book that occur there are not based on any known historical facts. The *types* of events described are, however, *very real*, both historically and contemporarily.

To God be the glory.

Chapter 1

The Spirit of the Lord is upon me . . .
He has sent me to proclaim that captives will be released . . .
(Luke 4:18, NLT)

August 1908

Rose finished her difficult climb and crested the rise behind their house. She slowly straightened her stiff back, her breath coming hard. Below her, nestled picturesquely between the knoll and a meandering creek, stood their home, the place where she and Jan had lived, loved, dreamed, and raised their family.

Across the creek and away to the east stretched the fields that belonged to Jan's son, Søren, and two of his cousins, Karl and Kjell. Their families, homes, and barns were surrounded by their well-ordered crops.

Rose turned toward the sinking sun. Their fields, hers and Jan's, lay before her. The drying stalks of their harvested corn waved in a gentle breeze. Rose searched through the shadows beginning to fall upon the field, her hand held to her eyes against the waning light.

There.

Rose spotted the young woman, on the far side of the field, her face turned toward the dropping sun. Even from this distance, Rose could tell the woman was staring out into the vast prairie, her shoulders bowed.

Rose's heart twisted a little. It would be best not to approach her right now. Rose's comfort would not be welcome. Not at this time.

Sighing, Rose looked back toward their little white house, the center of so much happiness. She looked for and found her husband of 26 years staring back at her. He leaned heavily against the rails of the veranda that wrapped around the house. Rose knew that he was as concerned as she was, but he was unable to climb the hill she stood on, no longer able to till or harvest their fields.

"Oh Lord," she murmured. "You are our Rock. Our strong High Tower. Our Fortress. Our strength in time of need. O God, we need you now."

She turned again toward the solitary woman across the field and remembered . . . remembered the summer day she came into their lives.

Late summer 1883

The heat in the house was oppressive. Sweat ran from Rose's face and soaked the pillow and her hair. She strained with a contraction.

"Jan," she moaned. "Jan!" The contraction peaked and she fell back against the pillow.

She had endured more than 24 hours of hard labor yet the baby just would not come. Rose had given birth three times before this, the children of her first marriage, but none had taken as long or been as difficult. As another contraction took her, Rose felt her strength ebbing and her hope and resolution slipping.

"Jan . . . Jan, please," she whispered as the constricting band about her eased momentarily.

Fiona leaned over her and wiped her brow. "Whist? Jan?"

"Yes . . . Jan . . ." she moaned through cracked lips. "I need him."

Moments later Jan slipped to the side of her bed and took her hand. Rose looked up and, voice shaking, whispered, "Jan, I don't think I can do . . . this . . . it's taking too long . . . and, and . . . something must be wrong . . . I'm so . . . sorry." She stared at his dear face in shame and regret.

"*Nei*, Rose."

His eyes, those blue, blue eyes, captured her soft gray ones as another contraction took her. Neither of them looked away; they remained fixed on each other until the pain eased again.

Jan began to speak, willing her to hear and be strengthened. His eyes never left hers as he spoke, his words awash with faith and resolve. "Listen, my li'l Rose!"

> *"Da Lord ist mine light an' mine salvation;*
> *whom shall I fear?*
> *da Lord ist da strength of mine life;*
> *of whom shall I be afraid?*
> *. . . For in da time of trouble he shall hide me in his pavilion:*
> *in da secret of his tabernacle shall he hide me;*
> *. . . I had fainted, unless I had believed*
> *to see da goodness of da Lord in da lan' of da living.*

> *Vait on da Lord: be of good courage,
> an' he shall strengthen thine heart: vait, I say, on da Lord."*

"In da lan' of da living, Rose. We vill see his goodness in *da lan' of the living*. Be of good courage, my Rose."

Another contraction began as Rose was muttering, "Be of good courage . . . he shall strengthen my heart . . . wait on the Lord . . . my heart will not fear . . ."

Her breath rasped as she struggled with yet another unproductive birth pang. Another. Again. Another. And another.

And then—water gushed from between her legs. The contractions came without reprieve now, one atop each other, relentless, without mercy. Suddenly an urgent need to push overtook her.

An hour later Rose lay exhausted and limp, while Fiona and Amalie gently cleaned and dressed her. Finally Amalie, her kind face smiling broadly, laid a tiny bundle on Rose's chest. Rose's arms trembled with fatigue as she struggled to hold the bundle. The bedroom door opened softly and Rose felt her husband leaning over her.

"Ist vell, Rose?" Rose heard the depth of concern and care in his voice. Her eyes drifted up to his deep glacier ones.

"Our daughter," she breathed. She felt the warmth of the tiny body against her breasts, felt the small rise and fall of the baby's breath.

"Ah, Rose! Our babe." Jan sat on the edge of the bed and tenderly slipped his work-rough hands under the bundle. Lifting the newborn he turned back the blanket and revealed to both of them a tuft of white-blonde hair and a crinkled pink face.

Rose thought her heart would stop, so great was the love that washed over her at that moment. She looked to her husband. His face was buried in the baby's blanket and she heard his muffled sobs.

Rose had never seen, never heard her husband cry so and, as his weeping intensified, tears began to stream down her face also.

She knew too well why he cried. He cried for the loss of his other daughter, Kristen, and her mother, Elli. For the many years of grief and loneliness he had suffered.

Rose cried for the husband and children she had lost three years before . . . James, and their children, Jeffrey, Glory, Clara. Gone in a few agonizing moments, claimed by a river of ice one fateful evening.

She also wept for the new love and companionship God had granted her with this good man. For the comfort and healing of this baby—for the renewal and purpose this child would bring them.

She knew they wept for joy.

"Oh dear God, I denk you!" Jan sobbed. He held the baby to his chest with one hand while his other hand tenderly caressed Rose's cheek. "I denk you, O Fat'er God!"

Finally, their tears eased, and Jan wiped his eyes on the corner of the baby's blanket.

"Such joy, my Rose! Such joy," he whispered.

"Yes," Rose answered tearfully. "Joy."

Their eyes met and they slowly nodded in agreement.

Jan looked down on the tiny face and murmured, "Little girl, you are Joy!"

"Joy Again," Rose added. "She is our Joy Again."

"Joy Again," Jan repeated, tasting the words for the first time. He smiled and nodded . . .

Rose roused herself from those precious memories and turned again to the tall figure across the field. How had so many years flown by?

And how had so much been undone so easily?

Chapter 2

April 1902

Arnie Thoresen smiled contentedly at his pleasant wife, his healthy young sons, and his cousin, Joy, who had just arrived in Omaha. They were finishing lunch outdoors at a sidewalk café, and it was a very lovely late spring day. Arnie hadn't seen his much younger cousin for more than two years. He leaned back, relaxed and replete from the meal, and indulged in his favorite pastime: people watching.

At almost 19 years old, Joy was proving herself to be a charming, unspoiled young lady. She was tall for a woman but as slender and supple as a willow branch. Her thick, white-blonde hair, inherited from her Norwegian father, hung to her waist in a silken sheaf. She wore it more in the mode of the last century than in the manner of a modern woman of the 1900s. Arnie liked that immensely.

Joy's father and Arnie's father had been brothers. Arnie, compared to Joy, was also tall but broad rather than lean, and he sported a shaggy head of dark-blond hair. Unlike his brothers, who remained on the family's farm, Arnie had chosen to study law and establish a practice in the city.

Arnie listened as Joy praised something Arnie's older son Petter said, her hand resting on Petter's arm. It was obvious that both of his boys were smitten with their second cousin.

Arnie grinned as Joy declared that Petter was "brilliant" and the young man reddened in both embarrassment and delight. Petter's little brother, Willem, punched Petter under the table, and attempted to distract Joy's attention toward himself. Arnie and Anna exchanged amused glances.

Arnie's hand was dangling over the arm of his chair when he felt a warm, wet nose snuffle his hand. Startled, he momentarily jerked his hand away and looked down into the soft brown eyes of a black-and-white border collie. The dog nudged his hand again and Arnie rubbed between his ears.

"Arnie! It's good to see you."

Arnie turned to find the greeter. "Grant! The pleasure is mine. How are you keeping?"

"Fine, fine; thank you for asking. I see Blackie found you. He never forgets a friend." Grant Michaels snapped a leash onto the dog and nodded and smiled at the group. And then saw Joy Thoresen. And stared.

Joy stared right back, her lips slightly parted. Petter and Willem looked from Grant to Joy and back and then glared. Arnie shook his head and smothered a chuckle.

"Grant, I believe you know my wife, Anna?"

"Pleasure," Grant muttered, still staring.

"And these are my sons, Petter and Willem."

"Pleased to meet you," Grant nodded in their general direction.

Petter and Willem's eyes narrowed and drilled holes in Grant.

"And this is my cousin, Joy Thoresen. She has just arrived in Omaha and will be staying with us this summer. Joy, this is my good friend, Grant Michaels."

Grant reached across the table to gently shake Joy's hand. He smiled into her deep blue eyes.

Joy smiled back and said sweetly, "Won't you join us, Mr. Michaels?"

"I'm so sorry; I believe we've finished lunch and were just leaving," Petter stated flatly.

Willem added in an icy tone, "Yup. Too bad you can't join us 'cause we're a-leavin'."

As if he hadn't heard, Grant Michaels seated himself across from Joy. Blackie laid himself down under Grant's chair.

"How long have you had your dog, Mr. Michaels?" Joy asked.

"Blackie and I have been pals since he was a pup. He's grown now at five years old, and he is a good dog and loyal friend."

Joy could not take her eyes off this new acquaintance. He was a little taller than she was with a riot of dark brown hair curling around his face and his laughing hazel eyes.

Such lovely hazel eyes . . .

Since Grant was both Arnie's friend and business acquaintance, conversation that day was uncomplicated and natural. On Sunday, Joy spied Grant across the filled pews of Arnie and Anna's little church. He smiled and nodded at her and she found him lingering after the service to greet the family. Of course, Anna invited him home for Sunday dinner.

Over the next several weeks, wherever the Thoresens happened to be in town, Grant Michaels somehow also "happened" to be there.

He happened to meet them when he was walking Blackie, he spied them outside the milliners, he encountered them in the library, he chanced upon them out at dinner. He and Blackie became frequent dinner guests at Arnie and Anna's. Before long he was calling at their home for Joy, taking her on drives and to church functions.

She and Grant talked effortlessly about everything, and he truly listened when Joy spoke. He was the only person she had ever shared her whole heart with. He wanted to know everything about her; he plied her with questions and she willingly responded.

She confided in him, "I come from a large family—only one brother, but oh, so many cousins, nephews, nieces, and second cousins! We are always teasing each other."

"From the time I was a little girl I could do sums in my head, quickly and effortlessly, even complicated ones. All my cousins, Arnie, too, teased me and tried to set sums I couldn't solve without pencil and paper. It became a family pastime—'see if we can stump Joy with this one'! But I could always solve those sums, no matter how large or difficult."

Grant was, of course, intrigued and had to try her also. Then he was simply amazed as she rattled off the solutions to each problem he set before her.

"I love our farm back in RiverBend. It is only a typical, small Nebraska farm, but it was a wonderful place to grow up! Even so, Papa and Mama knew how much I wanted to go to college." She ducked her head modestly. "I just finished my course of study at business college."

Her papa and mama had realized that their daughter would never be completely happy on a farm or teaching school. They had wisely sent her to a small business college for women—still a new and audacious concept for females in the year 1900. Joy had loved it and had thrived on every course of study she undertook.

"No! You cannot be that old," Grant teased.

Joy laughed back at him. "I went at 17, sir, and graduated after less than two years. I now possess a thorough understanding of business and accounting."

"What! You intend to work, then?" He loved to see her eyes spark when he teased her. Indeed, he was growing to love everything about this woman.

"I do. Why, this is a new century! The world is changing. I want to change with it," Joy replied saucily. "Cousin Arnie doesn't know it yet, but I intend to convince him that he cannot get along without my skills in his law office. So you see, kind sir, I have a plan."

She just hadn't planned on Grant Michaels!

Grant gently took Joy's hand, and for some reason her heart began to hammer in her chest, in her throat, in the tips of her fingers. "Dear Joy . . ." he murmured softly. "I have a plan also, and I'm wondering . . ."

She looked up into his face, his curly hair framing those lovely eyes and, with awe, saw love staring back at her. "You are wondering?"

"Yes, I'm wondering, dear Joy . . . if your plan is also your dream."

"My dream?" Oh, would her heart *please* stop choking her!

"Yes, you see . . . *my* plan is also my dream, the vision of my future that I believe the Lord has given me. It is the dream I cannot live without. So . . . I'm wondering, you see, if your plan is the dream *you* cannot live without. Because you see, my dear, dear Joy Again Thoresen, you are absolutely essential to my dream. Without you . . . well, you see, it wouldn't be my dream any longer. It would be merely a plan."

"Oh!" Joy could not breathe, could not swallow.

"Dear Joy, will you marry me? I love you as I love my life. I cannot have a dream, a future, in which you are not my heroine and partner for life."

Joy disintegrated into tears. Grant pulled her gently into his arms and, with her face buried in the lapel of his suit coat, he caressed and stroked her hair while whispering every endearment and vow of affection he had stored up in his heart.

As her sobs finally eased, he lifted her face to his. "Does this mean yes or no, my dearest?"

"Yeeees." Joy squeaked at last.

He nodded solemnly. "So in the future, when you soak my suit coat, shirt, and cravat with your tears, I'll know you are inexpressibly happy?" He was bursting with delight, but could not resist teasing her, if only a little.

"Oh, Grant!" and Joy gladly surrendered to his arms again.

Of course Jan and Rose insisted on knowing every detail about Grant Michaels. They traveled from RiverBend to Omaha and scrutinized him from all possible angles, but Grant passed their inspections handily: He was, of most importance, a man who truly loved God. In addition, he was showing himself to be devoted to their daughter and to providing for a family. Grant earned Jan and Rose's respect and approval, and in every way he was all Joy could want in a friend and husband.

Instead of the carefree summer she had anticipated, the next two months were filled with wedding plans and preparations. Friends and family showered Grant and Joy with good wishes and gifts to begin their lives together.

They said their vows before the Lord on a Saturday in late August, not long after Joy's nineteenth birthday. The church they attended in Omaha was overflowing with dear friends and family: Jan and Rose; Joy's half brother Søren, his wife Meg, and their five children; cousins Sigrün, Kjell, and Karl and their families; dear friends (and Meg's parents) Brian and Fiona McKennie; and Pastor and Mrs. Medford, all who traveled from RiverBend to attend the wedding.

One face sorely missed in the congregation that day was Joy's Aunt Amalie. She had gone home to the Lord three years before.

Arnie, Anna, Petter, Willem, and their church family in Omaha also celebrated with them. And Joy's dearest cousin Uli, her husband David Kalbørg, and their three children traveled from their home in Colorado to share Joy and Grant's happy day.

While Grant had many friends in the community who attended the wedding, he no longer had family other than two cousins who lived in Maryland. His parents and only sister had passed away when he was scarcely grown to manhood.

At the altar Arnie stood up with Grant, and Uli stood up with Joy. Although nine years separated the Uli and Joy, Joy had been the little sister of Uli's heart. Uli was Sigrün, Karl, Arnie, and Kjell's baby sister; their father, Jan's brother Karl, had died before Uli was born, and Jan had been the only father figure she had ever known.

When Jan and Rose married and had baby Joy, Uli had promptly appropriated Joy as her own. Some of Joy's earliest memories were of Uli smiling over her cradle, reading to her, playing with her, and being everything a big sister could be. When Uli married and moved away, Joy had been a devastated little 10-year-old girl.

As the organ played, Joy floated down the aisle on her papa's arm. Happy tears trickled down Rose's face as she watched the two people dearest to her—her husband, still blonde and handsome at 74, and her daughter, blooming, all pinks and whites, her eyes shining for the man anxiously waiting for her at the altar.

Grant slipped a gold band, the token of his love and promise to Joy, on the ring finger of her left hand. "With this ring, I thee wed . . ."

Chapter 3

Fall 1907

Over the next years, Joy became Grant's partner in business as well as in life. Grant owned a tool store on the growing edge of Omaha's downtown district and had funneled all his ingenuity and industry into making it a success.

While still specializing in tools, before long he was able to expand into general hardware and farm implements. The sign above the store declared in gold-edged letters, "Michaels' Tools, Hardware, and Farm Implements."

Joy was enthralled with their business and loved every part of the store—the heavy, oversized entrance doors with their brass hardware and beautifully lettered glass; the distinctive hollow thud of footsteps on the rough, wood-planked floors; the warm smell of oiled leather; and aisles lined with bins chock-full of nails, tacks, screws, washers, nuts, hinges, knobs, and bolts.

She loved the worn-smooth wooden countertops where their customers did their business and she loved the cheery oil stove in the center of the store where people gathered during the winter to warm their hands on mugs of coffee and swap news and stories.

Blackie, who befriended every customer, padded freely among the aisles, gently nudging willing hands. Grant kept a basket for Blackie near the stove and here he warmed his aging bones during the cold season.

"Good old dog," Grant would murmur, rubbing Blackie's ears affectionately. "Good old dog."

Joy loved doing the store's books and prided herself on keeping the ledgers and balancing them every day. Most of all, she loved the life of their store, how she and Grant and their employees served so many people's needs and how Michaels' was a needed and appreciated part of their community.

However, after more than five years of marriage, a void remained in their union. For some reason, children had not arrived. Joy suffered no miscarriages and her cycle was regular. Grant and Joy prayed, but their family did not increase. Joy watched and wondered as their friends' families bloomed and grew.

Joy recognized that if she allowed herself to dwell on their lack of children she could become despondent. Her parents had taught her that self-pity was not of God, so she focused her time and energy on what she and Grant were building.

They loved and served the Lord together, they had a contented home, and they worked side-by-side, gradually expanding their business and reputation. Instead of buying a house, they chose to make a comfortable home over the store and offices so that they could grow without debt. And they grew in their love.

"My dear, I shall miss my train!" Grant laughed as Joy caught him and kissed him again at the door. "And you know full well Arnie and Petter are waiting outside to take me to the station."

"I don't care! Must you go?" Joy responded half-playfully, holding his jacket tightly. "Six weeks is such a long time! And it might be longer if the crossing is difficult."

She wasn't pouting. Well, not exactly anyway. And she didn't mind shouldering Grant's responsibilities in his absence. It was only that her heart would not be whole as long as he was away.

Grant knew. He always knew what bothered her and always felt a separation as keenly as she did.

"I shall not be gone one day, one moment longer than I must, my darling," he whispered, cupping her chin to look into her deep blue eyes. "We agreed, did we not, on this venture?"

"Yes . . ." Joy answered reluctantly.

Because of their frugal living, they had managed to save enough to buy the building next to their store. Opening a second store, one specializing in fine household goods, would diversify their line of business. The new store was to be Joy's special domain.

"We know the need is there," she admitted. "You must go to Boston and on to England to select our inventory and establish our suppliers. But I do so wish I were going with you."

"Nothing would give me more pleasure," Grant smiled. "But who would we leave in charge while we were gone? Mr. Wheatley? Mr. Taub? Billy?"

They both laughed. Mr. Wheatley was near 70 years old and, although always proper, usually projected a frenzied demeanor, no doubt aided by a head of wispy, perpetually on-end hair. In reality he was as reliable as the sunrise and served their customers well.

Unfortunately he also had no head for accounts and began yawning each day at 4 p.m.

Mr. Taub, who managed their farm implements, was efficient but could be a bit imperious, even with the store's clientele! Billy Evans, their youngest employee, always wore an infectious grin and tore through his duties with the indefatigable energy of youth. Although he was just past 20 years old, he was already head and shoulders above most grown men. Like a young bull he sometimes bowled over or scattered customers in his wake.

No, it was clear to both of them that Joy must remain and manage while Grant was gone.

"All right, darling, I'll let you go before you miss your train," and Joy released his jacket, smoothing it as she did. "Do you have the list? You will pay special attention to the few notes I made?"

Grant laughed. "My dear, I would not dream of misplacing this 'list,' although a list of eight detailed pages surely qualifies as a treatise rather than 'a few notes'?"

"Do not tease me, Grant Michaels," Joy retorted. "Sending a man to select fine linens, china, and quality furnishings requires the detailed guidance of a woman with *discriminating* taste." She added with mock hauteur, "You must thoroughly acquaint yourself with my notes so that our store is stocked appropriately and *with taste*."

She stopped and then gripped him anxiously again. "Come home soon, my love. The Lord bless you in all you do while you are gone."

Grant held her close and whispered for both of them, "Father, we thank you for this new opportunity. We thank you for your grace and mercy every day. Your grace is sufficient for us, Lord. Thank you for watching over us. Thank you for comforting my beloved while I am gone. In the name of Jesus we pray. Amen."

"Amen," Joy echoed.

Joy received an enthusiastic letter from Grant 11 days later. He had spent five days in Boston searching the stores and warehouses for goods and was satisfied with his contacts and orders.

> *I embark on the Richmond the day after tomorrow.*
> *The Richmond, while not the newest steamer on the*
> *seas, will make excellent time, and should dock in*
> *Liverpool after no more than 10 days.*

> *When I return to Boston in four weeks or thereabouts,*
> *I will conclude arrangements with our new suppliers*
> *and take the earliest train home to you. Be advised*
> *that I shall not let you out of my sight or my arms for*
> *a week.*

Joy smiled and warmed at the thought of Grant's arms around her.

Chapter 4

Grant leaned far out over the rail of the *Richmond* as space grew between the ship and the Boston docks on that brisk fall morning. He watched with fascination the water churning under the hull of the ship far below. The rails of the many-decked liner, both above and below his level, were lined with passengers waving to loved ones on the crowded pier. Slowly the tugs alongside of them eased them away from the docks and out into the open water.

It would be an hour before the ship cleared the congested shipping lanes of Massachusetts Bay and began to steam at full speed. Their route would take them north and east, skirting Nova Scotia before arcing across the great expanse of the Atlantic to the British Isles. They would dock at Liverpool, England's great industrial port on her west coast, north of Wales and across the Irish Sea from Dublin.

The captain had cautioned that they would be dashing through a light storm as they neared mid-afternoon, but he expected the ship to pass through it quickly. Grant, after meeting his cabin mate and settling his luggage, set out to explore the vessel from stem to stern, intrigued with all he saw.

Richmond was a modest passenger liner just past her prime. She'd been well maintained and had crossed the Atlantic countless times in her 20-some years at sea. Grant noted some wear and weathering, but he also saw evidence of the care of *Richmond's* masters.

The first mate observed Grant's curiosity and called cordially to him. "She's an aging lady, but a grand one, sir. Don't worry about her! She'll be plying the sea for another 20 years, I wager." The mate touched his hat in respect and resumed his watch.

At noon Grant ate a light lunch and afterwards took a brisk walk on the promenade. Toward mid-day the sky began to darken to their south and the seas began to pick up. Grant reluctantly retired to his cabin to read. Before long, however, his cabin mate took to his bed in distress, obviously suffering sea sickness.

The ship forged steadily through the rough waters, but Grant soon found it impossible to be inside while the ship battled the growing wind and waves. His cabin mate groaned again on his cot and retched.

Grant's stomach tossed a little too, and his cabin mate's distress was not helping. Craving fresh air to set him right, he donned a hooded slicker and went out of the cabin. He made his way down the hall to the closed hatch that led to their level's covered passage on the port side of the ship. He pulled it open and stepped outside.

Aside from a few scurrying crew members, he was alone. The sky, a sickly shade of yellow, hung thickly down upon the ship. The sea pitched violently, and the *Richmond* alternately rose and dropped in an erratic manner.

The "light storm" the captain had predicted seemed to be something much more. Grant set out to find and ask someone about it. He grasped the rail as a blast of wind sheared down the side of the ship, staggering him.

A sailor in full oilskins, holding the rail and crabbing down the walkway toward him, hollered above the keening wind, "Eh! Another like that one'll put ya over the side if'n you don't have a care, sir! Best to be inside, I'm thinkin'."

Grant agreed and acknowledged the sailor's concern but shouted back, "I thought the captain said this was to be a light storm!"

"Aye," the man called into the wind. "But 'tis blowin' a nor'easter. Turribly unpredictable they are. No tellin' how long or bad she'll be."

As though to punctuate the storm's unpredictability, stinging rain began to pummel the ship. The sailor hustled away. Grant followed the man's example and pulled himself down the deck, grasping the rail hand-over-hand.

Then the sea did not pitch—it simply opened before the ship. He stared over the side as they swooped down into the hole the ocean presented to them.

"Dear God!" he exclaimed in horror, unable to look away.

As large as the liner was, the hole was surely larger. Finally, the *Richmond* nosed back up, but the wind veered freakishly again, hammering them from the side. The ship lurched over to starboard and momentarily wallowed. Grant lost his grip on the rail and slammed up against the ship's wall. He quickly regained his feet and the rail. He continued to haul himself down the railing until he came to the closed hatch that led back into the shelter of the cabins.

A crack of thunder right atop them momentarily stunned him. Then he threw himself at the hatch and grasped the handle—it would not turn! He pounded and pushed against the hatch to no avail. Grant felt the ship leap into the air again as the wild ocean rose—and then dropped from under them.

Realizing how precarious his situation was, Grant again threw himself on the rail. To his right was a round life preserver tied off to the railing. He looped his arm through the ropes that secured the preserver and hunkered down on the deck, wrapping his legs about a railing post. Through the white bars of the railing he saw the sea open again to suck them down. They were dropping . . . and overhead the shadow of a mammoth wave grew.

As the wall of water slammed into them from above, Grant clung for his life to the rail, grateful for the ropes securing him. His legs washed out from under him, but he held on, choking on the frothing salt water.

Suddenly he dropped to the deck. Safe! O thanks be to God!

The howling wind dropped off abruptly. The surface of the sea smoothed. Grant prayed the worst was over. After several moments he began to hope.

But it was not to be.

The ocean rose again, higher and higher, and a scream of agony ripped the air, the shriek, not of wind, but of rending iron and steel. The *Richmond* stood atop the sea, her bow hanging over an abyss. Down the length of the ship Grant saw it all . . . the bow end of the *Richmond* bending toward him, then with a screeching rend of metal . . . twisting and falling away.

There would be no surviving this storm.

As the rest of the ship began to tilt forward, Grant spoke softly. "O Lord, into your hands I commit my spirit."

Through the rain Grant saw people, machinery, and debris dropping from the broken ship into the chasm. And then the rest of the ship lurched over and followed.

Chapter 5

Arnie Thoresen held the morning newspaper in stunned disbelief. The headline, in three-inch black type proclaimed, "STORM SINKS *RICHMOND*." He stumbled to his feet grasping the paper, trying to read, trying to comprehend the article.

> *The ocean-going passenger steamer,* Richmond, *out of Boston en route to Liverpool, is reported to have sunk Monday last during a fierce nor'easter.* Richmond *had departed Boston less than 10 hours prior to encountering the unseasonable storm, and is believed to have gone down southwest of the Canadian province of Nova Scotia. Debris found washed up along the coast between Yarmouth and Clark's Harbour, Nova Scotia, has been positively identified as from the* Richmond.
>
> *American and Canadian vessels conducted a fruitless three-day search for survivors following Monday's storm. The ship is listed with a complement of 175 officers and crew and 523 passengers. All hands and passengers are believed lost.*

Joy was already in the store's office when a pounding on the front door distracted her from her task. Blackie, curled near her office door, whined.

"It is more than an hour until we open," she fussed, deciding to ignore the early customer. When the pounding grew more demanding, she tossed her pencil down and strode to the large double doors at the front of the store, Blackie padding along next to her.

"Why, Arnie! What on earth," Joy remonstrated as she unlatched the door and took one look at his distraught face.

Tears filling his eyes, he mutely held out the crumpled newspaper to her. Joy lifted it and began to read.

The world slowed and her arms and legs ceased to belong to her. Staggering backwards, she fell to the floor senseless.

Joy knew she would die, hoped she would die. Surely it was a mistake. She had only received Grant's letter yesterday! He was *not* already dead, drowned, when she had read his loving words!

She refused to believe it. Grant would be home soon—*had* to be home soon!

But day after day passed. Newspapers reported more wreckage washing up in Nova Scotia. And then a small number of bodies. And Grant did not come home. Would never come home.

Joy's papa and mama came as quickly as they could, as did her brother Søren and her cousins Uli, Karl, Kjell, Sigrün, and their families, their grief as profound as hers. Her papa held her tightly to his chest and they stood together as she wept and wept. Her mama had to pull her away before Jan fell to the floor, his legs no longer able to support him.

Later Rose found them in the same manner. Jan shook his head at Rose and endured the pain of his weak, crippled knees. He would suffer anything to comfort his little girl. So Rose stood and held them both.

A week later, after a memorial service for Grant, Joy's family returned to their homes with the exception of Rose and Jan. Rose cooked and cleaned and watched her husband carefully. He would be 80 years old the following spring, God willing, and she tried not to wonder how much longer she would have him with her.

Joy spent hours staring at the gold band she wore on her left hand. Except for the business and Blackie, it was the most tangible reminder of Grant she still possessed. As long as she wore it, she could keep him close to her. As long as it gleamed upon her hand she could deny that they were parted forever.

As she mourned, she cast about for something to grasp and hold on to. Poor Blackie received many tears into his furry back, and Joy took to keeping him always near her.

Although she prayed, the emptiness was constantly upon her, pulling her into despair. Soon she determined to return to the store. It would provide the order and structure she craved and would stave off the void that seemed to loom wherever she turned.

She would shoulder every responsibility of the business—and in so doing prevent herself from breaking into a million pieces. But she vowed she would never take off the golden promise she wore on the ring finger of her left hand.

Chapter 6

April, 1908, Omaha

In the months following Grant's death, Joy worked steadily to prove to their customers that they could still depend on the store to meet their needs. Her community was sympathetic, but suppliers were more difficult. Grant had taken a large portion of their savings with him to buy inventory for the new store. Joy tapped into the balance of their bank account to pay ahead on orders so that the store had an uninterrupted flow of goods.

Six weeks after Grant departed Boston on the *Richmond*, the fine household goods he had ordered arrived. Joy had put them out of her mind, and their unexpected appearance affected her like the arrival of a message from the grave.

With no heart or energy to open a second shop, she ordered the goods stored, unopened, in a warehouse near the station. She needed to give herself time. Time to grieve, time to decide how to dispose of the goods, and time to rent out the empty building they had purchased for the fine furnishings shop.

She hired two additional workers, both reputable, knowing that many eyes were watching the store for any sign of weakness or failure. Some in the Omaha community, she realized with a shock, were hoping for her failure.

Her parents wished to stay longer. Joy knew, though, that her father needed to be home, close to his fields, even though Søren and his boys managed them now. Jan stood and walked with such difficulty and pain. Joy knew that her father was 20 years older than her mother but he had always been the immovable rock of their family. She couldn't bear to face his decline, especially while she was still reeling from the loss of Grant. When Jan and Rose finally returned to RiverBend, Joy found she was somewhat relieved.

After six months without any lapse in supply or standards, the Omaha community seemed to accept that Joy was at the helm of the business. She handled that helm mostly from her office, but her windows overlooked the store floor, and her keen eyes knew what needed direction and improvement. She held her staff to high standards and, as she withdrew into herself more and more, they became the face of Michaels' Tools, Hardware, and Farm Implements.

Against the odds, Joy was succeeding, and some days she nearly forgot her crushing grief. Forgot until the staff turned out the lights and locked up and she was faced with climbing the stairs to the dark, empty apartment with only Blackie at her side. Joy began spending evenings in her office until her eyes could remain open no longer.

Once a week after work she spent an evening with Arnie and his family. Petter and Willem loved her selflessly and she doted on them. Those visits were both blessing and curse, for as much as she needed each of them and looked forward to the company, the visits reminded her of Grant and all that was now gone.

When she stopped driving herself long enough to reflect, she knew in her heart that she was not dealing with her grief; she was only masking it with hard work and the exterior of a tough business woman. She knew she had grown distant and abrupt with her staff and had developed an exacting attitude with them and others who did work for her.

Unfortunately, she sometimes carried that hardness to Arnie and Anna's house. Arnie made an exasperated observation one evening. "You remind me of your father, Joy. You have developed his toughness and stoicism. Except he has always been fair and kind."

Joy blushed in shame at the recollection.

One afternoon in August she received a caller at the store. Perhaps in his mid-30s, dressed well and quite professionally, he introduced himself as Henry Robertson.

"Mrs. Michaels, thank you for seeing me," he smiled as he took a seat in front of her desk.

"It is my pleasure, Mr. Robertson. How may I be of service?"

"Mrs. Michaels, I represent a very reputable consortium of business men here in Omaha. This group, Franklin and Chase Enterprises, is always on the lookout for successful ventures to which they might be of assistance." He smiled again.

"I have not heard of Franklin and Chase Enterprises," Joy responded evenly.

A number of salesmen had taken her for an easy mark. She had cut her teeth on them. They, and their slick delivery, generally went away empty handed but with a healthy regard for "that woman." She had felt guilty for being unnecessarily rude on more than one occasion . . . but had also taken a rather perverse pleasure in cutting them down to size.

"Really? How surprising! I assure you, they are quite reputable." Robertson smiled again, nonplussed.

"Yes, so you said." Joy's tone cooled a little. "And what can I do for you and your associates today, Mr. Robertson?"

"Ah! Actually, it is what *we* can do for *you*, Mrs. Michaels!"

"Indeed? May I ask in what way, Mr. Robertson?"

Robertson reached into his breast pocket and extracted a fine linen envelope. "Franklin and Chase would like to extend their assistance with this offer of partnership."

Joy's eyes narrowed. "I'm afraid you are misinformed, Mr. Robertson. I am not in need of a partner. Please thank your employer for me, but I decline their offer. Good day." She stood.

Robertson did not.

"I do encourage you to look at our offer, Mrs. Michaels. It is quite generous. I assure you that you will find the offer to be mutually beneficial. One never knows when a strong partner is really . . . a *healthy* addition."

Joy's stomach clenched. Robertson's inflection conveyed a subtle threat, but a threat none the same.

"Mr. Robertson, this interview is over. Please leave." Joy's voice was firm and a little overloud. Next to her desk, Blackie's hackles rose and a low growl rose in his throat.

Robertson merely smiled again, gathered himself to go, but laid the envelope on her desk. He tapped it lightly.

"I do encourage you to consider this." When he looked up at Joy, he no longer wore a smile and something dangerous flickered in his eyes.

"I said *good day*, Mr. Robertson." Joy's heart was thundering in her throat.

"A pleasure meeting you, Mrs. Michaels." Robertson, his mask back in place, smiled once more.

Joy didn't know how long she stared unblinking at the blotter on her desk. Mr. Wheatley timidly knocked on her door. Startled, she snapped, "What is it?"

He swallowed nervously. "Ah, Mrs. Michaels? Everything is in order and I've locked up. The rest of the staff is just waiting for you to dismiss them." Mr. Wheatley, a man near her father's age, drew back timidly and stared at the floor.

Joy tried to focus. She recognized his discomfort and was first confused and then embarrassed. When had she started intimidating this kind man? When had her staff become nervous and uncomfortable working for her? Had she really become a taskmaster, a shrew instead of a gentlewoman?

Her face burned as she stood. "Mr. Wheatley," she spoke gently, "I, um, I want to . . . apologize for my tone just now. Please dismiss the staff and . . . no, wait. I will do it."

She laid her hand on his arm. "Please forgive me, dear friend. My bad behavior has no excuse. I . . ." She shook her head.

He met her look. "Mrs. Michaels, we are all cheering for you. You are doing a fine job running this establishment . . . and . . ." he paused. "I accept your apology." His honest brown eyes glistened a little. "Things are going to get better, missus. I hope you can believe that."

This time it was Joy who looked down, eyes glistening. Would things get better? Would *she* get better?

"I thank you, Mr. Wheatley, and I appreciate your hope and good wishes. More than you know."

Blackie at her side, she walked the shop floors quickly, scanning the shelves, counters, floors, and window dressings. All in order. Neat and tidy. Her small staff waited patiently by the front entrance. Most of them did not meet her eyes. Recalling some of her recent rants, Joy could not blame them.

"I, ah, thank you all for the good work you did this day. I want you to know that I appreciate all you do . . ." Her voice failed her.

A few looked at her curiously. Billy, whose laughter and goodwill had always seemed boundless but whom she had excessively chastised—only this morning?—stared sullenly at the floor boards.

"Thank you all, for your support and hard work these last six months. I, uh . . ." she gulped. "Please enjoy your evening. And perhaps tomorrow, when you come in, I won't be quite the terror I've been lately." She laughed a little in discomfort, but no one joined her.

She turned to Billy. "Billy, I need to apologize for taking you to task this morning, especially in front of your co-workers. I was unnecessarily harsh. I . . . It won't happen again."

Nodding and murmuring good nights, the staff slipped out the door and Joy locked it behind them. She caught Billy looking back at her, hurt still stamped on his honest face.

Joy gulped in shame. Then she remembered the not-so-subtle threat lying on her desk in a fine linen envelope. She clutched her sides and sobbed once. She felt so alone! She needed advice—and perhaps help!

A gentle nudge turned her attention downward. Blackie stared at Joy, his eyes soft with the compassion a dog can often give. Joy wordlessly stooped to hug him and receive his comfort.

As she knelt there, a smoldering anger slowly replaced her fear. No one was going to insinuate themselves into what she and Grant had worked so hard to establish and make profitable. No; she could take care of this Robertson herself—*would* take care of him. By herself.

Chapter 7

April, 1908, Seattle

Mei-Xing Li stood beneath the flowering plum trees in her father's garden and sighed. It was here she had turned away the man she loved. The soft pink beauty of the tree's blossoms stood at odds with her heart. The plum trees had still been stark and bare when she had sent him away, more than a year ago now. Her heart had frozen that day, just as stark and bare as the trees.

Although she had done so many times, she retraced her decision. As much as she loved that man, he had chosen a life she could never share with him. A dishonorable life. If her father had known him as she had come to know him. Her heart clenched again in familiar pain.

In the last year she had also suffered her family's anger and recrimination. Her mother had not spoken to her for months afterwards. Even now her beloved father looked at her only with confusion and disappointment. Perhaps she should have confided in her father. Mei-Xing revisited her decision not to tell him her real reason for rejecting the offer of marriage but the situation was much too complex.

Mei-Xing's father was a wealthy man, owner of many ships and warehouses along the Seattle harbor. His best and oldest friend, Wei Chen, owned many restaurants, laundries, and import shops. The two friends had hoped that their only children would marry. It seemed propitious, the perfect means of joining two friendly, prominent families and thereby increasing their wealth and power.

Mei-Xing was only 14 at the time. The scion of the Cheng family was 10 years older, but they had grown up together and were deeply attached. They would have gladly married and had shared happy plans to do so—until Mei-Xing accidentally discovered the truth. The truth about her "Uncle" Wei and the truth about his son, the man she loved then. And loved still.

Not that it mattered now. After she had rejected him he had left her in anger and pain, left his family, and even left Seattle. He had been gone for more than a year and in all that time no one had heard from him.

But what if her father had known the truth? No, if she had told him, it would have broken his heart. And would he have even believed her? He was an honorable man who despised opium, gambling, and the other, unspeakable, trades Uncle Wei and his family controlled.

Oh, and she had been warned. First they had warned her to keep what she had learned to herself and simply marry the man she loved. Then after she had refused him and after her beloved had left the city she was warned of what might happen to her or to *her family* if she spoke up.

Blossoms floated to the ground around her. She sighed again. Oh, what if? What if she had never discovered the Chen family's secrets? What if she had married and been happily ignorant all of her life? She shook her head. Her father had taught her too well. To know the truth and to live with honor was better than ignorance. So why hadn't she confided in him? Why hadn't she told her father the truth? Because she also knew the truth about herself: She was weak and *afraid*.

Uncle Wei's wife, Auntie Fang-Hua, hated her—hated her with a malevolent passion. Mei-Xing shivered as she recalled the poisonous looks Fang-Hua gave her whenever they were in the same room and the equally venomous barbs directed her way in loudly whispered conversations with others.

Father wanted her to marry someone else and perhaps move away, but no appropriate man dared seek her hand. No, Fang-Hua Chen had made sure of that.

Now both her family and his blamed her for the division and discomfort between the families. She was an object of shame and friction. Her parents fought about her; her cousins shook their heads and whispered; she had come between her father and Uncle Wei, so the Chen family despised her. She could not show her face anywhere without bringing more shame to her father and mother.

Wei Chen's nephew, Bao, was her only remaining friend. He understood the powerful family dynamics and the strain she was under. He had commiserated with her and had tried to speak to his aunt, but to no avail. Mei-Xing felt certain he did not know about his family's "other" businesses. He was too kind and understanding.

Recently he had come to her with a bold idea. Mei-Xing read the instructions again.

> *This is a good family with no children of their own.*
> *They understand the circumstances and will let you*
> *take their name. You will be as a daughter in their*
> *home, and you will have a new life with them. By this,*
> *you will free your family of shame and free yourself*
> *as well. It is the best answer, little Mei. I cannot bear*
> *to see your sadness any longer. I wish you to be*
> *happy again.*

Bao had provided her with a train ticket and would put her on the train unseen. Perhaps it was the best way. Mei-Xing looked about her father's garden a last time. It would be dark soon. She would retire to bed early . . . as she often did lately. No one would miss her until the next day. She had already written a note of apology and good bye and left it where her mother would find it.

Bao returned from the train station late in the evening. He went directly to the Chen home and found his aunt waiting for him. Fang-Hua Chen's name may have meant "fragrant flower" but she was anything but a delicate flower—she was hard and vindictive and possibly the most powerful woman in the city.

"She is gone?" Her voice was brittle and cold.

"Yes, Auntie." Bao bowed low before her.

"And you have made all the arrangements?"

"Yes, Auntie. Her maid . . . Ling-Ling . . . will destroy the note Mei-Xing has left and replace it with the one you dictated. It tells her family where to look, and I have prepared the scene convincingly. They will believe she threw herself onto the rocks to spare them further shame. The tide will have come and gone twice by then."

Fang-Hua nodded in approval. "This place she is going. Near this town . . . Denver? They will take care of her as I wish?"

Bao suppressed a shudder. "Yes, Auntie. All has been arranged as you directed."

Fang-Hua smiled coldly. "Good. Then she will have the life she deserves." The woman turned to a lacquered tea table and picked up a delicate cup. She sipped in satisfaction. "You have done well, Bao. I will see that Wei Chen promotes you."

Bao shivered. "He will not know of this?"

"No. It is between us and the maid Ling-Ling you are so fixated on." She looked at him speculatively. "You are determined to marry beneath yourself, but I will give my approval and give you a good wedding gift, Bao. And you will, in the future, be useful to me again. Are we agreed?"

He bowed more deeply this time. "I am your servant, Auntie."

Chapter 8

Two weeks later, a knock sounded on Joy's office door.

"Come in." Joy had assumed it was one of her staff and was startled when Robertson walked in.

"You! You will leave immediately, *Mr.* Robertson," Joy said through gritted teeth. Blackie was instantly on his feet growling low in his throat, ready to attack.

He held up a placating hand. "A moment of your time, Mrs. Michaels? I deeply regret how we parted at our last meeting."

"*I* do not regret it, sir. I have nothing more to say to you except you are not welcome in my establishment."

He smiled, and when she saw that dangerous undercurrent flit across his face, she quailed a little. Without waiting for permission he seated himself in front of her desk again. "Mrs. Michaels, have you examined the offer I left you when I was here last?"

"I have not and will not. You will leave, Mr. Robertson, *immediately.*" Joy quivered in anger.

"My dear Mrs. Michaels. I believe you underestimate the, ah, *resolve* of my business partners. Let me help you understand our proposition and how it will . . . *benefit* you."

The veiled threats were scarcely covered by Robertson's ingratiating manner.

"Get out," Joy hissed.

"Now, now. Are you certain? By way of expressing our esteem for your business acumen, I would like to be the first to congratulate you on how you have recovered from your husband's untimely . . . demise, and how you have successfully steered your business back into profitability."

"I said get out!" Joy stood, nearly shouting.

Then Robertson stood, towering over the desk, leaning close to intimidate her. His face changed. It was like watching a dog turn from pet to a predator.

Blackie launched himself at Robertson's leg but the man deftly kicked the old dog aside. Joy heard Blackie yelp and then whimper.

Robertson, his smiling lips pulled back from his teeth, snarled, "Mrs. Michaels, my associates and I are quite determined. You can accept this as fact, cooperate with us, and continue to run a successful business or . . . unfortunate events will unfold."

"You think threatening me will work. *It will not*. I am quite capable of handling my own business affairs." She lunged toward the door. As she did, Robertson sprang to block her, clamping an iron grip on her arm.

"I guarantee that if you do not accept our terms, you will regret it, *Mrs.* Michaels."

Joy gasped and grabbed for the door handle, clawing to escape his grasp. As she wrenched on the knob, he abruptly released her. She threw open the door and shouted in panic, "Billy! Billy!"

All heads on the shop floor turned toward her frantic call. Billy, after a moment's confusion, thundered toward her office. When Joy turned around, however, Robertson was standing near her, hat in one hand, the other extended for a handshake—as collected and proper as could be.

In full view of all he took cordial leave. "Thank you, Mrs. Michaels. You have been most helpful. I appreciate it." Billy stopped, confused again.

Joy watched, incredulous, as Robertson calmly walked toward the store's entrance doors. She knelt, gathering Blackie into arms. He was already on his feet. As she checked him for injury he flinched just a little.

Grateful as she was that Blackie seemed to be unharmed, Joy's anger burned against Robertson and those behind him.

Robertson sipped a small glass of fine Kentucky bourbon with his employer, Shelby Franklin. The fire that hit the back of his throat was exquisite and gratifying—almost as gratifying as the work he did for Franklin.

Shelby Franklin was brilliant, Robertson gave him that. He was also utterly ruthless and a formidable strategist. Franklin moved in the highest social circles and with effortless elegance and grace. The man operated on a level that many men hardly dreamed of. On his worst day, Franklin managed with ease what most men would struggle to wrap their intellects around.

And Franklin was a superior man in every way—he had exceptional taste in clothes, food, drink, art . . . and women. Robertson smiled to himself as he recalled an especially nice "gift" Franklin had recently arranged for him. He was generous when it came to rewards. All of these facts made the prospect of someday taking Franklin down and assuming his position even more intriguing.

Robertson figured he would learn all he could from the master before making his move. In the meantime, he enjoyed the work, the challenges, and the many benefits of being one of a very small group Franklin employed. One of those men, a Chinaman named Su-Chong, sat at attention in a straight-backed chair near the door. As Franklin's personal bodyguard, Robertson would need to deal decisively with him when the time came.

Franklin held his crystal tumbler up toward the fireplace so that the flames danced through the facets of the glass. "You met with the woman again?"

"Yes sir." Robertson acted the role of loyal minion perfectly. "She is quite unyielding."

"Has she spoken of our 'offer' to anyone?"

"I don't believe so, sir. She is angry and willful. The challenge piques her pride, I'm afraid." He chuckled and Franklin smiled back. "She believes she will not be swayed but .perhaps with more persuasion?" Robertson's sadistic streak quite enjoyed when more persuasion was called for.

His employer stared through his drink at the flames for several more minutes. For some reason this particular woman's recalcitrant behavior rankled, and he would not tolerate it.

"Burn her out."

Robertson was startled but managed to keep his face unchanged. He had expected to move up the pressure on the woman a little at a time—and had assumed that Franklin wanted her business intact. This was an interesting turn of events. He would have to uncover the reason behind Franklin's play. Covertly, of course.

"Certainly sir. Timeframe?"

"Let's give her a week or more to begin to feel safe again. Say, early next month? No later than mid month."

Robertson could hardly contain his curiosity but had long ago learned to school his face. He nodded and tossed back the remainder of his drink. He knew the pleasantries were merely a framework for Franklin to conduct business, and he had just issued an order.

"Yes sir. I'll take care of it."

"Good man." Franklin stood to usher him to the door. "Oh, and Robertson, both properties."

"Yes sir." He nodded to Franklin. Su-Chong opened the door for him and closed it after he passed through.

Chapter 9

Nine days later, Joy fed Blackie and then closed up the store as usual and caught a horsecar whose route would take her near Arnie and Anna's home. She closed her eyes to enjoy the open-air trolley. The balmy May evening was filled with pleasant scents. The measured clopping of horse's hooves, the engines of occasional motor cars, murmured conversations, and the light breeze relaxed her and helped her to let go of the day's problems.

In the past weeks Joy had worked hard to mend fences with Arnie and his family. She gave the boys little gifts, brought flowers to Anna, and let them all know how dear they were to her, how she appreciated having family in town. She had determined to re-cultivate a sweet tongue and manner. Life had become, in some ways, pleasant and normal again.

Anna outdid herself that evening. The dinner and the company were a pleasure. Afterwards, Joy, Petter, and Willem competed at dominoes for an hour while Arnie read his paper and Anna a book.

At last Arnie put down his paper and stretched. "Ready to go, Cousin?" Arnie always drove her home.

Petter and Willem begged for another 30 minutes, but Joy knew that Arnie would spend an hour taking her home and driving back, making for an already late night for him. "Yes, I'm ready," she replied.

The spring evening was still pleasant as Arnie drove their carriage toward Joy's part of town. As they drew near, a water wagon, pulled by four straining horses careened past them. Joy looked ahead and saw an eerie glow down the street. Her breathing quickened.

"Arnie!"

"Be calm, Joy. It can't be yours. I'm sure."

Arnie lashed his team until they were galloping down the dimly lit avenue. They finally turned onto Joy's street. And stared aghast at the sight that met them.

The block was congested with hand-pump water wagons, two steam fire engines, and a large group of firefighters from the Omaha Fire Department. Flames jumped and shimmied inside both of Joy's properties. Joy could see the fire dancing inside the second floor of her store. Inside her home.

Blackie!

With a booming noise the windows of her upstairs apartment blew outward, showering glass on the firemen below who hunkered down to protect their faces. As the rain of glass ended, firemen aimed water hoses into the windows and at both roofs, but Joy knew that their efforts were hopeless. It was about saving the properties around hers now.

Arnie and Joy, well away from the inferno, watched helplessly. Even from a distance they could feel the heat of the fire. Then flames shot through the roofs into the inky sky. A minute later, the firemen gave a shout. Keeping their hoses trained on nearby buildings, they pulled back. And in an eruption of sparks and flames, Joy's engulfed buildings collapsed in on themselves.

Chapter 10

Joy stared at the steaming rubble that had been her and Grant's home and dream.

"My plan is the dream I can't live without. So I'm wondering if your plan is the dream you cannot live without."

Joy choked on the memory. Grant was gone. Now their dream was gone also.

Dear Blackie. Gone.

What did she have left? What would she do with her life?

Billy and Mr. Taub, wielding garden rakes, were poking through the still-warm debris. All Joy could do was watch numbly. Nothing remained of either building, the store or the adjacent property where they had planned their fine household emporium. It was gone. All of it.

Arnie and Anna gripped her arms tightly, and Joy thought dimly, *They must think I'll fall down . . .* Anna sniffled and drew her hanky over her eyes.

Joy caught sight of Mr. Wheatley across the street. Usually so proper, he was sitting on the sidewalk, his feet in the street as autos packed with gawking passengers slowly motored by. The sidewalks were filling quickly with folks from the neighborhood, fellow business owners, and shoppers. Mr. Wheatley held his scraggly gray head in his gnarled hand and stared at his feet.

"What will they do now?" Joy wondered aloud.

Arnie answered, his face a mask of stone, "Who, Joy?"

"Why, Mr. Wheatley and Mr. Taub and . . . Billy. What will they do? They won't have work!" Joy was suddenly brokenhearted for them, for the years they had shared that were now over.

Arnie shook his shaggy head.

"I . . . why, I will rebuild. I *must* rebuild," Joy whispered. "I surely must . . . for them, for Grant." She touched her wedding ring, assuring herself that something, *something* must remain of what they had, what they were.

Arnie growled. "Who did this, Joy? Do you have any idea?"

"Did this? What do you mean?"

"Joy, this is no ordinary fire. Look at it. Too perfect, too complete. Only *your* buildings—and both of them." His mouth twisted in anger. "It was set, Joy. Mark my words: *set*. Someone burned you out."

Joy's hand flew to her mouth. What had Robertson said?

Chapter 11

"But we have insurance! I paid the premiums!"

Arnie tossed a copy of her policy on to his desk in frustration. "Your policy's arson clause is very restrictive, Joy. Once arson has been established, *you* must be cleared of all wrongdoing before the policy pays. And even then, the arson clause entitles you only to the value of the buildings and a small percentage of the value of the contents."

Joy gaped. "But all the inventory! It will take me years to restock."

"That, I'm afraid, is the best scenario you can hope for. The insurer is insisting that they must have proof positive you did not set the fire yourself. They are conducting an investigation right now."

He scowled. "Until you are cleared, *Liberty Indemnity* won't pay anything—not a penny. And they are asking some very disturbing questions."

"But what kind of questions?"

"Questions like, wasn't Mrs. Michaels in over her head since her husband died? Was the business in trouble? What kind of financial difficulties was she experiencing?"

Joy shot out of her seat. "That's outrageous. We owned everything, free and clear. We were banking a profit every month—I know! I did the books!"

Arnie sighed and rubbed his hand down his face. "Don't take this wrong, Joy, but the fact that *you* did the books means that you are the only one who could testify to the condition of the business. The books themselves are gone, too."

"And the investigators seem to be implying that they have some inside information that brings the solvency of the store into question." He looked at her frankly. "Is there anything you are keeping from me, Joy?"

"No!"

He leaned his chin on his hand, pondering. "Something evil is at work here, I feel it in my bones."

"What do you mean?"

"Too many things that don't add up . . . too many 'facts' surfacing that are no more facts than my having two heads. I sense some sort of conspiracy."

Joy's heart thumped in her chest. "But why? Why me? Who?"

Arnie continued to ponder in a silence that stretched over several minutes.

"*Why*. That is the real question, isn't it? Why burn you out?"

Joy had no response. Why hadn't she told Arnie about Robertson?

"Arnie—I need to tell you something . . . something I realize I should have confided in you much earlier."

Joy spent the next 30 minutes describing Robertson's two visits and another 30 answering all of Arnie's questions. At the end of it, she felt more than a little foolish. In fact, as Arnie's face grew graver and his questions more pointed, she began to perceive how brash— no, how arrogant—her attitude had been. In spite of the conviction she had felt from the Lord regarding her treatment of her employees and family, she had not dealt with the root of the issue. Pride.

> *Pride goeth before destruction,*
> *and a haughty spirit before a fall.*

The verse came effortlessly to mind. Pride in her own accomplishments, pride in her self-sufficiency, pride in dealing with her pain in her *own way*. Yes, the pain had been the mask her pride had worn and used to rationalize her bad behavior.

If only she had allowed the Lord to help her deal with the pain! Instead, she had felt justified in her behavior because of her loneliness and pain—and all the while these were merely the facade that hid her pride.

"I-I should have come to you, Arnie, and told you about him, but I . . ." Joy stopped. "No, I'm still making excuses. If I am to be completely truthful . . . I must confess that, through my pride and presumption, I brought this on myself."

Søren, Arnie, and Joy retired to Arnie's study after dinner. It was two weeks since the fire. Søren had arrived that afternoon and they were still trying to puzzle out the "why" behind a conspiracy that seemed evident to them.

A pounding at Arnie and Anna's front door interrupted them. Joy's stomach flipped over as Søren took her hand. Arnie went to answer the door. They heard voices. They grew in volume, Arnie's loudest of all. Then silence followed by muffled conversation.

Finally Arnie reappeared. His face was ashen. "The judge has issued a warrant for you for arson. The police chief is here . . . to take you in to custody. He says they will not keep you in the jail. The judge has agreed to allow you to be confined to my home in my custody."

Joy swallowed. How could this be happening? Søren did not let go of her hand—until the officer placed his hand on her shoulder and firmly guided her out of the house and into the police wagon.

Joy endured the long process at police headquarters and was released hours later to Arnie and Anna's home—now her jail—to wait for a court date. The chief indicated to Arnie, who would serve as her attorney, that the judge was inclined to bring her to trial quickly.

Arnie, huddling with the police chief while the clerk took Joy's information and bail money, came away with information he began to share with her and Søren on the ride home. It was late. Theirs was the only buggy on the road.

"The insurance company is pressing for an early date. They want the court to confirm arson and your part in it so that they can deny and close your claim."

Joy nodded, mutely.

"And something else."

Both Joy and Søren looked to Arnie.

"No one in the police department seems to think that you can be proven guilty of the arson. Not without hard evidence. If you *were* proven guilty, you would go to prison. *Liberty Indemnity* would like a guilty verdict, of course, but even if you are found "not guilty" and yet can't be proven *innocent* of the arson—if the trial ends without determining who *did* set the fire—they can still refuse to pay the claim and take you to civil court. But—and this is the interesting part—even if you are acquitted at trial, the city has already decided not to issue you permits to rebuild."

"What! Even if I am proven not to have done this?"

"He asked me not to disclose that this information came from him, but that is what the chief told me."

"I don't understand." Joy's head pounded furiously and her neck and shoulders were tight with stress.

"There is something more, isn't there?" Søren asked.

"Yes. Our first clue."

"You mean the 'why'?"

Arnie nodded. "They may not have enough evidence to convict you, but in the court of public opinion, they no longer want you in Omaha. Seems that the city council already met and voted to condemn your property and put it up for auction."

"Mighty fast, if you ask me," Søren muttered darkly.

"How can they do that? How can they sell what isn't their property?" Joy was astounded.

"The city has the authority. It's the council's way of labeling you *persona non grata* and forcing you to leave. You will receive the proceeds of the auction, of course, but they will force the sale."

"Forcing me to leave . . ."

"Yes. But more importantly, forcing you to *sell*."

"Ah!" Søren's eyes gleamed. "So that's the game. And?"

"And an interested buyer has already stepped forward."

Chapter 12

Joy stared out the window at the street. A bitter spring rain discouraged foot traffic. Despite that, Joy would have given her right arm for five minutes to run free in the out of doors. Forced to remain within Arnie and Anna's house for three weeks now, she had never felt so confined, so oppressed in her young life. Or so bereft of God's care and comfort.

Nothing in her world made sense anymore. Papa and Mama could not come. Arnie was working like a fiend on her defense. Anna and the boys were timidly supportive but Joy could tell that public opinion was treating them harshly. In many eyes in the community, she already stood guilty. People were anticipating, some eagerly, the trial and her judgment.

Mr. Wheatley came to see her daily. Most mornings he stopped for no more than a cup of coffee and an encouraging word. He would pat her hand as they sat sipping coffee, the silence growing.

One morning he started talking, almost as if she weren't there with him. "See, I told Mr. Grant that I would look out for you, I did. Course we didn't know then . . . I mean we thought he would only be gone a few weeks." He sighed. "But a promise is a promise."

The silence lengthened but it didn't seem to bother him. When Joy poured him a second cup, he went in another direction entirely. "See, I . . . know how you feel, Miss Joy. I lost a sweetheart once."

This was something Joy hadn't known and, for a change, her interest was piqued. However, Mr. Wheatley seemed to have forgotten or not realized he had spoken aloud.

Finally Joy prompted softly, "You lost someone dear to you?"

"Hmm? Oh. Yes." He gazed into the distance again. "I was a young man once, you know. It was, oh, I think 50 years or more ago now." He chuckled. "You might not believe me, but I was a good-looking young buck once."

Joy smiled at him. "Oh, I think I can see that quite plainly!" They both grinned and Joy felt the stress ease for a moment.

"Well, now, I was raised back in Pennsylvania, see. My uncle had a shop and I worked for him. One day a gentleman came in and had his niece with him—prettiest thing I'd ever seen. As fresh as a flower and just as sweet as honey. I courted her and we fell in love. Then the war came."

"I was conscripted, o' course. Went off to fight . . . Those were dark days, missus. Dark days." He shook his head.

"You fought in the war?"

"Yes ma'am. I try not to think on it." Then he was off somewhere in his memories again, and Joy waited patiently for him to return.

"Well. I was talking about Helen and me. She wrote me regularly, and most times I got her letters. They kept me from losing my mind, I think. But then they just stopped. I didn't receive any letters for two months, and I was crazy with worry." He looked at Joy. "Got a letter from her mother finally. Helen had come down with a fever and passed away after five days."

He sighed and sipped his coffee. "Never did find anyone who could make me forget her. I used to see how you and Mr. Grant looked at each other and I'd think, 'why, that's just how Helen and I felt' or 'she used to look at me just like that.'"

Joy touched his hand. "I'm so sorry."

His aged face smiled back at Joy. "It's all right, you know. I know where she is. Someday I'll see her again. Until then . . . well, I made Mr. Grant a promise, so I'll be a-watching out for you."

In addition to the confinement, Joy had too much idle time on her hands. Too much time to think . . . about Grant. About the loss of the store. About the outcome of the trial. About the shame she was bringing on her family, on Mama, on Papa.

Papa.

Letters from Joy's mama arrived regularly. She didn't hide that Jan was confined to their little home; neither did she dwell on it. He suffered from pain in his back and knees and needed Rose's assistance to move from bed to chair. Joy's heart grew more anxious for her beloved Papa, but Rose's penned words were filled with peace.

> *I cannot yet fathom God's plan in all that has befallen you, our dear daughter. We stand in full confidence of your innocence and know without doubt that this attack is from the enemy of our souls. God will not be mocked. He takes very seriously every slander against his children. I pity those who have done so wickedly against you, and we pray for them, even as we pray diligently for you.*

While men and Satan may plot against us, our Lord, who knows the end from the beginning, has his own purposes in play. Trials accomplish great works in us, preparing us for those purposes. What must you learn at this time, my dear Joy? Learn to trust the One who will never leave you nor forsake you. On the other side of this, we will learn those purposes and be better equipped to carry them out to fruition.

Do not give in to discouragement, I beg you, Joy. Hold fast. God works all things—even wicked things—together for the good of those who love God and are called according to His purposes. Hold fast, dear one.

Joy read such words of encouragement numbly. She saw them, but they made no inroads to her heart, provided little comfort.

Chapter 13

June 1908

Robertson solemnly surveyed the packed courtroom. "I visited Michaels' Tools, Hardware, and Farm Implements on April ninth, I believe. Yes, here it is in my appointment book." He offered the prosecutor a small leather-bound book. He, in turn, handed it to the judge.

"I met with Mrs. Michaels just before closing time that day. Franklin and Chase made Mrs. Michaels a very handsome offer for her store and inventory. I have a copy of it right here." He again handed something to the judge, what looked like a linen envelope. A familiar-looking linen envelope.

Joy's mouth gaped. "No!" she whispered furiously to Arnie. "It wasn't an offer to buy, it was that 'partnership' offer, just as I told you—and he threatened me!"

Arnie shushed her quietly, concentrating on what Robertson was telling the judge. Søren, sitting close behind them, reached out his arm and gently put his hand on Joy's shoulder. She was grateful for that simple touch.

"We came to terms over the next two weeks and were set to sign papers, but then . . ." he paused, obviously embarrassed, "Dear me . . . I really don't like to say . . ."

The judged fixed him with a stern eye. "I remind you, Mr. Robertson, that you are under oath in this courtroom. You will complete your testimony."

Robertson sighed and nodded obediently to the judge. "Yes, Your Honor. I apologize to the court." As he turned to face the courtroom again his eyes drifted over Joy and she saw it. Something in the turn of the corner of his mouth. Something he *wanted* her to see.

So quickly did the glance pass that Joy knew no one else had seen it.

He continued. "Well, sir, we had asked to see the store's books, of course. And on the surface they were perfect—neat, well organized, complete. They reflected a thriving endeavor."

Joy hissed to Arnie again, "He never saw my books! He is lying!"

Arnie bid her silent with a stern look.

"And that was a bit concerning, Your Honor. You see, the condition of the business seemed . . . just a tad *too* perfect, sir, if you take my meaning. When we looked more closely, we found . . . irregularities."

"What kind of irregularities?" demanded the prosecutor.

"Well, sir . . . ah, the books reflected cash entries every week that were too similar—nearly the same amount each week. And not nearly enough overhead. Altogether, the debt-to-income ratio seemed too low and the overall profitability much too high. First we were suspicious, but then we became . . . convinced that the books were, uh, inaccurate, perhaps altered."

Someone in the back of the courtroom jumped to his feet, toppling a chair at the same time. Joy looked back and was startled to see Mr. Wheatley, his tufts of gray hair standing on end, large red blotches on each cheek.

He shook his fist in rage and shouted in his papery voice, "Liar! You're a liar, Robertson! You're a lying son of a—" The rest was choked off in a scuffle of bodies as deputies tackled him.

"Silence! Silence in the court! Silence right now!" The judge's gavel banged over and over, and the din in the courtroom slowly died.

Two deputies wrestled the old man from the courtroom and, with great concern, Joy saw him slumping in their grasp.

"I will have silence in my court!" the judge thundered. He glared at Joy as though she had orchestrated the outburst. Horrified, she saw condemnation in his fierce look. Glancing around, she saw other stares, some reflecting the same judgment, some speculation. Arnie gripped her elbow tightly.

"Steady, Joy. School your face."

Joy forced herself to return the judge's glare with an unflinching calmness.

The judge turned at last to Robertson. "Continue your testimony."

"Yes, Your Honor. Well, once we knew the books were cooked—"

"Objection, Your Honor. No irregularities in my client's books have been established." Arnie's tone was sharp, commanding.

The judge harrumphed. "Mr. Robertson, please remember that you are testifying. Do not draw conclusions that have not been entered into evidence."

"Of course, Your Honor. I apologize."

Arnie knew the damage was done as far as public perception. Robertson had spoken of "cooked books" in such a factual manner, the people in the courtroom were not likely to believe otherwise.

"When we, uh, believed we had found irregularities, I met with Mrs. Michaels again and informed her that we were withdrawing our offer."

"On what date did this take place," the prosecutor asked.

Robertson made a show of consulting his appointment book again. "April 23, sir."

"What did Mrs. Michaels do and say when you informed her that the sale was off?"

"Well, she was very angry. I was surprised, actually, at the words she used. Not like a lady, if you take my meaning . . ."

Joy slumped in her chair. Could things get any worse? She fought to breathe, fought against the tide of panic rising in her breast.

"Objection, Your Honor. Mr. Robertson should testify as to what he saw and heard and not characterize my client."

Robertson sniffed. "Mrs. Michaels threatened me, Your Honor. She told me that if I did not leave immediately, she would have me thrown out. She also said, and I quote, 'It is of no matter, Mr. Robertson. I am quite capable of handling my own business affairs myself.'"

Exactly what she had told him when she scorned his intimidation and offer of "partnership." Word for word.

Robertson ended his testimony and the judge excused him. She did not recognize the prosecution's next witness.

"The prosecution calls Mr. Tom Percher."

A slender man perhaps in his early 30s took the witness stand. He was dressed in new clothes and was obviously uncomfortable. The judge swore him in and the prosecutor began his questioning.

"Mr. Percher, tell the court where you work, please."

"Yessir. I, uh, work for Kimball's Market, over on Fifth and Grand."

"What do you do there, Mr. Percher?"

"Well, I, um, stock shelves and do a bit of sweeping up. Whatever Mr. Kimball has for me."

"I see." The prosecutor turned toward the courtroom as he asked the next question. "On the night in question, where were you around 6 p.m.?"

Percher gulped and looked toward the floor. "I was, uh, walking home from my job."

"And did your itinerary happen to take you by Michaels' Tools, Hardware, and Farm Implements?"

Percher looked confused. "My itinerary?"

The courtroom tittered and the judge banged his gavel and glared at the witness. Percher, now perspiring, slid a hanky from his pocket and wiped his face.

The prosecutor smiled benevolently. "Mr. Percher, did you walk past Mrs. Michael's store on your way home? Mr. Percher?"

"I, uh, yes. I walked by the store."

"Would you please tell the courtroom what you saw as you walked by Mrs. Michaels' store?"

Percher's eyes shot around the courtroom as if looking for the nearest door. Just then a spate of coughing from the packed courtroom drew his attention. Robertson, a handkerchief gingerly held to his lips, murmured a quiet "pardon me" while looking steadily at the witness. Percher visibly paled and straightened in his chair.

"I saw . . . *her*." Percher pointed at Joy. "She was, uh, coming out of the store."

"You saw Mrs. Michaels, the woman on trial here today?"

"Yessir." He paused.

The prosecutor, affecting a bored stance drawled, "And?"

"Oh! Um, she was locking up the store. Yes. That's right. She was locking up the store but . . . she had a sack in her hand. She, um, looked all around her and then walked away from the store and over to the trash can on the corner."

"What did she do then, Mr. Percher?"

"Well sir, she, um, put that sack in the trash can." Percher wiped his face again.

"Then what happened, Mr. Percher?"

"Well sir, she walked away."

The courtroom tittered again. This time the judge merely glared out across the crowded room.

"And then?"

"Oh. And then I was curious, see. And I went and fetched that sack out of the trash. To see what was in it. Cause I was curious-like," Percher recited in a monotone.

"What did you find in the sack, Mr. Percher?"

Voice low and eyes on the floor, Percher mumbled, "An empty jar of gasoline."

The courtroom erupted but Joy could no longer take in anything around her. She heard voices but took no notice of them. Some time later, Arnie gently helped her to her feet. Søren's chair behind her was empty.

"Is it over?" she whispered. She wondered vaguely about Søren, but her thinking was too muddled to ask where he had gone.

"For today. Tomorrow it's our turn."

Chapter 14

When they returned home Anna put Joy to bed and she was immediately asleep, partly due to the overwhelming strain of the day and partly through the help of a sleeping tablet. It was past midnight when Søren surreptitiously stole into Arnie and Anna's house. Arnie silently met him and they closed the door behind them in Arnie's study.

"What did you find out?"

Søren bent his head near Arnie's and began to answer his question.

The following morning Anna helped Joy dress. After a hurried breakfast, Arnie, Anna, Søren, and Joy prayed together. Both Arnie and Søren had bags under their eyes.

Joy, too, was exhausted. Although she had slept the night through, it was as if her bones had turned to India rubber in the night and her mind had filled with fine silt. Every action was an effort, mentally and physically. Emotionally she felt detached, disconnected.

The courtroom, if possible, was even more densely packed than the previous day. When Joy and Arnie entered and sat down at the defense table, the crowd's silence was oppressive and Joy felt the weight of every eye on her. As carefully as she could manage she kept her face impassive and calm. Arnie studied his notes intently.

At last it was the defense's turn. Arnie called Tom Percher back to the stand. Percher, dressed in the same clothes as the day before, looked to have shriveled overnight. His face was pinched and gray under the lights of the courtroom. The judge loomed over the witness and reminded him that he was still under oath.

Arnie stood and walked casually toward the witness stand. "Mr. Percher, is it your sworn testimony that at approximately 6 p.m. on the night in question you saw Mrs. Michaels lock the doors of her business and then place a paper sack in the trash can on the corner near her store?"

"Yes." Percher's voice was mumbled and low.

"Speak up, Mr. Percher. We cannot hear you."

"Yessir. That's what I saw."

"And you removed the sack from the trash can and looked inside."

"Yessir."

"And the sack contained an empty jar of gasoline."

"Yessir."

"What did you do with the jar?"

"What did I do with it?"

"Yes. That's what I asked."

"I, uh, well, I guess I threw it away again."

"You guess?"

"I did. I threw it away."

The prosecutor lumbered to his feet and protested, "Your Honor, the witness has already testified—"

The judge glared at him. "Sit down, Mr. Prosecutor."

"But Your Hon—"

The judge's gavel silenced him up. Joy, her mind clearing a little, looked for and found Robertson sitting a few rows behind the prosecutor. He glanced her way and gave her a slight nod and the glimpse of a smirking smile. Anger rushed into Joy again. She forced herself to sit up and pay attention to Arnie.

"Thank you, Your Honor," Arnie nodded toward the bench. "Mr. Percher, let me see if I understand your testimony correctly. You opened the sack, saw an empty jar of gasoline, and threw the sack back into the trash. Is that right?"

"Yessir, that sounds right."

"You *immediately* threw it back in the trash?"

"Um, yessir, I suppose."

"You looked at it and then threw it back in the trash."

Percher nodded.

"I'm sorry, Mr. Percher--you looked at it and then threw it *immediately* back in the trash, yes or no?"

Percher swallowed hard. "Yessir."

"What kind of jar was it, Mr. Percher?"

"Well, um, it was just a regular glass jar, you know. A Mason-type jar."

"With a canning lid and ring on it?"

Percher relaxed a little. "Yessir. That's right."

"And it was empty."

"Yessir."

"How did you know the jar had once had gasoline in it, Mr. Percher?"

Percher fidgeted a moment. "Well, sir, I saw a little in the bottom, sloshin' around I guess."

"You guess? I thought you said it was empty."

Percher paused and licked his lips. "Well, I'm thinkin' it wasn't *quite* empty. Just mostly empty."

Joy wondered where Arnie was going with his questions. The courtroom seemed intent also.

"Hmmm. So the jar had a *little* gasoline in it?"

"Yessir." Percher reached for his handkerchief and wiped his face. Absently, Joy wondered if it was a clean one or yesterday's well-used one.

"How did you know it was gasoline in the jar, Mr. Percher?"

Percher looked a little befuddled. "Well, sir, I saw it. Like I said."

"I see." Arnie motioned to Søren. Søren stood and handed Arnie a box. The contents clanked a little. Arnie removed three canning jars from the box and set them on a tray on the defense table. All three jars were filled about a third full with pale liquid.

The prosecutor jumped to his feet but the judge leveled his gavel at him and thundered, "If you stand up again during the defense's presentation, I'll have you removed from my courtroom. Do you understand?"

The prosecutor, his face flaming in indignation, sank into his seat.

"Your Honor, if it pleases the court, I have three jars here. I would like the witness to identify the jar with gasoline in it. May I proceed?"

The judge frowned. "This is a little irregular, Mr. Thoresen."

"Indeed, Your Honor. And so is testifying to finding an empty jar of gasoline that, on cross examination, is *not* empty."

"I take your point, Mr. Thoresen. Proceed."

Arnie picked up the tray and carried it to the witness stand. "Mr. Percher, would you please identify which jar contains gasoline?"

The prosecutor squirmed in his chair but remained seated. Joy looked behind him and saw Robertson staring steadily at Percher. She recognized the coldness of that stare and shivered.

Percher saw the look, too, and shrank a little. He looked over the jars and glanced toward Robertson and back.

"Well, sir . . ."

"Take your time, Mr. Percher," Arnie said softly.

Percher's eyes jumped from one jar to another. A drop of perspiration slid down his forehead.

"Oh! Well, you see, sir, um, actually, I *opened* the jar and *smelled* the gasoline." Percher's relief at coming to this remembrance was palpable.

"But you testified that you *immediately* threw the jar away, Mr. Percher," Arnie pressed.

"Well, sir, I did, you see, but first I opened the jar and smelled the gasoline inside."

Percher's testimony was so patently artificial that a low grumbling went around the courtroom. Arnie quickly pressed on.

"Well, which is it, Mr. Percher? I'm confused. First you say the jar is empty. Then you say it isn't. You also testify that you *immediately* threw the jar away after looking at it, and now you tell us you took the time to unscrew the cap, remove the lid, and sniff the insides." Arnie's shaggy head shook and his voice rose as he pressed Percher. "Which is it, Mr. Percher? Or do you have *another* tall tale to tell us?"

Percher shrank into the witness chair and stuttered, "No sir, that's the God's honest truth, it is!" He appeared ready to slide out of the witness stand.

Arnie turned toward the courtroom and, voice still raised, directed another question over his shoulder toward Percher. "Mr. Percher, please tell the courtroom. Are you acquainted with Mr. Robertson, the prosecution's other witness?" He pointed at Robertson.

The air in the courtroom evaporated as every observer inhaled. "W-w-what?"

"I'm sorry—was I unclear, Mr. Percher?" Arnie strode to the witness stand and enunciated with exaggeration, "Do you know Mr. Robertson, the prosecution's other witness?"

Percher's eyes grew wide. "N-n-n-no! I-I-I d-don't know him!" He cast around the room looking anywhere but at Robertson. "W-w-why would you say that? I don't kn-n-now him!"

While all stared at the drama playing out at the front of the courtroom, Joy stared at Robertson. His face was white and set. Then he turned toward her and smiled. Joy shuddered and felt like a mouse caught in the paws of a malicious cat. She forced herself to continue watching him intently.

"Your Honor," Arnie said, facing the judge. "I would like to dismiss this witness temporarily and ask Søren Thoresen to the stand."

"Relation of yours?" The judge queried.

"My cousin, Your Honor. Mrs. Michael's brother."

"Proceed."

Søren took the stand and was sworn in. Arnie did not waste time. "Mr. Thoresen, where did you go when you left the courtroom yesterday afternoon?"

"I followed the witness, Mr. Percher," Søren replied. He was matter-of-fact and calm.

"Where did he go?"

"He first went to his room, over on Eighth Street. Later he went to a bar on Tenth and Dodge. *The Cattleman's*. About 9 p.m."

"Did you follow him into that bar?"

"I did."

"What did he do in the bar, Mr. Thoresen?"

"He ordered a drink. A few drinks, actually. He spoke to some acquaintances."

"Where were you sitting, Mr. Thoresen? And where was Mr. Percher sitting?"

"He sat at the end of the bar facing the door. I sat at a table in a corner a little behind him."

"He didn't see you?"

"I don't believe so. The corner I sat in was dark."

"How long did you watch Mr. Percher?"

"About two hours."

"What else did you observe while you were in the bar, Mr. Thoresen?"

"Just after 11 p.m. Mr. Robertson came into the bar."

The courtroom erupted again. It was several minutes before the judge could restore order.

Arnie continued his questioning. Joy's attention was now riveted on him. "Did Robertson join Percher at the bar?"

"Yes he did. They spoke for several minutes."

"Did Robertson give Percher anything?"

"He did. He handed him an envelope. Looked like a linen envelope. Then he left."

The murmuring in the courtroom continued and this time the judge ignored it.

The prosecutor stood to his feet and respectfully addressed the judge. "Your Honor, really, I don't know how we can give any credence to Mr. Thoresen's testimony. He is, after all, the defendant's brother."

Before the judge could respond, Arnie asked Søren another question. "Mr. Thoresen, did you visit the bar alone last night?"

Søren spoke clearly. "No, I did not."

Joy glanced back toward Robertson—and all she found was an empty seat. Craning her neck, she searched throughout the courtroom . . . and saw a side door quietly closing. He was gone!

Arnie asked another question. "If you were not alone, who was with you, Mr. Thoresen?"

"William Evans and Isaiah Kimball."

Arnie faced the crowded room. "Are those men in this courtroom, Mr. Thoresen?"

"Yes. They are sitting just there."

Her former employee, Billy, and a man Joy didn't know stood.

Arnie spoke to the judge. "Mr. Kimball is Tom Percher's employer and can identify him." He called to both men. "Can you corroborate Mr. Thoresen's testimony?"

Billy nodded and Kimball said loudly, "I can."

"Thank you, Mr. Thoresen. That will be all."

Franklin stared at Robertson for several minutes. His expression was impassive as always. Franklin was always composed, always in control. In truth, Robertson had never seen him display a hot temper; nevertheless, something dangerous radiated from the man. For the first time in years, Robertson was nervous. He struggled to control his face and his voice.

Finally Franklin spoke. "Apparently Percher was not the ideal selection for the task, wouldn't you say, Robertson?"

"Yes sir. My mistake." Robertson hoped that by taking full responsibility Franklin would give him the chance to fix things.

"Indeed." That was all Franklin said. The silence grew.

At last Robertson, unable to restrain himself, coughed and looked down. *Damn!* he thought. *I just flinched.*

"Mr. Franklin, I take responsibility for this situation. I would like the, er, opportunity to rectify it, if I may have your permission."

Inside, Robertson scorned himself for his obsequiousness, yet his self-survival instinct was in full play.

Franklin fixed him with a cold eye. "Very well, Robertson."

As the door closed behind Robertson, Su-Chong stepped from behind the screen where he had been standing, unseen by Robertson. He stood near Franklin waiting orders.

"After he takes care of Percher."

Su-Chong bowed.

"Oh, and Su-Chong." Franklin flicked a speck of lint from his sleeve. "I'm afraid we won't be staying in Omaha quite as long as I had anticipated. Unfortunately, that will force me to take a loss on one or two of my investments, but I have prospects in mind west of here. I would like to be ready to leave as soon as our business here is concluded. Please make the arrangements."

Su-Chong bowed again.

Chapter 15

"The defendant will please rise."

Joy, with Arnie at her side, stood calmly. Søren, as he had been all during the trial, was seated close behind them.

The judge leveled his gaze at Joy. For the first time, Joy saw something less than condemnation in his demeanor. Something . . . perhaps kindness?

"Mrs. Michaels, the Court has weighed the evidence brought against you. The burden of proof lies on the prosecution's side."

He turned to the prosecutor. "You, sir, provided no physical evidence. Your 'eye witness' was proven to be a liar and a perjurer. As he was also found to be an associate of your other witness, Robertson, that witness's credibility is also suspect."

In the courtroom the crowd began to fidget and murmur.

"Silence!" The judge turned to the prosecutor again. "You have failed to meet your burden of proof, counselor."

"Mrs. Michaels, this court finds you not guilty of arson and insurance fraud."

The crowded courtroom burst into excited chatter. Joy heard several cheers but also a few boos.

"I SAID SILENCE!"

The judge, on his feet, towered over his bench and waved his gavel at the courtroom. "One more outburst and I will have this room cleared! Do I make myself clear?"

Order returned to the room.

"Mrs. Michaels, this verdict clears you of the charges. I regret to say, however, that Liberty Indemnity is still free to press civil suit against you and to refuse payment on your insurance claim until the civil suit is settled."

He cleared his throat. "I also regret to say that the City of Omaha has already moved to condemn your property. Unless you receive building permits from the city, you will be unable to rebuild. From what I have heard, that will not be happening."

He leveled his gaze at several men seated in the courtroom. "In point of fact, I have begun to have my own suspicions regarding this situation. Unfortunately, suspicions are not easily proved. And corrupt government officials are not easily unseated."

The courtroom took a collective breath at this statement and began to search out members of the town council seated in the courtroom.

"I cannot do anything regarding the actions of the council. Those actions may not be ethical or moral but they are within the City's legal rights. I have issued an arrest warrant for Robertson, but he seems to have flown the proverbial coop. Hopefully we'll find him soon and get to the bottom of this. In the meantime, this case is dismissed. Mrs. Michaels, you are free to go."

Joy walked out of the courtroom with Arnie and Søren on either side, Petter and Willem in front breaking a path for her. They put her into a motor car and drove directly to Burlington Station. She and Søren boarded the train and left Omaha within the hour.

Later that day she returned to Papa and Mama in RiverBend. Returned to her childhood home. Returned with nothing but ashes.

Chapter 16

Joy woke again in the room she grew up in. The curtains were the same. The modest furniture was the same. The early morning light coming in the window was the same. Yet she was so very different from the young girl who had left here after graduating from college. She was a woman now living again in her parents' home as she had when she was a still-innocent child. She was no longer a child and no longer innocent about the world or about the hardships of life.

She closed her eyes against the start of a new day and let her mind wander. Since coming home to RiverBend she had at last begun to grieve for Grant. She had no business to run, no crisis to deal with, only time and a shapeless future.

She pressed her head into the pillow and imagined that Grant was beside her in the bed, just inches away. She imagined his arms reaching for her, pulling her into his warmth, his breath upon her lips and then the soft touch as their lips met . . .

Joy let her imagination roam until the tears came. Then she dashed them away and pulled back the covers. She dressed and went quickly into the kitchen to make coffee. Her mama was already there, reading her Bible and sipping that first cup of the day.

Joy hugged Rose and then stepped away to get her own coffee. She was wanted here. And loved here. That was not the problem, of course. The problem was that she couldn't go back to being a child. And she had no idea how to go forward.

She obediently sat down and read several chapters in her papa's Bible. Mama regularly encouraged her to seek God for answers, but it seemed to Joy that answers were in short supply.

She had been at Mama and Papa's in RiverBend for a few weeks. The garden was at the peak of its production so she helped thin it, water it, and pick from its bounty each day. She helped Mama with the canning, with feeding the chickens, gathering eggs, and taking care of their other few animals. She kept Papa company in the late afternoons while Mama napped.

And the corn was ripening early this year. Of all the harvest activities, this had been Joy's favorite as a child—when Papa, usually with Søren's help, Joy running happily behind them, had picked the corn until it filled the wagon to the top of its slatted walls.

It was different now, though. Søren and his eldest son, Markus, would harvest the cornfields on the rise above Jan and Rose's house. Papa busied himself with anything and everything he could do while sitting, which was considerable, but had for all practical purposes given the cornfields to Søren.

That morning when Søren and Markus came to bring in the first of the corn harvest, Joy went out to help them. Later the rest of the family from across the creek came to shuck the corn and to celebrate. Jan, Rose, and Joy were joined by Søren, Meg and their brood along with Karl and Kjell and their families. The many hands made quick work of the mountain of corn.

Afterwards they built a bonfire and shared a feast around it. Joy looked around the large family circle. Her nieces, nephews, and second cousins—16? 17? of them?—ran about laughing and playing. The married women sat in a group exchanging recipes and stories and occasional calls to their children while the grown men sat in a knot swapping news.

She saw herself then . . . so apart from all of them, the only single woman there, the only woman without a purpose or a place.

Abruptly she set her plate aside and walked away. Walked up the rise and into the empty corn field. She kept walking until she reached the far edge of the field and nothing stretched before her except the vast prairie and the sinking sun.

"My heart is as empty as this prairie," she thought in aching wonder.

Behind her on the edge of the rise, her mother watched her. And prayed. With one more look toward the slender woman across their corn field, Rose slowly made her way back down the path to the house where Jan was waiting. Twenty-five years had gone so quickly. Now their Joy was a woman, and she was struggling with her own grief. What could they do for the one who had been their joy and happiness all her life but now had lost her own?

"Oh Lord, you are our great Hope and our Comfort," Rose prayed. "I trust you."

Chapter 17

The following morning when Joy came out for coffee, Rose patted the chair beside her. Joy sat cautiously. Something in the seriousness of Rose's manner made Joy sense that a sermon was coming.

Well, let it come. Joy was ready to cross swords.

"Joy, you remember how you received your name, don't you?" Rose asked softly.

"How could I forget, Mama? 'Joy Again Thoresen'! From the time I was old enough to know my name you told me why you gave it to me." Joy hadn't meant to spit the words at her mother. They sounded harsh, even to her ears. Even so, she rushed on.

"All my life I heard about the joy I brought to you and Papa, about the families you had before you married and had me, and how God gave me to you and I was the joy in your life. But it's not a name *I* want any more. You may have found "joy again," but there is no joy in *my* life any longer!"

She picked up Rose's Bible and thumped it on the table. "You told me to seek God, to read the Scriptures for my answers. Well I did. I read the Book of Ruth. And I found someone I could really relate to. Ruth 1:20."

And she said unto them,
Call me not Naomi, call me Mara:
for the Almighty hath dealt very bitterly with me.

Rose nodded but said nothing.

Joy kept on with heat. "Mara means 'bitter.' That's a better name for me. Not *Joy*, and especially not *Joy Again*."

"Joy," Rose began, but her daughter cut her off.

"Not *Joy*, Mama. Mara. From now on, Mara."

Rose looked carefully at her daughter for several moments before answering quietly but firmly, "I know you are grieving, daughter, but I want to remind you to whom you are speaking. I am your mother, and you will not disrespect me."

Joy flushed and looked down but said nothing. The silence dragged on. Finally Joy muttered, "I'm sorry, Mama."

"I am, too, dear one. More than you know," Rose answered gently.

Again the silence grew.

Finally Rose spoke again. "I asked you earlier if you remembered how you received your name. I know we told you as you were growing up, but we only told you what a child needed to know. Perhaps it is time to tell you as a grown woman."

Joy glanced up.

"I was 19 years old when I married James," Rose stated.

"The same age I was when I married Grant."

"Yes, that's right. We had 13 years together and three children. Jeffrey, Glory, and Clara." Rose paused and moistened her lips. "Joy, you may have never considered this, but you have a brother and two—no, *three*—sisters. In heaven."

Joy said slowly, "I don't think I have ever thought of it that way. I mean, I knew you were married before Papa. I knew he had a daughter . . . and I think I knew you had children but I didn't know their names or what happened to them." She frowned. "Mama, what happened to your husband and children?"

"Oh . . ." Rose looked away.

"You don't have to tell me, Mama," Joy quickly added.

"Thank you. It is still hard to speak of. But perhaps . . . perhaps it would be good for you to hear," Rose responded thoughtfully.

"Well. It was the evening of January 6, James' birthday. We had been to my mother's for a little party and were going home. Not far from our house we had to cross the river. We had a nice carriage and two lovely horses. Vincent was our driver. We were all tucked into the carriage because it was bitterly cold." Rose began to relive that night and she shivered as she recalled the frigid wind.

"We always crossed that river over an old stone bridge that arched over the water. We didn't realize it was coated with ice until the horses began slipping. It happened so quickly."

"One of the horses fell, and the back of the carriage began to slide toward the edge of the bridge." Rose's eyes were wide and she was far away. "The children were so frightened. Glory was only six and clung to James' legs when he stood up. He . . . he . . . I think he knew what was going to happen. He opened the door and threw me out of the carriage as it slid off the bridge." She quickly wiped her eyes and took a sip of water.

Joy's hands were over her mouth in horror. "Oh, Mama!"

Rose's words caught just once. "It was a long time ago. It is astonishing how it can feel like yesterday." She wiped her eyes again.

"Vincent made it to shore and found me on the rocks, half in and half out of the water. But James and the children . . . were lost."

"Did you . . . did they find them, Mama?"

Rose knew that part of Joy's pain was losing Grant at sea, never to see his body or kiss his lips a last time.

"No, Joy. The river froze over again that night." She looked bleakly at her girl. "Just as with you and Grant, I never saw them again. Clara was just a baby. I listened for her crying for so long afterwards."

Joy reached over and hugged her mother tightly to her. "Oh, Mama! I am so sorry! I never knew how awful it was. I'm so sorry."

They clung together crying for several minutes before Rose pulled away and looked her daughter in the face.

"Joy, do you think your Papa loves your brother Søren more than he loves you?"

"What? Of course not!" Joy frowned through her tears. "Why would you ask that?"

Rose was quiet for another minute. She looked out the window and composed herself. "By the same token, do you think Papa loves the daughter he lost *less* than he loves you? Do you think I love Jeffrey, Clara, and Glory *less* than I love you?"

Joy's mouth opened a little and then closed.

Rose continued. "We *never* stop loving those we lose in this life, Joy. Never. You will never stop loving Grant, I can promise you that. But in time, with God's grace and goodness, perhaps you *will* have joy again."

Her daughter stared at her dumbly, her eyes glistening.

"It is because Papa and I never stopped loving our children that your coming was so precious to us. We hadn't expected to be blessed with such happiness again. It was perhaps a little late in life for me and quite late for Papa. You were the only child we had together, but we were so blessed to have you."

Rose dabbed at her eyes. "I think we go through our lives taking for granted those we hold dear. Then when tragedy strikes, we learn a very hard but valuable lesson."

"What is that, Mama?"

Rose looked at her daughter and smiled sadly. "We learn that nothing in this life is forever. We are, after all, as the Bible tells us, only passing through, on our way to our eternal home. For that reason, all happiness here is only temporary, lent to us for a season and, as such, is fragile."

"The most important question to ask those we love is this, 'Will I see you with the Lord on the other side?' Because if the answer to that question is 'yes,' then we can somehow bear the separation. We can bear it because we know we will see them again, and when we do, it will be forever, never to be parted again."

Rose sighed. "My precious daughter Joy. Do you believe you will see Grant again?"

Tears began to trickle down Joys cheeks once more. "Yes, Mama, I know I will. Grant loved Jesus even more than he loved me."

"As he should, my Joy. As he should." She took Joy's hand. "Then let us do this. Let us thank our Father God right now for the great assurance we have. We know where Grant is. We know he is safe. And let us thank him too, that knowing we will see him again *will* make living without him for now bearable."

And Rose and Joy joined hands and wept their thanks unto the Lord.

Chapter 18

Joy studied the envelope, a letter from her cousin Uli and her husband. They were ministers in the small community of Corinth, Colorado, a few miles outside of Denver on the flanks of the mountains. Joy had last seen them at Grant's memorial service.

Joy thought of her cousin, forever more her big sister than cousin. She tapped the envelope against her hand a few times. The letter likely contained additional expressions of sympathy, something Joy didn't think she could take more of. Finally she opened the envelope, unfolding and smoothing the single page on the table. Joy's eyebrows rose in surprise as she read.

> *Dearest Cousin Joy,*
>
> *David and I send you our love. We also send you a challenge.*
>
> *We have been less than candid with our families regarding some of our work in Corinth this past year. The opportunity the Lord has placed before us is unconventional and sometimes touched with danger. For this reason, we have been cautious and reticent to speak of it. However, the task before us is so important and of such consequence, we must address it to those who will listen and will act with us.*
>
> *I speak of a great evil. Corinth is at the center of an industry that preys upon the defenseless, and we are a small but vital part of God's plan to combat this evil. Those who profit from this business operate out of Denver but use our little town to advance their despicable goals. These are powerful and unscrupulous men. We trust God and our wits to keep us hidden and protected, but we are often only a few steps away from discovery and possible disaster.*
>
> *Come to us, Joy. Bring your broken heart to this battle, for we desperately need good soldiers. Your pain will pale in comparison to that of the victims of this wickedness. God will mend you, even as you work to save those who often cannot save themselves.*
>
> *Your loving cousin,*
>
> *Uli*

Joy did not know what to think of the letter and told herself that she did not care. She reread it, puzzled over it, and tossed it unceremoniously into a drawer. But when she woke the next morning, the puzzlement niggled at her. She read the letter again.

"Mama, would you read this letter from Uli and tell me what you think?" Joy asked Rose. "It is a bit mysterious, don't you agree?"

Rose settled into a chair and took up the letter. After several minutes she nodded. "Mysterious, indeed. And yet, I do believe your cousin is a wise woman."

"Oh? In what way do you mean?"

Rose returned the letter to her daughter with a pat on the hand. "Well, she has gotten your attention, hasn't she? She certainly has mine. Now you will have to ask her to explain herself if you are to know the mystery. Or am I wrong?"

Joy paused. "Hmm. I see your point."

She stood up with resolve. "Well, I'm *not* going to write and ask her. If she thinks that I will uproot myself to Colorado, she will be disappointed," and she stomped to her room.

Rose heard the dresser drawer open and close with a thump. But she muttered under her breath, "A very wise woman. Thank you, Lord."

> *Dear Cousin Uli,*
>
> *Received your letter. Please explain in detail.*
>
> *Love to you, David, and the children,*
>
> *Joy*

Joy was as grumpy as the tone of her letter. As much as she would have preferred not to, Joy fretted in her mind about the curious contents of Uli's letter. She conjured up several scenarios that might fit the enigmatic message: Combating the evils of drink? Child labor? What would a minister and his wife give themselves to that presented the level of danger Uli wrote of?

Although she would have flatly denied it, Joy anxiously looked for a letter in response to her terse missive, one that would at least solve her puzzlement. Not that it would induce her to move to the mountains of Colorado, thank you very much. Her life was here, in Nebraska. Or at least it had been.

The letter arrived sooner than Joy expected.

Dearest Joy,

You have asked for detail. I will fill this letter with as much detail and passion as my pen and my heart will permit. Please allow me to write plainly, for my heart is overflowing with grief and I know that you, a sister in mourning, will permit me to share that grief with you, as you know I would receive yours.

What I speak of is the entrapment of unsuspecting young women, some no more than children. Through a cleverly designed scheme, they are lured here to Colorado and forced into a life of unspeakable horror and bondage.

The evil men behind this scheme write sincerely worded advertisements which they place in major newspapers in the east. The advertisements seek young women for seemingly respectable positions, but actually prey on young ladies who are desperate and without opportunities.

When a woman responds to the advertisement, she receives a letter with a number of questions. The letter asks, among other things, if she has family and if she can provide recommendations—but assures her that a lack of recommendation will not necessarily disqualify her from the position. As far as we can ascertain, only women who have no family and no one to recommend them are "hired" and are sent train tickets to Denver.

As soon as an applicant arrives in Denver, she is brought to our little community. Two houses in an otherwise respectable neighborhood are operated by these unscrupulous people. The girl is taken to one of them where, instead of a respectable position, she is forced into intimacies with men who pay well to deflower an unsoiled young woman.

After she loses her appeal to these evil men, she is taken back to Denver and placed in a more common brothel for use by any who will pay. Girls who resist, who try to run away, and who will not learn to "accommodate" the demands of the customers are beaten, starved, and abused unspeakably until their spirits are broken.

Some applicants who were widowed or who had children out of marriage were also offered positions and allowed to bring their children. As you can imagine, a mother alone and without means would look on such an opportunity as manna from heaven. However, once they arrive in these "houses," their children are taken away and their continued safety is used to blackmail the mothers into a life of prostitution and veritable slavery.

Worse than this—and I can scarcely bear to put this to paper—the children, both boys and girls, are raised until they, too, are of an age to be used by evil men. Joy! How can men whom God created in his own image descend to such evil? I cannot comprehend it, and yet the evidence is before our eyes.

Because these poor creatures are alone in the world, no one wonders when they go missing. No one comes to look for them or their children.

We have been able to rescue three of these women and, after ministering to the needs of their hearts and bodies, spirit them along a loosely constructed underground to new lives far from here and far from the men who have so misused them.

You may wonder why the men behind these acts have chosen Corinth to "break in" these young women. We are less than two hours by train from the heart of the city. While Denver has many houses of ill repute, to kidnap, rape, and break the will of a young woman— especially very young ones—is a much more serious crime. It is done here, away from the city and where, I am ashamed to say, bribes induce some town officials to wink at these despicable acts.

A very "elite" type of customer, one whose appetites include the perverse and sadistic, arrives on the train in the evening and returns home before morning. As the railway through Corinth is a main line to destinations farther east, the interchange between Denver and Corinth is regular. Those who come to Corinth for "sport" are not obvious to the casual observer.

The young women who have escaped to us are beset with shame, fear, and self-loathing. They have nowhere to go and no way to support themselves. Joy, God has bestowed organizational skills upon you we have such need of. More than that, your broken heart will understand and pity their condition.

All that they were has been taken from them, Joy. Only Jesus can heal and set them free. I shared Isaiah 61 with one of the young women who stayed briefly with us—it seemed so fitting!

> *The Spirit of the Lord God is upon me;*
> *because the Lord hath anointed me*
> *to preach good tidings unto the meek;*
> *he hath sent me to bind up the brokenhearted,*
> *to proclaim liberty to the captives, and*
> *the opening of the prison to them that are bound;*
> *To proclaim the acceptable year of the Lord,*
> *and the day of vengeance of our God;*
> *to comfort all that mourn;*
> *To appoint unto them that mourn in Zion,*
> *to give unto them beauty for ashes,*
> *the oil of joy for mourning,*
> *the garment of praise for the spirit of heaviness;*
> *that they might be called trees of righteousness,*
> *the planting of the Lord, that he might be glorified.*

Is this not the same passage that our Savior quoted? And did he not say, "Today I have fulfilled this prophesy?" What greater ministry can there be than to bring Jesus to every wounded girl and woman and to proclaim them free?

We need you, Joy. Come to us, for the work is great.

Your loving cousin,

Uli

Chapter 19

Edmund O'Dell greeted several acquaintances as he entered the Chicago office of Pinkerton Detective Agency.

"O'Dell? Get in here!" The rough-spoken words were bellowed from an office down the hall.

"Hey, Boss." O'Dell tossed his trademark bowler hat onto a hook on the coat rack inside Parson's office.

"Took you long enough to get back."

"Had a lot to look into."

"And?"

"Strangest missing persons case I've encountered." O'Dell plucked a cigar from his breast pocket and quickly returned it when Parson glared at him.

"Missing persons and kidnap are your specialty, your bread and butter. What's so strange?"

O'Dell shrugged. "Working it from the other end, that's what. And not much to go on. So what's the news here on our 'train kidnapping' cases?"

"News? Every time we think we have a solid lead, it turns up dust. They must have every official in Denver on their payroll. They keep moving their letter drops but have some means to forward stray letters to the next drop before we can intercept them. What did you turn up in Boston?"

"Same thing as in New York, Philadelphia, and Baltimore. Interviewed a few women who answered the ad, received and answered questionnaires, but did not receive further correspondence. As we surmised, in every case we interviewed, the woman had family members who would have made official inquiries if she went missing."

"Any other families in Boston with missing women?"

"Found one, but just a drunk father. I think his 'concern' was mostly that his missing daughter wasn't around to support him anymore. She probably lied on the questionnaire to get away."

"You get enough information to trace her to Denver?"

"I think so. Plan to head that way." O'Dell was already bored and ready to head west.

"And your 'strangest' case?"

"Yeah. Well, that's a whole other ball of wax, isn't it?"

"Any leads at all?"

"I have a few ideas."

Parson snorted. "Your *ideas* usually pay off like most detectives' solid leads." He spoke with reluctant admiration.

O'Dell shrugged modestly. "Well, I have some things to attend to up north. Be back in a few weeks. Then I'll look into my, er, *ideas* and follow up on the leads with our office in Denver."

Chapter 20

Shelby Franklin looked about him in satisfaction. His offices and apartment were impeccable and located in the best areas of Denver. He had quickly identified several of the right acquaintances—those who would soon acknowledge him as their new best friend. His uncanny capacity to analyze and gain access to both the social and business workings of a city was his greatest strength—on par with his ability to seize the reins of power before his quarry even perceived the threat.

Denver would be different, though. Here he would establish himself and make his new identity permanent. No more temporary schemes to pluck low-hanging fruit and run. No, he had accumulated the small fortune he needed in that manner, but would now settle here, partly because he liked the area, partly because he had already left a trail to the east of Denver, and finally because to the west lay the land of his origins. And he did not wish to revisit there.

He had grown to adulthood in California but had relocated to the east coast to begin what he fondly viewed as his metamorphosis. From one identity to another he had changed and grown until he was as comfortable in whatever new persona he chose for himself as the one he had been born in.

No, that was not quite right. He had never been comfortable in the role he had been born to.

He didn't linger on those memories, for that is all they were. He had transcended what the fates had assigned him—he had superseded a sentence of poverty and mediocrity by the sheer power of his superior mind and will.

Using his fortune and his intellect, he had, in only a few weeks, laid the foundation for his empire. His financial advisement was solid and, *this time*, would be completely above-board. This time, he would make money both for himself *and* his clients. On the side he would also invest himself where he knew money was most abundant—the vices of men—but didn't many wealthy men do so?

Franklin smiled to himself. He knew how to spot weaknesses and exploit them for his purposes. In fact, he hadn't been able to resist taking control of that insurance company in Omaha, *Liberty Indemnity*. After the trial of that Michaels woman ended, public opinion had turned against and nearly destroyed the company.

So, even as he manipulated the circumstances behind its financial troubles, he had moved in to buy the controlling interest. Under his present name, of course! And at quite a discounted price. The company would remain headquartered in Omaha, but he would rebuild it from here in Denver . . . a virgin market that would respond well to his touch.

Yes, his new identity would be his last. He had saved it for this phase of his life. The man whose name he would bear had left a sterling reputation in England some seven years before and had traveled to America to establish himself here. He had left no family in England and had died without notice. Franklin had arranged that, of course. He had kept the man's effects and done regular business in his name over the past five years—letter writing, banking, investing—so that all Franklin need do is step into his new identity. He had done so with his move to Denver.

He signaled Su-Chong who opened the door for him and silently took up position close behind him.

This was the persona he would wear from here forward.

Chapter 21

Joy did not know how long she remained seated with Uli's letter before her. As she came to herself, the tears running down her face became sobs, and she wept, wept as she had not even been able to when Grant died. She wept for herself but, strangely, she wept also for the women Uli described, those women whose pain seemed so real and near to her.

She reread the passage in Isaiah again, fixing her eyes on verse three:

> *. . . to give unto them beauty for ashes,*
> *the oil of joy for mourning . . .*

Wasn't this her? Wasn't her life ashes and mourning? Could Jesus give *her* beauty and joy again? As she sobbed a rough but gentle hand rested on her back.

"Oh Papa!"

Jan sat beside her and gathered her to himself as he had when she was a child. "Dear daughter." He held her tightly and gently stroked her back.

Eventually Joy's sobs eased and she sat up, wiping her face on her papa's handkerchief.

"I'm sorry, Papa."

"*Nei*, child," he smiled. "What ist reading?"

Joy hesitated and then offered him Uli's letter. Joy watched the play of emotions on her papa's face as he carefully read and then re-read Uli's long message. She saw the stern tightening of his jaw. Finally he handed the letter back to Joy.

"We mus' pray for Uli an' David, Joy. Pray da' Lord help dem overcome dis evil." He looked at her intently. "Pray you know for God's vill in dis."

"God's will in this? How is this possibly God's will? This, this is *horrible*. And what could I possibly do to help them?"

"Daughter, you not know how da Savior taught his friends to pray?" Jan quoted,

> *Our Fat'er which ar' in heaven, Hallowed be dy name.*
> *Dy kingdom come, Dy will be done in earth, as ist in heaven.*

"He say, 'you pray dat Gott's vill be done *here*, as ist done in heaven,' Joy. Gott's vill *not* done here on da earth most time. Ve who carry Gott's Kingdom inside us, *ve pray* and *ve bring* Gott's Kingdom to dis earth."

"Dis ver' evil t'ing in Uli and David's town, ve mus' pray and mus' bring heaven's vill as Gott leads us. Mus' pray too, ist Gott's vill for you?"

Joy frowned. "We must pray and find out if this is God's will for me?"

"Ja, daughter, ist so." Jan patted her hand. "Time of mourning mus' end, dear one. You mus' ask da Lord for . . . direct . . . for his vill for *you*."

"But Papa . . ." Joy so wanted to resist his words.

"Joy." Jan looked at her steadily and Joy felt 10 years old again. "Time for life mus' be coming again. You ask. Mama and I ask. Gott vill tell."

He struggled to his feet, leaning heavily on his cane. "Ven Gott tell, den ve do."

Joy sat at the table resisting her papa's exhortation to pray, but . . . both he and mama were such examples of living beyond grief and living for the Lord despite pain and difficulty. Even with crippled knees that continually ached and throbbed, Jan gathered the young men of the community around him and taught them from the Bible, praying with them and helping them to grow up in the Lord and into their responsibilities as husbands and fathers.

She looked at Uli's letter laying there and resented it, resented Uli, and resented the pull on her damaged heart. Sighing, she took it up again and re-read,

> *to comfort all that mourn;*
> *To appoint unto them that mourn in Zion,*
> *to give unto them beauty for ashes,*
> *the oil of joy for mourning,*
> *the garment of praise for the spirit of heaviness;*
> *that they might be called trees of righteousness,*
> *the planting of the Lord,*
> *that he might be glorified.*

"That he might be glorified." She weighed again what her papa had said. *You pray that God's will be done* here, *as it is done in heaven, Joy. God's will is* not *done here on the earth most of the time. We who carry God's Kingdom inside of us, we pray and we bring God's Kingdom to this earth.*

Joy went into her room and opened several drawers, until she found the Bible of her childhood. Turning to Isaiah 61, she read the passage for herself.

"*To comfort all that mourn . . .*" she pondered. "That would certainly include me." Resigned, Joy dropped the book on her bed and knelt down. "I might as well get this over with, because Papa will ask me if I have prayed."

"Lord," she began, "I feel like I don't have any life left in me, but my papa says you will give me direction . . . for whatever *might* be left." She sighed again, straining at the bleakness in her soul. "I guess I am asking you . . . do you have any comfort for me like this passage says? Any 'oil of joy'? Because if I am honest, I feel that I am crushed under a 'spirit of heaviness.' Lord, what can I do? How can I begin again? What would you have me do?"

She thought on Jan's words again. *This very evil thing in Uli and David's town, we must pray and must bring heaven's will as God leads us. Must pray too, is it God's will for you?*

Joy wanted to refuse his counsel, but at last she bowed her head again. "Father God, I am asking you to lead and guide me. Let me know—and let Papa know—that it is *not* your will for me to go to Colorado and help Uli and David. Amen."

She frowned a little. "Well, perhaps that is not quite right. I'm sorry. Let me begin again. Lord, I am asking you to lead and guide me. Let me know *your* will for me. If you truly want me to do something, and if you let me know, then I will do it."

Satisfied that she had obeyed her papa's request, she pulled the Bible toward her and opened it again to Isaiah. As she flipped through, looking for chapter 61, the book fell open to chapter 54. She paused and began to read.

> *Sing, O barren one, thou that didst not bear;*
> *break forth into singing, and cry aloud,*
> *thou that didst not travail with child:*
> *for more are the children of the desolate*
> *than the children of the married wife,*
> *saith the LORD.*

Joy's breath caught in her chest. "*I* am the barren one!" she whispered. "This is *me!*" Her eyes raced ahead on the page.

> *Enlarge the place of thy tent,*
> *and let them stretch forth the curtains of thine habitations:*

spare not, lengthen thy cords, and strengthen thy stakes;
For thou shalt break forth on the right hand and on the left;
and thy seed shall inherit the Gentiles,
and make the desolate cities to be inhabited.

"Thy seed? Shall inherit?" She laughed harshly. Until she read the next verses.

Fear not; for thou shalt not be ashamed:
neither be thou confounded;
for thou shalt not be put to shame:
for thou shalt forget the shame of thy youth,
and shalt not remember the reproach
of thy widowhood any more.

She relived the shame of the past year . . . enduring the loss of her husband, having to work so hard against prejudice and ill-will to keep their business intact, the pressure and threats and then . . . the way her own community had believed her guilty of arson and had forced her to sell her properties. "I know a little about shame," Joy muttered darkly.

For thy Maker is thine husband;
the Lord of hosts is his name;
and thy Redeemer the Holy One of Israel;
The God of the whole earth shall he be called.
For the Lord hath called thee
as a woman forsaken and grieved in spirit,
and a wife of youth, when thou wast refused,
saith thy God.

For the Lord hath called thee . . . as a woman forsaken and grieved in spirit, and a wife of youth. Yes, she was a woman forsaken and grieved in spirit.

For a small moment have I forsaken thee;
but with great mercies will I gather thee.
In a little wrath I hid my face from thee for a moment;
but with everlasting kindness will I have mercy on thee,
saith the Lord thy Redeemer.

Mercy. I will have mercy on thee . . . Joy bowed her head and prayed once more. "Lord, I come to you with all the shame and grief I feel. I give them to you. I come to you and lay them at your feet asking you, do you . . . *will* you have mercy on me? Will you gather me to yourself?" She read again:

Enlarge the place of thy tent,
and let them stretch forth the curtains of thine habitations:
spare not, lengthen thy cords, and strengthen thy stakes;
For thou shalt break forth on the right hand and on the left;
and thy seed shall inherit the Gentiles,
and make the desolate cities to be inhabited.

Her eyes returned to the top of the chapter.

For more are the children of the desolate
than the children of the married wife,
saith the LORD.

She carefully marked the passage and sat thinking on it. "More are the children of the desolate . . ." she muttered. "The desolate."

Evening shadows were falling when Joy finished praying and closed her Bible. "If Corinth is as Uli says, then it is a desolate place, if I've ever heard of one. Perhaps . . . it is a good place to begin again."

She and God had wrestled with more than one thing as day gave way to night. Joy touched the gold band on her left hand and gently pulled it off. Tears fell anew as she kissed it and then tucked it into the back of a tiny drawer in her jewelry box.

"You believe the Lord has directed you to go, Joy?" Rose spoke calmly. She and Jan waited for her response.

"Yes, Mama. I am surprised, but I do believe it."

"Den ve say 'amen' to his vill for you, daughter," Jan replied and Rose nodded in agreement. Jan's eyes glinted with love and approval.

"I will write Uli and David right away," Joy told them.

Dear Uli and David,

I have prayed about your letter as have Papa and
Mama. I believe that the Lord has directed me to
come. I confess to thinking I may be less a help than a
burden, but I must set myself to thinking differently
somehow.

If you please, I will prepare to leave RiverBend in about two weeks. As you can imagine, I don't have much to bring, but Mama and I will make sure I have adequate clothing before my departure.

Your loving cousin,

Joy Thoresen

P.S. My infamy under the name Michaels will do your work no good. I have, therefore, decided to take up my maiden name again and would be grateful if you would introduce me in Corinth by the same.

Joy

Chapter 22

"Mr. O'Dell?"

O'Dell didn't know why it felt like the man had crept out of the woodwork when he had merely stood up as O'Dell strode through the reception area.

"Branch? What are you doing in Chicago?"

Branch twisted his hat awkwardly in his left hand. He slanted an anxious look around the waiting area. The Pinkerton clients in the waiting area quickly feigned disinterest. "May we talk?"

O'Dell snorted. If he had a dollar for every time he and Branch had "talked," he'd be a rich man. "Right. Come on then." He led the way to an office he used when in town.

"All right, Branch. What's on your mind?"

Branch hesitated. "Any news?"

"If I had news, I would have contacted you. We've discussed this before, right?" O'Dell pinned his client with impatient eyes. "Now look. I can't contact you if you keep moving around, can I? What if I did have news? How would I have reached you?"

Branch looked down at the battered hat balancing on his left knee. "It drives me, you know? Won't let me rest."

"Why did you leave Boston? I thought you had a job. A decent one."

"I did. But . . ." The man swept his hair out of his eyes. It had been dark brown once; now it was shot prematurely with silver. A patch on his cheek was roughly abraded. "Can't keep my mind on the work, you know? I dream . . . such vivid dreams. I sometimes see her. Then I wake up and . . ." He shook his head adamantly. "I know she's out there . . . and I can't stay put."

Something in the man's manner always stirred O'Dell. "I'm looking. I'm following every lead. I don't know when, but I will find her," O'Dell promised.

He promised because he had never failed on a case he had really put his heart into. He promised because the man's earnestness and pain haunted him. He didn't want it to. He even fought it sometimes, tried to harden his heart against it. But every time he saw the man again, he promised.

O'Dell, yer a fool, he thought to himself. *A bloody, soft-hearted fool.*

"Look here, Branch. I need to know where you'll be or how to reach you. If I think I've found her, I'll want you to come right away. Perhaps seeing her will . . . you know . . ." He let that linger a moment but Branch did not reply.

"I'm following up on some promising leads soon. If you move around, let this office know where you are. If I can't find you, I'll leave word here for you." O'Dell stood up. "Agreed?"

"Yes. Thank you," came the soft reply. Branch plucked his hat off his leg and moved toward the door and then turned.

"You will find her?"

God almighty, O'Dell thought.

"Yes."

"Thank you. I . . . I'm praying, you see. When I pray I feel like I've found a piece of myself. When I pray . . . I feel hopeful. Like things will break through," Branch muttered.

Yeah; me too, O'Dell thought sardonically and then repeated aloud, "I'll find her."

"Thank you. I pray for you, too, Mr. O'Dell. The Lord bless you."

"Yeah. Thanks." O'Dell replied automatically.

Sifting through the particulars of Branch's case again, he made a reluctant decision. He knocked on Parson's door.

"Just letting you know. I'm off tomorrow."

"Oh? Where to?" Parson didn't really care. The question was more perfunctory than interested.

"Omaha, I think. Then on to Denver. I've delayed this too long."

Chapter 23

September 1908

On that dripping-wet morning, the Union Pacific train eased out of RiverBend's little station. Joy finished stowing her bag and packages and found Søren and Meg waving to her from the platform. She blew them one kiss before turning away from their somber faces. She had happily endured many cautions and words of advice from the two of them before boarding her car. She knew how much they cared for her. They would do anything to fix the ruin her life was in. If only it were so easy.

Sensing her emotions beginning to tumble, Joy shook herself and pulled her handbag open. She tugged out her little green journal and opened it to the back. She removed five small newspaper clippings. Each was from a different paper in either Boston or New York, several weeks past: The Boston Globe. The Boston Times. South Boston Inquirer. The New York Times and the Tribune. All five clippings, while not exactly the same, read in a similar manner.

> *Help Wanted*
> *Young woman for light domestic work.*
> *Must be able to relocate, Denver, Colorado.*
> *Travel paid; good wage.*
> *Children allowed with prior approval.*
> *Send letter of inquiry to . . .*

Joy pondered the dark intentions that Uli and David maintained were hidden in those simple words. If what they insisted was so, then the wrong being done in and around Corinth was truly monstrous.

Joy stepped into the aisle of the swaying train and took stock of her surroundings. Her train had originated in the east and come through many cities, including Omaha, before stopping briefly in RiverBend. She had hastily counted passenger cars before boarding and was determined to walk through all of them.

Making her way down the narrow aisles, she kept her eyes open, believing she would know what she was looking for when she saw it—*if* it was actually to be found on that train. The odds were against it, yes, but she was determined to look.

In the third car a young woman sitting alone caught her eye. She seemed a little nervous and frequently looked around. Her dress and hairstyle were decidedly "countrified." Actually, Joy recognized the way the girl's hair was done—two long, blonde braids, wound in opposite directions from the base of her neck across the top of her head, and pinned so that they formed a crown around her pleasantly plump face. Decidedly Scandinavian, Joy knew, from her Norwegian roots.

She chided herself for not having a plan to "arrange" a meeting with the girl. She would be more prepared as she returned to her seat.

Joy kept moving toward the back of the train looking for other young women traveling alone. In the second-to-last passenger car she glimpsed a dark-haired girl. The girl was not much taller than a child—certainly much shorter than Joy—and could scarcely be seen over the tops of the seats. She stared fixedly out of the train window into the rain, holding tightly to a faded handbag in her lap.

As Joy drew alongside of the girl, her book "slipped" out of her hands and onto the seat next the young woman. The dark-haired girl glanced over, quickly picked up Joy's book, and returned it to her.

"Oh! Clumsy me," Joy smiled as she took the book. "Thank you *so* much."

The girl offered only a tight smile in return and didn't speak, so Joy plunged ahead. "I love a good train ride, don't you? What beautiful sights we will see! I'm going to Denver. We'll see real mountains there—tall ones! Where are you bound? My name is Joy Thoresen, by the way."

"I'm bein' called Breona," the girl replied shyly. "Breona Byrne. Denver! 'Tis t' Denver I be goin', too."

Many of Joy's childhood friends were McKennies. If she was hearing correctly, Breona's accent was Irish. As were the snapping black eyes that reminded her of "Aunt" Fiona's.

Joy forced herself to blather mindlessly. "Are you traveling by yourself? I am. We'll be on this train for two whole days. It would be lovely to have someone to talk to."

Breona tilted her head to the side in a charming way and studied Joy. Finally she said, "Yis. I'm belaivin' I would enjoy yer comp'ny. Would ye care to set a spell?"

"Thank you so much. My things are farther up in another car, but they will be fine for a bit."

They settled in and talked a little about the passing scenery and the weather, gradually warming to each other. Joy took careful inventory of Breona's plain but clean skirt and blouse, her scuffed shoes, and the way Breona tried to keep her small hands in the folds of her skirt or under her bag.

But Joy had seen the girl's hands when she returned Joy's book, and the girl could no more talk without using her hands than could any of the McKennie clan. Her hands were red and rough, hands accustomed to hot water, harsh soap, and hard work. Joy was acutely aware of her own smart new suit, gleaming shoes, and spotless gloves. No wonder Breona had set her head to the side and appraised Joy before inviting her to sit down.

If Joy were to guess, she would fix Breona's age at 17 although, with her tiny frame, she could easily be mistaken for 14. And her face had that pinched, wizened look that bespoke too many days without enough to eat.

Finally Joy said casually, "I'm from Omaha. My family lives in RiverBend, where the train just stopped, but I lived in Omaha for several years."

Joy forced back images of Grant and thoughts of her lost love, home, and business. She pushed down all the things her short statement left unsaid. With effort she kept emotion from her voice and continued, "I'm visiting my cousin and her family. Once we are in Denver, I will change trains and ride to their little town, Corinth, not far from Denver."

Breona replied quietly, fidgeting with her little bag. "I'm bein' from Boston, at leas' nearby, and am t' be met by me new employer in Denver."

"Ah!" Joy answered, keeping her tone innocent. "How interesting! But why ever did you secure a position so far from Boston? Won't your family miss you?"

Breona was silent for several moments before saying stoutly, "Miss Joy, m'family is goon. As I'm a grown woman, I mus' make me own way in t' worl'."

Joy was silent for a moment, too, suddenly recognizing how blessed she was in comparison to this young girl. Then she said with forced cheerfulness, "Why, I do believe it is past lunch time! And I scarcely ate any breakfast, what with last minute packing and getting to the station on time. My mother made me such a huge lunch! I'm ravenous, aren't you? I'll just go fetch it and we'll have ourselves a little feast."

Joy bounced out of her seat without waiting for a response from Breona. She glanced back and saw a hungry hope flicker across the girl's face.

"And just try to talk me out of sharing it with you, Miss Breona Byrne!" Joy muttered to herself.

She made her way up the train, but the blonde girl she had noticed earlier was not where Joy had seen her sitting. Joy made it back to her seat, pulled out the paper-wrapped bundle containing the lunch her mama had packed for her, and began her way back to Breona.

Her thoughts and feelings were awhirl. Had Breona answered one of the advertisements tucked into the back of Joy's journal? Was she unknowingly about to be snared by unscrupulous men? Joy felt fear and loathing swelling in her breast, and something else: She was gripped by a feeling of righteous anger she had never before experienced. Joy's jaw clenched. Without intending so, her steps down the aisle quickened with purpose.

She paid no notice to a passenger seated near the door of her car. His eyes were shadowed by the short, curled brim of a derby hat.

As she crossed from one car to another, she saw a man crushing a young woman against the end of the next car. The man's tall, lean body mostly hid the woman, but Joy could hear her voice, and she *did* catch a hint of the woman's blonde braids pinned around her head.

"Please! Let me go! You're hurting me!"

Joy didn't think; she only acted. She grabbed the man's arm, pulled on it as hard as she could muster, and shouted, "*You!* Let her go, *immediately!*"

The man stumbled back, his face flaming with anger and lust, his fist raised against Joy. A glance at her face gave him pause, for she was emboldened by something or someone so much greater than herself and he saw so in her narrowed eyes. Instead of flinching back, Joy stepped closer and stared him down. He was tall, but Joy was too, and they locked eyes.

Something of Joy's papa awakened inside of her.

Something right and holy, yet hard and unyielding.

"You are a scoundrel. If I were a man I would thrash you within an inch of your life," she said coldly. "As it is, I'll have you thrown off this train if you so much as look at this woman again." Her blue eyes, icy in their reproach, never flickered.

For a tense moment they stared at each other, he with a cooling lust and she with an icy fury she had not known she possessed. Without looking away from the man, Joy reached behind the man, grasped the girl by the hand, and dragged her toward the door and into the next car.

They reached the girl's seat, and Joy drew her, a bit roughly, into it and took the seat beside her. Somehow she had maintained possession of her lunch and handbag, although the package was now a bit crushed.

Neither of them spoke a word. Joy's breath was coming in gasps as she tried to calm herself and take stock of her actions. What *had* come over her! What *had* she just done!

A tiny gulp from the seat next to her finally broke through Joy's jumbled thoughts. She turned her head. The girl was shaking, trembling, tears streaming down her face.

Joy sighed. "Are you all right?" she finally asked. Carefully, Joy touched the girl's hand. The young woman started and sobbed again.

"It's all right. It is going to be all right," Joy soothed. "I promise you. It *will* be all right."

They sat quietly for a quarter of an hour. Joy wondered briefly if Breona had given up on sharing her "little feast." At last Joy turned to the girl next to her.

"My name is Joy Thoresen. I'm from Omaha. Are you Swedish or Norwegian?"

The girl, still trembling, nodded her head. "Svedish."

Joy nodded too. "Are you feeling better now?"

"Ja—I mean *yes*, denk you."

"What is your name, if I may ask?"

"Marit Dahlin." She hiccupped. "Sorry."

"No need to apologize, Marit. 'Little Pearl,' ja?" Joy smiled because she had inadvertently lapsed into the familiar response of her home and childhood.

Marit nodded, smiling timidly in return. Two dimples briefly showed themselves in an otherwise unremarkable face. Marit was not a striking young woman, but she was sweetly lovely and round in all the right places. Why would this lovely girl, perhaps only 15, leave a home where she was obviously well cared for?

"Marit, I need to talk to you about something important. May I speak plainly?" Joy was beginning to be weary. And she *was* hungry.

Marit looked confused but hiccupped and nodded again.

Joy sighed. How to begin? "Marit, I am going to show you some newspaper clippings. Is that all right with you?"

Without waiting to see Marit's response, Joy opened her handbag, pulled out her journal, and opened the green book to the back. She lifted the clippings out carefully.

"Do you read?" Joy asked.

"Yes," the girl answered, taking up the clippings. She leafed through them and her brow furrowed as she did.

"These? They are all from same paper? Paper in Minnesota?"

"No," Joy replied. "All from different papers in Boston and New York City."

Marit felt under her seat and pulled out a small suitcase. Setting it on her lap, she undid the latches and reached inside, retrieving a newspaper. It was folded open to the classified ads. One ad was carefully marked in pencil. She handed it to Joy.

> *Help Wanted*
> *Young lady for light work in family dairy.*
> *Must be able to relocate, Denver, Colorado.*
> *Expenses paid; good wage.*
> *Children allowed with prior approval.*
> *Send letter of inquiry to . . .*

Joy blanched. She looked again at Marit, happened to glance down at the suitcase in her lap, and saw the small roundness between the suitcase and her waist.

Dear God in heaven!

Chapter 24

An hour later, Joy and Marit walked together down the train to find Breona. When she saw Joy, her response was cool and distant.

"Breona, I need to apologize to you. I was delayed in bringing our lunch, but I have it right here. I hope you will forgive me." Joy pointed to the paper-wrapped bundle under her arm.

Glancing at the package, Breona involuntarily swallowed and licked her lips.

Joy gestured toward Marit. "Breona, this is Marit Dahlin. She is also going to Denver. May I suggest that we turn this seat in front of you around to accommodate all three of us and our very overdue lunch? Then I will explain my delay."

As the bench in front of Breona was empty, they flipped it over so that it faced Breona's seat. Soon all three of them were sitting and Joy was sharing out the lunch. Breona placed a dilapidated case across their knees. It was held together with twine, but worked admirably as a table.

Joy's mama had packed two large roast beef sandwiches (slightly squished now but edible), two apples, pickles wrapped in paraffin paper, a small cake of gingerbread, an apricot tart folded up in a napkin, a small knife, and a jar of apple juice. Joy deftly divided all the food, placing Marit and Breona's parts onto the napkin, leaving her portion on the brown paper wrapping.

She bowed her head. "Father God, today is a good day—a great day. We are fed by your bounty and give you honor. We are in your hands and thank you for every good and perfect gift in our lives. Amen."

They tucked into the food and left no crumb remaining. Joy handed round the jar of juice and they took turns sipping it until it, too, was empty. Then they cleared the suitcase and stowed it again under Breona's seat.

Joy sighed. "I needed that. Did you have enough, Breona?"

Breona's dark eyes looked brighter. "'Twas bein' th' most I've eaten since leavin' Boston, Miss Joy. I thank ye kindly."

Marit nodded, "Ja, Miss Joy. I denk you, too." She looked embarrassed. "I brought some food, but ate the last yester eve. I hadn't eaten yet today. I have a little money . . . "

"*Nei*, child," Joy replied quickly and then laughed because Marit had the knack of bringing out Joy's roots. Or at least her father's mannerisms. She smiled, thinking fondly of her papa. "That won't be necessary."

Then she sobered. "Breona, I think we need to talk." She lowered her voice to a whisper and leaned forward. The car had many ears that could be listening.

An hour later, Marit and Breona, both now sitting across from Joy, were grasping each other's hands. Breona had finally gone quiet and still, but Marit was shaking.

"Marit," Joy whispered. The girl's haunted eyes turned to her. "You are in a family way, aren't you?"

Fresh tears streamed down her face. "O Miss Joy, vat am I to do? I can't go back home—they don't know, and my *far*—my fat'er—will not understand." She began to sob and Breona pulled the younger girl's face into her shoulder, gently stroking her hair.

As she calmed, Joy asked her a few more questions. "Marit, what about the father of your baby? Does he know? Will he not do right by you?"

Breona waited with Joy for a response, but Marit only looked down in shame and said nothing.

"I'm sorry, dear one. I shouldn't pry."

Marit shook her head. "I . . . I can tell you. It's just that . . . ." She gulped and said softly, "The man . . . who did this is already married."

Breona's eyes were as wide as saucers and, indeed, Joy was taken aback. To err with a sweetheart was serious enough, but to dally with a man who was married! Then Joy recalled the exact words Marit had used.

"Marit, you said, *the man who did this*." Joy paused, wondering how to say it delicately. "Did this man . . . force you?"

Marit began trembling again and Breona's arm tightened around her. "There, there, miss," she crooned softly.

Joy persisted gently. "He did. He forced you, is that it?" Joy thought she would burst with anger.

Marit nodded weakly.

"And you didn't think you could tell your mama and papa?"

Marit sobbed. "*Mor* died two vinters past. *Far* is terrible angry most times. I can't . . . he doesn't see me or hear me . . . I know he vould not haf believed me . . . he respects . . . that man so much . . .

and ve are beholden to him . . ." She wiped her face and shuddered. "I vorked in the dairy, you see, that man's dairy. Ve sorely needed the money and he vould always send me off by myself for some reason . . . and then he vould be there . . ."

She sobbed. "I couldn't get shut of him! I couldn't!"

"Aye, lass. Shush. I'm knowin' of what yer sayin'." Breona's eyes, already older than they should be, turned to Joy. "I was workin' fer a fam'ly of quality. Th' elder son vexed me life in th' same manner. Tha's why I answered th' post in th' paper. T' be gettin' shut of his advances. And now air ye tellin' us th't we've left th' fryin' pan fer th' fire?"

Breona's face crumpled. "What air we t' be doin', Miss Joy? Th' folks as sent me fare will be waitin' for me. Th' letter said plain that I had t' pay the fare back if I dinna stay."

Yes, Joy pondered. That would be one of the ways they used to snare their victims. If a girl was penniless and without friends, how could she pay back the fare? Where would she go, once she had arrived, if she did not go with those waiting for her?

This was indeed the dilemma, and Joy thought hard for several minutes. Could she arrange for them to leave the train before Denver? If so, where? And where would they go from there? Could she send them to Omaha, asking Arnie and Anna to take them in and help them? Should she take them to Omaha herself? But Uli and David were expecting her, needed her.

Uli and David. They would know what to do. They had friends, part of the underground they belonged to, to whom she could entrust Breona and Marit.

So how would they escape the "employers" who would be waiting for these girls? Her face warmed in anger and impotence. She clenched her teeth as her indignation built. Then Joy felt something else rising in her chest again, that holy, calm determination and unyielding firmness so like her papa. Joy's anger gave way to cool resolve. *For the wrath of man worketh not the righteousness of God*, she reminded herself.

"This is what we shall do."

Both girls looked up expectantly.

Joy and Marit returned to their seats, gathered their things, and moved them to where Breona sat. The three of them kept their heads close together over the next several hours as Joy gave them instructions and fleshed out her plan. In a serious tone she issued three rules: Breona and Marit were never to go anywhere on the train without each other; when they all disembarked the train, Breona and Marit were to keep hold of each other and stay close in Joy's wake; if anyone attempted to grab either of them, they were to both scream loudly and not let go of each other.

At the next major stop, they stepped off the train and Joy searched for a novelty shop. At the end of a frustrating hour, she found what she was looking for, purchased it, and tucked it safely into her pocket where she could easily reach it. After buying a few additional food items, they returned to the train with more than an hour to spare before departure. The girls had dutifully stuck to her like glue but were looking worn, as was Joy.

They passed a small storefront restaurant near the depot and caught whiffs of savory cooking. Joy's grumbling stomach could take no more. She turned into the café and the girls obediently followed her. They sat at a small table while Joy perused the menu.

"What do you ladies like to eat?" she inquired. Breona and Marit both shook their heads.

"Miss, I'm havin' all of ten cents," Breona confessed. "I mus' be savin' it fer a real need. I've been hungered afore." Marit nodded in agreement, but Joy saw the whiteness of her face.

"Look," Joy explained frankly. "I have some money. Let us have a hot meal, shall we? We need to keep our strength up and our wits about us."

She ordered soup first followed by roasted chicken, seasoned boiled potatoes, and peas. They tore into the food with a will, but Joy saw Breona tuck her dinner roll and several crackers into her pocket.

Their departure was delayed for a further hour so that when the train pulled out, it was dusk. By unspoken agreement they began to settle in for the night. Joy could scarcely believe she had left RiverBend only that morning and had not known these young women before then. The sense of protectiveness she felt for them was peculiar.

As she tucked her feet up along the hard seat she prayed, "Lord, by your grace, we shall make it safely to Corinth and I will help these girls into hands capable of keeping them hidden from those who seek to do them harm."

Then sleep found her.

Chapter 25

The Denver station was a mix of old and new, civilized and untamed, order and chaos. Six railroads converged on Union Station; Joy, Breona, and Marit would need to leave the Union Pacific and find the Denver & Rio Grande Western, the narrow-gauge train that climbed out of Denver into the Rocky Mountains to the west of the city.

Omaha had been a hub of agriculture and transportation and a gateway to the west for decades and had grown into a large city over those many years. Denver, the jumping off point into the wilderness, had scrambled up with less aplomb, growing on the frenzy of gold and silver mining. Not all, but many, came to the city, not to settle a community, but to strip riches from her near mountains as swiftly as they could manage. They came not to bring industry, enterprise, and civilization but to find quick wealth.

Some succeeded, but more did not. Their frustrations often fueled other "needs," needs that vile opportunists quickly comprehended and moved to satisfy. The city itself was a contradiction—stately homes, gardens, and parks with gleaming monuments standing in stark contrast to shacks, shanties, poverty, filth, saloons, prostitution, and gambling.

Uli had written Joy that while Denver's size was now near that of Omaha's, Denver had the "distinction" of falling only slightly short of the crime and depravity found in San Francisco's Barbary Coast district and the red-light quarter of New Orleans' Storyville.

Not all of Denver's citizenry ignored the poverty and depraved state of many of Denver's populace. Their concerns had given birth to what was being called a "social" gospel movement. Uli wrote regarding it.

> *We do not claim the same methods and opinions of this movement, although we certainly share similar goals and aims. We believe the Bible teaches that sin cannot be cured on a global level, only one contrite heart at a time. Some sister churches, on the other hand, while passionate to follow our Lord's commands to feed the needy, feel that the ills of society can be remedied through government*

programs and by discerning between the deserving and undeserving poor.

If a Christian understands the Bible, he knows that the terrible conditions of this life are the result of sin and sinful men in the world. Sin is the root of poverty and evil and is why Jesus told us, "The poor you will have with you always." Sadly, no program can fix the ills of society—only the message of redemption and transformation can change a man's or woman's heart and life.

Minister Uzzel and others like him do much good work but, to our great disappointment, seem to have forgotten that Gospel means "Good News" and that men must be saved from their sins before they can be truly saved from their circumstances. They seek to reform society without the Blood of Jesus also reforming hearts.

So we work somewhat differently than this great social gospel movement. We have determined not to fall into this imbalance but to seek every day to balance the Great Commission with the second greatest commandment, "Thou shalt love thy neighbor as thyself." One without the other serves not God's purposes.

Joy, Breona, and Marit stepped from the train. A dark-haired gentleman handed them down the steps of their car. He said nothing but touched the brim of his derby hat politely and set off quickly across the platform.

Breona and Marit, as Joy had drilled them, kept hold of each other's hands and stayed close behind Joy. Their eyes darted around the crowded platform, and Marit gripped Breona's hand fiercely.

"Marit," Breona hissed. "Have a care! I mus' be usin' me fingers later t'day."

First they needed to arrange for Joy's trunk to be taken off the train and placed on the train to Corinth. Breona and Marit had their belongings with them. Joy signaled a conductor and handed him her claim check, quickly making arrangements.

Joy scanned signs in the station looking for the ticket counters and directions to D&RGW departures. She signaled Breona and

Marit and they set a brisk pace. Hopefully, a casual observer would only see three young women traveling together, confident of their destination, rather than a single, vulnerable girl looking about for someone to meet her.

Near a corner of the platform, Joy spied a large man on the platform holding a sheet of paper with the word "BYRNE" written on it in large letters. Breona's last name! He was scanning passengers as they stepped off the train. She glanced back at Breona and Marit; their eyes were studiously averted from the sign. Joy slipped her hand into her pocket, reassured by its contents.

Keeping close together, they pushed through the jostling crowds moving toward stairs leading up to the ticket offices. Across the seemingly endless station floor, Joy spotted the ticket counters.

Close behind her she heard a startled "eep!" from Marit. Praying Marit was keeping her eyes downcast, Joy looked to the balcony above them and made a show of waving cheerfully to someone. An elderly gentleman, seeing her enthusiasm, looked about himself before dubiously lifting his hand back to her.

"Look! There's Uncle Arthur!" Joy gushed loudly. She kept the girls moving steadily toward the ticket counter. As they arrived she chanced a look back and glimpsed another man, also holding a sign. This one read, "DAHLIN." He had a disagreeable expression on his face and kept scanning the crowded station floor.

Behind them, but never close enough to be noticed in the crowd, the man in the derby hat followed them. His manner was casual as he pushed his way through the throngs.

Joy quickly skimmed through the departure notices. "Three for Corinth on the 3:45." She paid out the money, grasped the tickets, and demanded breathlessly, "Which way to the platform, please?"

Finding that they needed to go down the stairs again and quite some distance along the track, Joy gave each girl her ticket and reminded them firmly, "Stay close behind me. Do not, under any circumstances, let go of each other's hands. If we are separated for any reason, stand where you are—we will find you. And if someone grabs you, scream for all you are worth."

Knowing she would not feel safe until they were on the train under the watchful eye of a conductor, she set a brisk pace.

"Miss Joy!"

Joy turned and saw Breona and Marit several yards back. Confronting them was a hulk of a man. Joy sped back toward them and thrust herself between the girls and the stranger.

He was dressed well. His clothing was clean and of good quality, but . . . something was not right in Joy's estimation. His collar was too tight, the shoulders of his great coat cut too small, and he was perspiring in discomfort. Even the top of his slightly balding head gleamed with perspiration. In a meaty hand he grasped the lettered sign that read DAHLIN.

Coolly, Joy asked, "May I help you?"

"Who are you?" the man demanded.

"Who am *I*? Sir, you accosted *us*, not the other way around. Who are *you* and what is your business with these young ladies?"

The man's eyes narrowed. "Name's Darrow. I'm here to escort Miss Dahlin to her new, ah, employer. Now who are you?"

"I am guardian to these young ladies," Joy replied.

"Guardian? Yeah, right." Darrow snickered and shrugged in disdain. "I am here for Miss Dahlin. I have my instructions."

"I see. For whom do you work, Mr. Darrow? And where is his residence?" For a second time in two days, Joy blessed the Lord who gave her the height of her father's side of the family. Even so, Darrow towered over her. She stared calmly at him while quivering inwardly.

"Lady, that's none o' your business. Miss Dahlin writ a letter and received a train ticket to come and work here."

"That may be, Mr. Darrow, yet I will not release one of my charges without ensuring that the arrangement she has made with your employer is, shall we say, *legitimate*, and to her advantage." Joy lingered slightly on the word "legitimate." "I have asked for your employer's name and place of residence. I am waiting, Mr. Darrow."

The man pushed close to Joy's face. She could smell him, the stink of his breath, his body odor, and his greasy hair. His clothes may have been relatively clean, but he was not.

He reached behind Joy and grasped Marit's arm. "From the description you writ us, you are Marit Dahlin. I was sent to take you to your new employer, and time's a-wastin'."

Marit dropped her bag and, holding fast to Breona, who was holding fast to her, refused to be moved.

"Unhand that young lady, Mr. Darrow." Joy again thrust herself between Marit and Darrow.

"Lady, you are puttin' yer nose in where it is not wanted," Darrow warned. With a rough shove of his powerful arms, he separated the two girls. Breona had held so tightly to Marit that their separation caused her to sit down hard on the station floor.

Darrow grasped Marit's arm more tightly, and Joy could see that he was hurting her. He grabbed Marit's bag from the floor and began to drag her away. Before he could go far, Joy pulled the device from her pocket and put it to her lips. Close beside Darrow's head she blew with all her might.

Joy was prepared for the ear-splitting whistle, but Darrow was not. He slapped one ham-sized fist to his ear and yelped in pain and surprise. Joy danced around him and, near his other ear, blew the whistle again. And again.

Darrow bellowed a curse word and swiped an arm at her, but Joy had dodged away. Marit and Breona, linked up again, were standing several yards away, staring—as were all eyes in the station. Joy quickly ran to the two girls and turned to face Darrow.

Still holding his ears and blinking in pain, Darrow took stock of the situation.

"I say," a portly gentleman called from the crowd. "You, there! Leave these young ladies be, or we will call the officers!" Murmurs of assent rose from others watching closely.

"Can I be of some assistance, ladies?"

A voice on their right interrupted the confrontation between Darrow and Joy. While continuing to shelter Breona and Marit closely behind her, she chanced a look. A dark-haired man in a derby hat waited for her response. He looked familiar and Joy frowned, trying to place him.

"If I may be allowed to assist, I should be pleased to escort your party to your train," he offered again. While not nearly the size of Darrow, the man's confidence was comforting.

Joy made a quick decision. "Thank you, sir. We accept your assistance. Would you be so kind as to escort us to our platform?"

Darrow scowled at both of them and made a move toward Marit. Tiny Breona, still holding Marit's hand, stepped out in front of her and scowled back at Darrow. Joy grinned at her spunk.

"Ladies, shall we go?" The man in the hat, keeping one eye on Darrow, gestured them in the right direction.

They made their way quickly to their departure platform. Breona and Marit scrambled up the steps of a passenger car. Joy turned to their benefactor.

"Thank you, sir. We owe you our gratitude." She extended her hand.

"It was a service I was happy to offer." He shook her hand respectfully. "Edmund O'Dell. If I can ever be of assistance again, Miss . . . ?" He tried not to stare at her, but couldn't help himself. She was lovely.

Joy politely nodded her thanks again and, without giving her name, mounted the steps to the train. *As if we are likely to meet again*, she thought. She quickly found the girls and settled her things.

Back on the platform, the man took off his hat and ran his hand through his dark hair. He stared after the departing train.

Lovely was all he could think.

Chapter 26

The narrow gauge train steamed south out of Denver and after only a few miles began a long westerly sweep. At only minutes past 4 p.m., the sun was beginning to sink down in the sky. As they looked out the windows and saw the tracks bending west ahead of them, the three women collectively gasped.

A crown of sharp, jagged peaks soared into the sky. Early snow covered those peaks, and the sinking sun bathed them in red, purple, orange, and pink.

"Is that vhere ve're going?" Marit breathed. Breona stared.

"I've never seen such mountains!" Joy exulted. She recalled when she and Uli had been children. Uli had told her, in a quite superior and matter-of-fact manner, that her Aunt Rose had informed her, "Uli, there are more and bigger mountains in America than anywhere in Norway, but unfortunately we live a long ways from them. Perhaps someday you will ride on a train like I did and see them."

Uli had told Joy in the same matter-of-fact manner that she intended to do just that. Joy laughed aloud. Now Uli *lived* in those mountains!

As the train angled toward the imposing peaks, the tracks ahead vanished into their foothills. They could no longer see the mountains directly ahead, but could see the range extending on either side of the train as they drew closer.

They watched, mesmerized, as the train entered a shadowed canyon and began to climb, making narrow turns that a wider train would never have been able to navigate. They stared down as the train curved, hugging a hillside on one side, hanging over a precipice on the other.

The conductor interrupted their gawking. "Tickets?"

They handed them over quickly.

"Getting off at Corinth, eh?" He looked at them curiously. "Most of our passengers go through these days, headed for California, Utah, or New Mexico."

Joy smiled. "We're meeting my cousins in Corinth."

He nodded, still unsure. "Glad to hear you have family there," he replied before continuing down the train.

"Not very reassuring, was he?" Joy muttered.

Uli had written that Corinth was not far into the mountains. The ride from Denver would take just two hours. While it had originally been a mining town, it was close enough to Denver not to have suffered as much economically as so many other mountain communities had when mining declined drastically. True, Corinth still had some small mining operations nearby, but it also had timber and farming in the valleys outside the town.

After an hour or so Joy rose to stretch her legs. Breona and Marit promised to stay in their seats, so Joy began to walk. She left their car and walked through a second one similar to theirs, and entered a third.

The eyes of five well-dressed gentlemen surrounded in cigar smoke turned toward her. They were the only occupants of the car. Joy could not help but immediately notice two things: The car she had entered was sumptuously furnished, and the collective gaze of the men in that car made her exceedingly uncomfortable.

Excusing herself, she retreated and hastened to return to her seat.

It was nearly dark when they arrived at the little siding with a dim sign that read, "Corinth, Colorado. Altitude 7,586 feet."

"Uli!" Joy called from the steps of the train. She spied her cousin and her husband looking anxiously for her.

"Joy! Oh, I am so happy to see you!" Uli embraced her for a long moment, and Joy sank into her welcoming arms. She hadn't realized how much responsibility she had been carrying for Breona and Marit until she knew she would be able to place that care on other, more experienced shoulders.

The girls, holding hands again, stood a little ways off, watching carefully.

Joy whispered in her cousin's ear, "Uli, both these girls answered newspaper ads to come to Denver. A horrible man tried to take one of them against her will in Denver, but I rescued them and we—" Uli stiffened. Joy drew away from her embrace and looked at her.

Uli's smile was frozen on her face, but Joy knew her well enough to recognize dismay.

"Oh Joy . . . what have you done?"

Sizing up the situation, Uli's husband David acted quickly. "Cousin Joy! I'm so pleased you could come! And your friends are welcome. Please." He gestured for the girls to join them.

As Breona and Marit approached, David said quietly. "Act normally. We'll explain once we are home. Uli, my love, please welcome these young ladies."

Uli widened her smile and reached for Marit, enveloping her in a hug. She repeated the same with Breona and said brightly, "Well then! Let's all get into our old-fashioned wagon and go home to a hot, home cooked meal, shall we?"

Joy saw her trunk being unloaded and pointed it out to David. Then she noticed several men lounging about the small station. Two of the men stared fixedly at their group. David and Uli carefully kept their eyes turned away.

She also could not miss the well-heeled men who had disembarked from the elegant car she had stumbled into earlier. The men lounging nearby greeted them with deference and showed them to two idling motorcars waiting just off the sliding. One of the gentlemen from the train, his dark hair shot distinctively with gray, eyed Joy with bold admiration and tipped his hat to her. She blushed and turned away.

A few minutes later, David clucked to the horses and, although a bit cramped in the wagon, the five of them headed down a road into the town. They passed a few widely-spaced houses before they spied a modest plaza and city hall. The plaza boasted a formal little town square at its center and a small monument set in a grassy commons. The streets along the plaza were lined with shops, all shuttered and dark. Down a side street Joy saw a bar or two, well-lit, with men going in and out. Corinth appeared to be a normal, sleepy small town.

Several streets later, the wagon entered a well-kept residential area. As David turned onto an unexpectedly wide avenue, Joy couldn't help but notice two particularly lovely houses. They were both several stories tall and graced by covered verandas, attractive balconies, and meticulously groomed grounds. The houses' long, curving drives were lit by gaslight. Every window glowed from within.

Joy was amazed that the tiny town boasted such . . . *mansions* . . . was the only word fitting their luxury. Other homes in the area were modest in comparison.

Marit, never having seen such imposing homes, gaped at them. David and Uli kept their eyes straight before them, but Joy noticed David's drawn brows and firmly set mouth.

Then she saw the motor cars. They had pulled high up onto the curved drive in front of the larger of the two houses. The men from the train, in boisterous spirits, were disembarking and walking to the front door.

Eventually the wagon reached the edge of the town and turned down a lane well-treed with evergreens. Near the end of the lane, Joy spied a small white church roofed with cedar shakes. David pulled the wagon around the little church to a cozy looking house tucked into the trees.

David and Uli looked at each other and let out pent-up breaths.

Chapter 27

"But I understood that you had . . . friends . . . who could help Breona and Marit away from here? Isn't that what you wrote to me? I'm afraid I don't understand."

They had enjoyed a well prepared dinner with David, Uli, and their boys, Sam and Seth, and their daughter Ruth. The women had worked together to make up two more beds on the floor of the bedroom they had prepared for Joy. Joy, Breona, and Marit would share the room until a decision could be made about how to spirit them out of Corinth.

At Uli's request, Joy left the girls in their room to settle in for the night and joined David and Uli in their kitchen.

Uli's husband David chose his words carefully. "You saw those two beautiful homes we passed. You know the ones I speak of."

Joy nodded soberly.

"Those are where they take the girls and young women they pluck off the trains in Denver. Behind those beautiful walls they are forced . . . into a life of slavery. We know from the stories told us by the women we have helped escape."

"We are being watched at all times, Cousin Joy. So far, each time we have aided a young woman in her escape, we have eluded detection—but those who are watching have their suspicions."

"For you to openly bring two girls you 'rescued' in Denver to Corinth, to our home, plainly tells those who watch us that we must be involved with the other runaways, especially if Miss Byrne and Miss Dahlin just as quickly disappear from Corinth."

Uli watched Joy as she digested David's words.

"So . . . by bringing them here I have endangered you . . . and the work?" Joy was stricken.

David was a kind man, lean and already much bowed by cares and responsibility. He nodded and gently continued. "We have been . . . threatened, Joy. Once in an anonymous note, once by two thugs who actually made a donation to the church while they were threatening us!"

Uli nodded her agreement and added softly, "Joy, they threatened to burn us out. Church and home. I'm sure you . . . understand."

"I . . . I am so sorry. I thought . . ." Joy swallowed nervously. She had pictures of steaming rubble forever etched in her mind, could still smell the acrid smoke. It must not happen again!

"What will we do?"

"We will pray," David said firmly.

"Yes we will," echoed Uli. "God himself will give the answer."

The three of them bowed their heads together. When they finished, they quietly said goodnight. Joy slipped into her room, listening to the even breathing of Marit and Breona before crawling under blankets on the floor near Breona. She had insisted that Marit take the bed.

As she tried to settle, she kept turning the events of the past few days over in her mind. Finally she breathed out her own prayer.

"Lord, I know that you led Breona and Marit to me. You did not save them from such grief and destruction only to have us and this important work overthrown through my ignorance. I cannot—I do not—believe that."

"I trust you, Lord. I believe you have an answer for us, something that is already part of your plan. And I refuse to be afraid. I have been afraid for too long. No; I will wait calmly and without fear for you to tell us how you wish us to go forward."

"I trust you, Lord. I will not be afraid . . ." she murmured and then slid into a deep sleep.

Chapter 28

Edmund O'Dell and Beau Bickle lit cigars and leaned back in comfortably overstuffed chairs with a view of the busy Denver boulevard in front of the Denver Pinkerton office.

"I take it McParland isn't around?" O'Dell observed casually.

"Ha! He'd have my badge if he caught us smoking on Pinkerton time," Bickle agreed. Denver's famous—or infamous, depending on who was asked—James McParland, head of Pinkerton Detective Agency in Denver, ran a tight ship. "And Siringo retired last year."

O'Dell nodded at the mention of another famed Pinkerton. "You've moved up. Congratulations. You said you had something for me?"

"Yup." Bickle took a long drag on his cigar. "Something near here and maybe why your trail goes cold soon as it hits Denver."

"Oh?"

"We think the girls are taken out of Denver as soon as they get off the train."

"Where?"

"Not certain sure, but we've heard rumors of a little town south of Denver. Think the girls are taken there to be broken in."

The cavalier manner in which Bickle used the words "broken in" infuriated O'Dell. His voice darkened. "You mean where a dishonorable brute can rape a little girl for the right price."

Bickle went on, oblivious to his companion's growing ire. "That's right. The guys running this game get top dollar for young, unspoiled girls. Then they likely give the girls their options—learn the trade, get good at it, and get a bed in a nice house with nice clients, nice clothes, and good food. Don't show the clients a good time, have a bad disposition, that sorta thing, you end up in a third-rate crib down on Market—"

O'Dell gripped Bickle by the cravat. Tightly. "These girls are someone's daughter or sister. The crimes are kidnap and rape, pure and simple. Why don't you show a little respect, Beau." He released Bickle's cravat and pushed the man against the back of his chair.

"Jeeze, O'Dell! I'm just tellin' it like it is."

"What's the name of this little town?"

Bickle rubbed his throat. "Called Breezy Point. Just a couple hours south."

"Thanks." O'Dell picked up his hat. "Sorry about the necktie."
He didn't sound sorry.

Bickle watched as O'Dell marched down the street in the
direction of Union Station. "Sure pal."

He rubbed his neck again. "O'Dell. Keep diggin' and sure as
spit, I think you're gonna find trouble here."

Chapter 29

The next morning after an early breakfast, Joy, Breona, Marit, and the Kalbørg family gathered around the table again. David read aloud from the Bible. The three children each recited a passage they were memorizing, and then the family bowed their heads and prayed together. Breona and Marit followed along politely, but Uli recognized that family devotions were foreign to both of them.

"Our morning routine must seem a little strange to you," Uli explained. "This is something we do together each morning and each evening. You see, we want to involve the Lord in every part of our lives, rather than just on Sunday or holidays. So we welcome Jesus into each new day, reminding ourselves to put him first in our thoughts, our chores, our problems, and our decisions."

David smiled at the two young women. He and Uli both looked rested; it was obvious to Joy that they had also slept peacefully after their prayers last evening.

"Miss Byrne and Miss Dahlin, we believe you are here in Corinth, in our little home, because the Lord brought you here. We're grateful that he did. We believe that he has a plan for each of you. So, now that you are here, what is next? We would like to pray and ask him to show us. Would you join us in asking him to give us direction?"

They both nodded self-consciously but bowed their heads with everyone else and David prayed aloud. "Father God, the Bible tells us that you know the end from the beginning. *We* are the ones who need guidance, not you. Help us to walk in your ways this day and to follow you closely. We thank you for bringing Miss Byrne and Miss Dahlin to our home. You have a plan and purpose in doing so. Will you show us how to help them next? We ask you in the name of Jesus. Amen."

Joy and the girls pitched in willingly to clean the kitchen and help the children out the door to school. Then they straightened the small room they shared. Afterwards, Joy suggested a walk. They donned warm cloaks against the brisk mountain air and wandered down the pine-edged lane.

Marit broke the silence first. "The air is different here."

Breona agreed. "Loik Christmas!"

"We are so high and these trees smell so good," Joy agreed.

"'Tis it!" Breona's tiny face split into a grin. "Th' trees! They smell of Christmas."

The three of them laughed, and Joy was gladdened to hear their laughter.

Before long they were walking by other little houses and shanties nestled in the trees and then came to the edge of the town. Heeding David's caution that they not go into Corinth proper, Joy steered them toward a rocky vantage point.

In the daylight the mountains displayed themselves—towering crags that seemed close enough to touch and lofty peaks shimmering in the mid-morning sun. Dizzying valleys and canyons spread out far below them. "So beautiful," Marit murmured in awe.

All of them were struck by the natural splendor surrounding Corinth. They perched on a wide rock and gazed in silent companionship, the sun gradually warming their backs.

Joy knew she would never be able to catalog every wonder displayed before her. She had loved the simple beauty of her childhood prairie home but this . . . this was more than beauty. This was majesty.

How could people defile the majesty of this place? That thought abruptly ended her peaceful reverie.

"Miss Joy?" Breona's eyes were still drinking in the view.

"Yes?"

"What we were seein' last night. Th' fancy houses and th' men from the train." It wasn't a question.

Both girls looked to her and Joy nodded. "Yes."

Marit asked the obvious question. "Vat vill ve do?"

Joy turned to them. She had determined to be frank with both of them. "Unintentionally, my bringing you here has placed David and Uli in a bit of, um, a quandary. Those men at the station saw all three of us. We must assume that they are accomplices or at least acquaintances of Darrow."

Marit paled visibly and Breona did that "thing" Joy had noticed several times now. She grew very still and, if it were possible, she shrank into herself, making herself even smaller. *Like a rabbit when it senses danger*, Joy thought.

"I had thought that friends of David and Uli's friends could 'spirit' you away as they have done when a few of the . . . girls . . . ran away. However, since those men saw us with David and Uli, if you just disappear without notice, then David and Uli will be proven to have helped not only you, but those other girls as well. This is why Uli was a bit . . . disconcerted when I told her how I met you."

She blew out her breath and then added, "They have been threatened. People are watching them."

Joy looked out into the vastness of the mountains and drank in their splendor again. *Lord, please show me the way.*

"Marit," Joy broke the quiet.

"Yes 'm?"

"How long before your baby comes?" Joy asked.

Marit's plump face creased in concentration. "I . . . I'm not sure, Miss Joy. I don't know how to figure it."

As if I do, Joy sighed to herself cynically. *Is this what "for more are the children of the desolate than the children of the married wife" means?* She chided herself and squared her shoulders. "Let's see if we can 'figure' it, shall we?"

Joy and Breona asked Marit several questions. Joy ran the months quickly in her head. "Uli will be able to help us determine this better, but from your looks and what you've told us, I think you have less than four months before the baby comes. Perhaps the end of December or first of January."

"David, Uli, and I prayed about what to do last night after you went to bed and again this morning. I am confident the Lord will give us an answer. We will likely need to leave soon. Perhaps I will take you myself back to Omaha."

"Whist? Should we be thinkin' on leavin'?" Breona asked sharply. "Truth, will that not be pointin' th' very finger at yer cousins?"

"But how could we stay, Breona?" Joy asked gently. "What possible story could we put on our being here that would protect you both and David and Uli's family and church?"

Breona bristled a little, and Joy smiled and thought with admiration, *this girl has such spirit!*

"I'm thinkin' Marit is lookin' a bit loik you," Breona responded. "Easy enow, it's bein' yer sister or yer cousin she could." Almost fiercely, she added, "She'll be havin' thet wee one, an' has no' a husband, yis? So! So 'tis *here* you brung her. T' hide her away."

Joy nodded slowly. "All right . . . and what about you?"

"Miss, I am bein' a housemaid since I were 11 years grown. I'll be workin' for ye doin' th' cleanin' an' th' washin'. Helpin' w' th' babe, an' all."

Joy's thoughts were buzzing quickly through Breona's ideas. Marit watched the interplay between Joy and Breona quietly.

"An' we canna be stayin' wit' yer cousins loong, Miss Joy," Breona said flatly. "They have no' th' room, an' we should be puttin' some daylight twixt us an' them, aye?"

She almost glared at Joy. "I'll no' b' leavin' Marit, miss."

Marit stared down. "I don't know vat I'll do, Miss Joy. I vas counting on the job to take care of the baby. How vill I take care of him? Vhere vill I live?"

"A job," Joy mused. "Yes . . ."

Joy was concentrating hard. "What if . . . what if you had a job, too, Breona? Not a housemaid's job, but one in a shop or store? What if you both did?"

Marit stared hopefully at Joy but Breona protested, "I'm no' bein' shop quality, miss. I canna speak well an', an', well, I'm no' presentable, miss. No' t' mention, I'm knowin' nothin' of shops an' stores!"

Joy nodded, still concentrating. "No. But *I* do. Oh yes. *I* do."

Chapter 30

"What if we don't hide?" Joy asked, taking them by surprise. David, Uli, and Joy were gathered in the warm kitchen that evening. Out of doors, a chill wind gusted and moaned. David and Uli listened, more than a little chagrinned, as Joy elaborated.

"Breona suggested it first. She is adamant that Marit needs a secure place to stay and have her baby—and as equally adamant that she will not leave her side!" Joy smiled. "Breona has only known Marit a few days but has already developed a strong attachment to her."

She looked down. "I confess, I have also. I don't want to send these girls off with strangers and not know if they are all right. I don't want to think of Breona and Marit alone in the world with no way to care for themselves."

She mused, "Perhaps 'hide in plain sight' describes it better. Marit and I look similar enough to be sisters. We could introduce her as my sister and say that we have brought her here to have her baby."

David was shaking his head. "I don't like that, Joy. We shouldn't cloak our work in untruths."

Joy frowned. "You are right. Perhaps that isn't the right way, but . . . David, when girls come to you for help, don't you hide them? Don't you intentionally deceive those who are looking for them? When those two thugs threatened you, did you tell them the truth?"

"Those men have no rights on those poor women!" David burst out in anger. Uli touched his arm. She shook her head gently and he looked away, chastened.

"What you said is true," Joy responded evenly. "They also have no right to *Marit* or *Breona*. If we deceive those men about them in some way, isn't that the same thing?"

Joy turned to Uli. "Wasn't there a woman in the Bible who let the Israelite spies into Jericho and hid them, deceiving her own people?"

"Well, yes. Rahab. I see what you are saying, but . . ."

"Didn't the Lord reward her?" Joy asked David.

He frowned.

"And wasn't she . . . a harlot?" Joy asked softly.

"Have a care, Cousin Joy," David warned.

"Well, I don't think we need to lie about who Marit is here in Corinth. Perhaps she is a dear friend or distant relative who is in a family way and we have removed her from prying eyes and wagging tongues. Who she is exactly is no one's concern," Joy answered doggedly.

Joy had told David and Uli the circumstances of Marit's pregnancy, and it was not in their nature to judge her anyway. Uli simply asked, "So what are you thinking?"

"The Lord directed me to come and to help you with this work. I know in the heart of my very being that he led me to come here, so I don't want to just pick up and go—because I also know that meeting Marit and Breona on the train was no accident. They do not think it right to leave either, and they both need employment."

Joy was thinking aloud now. "I have some money left from the sale of our property in Omaha. I thought I would look for something here that can support the three of us—four, after the baby comes. I didn't see any services near the train siding. Perhaps a shop or little eatery that caters to travelers? It would need to be large enough for us to live in, so that attention is deflected from you and the church."

Uli nodded encouragingly at this. Joy continued. "Cousin David, Cousin Uli. You pled with me to come to Corinth to help. I know that the Lord directed me here. I have been wondering . . . It is no small thing to rescue the one or two who somehow escape . . . but how do we embolden others to help and perhaps end this wickedness? We prayed just this morning, asking the Lord to show us his plan. Is it possible that making a stand, even such a small one, is part of that plan?"

Joy's brow furrowed. "I don't know precisely what the Lord has in mind but—would you know of any buildings available here in Corinth?" She looked at David.

David thought for a moment. "Perhaps. I would need to speak to the owner of a place I know is empty."

The next day David went to pay a call on one of his parishioners. When he returned, he offered to show Joy a vacant house and introduce her to the owner.

"Corinth was a booming mining and logging community at one time," David told Joy on the drive into town. "During the mining heydays a few folks made their fortune. Afterwards, Corinth began drying up like many of the boom towns up the creeks and rivers that flow out of the Rockies toward Denver."

"All Corinth had to offer then was a beautiful place to live—if you were willing to live modestly. About 10 years ago a few wealthy families built summer homes here. But she also had something of interest to a group of unscrupulous men—she was less than two hours from the city by train. Three years ago one man in particular began buying up the best properties, including those two houses near the center of town."

David drove Joy beyond the train siding and onto a promontory that jutted far out over a valley. He pointed Joy toward a large two-story house. The lines of the house were clean and lovely. "That man and a few others tried to buy this house, but the owner would not sell it."

Although in disuse, the house was still striking. Even better, it had a commanding view of the valley and the mountains around it. Joy spied trails leading away from the house and she found herself eager to explore them.

A rustic lock secured the front door. David drew a key from this pocket. "The owner is a member of our church. After his boys moved away and later his wife passed on, he closed up the house. He operates a little smithy over there, on the other side of the siding. The railroad uses his services, as do town folk."

They stepped inside. Dust motes floated in the dim sunlight. The bottom floor had a single great room in the front with ornate windows facing the valley. A stunning rock fireplace dominated one end of the room; a more practical oil stove stood at the other side. A wide staircase with a curving banister at the back of the great room led upward.

The rear of the first floor contained a spacious kitchen and two attached rooms. The smaller of the two rooms, lined with shelves, had obviously been the pantry. A narrow flight of stairs led from the kitchen to the second floor and on up to the attic. Joy flinched as a mouse skittered across the floor.

On the second floor they wandered down a long hallway and peeked into six bedrooms. One of the bedrooms was obviously the master and had a small, attached sitting room. At the end of the hall, just past the larger bedroom, a door opened to a balcony that spanned that end of the house. David wrestled the door open for Joy but cautioned her about the condition of the balcony. She stood safely in the doorway and stared with pleasure over the trees at the view of the mountains before her.

Above the second floor was a wide attic beneath the high-pitched roof. Joy glimpsed daylight through the roof in two places. Boards creaked and groaned. Cobwebs clung to the bare rafters and dust lay thick and undisturbed across the floor.

"Entirely too much work, I'm afraid," David apologized.

"On the contrary, it may be perfect," Joy murmured. "May I meet the owner?"

"His smithy is on the other side of the platform, just back in those trees," David pointed and Joy spied a wisp of smoke and a stove pipe peeping out beyond the trees.

A few minutes later, Joy shook hands with Joe Flynn, "'Flinty' to my friends," he said, grinning. His red hair, streaked with gray, still hinted at how he had earned his name.

"Thank you, Flinty," Joy grinned back. "What can you tell me about the house you have for sale?"

"Well, miss, it ain't 'zactly fer sale now, but . . . it's a fine place, jest a little long in the tooth, kinder like me, ya see?" He laughed and then looked her over quizzically. "Needs a mote o' work."

"Yes, I agree. Is it basically sound, though?"

"Yep. Built her m'self, 'bout 30 year ago now, back when Corinth was flush with silver. Raised four boys there, we did. After they growed and moved away the missus liked to have lodgers but she's been gone eight years and it's too much work fer my taste."

"So it's been empty eight years?"

He nodded. "Yes 'm."

They talked weather, church, and neighbors. Flinty showed them his forge and a machine part he was repairing. Joy and David sipped coffee and listened attentively for an hour while Flinty told them about his wife and their years together. He talked openly about the hard life he'd lived before he met Jesus, and the changes God worked in him over the years following. After a time the conversation came back around to the house.

Flinty looked from David back to Joy. In response to some unspoken question, David nodded.

Flinty looked at her speculatively. "Well, miss, it's like this. City big shot came lookin' t' buy m' house, few years back. Got the best views in Corinth, it does. But he'd already bought two in town and, not meanin' to be indelicate, miss, I knowed what they's usin' them houses fer." He spat in disgust and then blushed. "I 'poligize, miss. But that's why m' house ain't *'zactly* fer sale."

Joy nodded. "Flinty, what if I told you that not only would this house *not* be used for those purposes but would actually be dedicated for God's purposes?"

Flinty looked at David again. "Well, seein' as how yer th' preacher's cousin an' all . . . we might dicker a bit." Several minutes later Flinty found out from personal experience how astute a business woman Joy was. She agreed to his asking price—less ten percent!—*and* with his agreement to oversee a scribbled list of repairs that Joy drew from her pocket.

He beamed at her anyway. "You drive a good bargain, miss, but I can't say I didn't enjoy it. Most excitement and best comp'ny I've had in a year!" He shook on their deal enthusiastically. "Yes 'm! You're jest what the doctor ordered, I'm thinkin'!"

Joy smiled back. "I have thoroughly enjoyed our visit too, Flinty. And I'll have a check to you by evening," she promised him.

Chapter 31

They came to their new home early the next morning with buckets, mops, brooms, soap, rags, and hope. *Hope.* Breona took one look at the large, empty great room and, grinning widely, started dancing a little jig. Marit clapped her hands and then shot Joy a mortified look.

Joy just laughed out loud. She grabbed Breona's offered hand and they skipped together across the floor. Joy bowed, Breona curtsied, and they sashayed down the length of the room. Soon the two of them were twirling around together, giggling and laughing in abandon, while Marit kept time.

Tiny as she was, Breona demonstrated that day that she was a force to be reckoned with. Before Marit and Joy realized it, she had organized them and issued assignments. Joy was amazed how quickly and thoroughly Breona worked. Not only was she undaunted by the task before them, she seemed to relish the challenge. Joy's heart warmed to the young woman.

Marit, cumbered by the growing baby, worked slowly but steadily and with a will. Breona gave her tasks that required less bending and stooping and encouraged her to take regular breaks. Joy, on the other hand, had to push herself to keep up with the whirlwind known as Breona Byrne.

By noon the first floor sparkled. The great room's oil stove sent out welcome warmth. They decided to sleep, for the present, in the room behind the kitchen and cleaned it thoroughly for the coming night. The kitchen stove, scrubbed and newly blackened, popped and crackled with a wood fire. A small pot of soup simmered on the back of the stove.

They took a quick lunch break, sipping their soup out of chipped mugs, and then tackled the bedrooms on the second floor. They wiped down and washed every wall and ceiling. Soon windows gleamed and floors were spotless.

Around three o'clock David arrived with a wagon load of used furniture, many pieces donated by church members. Uli had also sent along bedding for them although Joy and Breona would still be sleeping on the hard floor until more beds could be acquired.

"As soon as I am able to, I will make arrangements for what we need to set up housekeeping," Joy told the girls that evening. They sat around a battered (and wobbly) table in the kitchen, nursing their worn hands and tired backs.

"But miss, vat kind of business vill ve do here?" Marit finally asked.

"Aye—and I'm still feelin' loik bait on a hook, pardon me frank speech, Miss Joy," Breona added. "How air we bein' safer all alone over in this place th'n at yer cousins?"

"We require some help," Joy responded. "I have letters to write, but for the next several nights, Mr. Flynn will be sleeping here to safeguard us. As to our business, trains come through Corinth twice a day. What do passengers traveling through need or want?"

They grew thoughtful. Joy had a few ideas but wanted to hear what Breona and Marit might come up with.

Marit offered timidly, "Vell, hot coffee is alvays nice."

Joy smiled in approval.

"Yis. An' hot meals. And other foods folks can be takin' on th' train." Breona's brow furrowed as she concentrated.

"I can cook," Marit offered boldly.

"Excellent! Do you have any baked specialties?"

"Vell . . . breads, of course," Marit suggested.

"Limpa bread?"

"Oh ja! And sveet baked goods, like julekake and cardamom braids—oh! And cookies! Lefse, krumkake, pepparkakor, and brunscrackers—so many kinds I made with *Mor* vhen I vas little." Marit radiated enthusiasm.

Breona looked skeptical. "Niver heard on ony o' those . . ."

"Traditional Swedish baked goods, Breona," Joy said reassuringly. "I think travelers may think of them as novelty items, and if they get a whiff of fresh pepparkakor—those are Swedish gingersnaps—they won't be able to resist."

Breona nodded reluctantly. "Don' seem enow t' get us by, tho', do it?"

"No. It wouldn't be. But I have another idea. What if we advertised in Denver papers . . . tourist accommodations in the fresh mountain air, by the week or the month? Scenic views, healthful walks along the overlooks, and excellent food! I believe that quality people wanting to leave the city for a week or a little longer might find the short train ride here very inviting . . . and would pay well for the experience."

Marit looked about at the condition of the building and the sparse furnishings and said nothing. Breona might have alleged Joy had lost her mind, but wisely kept her own counsel, too.

Finally Marit said meekly, "Do you think ve can fix up this house for quality people?"

"Ah, that is the question, isn't it?" Joy said softly, "However, I know something you young ladies do not. I own a large quantity of fine furnishings. We were to open a shop, my husband and I, one specializing in select household goods but we . . . Well, we were unable to. All of those beautiful things, far more than we will need, are still waiting for me in a warehouse in Omaha."

She stood up resolutely. "This building in itself may not look like much at the moment, but it has the space we require. I will hire workers to improve it and to make it livable again. And then we will decorate it as if it were a fine city hotel."

She strode about the kitchen, arms gesturing grandly. "Damask draperies, lush carpets, select furniture, and the best linens and dishes. We will make a proverbial silk purse from a sow's ear. We will dress up this fine rustic building and our guests will sleep and dine like kings and queens!"

She looked fondly at Breona and Marit. "You will both have good jobs here and be able to care for yourselves—and you will be able to have your baby here, Marit. More than that, you will all be safe. I will make sure of that."

Later that evening, Flinty, a bedroll on his shoulder and a shotgun under his arm, knocked on the door. Joy showed him what they had done so far and he grinned in approval. "If y' don't mind, miss, I'll bunk here in th' great room where I kin keep an eye and an ear open fer trespassers. I sleep easy natural, s' it's no trouble fer me."

In the morning while Breona and Marit continued cleaning, Joy wrote a letter.

Dear Arnie and Anna,

So much has happened since I left Omaha . . .

Joy filled the pages with a great many details, particularly regarding Breona and Marit, Marit's baby, and the work ahead of them. She took pains to explain the trafficking of young girls and women to Denver, the methods used by those behind the trafficking to bait and snare their unsuspecting victims, and the terrible role Corinth played in their schemes.

Then, putting on her business woman's hat, she explained her intent to establish a small resort she would call "Corinth Mountain Lodge." She described the overlooks and trails around the little town; she explained how she believed their nearness and accessibility to Denver would make their little getaway inviting to city dwellers.

> *In this way, Breona and Marit will have a home and meaningful work. I have hopes to win them to the Lord and, as he gives opportunity, perhaps we shall rescue some of the girls in town whose freedoms have been taken.*

> *The Lord willing and if our endeavor thrives, we may even be able to focus the attention of upstanding Denver leaders onto the criminal activities in this town. If the right attention is brought to bear, perhaps the evil deeds taking place here can be brought down.*

Finally she began a list of things from the warehouse she would need shipped to her.

> *Arnie, would you be so kind as to locate Billy for me? If he is in need of work, I have a place for him here in Corinth. His first assignment would be to select the items from the warehouse, see to their packing and shipping, and then accompany them on the train to Colorado.*

> *I would come to make the arrangements myself, but I do not dare to leave the relative security that our numbers and the common knowledge of our being here provide.*

> *Once Billy arrives, he would assume duties similar those he had in our store, but he would also live on the premises and fill a security need. Because we have, by rescuing Breona and Marit, outwitted the men who prey on friendless girls, I do not want to make the mistake of thinking we are beyond their reach and retribution. I need a couple of hale and hearty young men, and Billy would be most welcome here if he is willing.*

Anna, I have also listed other items we will need to properly set up housekeeping here and to prepare for the arrival of a baby in a few months. Dear Cousin, it would be a great blessing if you would select and buy these things for me. I enclose a bank draft for that purpose.

When I last saw all of you, I was a beaten woman. This past year has frequently been unbearable. Yes, it has been a year now. The anniversary of Grant's passing was a few days ago, but I am grateful to the Lord for the new purpose my life now has.

I confess that I would rather be telling you face-to-face over coffee and cake in your cozy parlor all the things our Savior has done in my heart rather than in these few inadequate lines. However, I don't know if I could bear to ever come back to Omaha. Perhaps in the spring you will come and see us and how we fare. David, Uli, and the children send their fondest wishes for this also.

Joy spent the best part of the morning making her lists. Breona and Marit saw her measuring rooms and windows and muttering to herself. When David came by later, she spent an hour questioning him and Flinty as to the better carpenters and roofers in Corinth and the best means of buying materials. When David left, he bore her very thick letter to the train where it was taken down into the valley with the rest of the mail.

It was Saturday evening and the morrow was Sunday. Somehow they all managed to bathe in front of the kitchen stove and ready themselves for church in the morning. Their preparations were not without some resistance. Breona lacked enthusiasm and Joy could see that Marit was anxious about showing her pregnancy to strangers.

"I niver had no need fer th' church, miss," Breona stated frankly. "But out o' respect, I'll be goin'—this oncet."

"Marit, did your family go to church?"

"No, miss. My father usually . . . slept on Sundays."

"By that air ye meanin' he slept off the drink?" Breona's question wasn't unkind, just curious.

"Yes," and Marit shook her head. Breona squeezed her hand.

Joy had not anticipated resistance and it took her a little by surprise. "I understand, Breona, and it is not my place to insist you go, of course. I was hoping . . . I think I was hoping that in our home we would pray and read the Bible together like the Kalbørgs do."

Neither Breona nor Marit answered and Breona, her mouth set in a firm line, studiously picked at a thread on her sweater, avoiding Joy's eyes.

Chapter 32

David pastored a small congregation that was welcoming to Joy and the girls. Uli had told Joy that everyone knew what was happening in Corinth but, because of the risk of retribution, only a few of the members knew about and were involved in the work to help girls escape.

She introduced Joy as her cousin and Breona and Marit as Joy's employees, solving that issue for now. Uli had also discreetly informed a few women of Marit's circumstances, and Joy was gratified to hear of their concern for Marit and her baby's wellbeing.

The service was sweet and Joy found it easy to feel at home. As to what Marit and Breona felt or thought, Joy could only guess. She sang happily, many of the songs being familiar and loved ones. Marit and Breona, on the other hand, shared a hymn book and looked overwhelmed by the strange songs and activities.

David preached a simple message and chose John 4, the woman at the well, as his text.

> *The woman saith unto him,*
> *Sir, thou hast nothing to draw with,*
> *and the well is deep: from whence then*
> *hast thou that living water?*
> *Art thou greater than our father Jacob,*
> *which gave us the well, and drank thereof himself,*
> *and his children, and his cattle?*
>
> *Jesus answered and said unto her,*
> *Whosoever drinketh of this water shall thirst again:*
> *But whosoever drinketh of the water*
> *that I shall give him shall never thirst;*
> *but the water that I shall give him shall be in him*
> *a well of water springing up into everlasting life.*
>
> *The woman saith unto him, Sir, give me this water,*
> *that I thirst not, neither come hither to draw.*
> *Jesus saith unto her, Go,*
> *call thy husband, and come hither.*
>
> *The woman answered and said, I have no husband.*
> *Jesus said unto her, Thou hast well said, I have no husband:*

For thou hast had five husbands;
and he whom thou now hast is not thy husband:
in that saidst thou truly.
The woman saith unto him,
Sir, I perceive that thou art a prophet.

As David finished the passage, he said, "Jesus demonstrated to this woman that he knows both our lives and our hearts. Can you imagine having five husbands? Surely she was not a respectable woman, for his disciples were astonished when they returned and found him speaking to her."

"But listen to what Jesus said! 'Whosoever drinketh of the water that I shall give him shall never thirst; but the water that I shall give him shall be in him a well of water springing up into everlasting life.' Whosoever! Not sinless people, not righteous ones, not upright citizens, but whosoever! And what does whosoever mean? Whosoever means 'whomever will'. It means anyone who is willing. *Anyone.*"

"Jesus was inviting her to drink of the living water that only he could give. Did he invite her in error? Did he mistake her for a respectable woman? Obviously not. He knew all the facts of her life. He knew her every wrong decision and every failing. He also knew her heart, and so he said, 'whosoever' *to her.*"

"Church tradition teaches us that this woman became a devout follower of Jesus and led many of her fellow Samaritans to the Savior. We should be careful, friends. We should be careful to never discount people's hearts and God's plans for them. God looks at us and he sees everything we have done—but the Bible tells us that he *looks on our hearts*, and he says, 'come to me, and I will give you Living Water—and you will never thirst again'."

When Joy, Marit, and Breona returned home afterwards, they set themselves to cook enough for both lunch and dinner later. Joy, without thinking, hummed one of the hymns they had sung during the service.

"I liked that one," Marit said, while peeling potatoes.

Breona only harrumphed.

The following morning as they cleared the breakfast dishes from the table, Joy poured herself another cup of coffee and sat back down. She opened her Bible and began to read.

Breona and Marit watched her for a moment, unsure of what was expected of them. Joy glanced up at them. "I am going to have morning devotions like we did at David and Uli's house. You may join me if you wish or not. You are entirely free to choose."

After a moment's hesitation, Marit poured herself a glass of milk and sat near Joy at the table. Breona scowled and reluctantly plunked into a chair.

"Breona, I am sincere when I say you are not required to do Bible reading with us," Joy told her.

"Well, be gettin' on wi' it," she replied gruffly. "We've more 'n' enow work awaitin' fer t'day."

Joy nodded and pointed to the passage she was reading in her Bible. "I thought I would reread the chapter in John that Pastor David spoke on yesterday. If that is all right?"

"I vould like dat," Marit replied. Breona merely shrugged her shoulders noncommittally.

Joy slowly read John chapter 4 aloud. When she finished, she asked, "Do either of you have any questions?"

When neither of the girls responded, Joy bowed her head and prayed aloud, "Lord, thank you for your word. Thank you even more for sending Jesus to be the Living Water that each of us needs. Help us to understand what you are saying to us. In Jesus' name I pray, amen."

Joy closed her Bible and started to get up when Breona asked a little roughly, "I'm no' understandin' how a daecent woman can be havin' five husbands . . ." She pursed her lips tightly. "Pastor Kalbørg said she was no' a respectable woman . . . was she then bein' a night woman?"

"Weeeell, we don't have any way to know that for *certain*," Joy replied thoughtfully, "But perhaps we can look at some of the clues about her in this passage."

"Vat are 'clues,' miss?" Marit asked innocently.

That seemed to break the tension. Breona chuckled in her usual good-natured way and Joy smothered a smile. Breona, who confessed to having a taste for dime store novels, hastened to explain with some zeal.

"Clues air bein' like a trail o' bread crumbs tha' daetecktive fellers follow t' fin' th' bad guys, mainly if'n they cormitted murders." Breona's eyes shone at the prospect of murders and mayhem.

Joy truly struggled not to laugh aloud. Coughing to cover her mouth she responded, "Yes, that is so. A clue is a hint or a sign—very much like the bread-crumb trail in Hansel and Gretel."

"Ah! I know dat story." Marit looked pleased.

Joy nodded. "All right, let's look at some of the clues in this chapter. Here is one. 'It was about the sixth hour'. Time was counted from sunup in those days, so if the sun rose, say, at 6 a.m., then at the sixth hour it was about noon. The disciples had gone to find food, probably for lunch, and they left Jesus sitting on the edge of the local well. It's very possible that the well was a ways outside of the town because verse 8 reads, 'For his disciples were gone away unto the city to buy meat.'"

Both girls nodded in understanding.

"So Jesus was sitting there when the woman came to draw water—by herself. That is a little clue in itself, when you know the way things were done back then."

"Whist?" Breona's brow furrowed.

"Well, because women never went anywhere by themselves, partly because it was dangerous. But also because only women who were not 'respectable' went out in public by themselves—women who were not considered fit company for the other women of the village. And yet there *she* was . . . drawing water in the middle of the day, alone. You know, I would think that the respectable women of the village would go to draw their water early, in the cool of the day, not in the heat of it, and not alone, like this woman."

Marit made a little "o" with her mouth as the implications sank in.

"And then Jesus, who was a Jew, spoke to her. First, you should know that Jews did not associate with Samaritans—*any* Samaritans—because they were half pagan in their beliefs. Second, a respectable man never spoke to a woman he did not know, especially a woman who was alone . . . you see, it was interpreted as a man seeking . . . a 'night woman,' as you put it, Breona."

Both girls were looking slightly stunned at this point.

"But . . . air ye sayin' Jesus was talkin' to a . . ." Breona's voice dropped to a whisper and she leaned forward, conspiratorially, "*a prosdadute*? Of a purpose?"

Marit's eyes were like saucers now.

Joy answered, "And he asked her to give him a drink. Not only was he talking to her, he was willing to take a cup of water from her, to touch her hand to receive it. What do you think of that?"

Marit swallowed and thought hard, but Breona answered first, somewhat fiercely. "I am thinkin' he was havin' no bus'ness talkin' t' a woman loik that. He's the holy Christ, he is. Don' seem 'propriate."

"Yes, that is what his disciples thought, too. But then he said to her, 'if you knew the gift of God, and who it is that is saying to you, give me a drink, you would have asked him, and he would have given you living water.'"

"And then he said," and Joy opened her Bible again and read aloud,

> *. . . whosoever drinketh of the water*
> *that I shall give him shall never thirst;*
> *but the water that I shall give him shall be*
> *in him a well of water springing up*
> *into everlasting life.*

"Everlasting life . . ." Marit breathed.

Breona looked at Marit sharply. "Not meanin' it fer her, surely!" But she looked to Joy for confirmation.

"Actually . . ." Joy said slowly. "Do you remember what Cousin David said about God knowing everything we have done but also our hearts?"

"Yis, surely."

"I can't help but wonder how this woman ended up where she was . . . five husbands but living with a man who was not her husband. Shunned by the other women in the village. Not fit company for them. Having to walk to the well alone every day. Do you think she planned for her life to be like that or was happy with how it turned out? Why don't we think for a minute of some things that could have happened to her when she was younger?"

The kitchen became very quiet for a long moment. As Joy waited for either of the girls to respond, she saw a tear drop from Marit's chin.

"Marit? What are you thinking, dear heart?"

Marit gulped back a sob. "I'm vondering . . . if, if, someone made her have a baby ven she didn't vant one. Ven she didn't have a husband."

She looked earnestly at Joy. "Maybe people vill think I'm not a respectable voman, Miss Joy. Maybe they vill shun me, like they did her. Maybe . . . no good man vill ever vant me for a vife, now I have a babe coming."

Breona growled at her, "Tosh! Ony man'd be fool not to want you! Ist no' fault o' yourn."

"But . . ." and Marit looked at Joy, tears streaming down her face, "Vat . . . vhere vould I be if you hadn't found me on the train before ve got to Denver? An' vat of those other girls you told us about?"

Joy agreed soberly. "Yes. How many of those girls had no part in their ruin? Sometimes people fall into bad situations not of their choosing. And afterwards, when they are damaged or broken, perhaps they have few choices left . . . except bad ones. I wonder what bad situations the Samaritan woman fell into? I wonder if she had no choices left . . . except wrong ones. I wonder what Jesus knew about her that we don't know."

Breona stared at the table, color rising on her cheeks.

"What David told us Sunday is that Jesus sees not only all that we have done but sees our hearts, too—our past and all of our secrets. Even when we intentionally choose to sin, he sees our hearts, and he has compassion on us. Jesus said to that woman, 'God is a Spirit: and they that worship him must worship him in spirit and in truth'."

"Well, what is the truth? The truth is that *all* of us are broken in some way. We just refuse to see it or perhaps are blind about our own flaws. When we worship God, he wants us to see the truth about ourselves—that we are broken and we need a Savior."

Joy took a deep breath. "Jesus didn't come to save 'the righteous.' He came to save sinners. I, too, am a sinner—"

Breona made to disagree, but Joy waved her protest away. "No, Breona, you do not know everything about me. Only God does. He knows everything I have done and he knows my heart. I *am* a sinner—but, thank you Lord! I am also forgiven. I have been lost, so lost! You have no idea how lost I was this past year, how broken I was and, in some ways still am."

"If it weren't for the Living Water that Jesus gives me every day, I could not have survived. I would not have found hope again. And . . . I don't believe I would have been on that train the same day both of you were also."

"Not a mile from here are girls who were taken against their will and forced to do despicable things. They have been beaten and starved into obedience by evil men. They may have no hope left in their hearts."

Joy paused and came to a decision. "I came to Corinth because Uli and David have been secretly helping a few of them to escape. I came to help them in their work."

Marit and Breona gasped at this revelation.

"And the first ones the Lord led me to were *you*, my dear friends. It was no coincidence, no accident! The Lord caused us to find each other. My hope is that we can find and help more of these young ladies. Help them to escape from slavery and help them to heal. Right here in this house we can love them and tell them about Jesus, the Living Water. We can give them jobs and help them to learn new skills so that, eventually, they can go forth into the world, forgiven, healed, and able to care for themselves."

Joy was exhausted. They had finished breakfast well over an hour ago. This morning's conversation had been an important one, she knew, but it had taken a lot out of all of them.

"Marit, Breona, if you don't mind, I'd like to pray again." Joy bowed her head and the girls followed suit. "Father God, once more, we thank you for your word. Thank you again for sending Jesus to be the Living Water that each of us needs. Help us to understand what you are saying to us. In Jesus' name I pray, amen."

Chapter 33

The next weeks flew by. Flinty, good as his word, brought in a small crew to make the repairs and improvements Joy requested. The first additions were new, reinforced doors, front and back. Flinty himself installed the keyed locks, the new "dead bolt" type, he called them.

Carpenters repaired the leaks in the roof and, after consulting Joy's plans, stripped off all of the old shingles, rolled out and tacked down new tar paper, laid down a second layer of wood, and replaced the shingles with sheets of heavy metal.

As the workers re-roofed, some of them sectioned the attic into three bedrooms, a tiny office for Joy, a storage room, and a small sitting room they would share. The workers nailed tar paper to the ceiling of the attic and the exterior walls to hold in heat. Then they lath-and-plastered the ceilings and all the walls to reduce noise and nicely finish the rooms. Finally, Flinty installed a small oil-burning stove in the sitting room.

The men also repaired the second story balcony and replaced the weathered door to it. Two of their crew began work to add a wide porch that would wrap around one side of the lodge. "We will need some sturdy all-weather chairs for our guests to sit in and watch the sunset," Joy announced one afternoon. Flinty retired to his shop to craft half a dozen he declared would be 'just what the doctor ordered!'

Joy also requested that they add a small balcony and a door that would open from the attic under the ridgepole, the highest beam of the roof. *Almost like a widow's watch*, she thought wryly. From there the view would be unparalleled. In addition to the mountain vista, they would have a bird's eye view of the siding and be able to keep watch on the comings and goings of the trains—and those who disembarked in Corinth.

David lent a hand in the kitchen and pantry. He repaired cupboards, added shelves, and then sanded, stained, and oiled the wooden-planked floor. Breona and Marit scrubbed the pantry and all its shelves with boiling water and lye soap. When the room finally came up to Breona's exacting standards, they applied a coat of strong whitewash to the ceiling, walls, shelves, and floor.

The carpenters worked quickly with an eye to the changeable weather. Fall was short-lived in these mountains; any day a winter snow could halt their progress and the lodge was in no way ready for severe weather.

Uli had questioned Joy about the wisdom of opening Corinth Mountain Lodge just as winter was setting in. Joy replied simply. "I sense in my spirit that we can't wait for good weather, Uli. The girls and I need a place now, and if we don't have many visitors during the cold season, well, that will give us time to fully ready the lodge for the spring and summer season."

"In the meantime, we'll sell Marit's goods at the siding and live from my savings. More importantly, we will prepare ourselves to receive a harvest of young women who may need the quiet of the lodge this winter."

Uli had still frowned with a tiny bit of concern so Joy answered her more seriously. "It is not the best business plan—I acknowledge this. But I was praying and the Lord showed me a passage of scripture that seemed to settle my heart. It comes from the book of Ecclesiastes. Just listen to this!"

He that observeth the wind shall not sow;
and he that regardeth the clouds shall not reap.
As thou knowest not what is the way of the spirit,
nor how the bones do grow in the womb of her that is with child:
even so thou knowest not the works of God who maketh all.

It was the second reference to birthing children that especially spoke to Joy, but she kept that precious bit to herself. Instead she told Uli, "I figured that if Solomon, the wisest man in the world, understood that our ways are often not God's ways, then I could trust the Lord a little, too."

Uli finally relented. "Well then, Joy, we will pray with you for a harvest to grow in the snow!"

Joy also received a response from Arnie and Anna. Arnie had at last located Billy digging ditches for the city of Omaha. With winter coming on, Billy was more than happy to become a shop keeper again.

Two weeks later Joy received a wire from Arnie. It was short and mysterious, and she laughed aloud.

Expect B within week. A

She showed it to Breona and Marit. "My cousin Arnie is taking care that snooping eyes here in Corinth have nothing of note to report," she surmised.

"Aye. Flinty says naught happens in Cor'th a man bein' called Morgan don't know 'bout," replied Breona, lifting one eyebrow.

"Morgan? Hmm." Joy was distracted by a letter that had arrived from RiverBend at the same time as the wire from Arnie. A letter from home! She eagerly tore it open.

> *Dear Joy,*
>
> *I am so stirred in my heart by the work you have undertaken! Just as some of the brave missionaries we read of who have sailed to the far-off lands of China or India, you have "sailed" to your mission field. Papa and I pray for you every day that the Lord will lead you, guide you, and make you fruitful for him.*

Joy read several tidbits of news from her extended family and the community of RiverBend, some happy, some needing prayer. However, her mother's last paragraph caught her unprepared.

> *I don't mean to overly concern you, Joy, but Papa is not doing as well as I would hope. He has had some pains in his chest and difficulties breathing. Today he seems well enough, although I notice that he is not often out of his chair.*
>
> *Please do not come running home at this time. You have important work in your hands that should not be interrupted. Søren visits us each evening and helps Papa to bed. If things change, I will wire you immediately. Joy, I know you are praying for Papa, and I want you to know that I trust the Lord in all things.*
>
> *Love,*
>
> *Mama*

Stunned, Joy tried to digest her mama's words. What would life be without her papa? What would Mama do if Papa passed away? Joy bowed her head and prayed earnestly for both of her parents.

Vikki Kestell

Chapter 34

On Friday Flinty jogged to the lodge from his smithy near the siding bringing good news. "Yer friends hev arrived, they hev!" He was out of breath but grinning as usual from ear to ear.

"Friends? More than one?" Joy was puzzled but smoothed her hair and dress while Marit and Breona quickly loaded a basket with foods to sell to passengers. They donned sweaters or cloaks and Flinty walked them toward the siding.

A plume of coal smoke billowed into the sky from the engine as it idled a ways down the track. A light haze of gritty soot fell from the plume and wafted in the chilly breeze. Along the tracks small clusters of passengers stretched their legs while the crew topped off the engine's water tank and coal bin.

"I sint a boy on over t' yer cousin's place t' git th' wagon," Flinty puffed as they walked.

"You are a good friend, Flinty," Joy said sincerely. As they came closer to the platform, Flinty protectively strode out a little ahead of them. Joy saw why. The two sleek black motorcars and a group of men waited on a trio of elegantly dressed male arrivals. Joy and the girls slowed down until the cars pulled away.

Relieved to avoid a possible confrontation, they made their way to the siding platform. Marit quietly introduced herself and her wares to passengers, several of whom eagerly gathered around to make purchases. Breona stayed close to Marit and kept an eye out for trouble.

Joy, on the other hand, searched down the tracks for a *very* large young man. There he was! She waved enthusiastically at Billy who was standing in front of an open box car. He grinned back, his face alight with the same fun and laughter she knew so well. What a welcome sight! With him were two others.

"Arnie!" Joy flew down the track to her cousin. Arnie turned toward her voice—and so did the third man in their party, his gray hair standing up in tufts around the crown of his head. "Mr. Wheatley!"

His faced creased into a happy smile. "Now that's a sight for sore eyes," he declared, shaking her hand, his eyes growing a little misty.

Joy could hardly restrain herself. She hugged Arnie and barely refrained from hugging Billy and Mr. Wheatley. "I am so happy to see all of you—and so surprised!" Oh, how she had missed them all!

"I couldn't talk him out of it, Joy," Arnie declared. "When he heard from Billy where you were and what you were about, he insisted on coming along. He told me, 'I'll just make myself so useful she'll have to take me on.'" Arnie chuckled. "Not much I could do to stop him from buying a ticket."

Mr. Wheatley looked a little abashed, and perhaps a tiny bit worried, but Joy reassured him immediately. "I would be proud to have you join us, Mr. Wheatley. We can talk later about how to best employ you, but we have so much to do!" She added seriously. "You will always have a place with me as long as I am in business. I am honored that you came, too."

A real tear formed in his eye then, and Joy remembered that he had no family. "But Arnie!" she added to quickly change the subject, "What are *you* doing here? Are you looking for a job, too?"

Arnie just put an arm around her shoulders and squeezed her again. "Anna insisted I come and make sure all was well with you. Believe me, it took an act of Congress to keep Petter and Willem at home and at their studies. You can imagine how they are chafing right about now. Anna had to stay home and keep their noses to the grindstone, so she sent me along with Billy and Wheatley. I'm fairly certain I will be required to submit a report in triplicate when I return to Omaha. Oh, and your old employee, Mr. Taub, sends his warm greetings. He is doing well."

Billy had mostly watched the greetings from the sidelines, his cap in his hand. Finally Joy addressed him more personally. "Billy, I cannot tell you how delighted I am that you have come. I couldn't think of anyone I wanted more to oversee the inventory and to come help me."

She took a breath and included Mr. Wheatley in her next words. "We are walking a fine line here in Corinth. Perhaps when you learn all about it, you may wish to return to Omaha."

Billy, smiling softly, just shook his head. "Mr. Arnie filled us in on our way here, Mrs. Michaels. I'm in for the long haul."

Joy looked him up and down. He had been head and shoulders over most men when she had seen him last, but he had also had the lankiness and sometimes clumsiness of youth. Six months of digging ditches in the city had filled him out in hard muscle. Gone was the gangly and ungainly young man she had known; now he seemed solid and grounded. Moreover, Joy knew he was quick-witted and loyal. She nodded in approval.

"You are all, as our dear Flinty says, just what the doctor ordered! I couldn't be happier." She saw Marit and Breona waiting not far off and waved them over. "I would like you to meet the other members of our little household."

As she introduced everyone around, she spied David and Uli's wagon coming toward them. "Good. We can start moving the inventory right away. It will be getting dark soon, and if you think this nip in the air is bracing, wait until the sun drops behind those mountains!"

Joy gestured toward the panorama in the near distance and laughed as the three newcomers gaped. When had she last laughed so freely, so spontaneously? She smiled again. "And wait until you see the view from upstairs at the lodge!"

Uli was just as amazed to see her brother as Joy had been. Greetings, hugs, and handshakes took several more minutes. At last Joy had to urge them into action.

"It truly will be dark soon! We should hurry along." With a will the men began to unload the freight car onto the siding platform, knowing that they would have to make many trips with the wagon. The women walked together back to the lodge and put on fresh coffee and added more potatoes to the stew.

The shifting of the goods from the siding to the lodge took until long after dark. When the last crate was stacked in the great room, Marit had supper and fresh bread waiting. Breona, Joy, and Uli had busied themselves making up beds for Arnie, Billy, and Mr. Wheatley.

When they finally sat down to eat, the great room was crammed with boxes and crates. They shared the meal in the kitchen around the same rickety table. The men had to employ small boxes as chairs but the mood was cheerful and companionable.

At Joy's request Arnie prayed. "Bless this food, O Lord, and the hands that prepared it." Joy smiled as everyone enthusiastically dug into the hearty stew Marit had made.

Chapter 35

As bedtime drew on and most of the house retired, Joy and Arnie found a quiet corner of the great room to talk quietly for a few minutes. Arnie began soberly. "Joy, first I should tell you that Robertson and his lying pal, Tom Percher, are both dead."

Nothing could have shocked or surprised Joy more. "Wha—how?" she stammered.

"Percher was found poisoned in his jail cell about a week after the trial ended. That caused quite an uproar." Arnie smiled sardonically. "He hadn't been able to tell the law much, but someone evidently wanted him silenced permanently. The law couldn't seem to catch up to Robertson either—until a maid found him, the day after Percher died, in a hotel room. *He* had been strangled."

Arnie put his feet up on a box and stretched his legs. "And I did some digging and have discovered quite a bit about him since you left Omaha. You told us that Robertson represented a consortium called 'Franklin and Chase Enterprises.' We couldn't find anything on this business during the trial, but did finally find them, or what had been them, last month."

"Seems the 'consortium' was really one man, a Shelby Franklin. He operated with a small, select crew. Franklin used intimidation to extract 'protection' money from local businesses and to acquire part ownership of lucrative ones. He hadn't been operating in Omaha for long, but had already made considerable inroads into the legitimate business community. Apparently Robertson worked for him."

"They expected that you would be easy to intimidate and control. In refusing their intimidation, you threatened their plan to force the downtown businesses into their protection racket. They could not allow your resistance to go unchecked—they stood to lose a lot of money if others were to follow suit."

"That," he paused, "and they wanted your property, Joy. Plain and simple. We believe that if you had bent to their 'partnership' agreement, you would have found yourself out on the street in very short time. The City is expanding rapidly in that direction. I don't know if you realized how strategically located your two lots were."

For a moment Joy felt yanked back into the hopelessness of those few weeks. She had to shake herself to snap out of it. "How did you find this all out, Arnie?"

Arnie's smile twisted shrewdly. "I have a sympathetic friend who suggested that I hire some professionals to investigate the situation. He and others in our community did not like what was done to you, Joy."

"Professionals? But who?"

"The Pinkertons."

"What? Detectives?" Joy was astonished.

"Yes, and they were happy to take the case. Seems Franklin's activities were stirring up a lot of interest. You see, the other thing Franklin was into was investment fraud. He's a clever one, let me tell you. On the one side of his 'business' he was nothing more than an upstart gangster and opportunist; on the other side he presented himself as a respectable financier with a finely appointed office and a slick and *quite* exclusive investment strategy. He brazenly targeted only the plums of Omaha society and suckered significant amounts of money out of a number of our most outstanding citizens through false investment opportunities."

"When the city auctioned your lots, Franklin had prearranged to snap them up. That's how we finally got a bead on him. He already had buyers from back east lined up—and he immediately turned a substantial profit on your property." Here Arnie looked pained.

Joy patted him gently on the leg. "It's all right, Arnie. Truly."

Arnie shook his head in regret. "I just wish I'd known sooner, Joy. Maybe I could have prevented all—"

"That was my fault, was it not?" Joy replied candidly to her cousin. "*I'm* the one who was wrong. I foolishly thought I could do everything on my own. I was filled with anger and pride at the time. I should have asked for help the first time Robertson darkened my door. But I didn't. I thought I could—no I *wanted* to handle it myself. I have repented of my prideful foolishness, Arnie. Now I have to let it go. And so do you."

"I understand, Joy. I'm grateful that you are past that part of your life. However, just 'letting it go' may not be an option."

"Why? What are you telling me?"

"As I said, Franklin defrauded some outstanding Omaha citizens. They didn't take kindly to it, so the Pinkertons are still on the case. And this was arson, you know. We cannot let *that* go."

"More investigation by the Pinkertons uncovered a similar pattern of criminal activities in other major cities. Someone, using different identities in each city, had worked his way across the country from east to west. According to victims interviewed by the Pinkertons, a very genteel man with 'sure-fire' investment opportunities charmed well-heeled clients in each situation. The description of the man is essentially the same, city to city. And matches that of Franklin."

Joy was both fascinated and repulsed by what she heard. "And Franklin now? Do they know where he is?"

"Franklin is no simpleton. He is well organized and his schemes are all always very short-lived, easily cashed out. He even turns a profit on his protection schemes by selling them to other outfits from back east—thus giving them a foothold where they hadn't operated before."

"We found that he never intended to stay in Omaha—just fleece as many as he could and then disappear. That has been his pattern in other cities. As soon as he sold your properties, he vanished. All the Pinkertons found was an empty office and a trail of indignant investors. Oh, and the bodies of Robertson and Percher. Since they had both testified at your trial, Franklin knew the police would eventually seize them and pressure them for information. Apparently Franklin leaves no witnesses."

"The Pinkertons know he left Omaha with a sizable amount of cash. Reports are that he headed south, but they are also following a lead west. To Denver."

Joy's heart jumped into her throat.

"Not to worry, Joy. First of all, this is a man who lives in the shadows. He has nothing personal against you and you cannot identify him. Besides, you are not in Denver and no longer go by the name of Michaels."

Arnie changed the subject. "By the way, the City of Omaha is a little nervous about you."

"About me?" Joy didn't understand.

"It is more than apparent now that Franklin burned you out, framed you to take the fall for the arson, and then further defrauded you by orchestrating the sale of your properties at bargain prices. The City, when it jumped according to Franklin's plan, became an unwitting accomplice to his crimes—that and a few city council members may have profited under the table from the arrangement."

"The judge who presided over your trial has been more than a little vocal, publicly taking the City to task for its overzealousness and raising the possibility of criminal behavior by a few officials. *That* investigation is ongoing. He has suggested that perhaps the City is liable to you for damages."

Joy was stunned. Arnie withdrew a fine linen envelope from his breast pocket and extended it to her. Joy couldn't help it—she flinched from it as surely as if he had held out a scorpion. She doubted she would ever willingly touch a linen envelope again!

"It's all right, Joy. This is a letter from the mayor of Omaha. An apology—of sorts. And a little something more than that. In any event, you should know that you have been fully exonerated in the community's eyes. You are welcome in Omaha, should you ever choose to return."

He continued to hold out the envelope. At last Joy touched it, felt the smooth elegance of the paper, and finally took it in her hand.

She stared at it for several moments before finally opening it.

The letter was short but kindly written. What fell out of the letter into her lap is what truly amazed her. It was a check.

"The amount is the difference between what Franklin paid for your properties and what he sold them for—the fair value you should have received," Arnie told her. "You will notice that the letter is carefully crafted. The City of Omaha does not take responsibility for what befell you or how you were treated. It is written with a conciliatory tone. I believe the check is meant to placate you, should you think of suing the City for how you were basically run out of town, even after you were found 'not guilty' in a court of law."

"Oh. And as your attorney I have contacted your insurance company with the evidence the Pinkertons uncovered. I have formally warned them to pay on the policy forthwith."

Joy nodded, still staring at the check. Her head was whirling. The amount was enough to cover what she had already laid out on Corinth Mountain Lodge and its refurbishment. It was as if she had spent nothing on it.

She met Arnie's eyes and smiled a small, crooked smile. "You know, coming here and believing that the Lord is in what we are doing has been frightening and more than a little overwhelming. However, apparently God himself has paid for this lodge." She looked down on the check again and thought about what Arnie had said regarding the insurance on the store.

She got a faraway look on her face. "Yes. God himself has paid for this place—and more. This is confirmation, don't you think? We are on the right track."

Chapter 36

Arnie, David, and Billy tackled unpacking the crates and boxes the next morning while Joy, Uli, and Breona determined how the furnishings would be arranged. David and Uli's boys, Sam and Seth, carried the wood crates around back and stacked them by the kitchen door. There Mr. Wheatley methodically removed all the nails and tacks and reduced the wood to kindling. Little Ruth Kalbørg ran simple errands and generally managed to stay out from underfoot as the pieces of furniture were uncrated.

Marit, already slowed by the weight of her growing baby, came to a complete standstill as the elegant pieces to a dining room suite were unpacked. Her hands cautiously and then lovingly stroked the polished woods.

"Pretty posh, eh?" Breona joked in her usual merry manner. Marit shook her head in wonder as each piece was revealed.

Under Joy's direction, the men laid carpets in the clean guest rooms and set up bedsteads and mattresses. Later they hauled chifferobes, dressing tables, and men's valets to the rooms, shifting them about as Joy and Uli discussed the optimal positioning of each piece. David diplomatically pointed out Arnie's reddening face to Uli as he struggled to control his impatience. Joy and Uli exchanged amused grins.

"Over there, please," Joy commanded Arnie. It was the third time he had muscled the same piece of furniture to a new location. Joy and Uli both burst into laughter as Arnie sputtered and tried not to explode.

"Cousin," Joy said in a conciliatory tone but her eyes still laughing. "You will be sleeping in one of these beds this evening and not on the hard floor. Think of how it will feel to be soothed by Egyptian cotton sheets and warmed by a silk-covered goose-down comforter tonight."

"Sounds good, now that you mention it," Arnie replied, his normally even nature instantly restored.

After the bedroom furniture had been placed, they laid carpets in the great room and set the parlor furnishings on one end. Two dining tables and their chairs were placed on the opposite end nearer the kitchen. All of the men lifting together moved a majestic china hutch and matching sideboard against a wall in the dining area.

Marit was beside herself when Joy asked her to unpack two beautiful sets of dishes and an elegant tea service and place them in the hutch. Breona helped her arrange table cloths, napkins, serving pieces, and silver in the cavernous drawers and cupboards of the sideboard. Breona was accustomed to handling fine things for the families she had worked for, but Marit, who had neither seen nor touched such richness, handled each piece with both fear and wonder.

In the morning the entire household went to church together. It was a long walk and the air was crisp, but the women in particular enjoyed the security and freedom of movement that having three men in the group afforded them. It was probably too long of a walk for Marit in her condition, however. Joy determined, with her new influx of funds, to buy a wagon and two horses as soon as suitable ones could be found. And somehow they would have to afford a more genteel conveyance for guests when they began arriving.

Marit seemed to genuinely look forward to Sunday services. She had made a few friends and, although the situation was awkward, was beginning to believe that she might be accepted in the church as a mother without a husband. Because David and Uli had diplomatically explained her circumstances to the pillars of their church, no one had asked Marit embarrassing questions.

Breona, on the other hand, was a continuing puzzle to Joy. Although free to make her own choices, she willingly took part in morning devotions and came along to church—all the while holding herself aloof. Normally gregarious and social, Breona stood off to the side before and after services, her snapping black eyes daring anyone to speak to her. Joy wondered if she came only to watch over Marit. She was only a few years older than Marit and perhaps half her size, but Breona was something of a mother hen to the sweet, simple girl, and would not allow anyone or anything to hurt her if she could prevent it.

Joy and the girls rode back home in the Kalbørg's wagon while the men and David and Uli's boys walked behind them. Sunday dinner was a happy though disorganized event. So much of the house was still in disarray. Their party of 11 squeezed in around the larger of the two dining tables that normally seated eight. They dined on roast beef, potatoes, carrots, and thick, rich gravy over Marit's hot biscuits, mixing fine china with a cast-iron Dutch oven. Dessert was

apple pie and slices of cheddar accompanied by sweet coffee—
served in tin cups.

Plain or elegant, it didn't matter: The meal around that table was
a festive affair. Breona teased Samuel and Seth mercilessly, and little
Ruthie followed Marit everywhere. The conversation flowed
effortlessly, and a contented light danced in Mr. Wheatley's tired old
eyes. Billy didn't say much; Joy was happy to see he was the same
smiling, good natured young man she had known before.

"As much as I have enjoyed these few days, I will need to return
home soon," Arnie announced over coffee.

"But you only arrived Friday evening!" Uli protested.

He nodded. "I'll stay another day—I can see how much still
needs to be done—but I need to start home Tuesday. The important
thing is that Anna and I can be more assured about Joy's little
endeavor here in Corinth."

"Little endeavor!" Joy bristled but laughed too. "We'll see."

Chapter 37

November 1908

Over the next two weeks they brought the lodge into working order. Billy and Mr. Wheatley moved into the room behind the kitchen. Joy, Breona, and Marit settled into their finished and newly furnished apartment in the attic. Breona and Marit delighted in their new fittings. Marit's room, in addition to a bed and armoire, also held a cradle and a tiny dresser filled with newborn clothing. When Joy had given her the box containing the baby things Anna had selected, Marit and Breona had spent a delighted hour exclaiming over each item.

Thanksgiving was only a week away and the weather was cold. Joy was grateful that they hadn't yet received much snow, but it was inevitable.

That morning Billy had escorted Breona and Marit to the grocers. Mr. Wheatley and Joy had taken a loaf of fresh bread to Flinty. Mr. Wheatley, with Joy's urging, had given into Flinty's plea for "just one game" of checkers. Mr. Wheatley walked Joy home and hustled back to Flinty's. Joy found herself alone in the lodge for the first time.

She critically examined the great room, now furnished as parlor on one side and dining area on the other. How would wealthy guests view it? She rearranged several knickknacks and decided a few wall hangings were needed. She was making another list when she heard boots on the front porch.

The two men who strode in did not knock. They were large and rough and Joy was alone.

The smaller of the men stood by the door as if waiting instructions. Joy immediately recognized the other. Darrow strolled around the room, touching the furnishings, picking up objects with his ham-sized hands and setting them down carelessly. He concluded his examination in front of her. Something in the set of his mouth made Joy go still.

She was in trouble. Why had she broken her own rule and allowed herself to be cornered here alone? Then she thought of Mr. Wheatley confronting this mountain of a man and knew it would have ended badly for her friend.

"Thought you were so smart in Denver, didn't you, lady?" Darrow's hair was still greasy. He still stank and Joy shrank back from the stench. "We know you brought those two women here. You know they belong to us. Let's just say the present situation ain't permanent."

Joy straightened her spine. "Those girls will *never* 'belong' to anyone, you, you . . ." Joy's vocabulary failed her but her courage did not. "However you threaten us, you will not have them. Now get out of my lodge!"

Darrow turned to the other man who immediately kicked over an end table. It splintered and the items on it shattered on the floor.

"What's going on here, Darrow?" A lanky figure wearing a Stetson and a badge loomed in the doorway.

Darrow's eyes narrowed. "Sheriff. Surprised to see you here."

"I'm more surprised to see you here. Looking for lodgings?" The man's face was weathered and lined yet he was not an old man—and he seemed to wear his authority easily.

He took his hat off and nodded at Joy. "Sheriff Duane Wyndom, ma'am. Sorry I haven't been over to introduce myself sooner."

Joy nodded back, quaking with relief. "Pleased to meet you, Sheriff Wyndom. I'm Joy Thoresen."

"These men bothering you, ma'am? What happened to this table?"

Before Joy could answer, Darrow guffawed. "Damn! I swear, ol' Harold here was born in a barn. Not used to walkin' around fancy stuff—just kicked that little table right over, Sheriff. Purely accidental-like, right, Harold?"

"You watch your tongue around the lady, Darrow," Wyndom's tone did not leave room for disagreement.

"Why, I beg your pardon, miss. And, of course, we'll pay for the damages."

Darrow immediately drew a wallet from his back pocket and pulled out a sheaf of notes. He handed them toward Joy, but she refused to touch the extended bills. Darrow shrugged and let them flutter to the floor.

"We'll just be on our way, Sheriff." Darrow jerked his chin toward Harold.

"I don't want to see you here again, Darrow. For any reason."

Darrow looked aggrieved and managed to smirk at the same time. "Why do you have to take that tone, Sheriff? After all . . . we're basically on the same team, right?"

The sheriff's jaw tightened but he did not take the bait. "You don't come here again, Darrow, or any of your crew. Got that? Not for any reason."

Darrow shrugged his massive shoulders. "Well, all right. No need to get testy. I'll be sure to give *the boss* your message."

"You do that." Wyndom's jaw clenched so tightly Joy thought his teeth would crack.

As Darrow and the other man stomped away, Joy sank onto a sofa. Wyndom picked up the money and counted it. "This enough for the breakage, miss?"

Joy just shook her head dismissively. "I don't care. I don't want it."

Sheriff Wyndom laid the money on a chair anyway. "Money doesn't grow on trees. You got a broom around here?"

"I, um, thank you, but there's no need. I'll clear it up . . . soon as I catch my breath."

He nodded. "My office is over on Main Street, kitty-corner from the town square. If Darrow or any of that crew comes around again, I want to know right away."

"I am so grateful, Sheriff Wyndom. How . . . how did you happen to be here at just the right time?"

"Didn't 'happen'. I keep my eyes on that one. I've recruited a few of the boys in town to be my eyes and ears, too. One of them let me know they heard Darrow talking about coming over here, that you were by yourself." He looked at Joy a little quizzically. "Not sure what you're about doing here in Corinth, miss. But I *am* sure that the wrong people are paying attention."

Joy flushed. "I, ah, well it's a lodge, as you can see. We'll be in business soon and will have paying customers coming to Corinth for the fresh air and the views . . ."

Wyndom still looked skeptical. "I know what goes on in this town, Miss Thoresen. To my shame, I know it. And there's not a lot I can do about it. Seems to me you've stepped into something you might regret."

Joy didn't have an answer. Wyndom slapped his hat on his knee and put it back on his head. "You've got a couple of men working for you. The young one is fit enough, but the other is too old to be much protection. If you'd like some additional muscle, I can recommend one or two respectable young men looking for work."

Joy nodded. "I'd like that."

The sheriff touched his hat to her. "I'll have them come by one at a time so you can speak to them. I think you know not to be alone . . . like this . . . again?"

"Yes. Thank you."

Chapter 38

The faces around the table that evening were grim as Joy related what happened. Mr. Wheatley, red with shame, was beside himself. "It's my fault, Mrs. Michaels! No way should I have left you here while I went to play checkers!"

Joy put her hand on his and said gently. "Mr. Wheatley, what would you have done if you had been here? Two against one . . ." She let the implications go unspoken without bringing up his age, but he was not fooled.

"I might be just an old man but, but I can handle a gun!"

Joy grew stern. "No, Mr. Wheatley. I'll not have you doing that. You are not here as a bodyguard, like Billy is. You are here to help us manage the lodge. We need you for that—we cannot do *without* you for that. No, I will take the sheriff's suggestion and hire another man for security. And we will strictly follow our own rules—none of us goes anywhere alone. Am I understood?"

She addressed everyone at the table. "I know old habits are hard to break, but also please remember that I am known as Joy Thoresen now, rather than Michaels." Billy and Mr. Wheatley, who were the ones who frequently forgot, both nodded. "I'll start interviewing for another 'handyman' as soon as possible."

Joy immediately took to the first young man sent by the sheriff. Flinty introduced them formally. Domingo Juarez was small and wiry and quick as a cat. Moreover, his dark brown eyes were respectful and kind. He spoke in a soft and confiding way to her during the interview.

"I think I know what you do here, *señora*." He gestured around him to include the lodge. "Some of us hope you will help more girls. Many Corinth peoples know *that man* and what he does, but the Corinth—what they call? *city clerk* and some *hombres de nogocios*-- the businesses peoples—are in that man's pocket."

"They's in his pocket, all right," Flinty agreed with vigor.

Joy couldn't stop herself. "Er, what man?"

Domingo's eyes flashed. "It was Judge Brown, *señora*. That is how it started. He was *malvado*—evil man, and his wealthy *cómplices* in Denver were just as evil as him. But we did not know that then, did we?"

Flinty, chewing a toothpick thoughtfully added, "Tha's right, Miss Thoresen. First Judge Brown, he opens a savin's 'n' loan in Corinth. An' folks all a-thinkin' it were a great cornvenience, being able t' bank their money right here 'stead-a in Denver. They 'preciated that he was investin' in our little town."

Young Domingo frowned. "Then other bad things start to happen, ver' *secretamente*."

"Yup. Real quiet-like. No one s'pected what was goin' on at first," Flinty said. "Judge Brown bought them two nice houses—and made 'em even bigger! And *fancy*? Nothing else like 'em way up here in *these* mountains. Can y' figger what one man would be wantin' with *two* big houses? No sir! But then we started seein' them city swells comin' up on the train t' visit those houses."

He nodded his head sagely. "Then things jest kinder exploded— Brown hired a crew o' rough men and put 'em in a boardin' house 'long Main Street, not far from th' sidin'. Suddenly, if someone was t' ask too many questions, those thugs'd deliver a thrashin' you wouldn't want t' repeat."

Domingo nodded in agreement. "*Sí*. It is very bad now."

Joy frowned. "You said it *was* Judge Brown?"

Flinty answered her. "Last August, a new feller shows up, new friend o' Brown's from Denver. A real gentleman, that 'un—the best clothes 'n' manners. Folks say butter wouldn't melt in *his* mouth. Only Brown don't know 'til too late that he done brought a snake into his house."

"Within a few weeks Brown jest up 'n' disappears. This new guy, Brown's 'friend,' name o' *Dean Morgan*, steps right in, slick as oil, and starts a-runnin' ever'thing. He lives down th' mountain but he uses them thugs t' keep Corinth on a tight leash."

"What happened to Brown?" Joy's eyes were huge.

"No one knows, *señora*," Domingo replied softly.

Flinty added, "Yep. He jest disappeared. Someone tried t' spread th' story that his mother took ill back east, 'cept old Missus Childers knew Brown's mother 'way back. Says she died years ago. We're all pretty certain Morgan had som'pin t' do with Brown disappearing, and we mighta cheered fer him, 'cept he's ten times worse'n Brown."

"How? How is he worse?"

Domingo grimaced. "This Morgan? He is *hombre rico*, very big money. Now many Corinth peoples, they—how you say?" Domingo turned to Flinty.

"Thet Morgan cornvinced a bunch o' folks here t' invest th' money they had in th' savings 'n' loan with him, is what," Flinty explained. "Like Domingo here said, th' city clerk and some o' th' business folk are in cahoots with 'im, so not only did they invest *their* money, but th' town o' Corinth did, too. Oh, he's a smooth 'un all right."

"Couple o' brave folks decided t' withdraw their money. That's when we found out how bad things was. He let those folks know, kinder subtle-like, ya know, that it wasn't a good time t' pull their savings. He said th' S&L was heavily invested and it were an uneasy time in th' market. Said if they pulled their money, it might cause a run and everybody—'specially th' town—might be *negertively* *'ffected*, sez him."

Flinty aimed a shrewd look at Joy. "S' far, people *say* they're happy with their 'vestment returns—but it's all on paper, so how d' they know it's *real*? Fact is, they're 'fraid t' find out th' truth. No, we all got th' message. He's holdin' th' people *and* th' town o' Corinth hostage with their own money. No one is brave enough t' pull their money and no one dares t' cross him."

Chapter 39

Joy felt as though Thanksgiving had landed on them rather than arrived. She took a deep breath and gazed around the crowded table at the familiar and now loved faces . . . Breona, Marit, Mr. Wheatley, Billy, Flinty, David and Uli, Sam, Seth, and Ruthie. She bade herself to relax and truly give thanks for the beauty of the season.

They had used only the best of everything today—china, silver, and crystal that would have been sold for a small fortune back in Omaha; linens and lace that had been intended for the tables of wealthy homes; a pair of silver candelabra holding an array of flickering candlelight that might have graced a governor's home.

And the food! Marit and Uli had assumed direction of the feast while Breona and Joy had tackled the cleaning and polishing and the table arrangements. The women ran Billy and Mr. Wheatley ragged with errands and chores.

Now the assembled guests stared about them at the bounty: an enormous bird, its buttered skin browned and crackling, a savory stuffing bursting from its insides; elegant footed crystal dishes and cups, each one brightly gleaming red, purple, green, orange, or yellow with jellies, jams, pickles, relishes, or sauces; a mountain of mashed potatoes accompanied by a boat of thick, steaming gravy; fresh, sweet-smelling yeast rolls, saucers of churned butter, and three kinds of vegetables.

The men and boys eyed the sideboard greedily, for Marit, Uli, and Ruth had concocted enough desserts for an army: a three-layer coconut cake, a two-layer chocolate torte, and pumpkin, pecan, mincemeat, cherry, and apple pies. A gallon of sweet whipped cream waited in the ice box.

In the pause before they gave thanks, Joy watched Breona and Marit especially. How those girls were blooming!

Breona, always the joking little spitfire, tormented Sam and Seth relentlessly—and they adored her. It was clear to see that she adored them back.

Marit glowed with pleasure, one hand in Mr. Wheatley's and the other in Ruth's. Marit and Ruthie were practically inseparable. Ruthie viewed Marit as a beautiful older sister and Joy realized their relationship had grown into something akin to what Uli and Joy had known as children. Soon there would be an infant to care for. In the joy of caring for that baby, perhaps Ruthie would help Marit put her shame behind her.

Around the table they joined hands and bowed their heads to thank God for their bounty. And within herself Joy particularly gave thanks for the "family" that had grown under her roof—the band of misfits, orphans, and lonely hearts that had found each other. No, the Lord had found *them.* Seen them in their aloneness and brought them together. Here in little Corinth.

Dinner began, and Joy looked about her, feasting not on the food, but on the contentment that enveloped her. Despite the many uncertainties ahead, here her heart was finding peace again.

Thank you, Lord. Amen.

Chapter 40

In her trial attempt to garner guests for the lodge, Joy had placed a carefully worded advertisement in the Denver Post. If she attracted even a few select guests over the holidays, she would count the attempt as a success.

No one at the lodge had skills in guest keeping—Joy had management experience and Marit's cooking was quite good, but only Breona had experience in personal service for "people of quality." The household quickly learned to defer to her "how-to" guidance and judgments. With their first few visitors, they planned to carefully practice and hone their guest skills. Then in the spring, if they were successful with their trial guests, Joy intended to reach east of Colorado to attract more and varied guests.

The day after Thanksgiving they finally received their first significant snowfall. Breona, Marit, Joy, Billy, and Mr. Wheatley tramped a path to "their" overlook and gazed in awe at the snow-laden majesty spread before them. This spot, they decided, would be a destination "must" for lodge guests. Mr. Wheatley set out for Flinty's to commission some benches to be placed strategically at the overlook. Then he and Billy set upon building railings they would install along the path and at the overlook to make the walk easier and to ensure that guests did not stray into unsafe areas along the ridgeline, especially in the snow.

That day Billy fetched their mail, and in it was a small, feminine-looking envelope. The quality of the letter was understatedly evident; the handwriting perfectly uniform and elegant. Joy opened the letter carefully.

Dear Corinth Mountain Lodge,

I read with interest your advertisement in the Post. You have described your mountain inn in delightful terms.

If it is available, I would like to reserve your Mountain View Suite for a week beginning December 1. I would expect to arrive by afternoon train and would request that you make arrangements to meet and provide conveyance for myself and my luggage.

If this arrangement is satisfactory, please reply by return post.

Cordially,

Mrs. Randolph Van der Pol

Joy gasped in delight. A guest! It was Friday—December 1 was the coming Tuesday! She called Breona and Marit together and quickly told them that their first guest would arrive in four days.

If the quality of the letter were any indication, their guest would be both wealthy and genteel. Those were the qualities they needed in their first guests to ensure that Corinth Mountain Lodge would be well spoken of in Denver society.

Tuesday morning Joy had Domingo drive her into town for some guest soaps and items Marit had placed on a list. Corinth had a small grocery, a bakery, a butcher, and a few sundry shops near the town plaza—and near the sheriff's office. David considered the area safe to visit as long as the women had a male escort.

Joy was leaving a tiny specialty shop just as another woman had her hand on the door to enter. They tussled with the door for a moment before realizing their impasse. The middle-aged woman standing in the doorway had strikingly red curls above a full mouth. She was pleasantly plump . . . but that plumpness was displayed in a day suit so tightly corseted that Joy must have gaped as she ran her eyes over the woman. The suit exhibited every possible curve on the woman's body to its best advantage.

"I-I beg your pardon," Joy stuttered. She didn't know what she was apologizing for, but she found herself mentally examining her dress and finding it somehow lacking.

"Not at all. I believe the fault was mine." The woman wore a mildly amused expression. "Miss Roxanne Cleary. You must be . . . Miss Thoresen?" She extended a gloved hand.

"Why, yes, I—" Joy was cut off as Dom took her firmly by the arm just as she was raising it. Joy glanced reproachfully at him only to be met by a fiery-red face and a clenched jaw.

"*Señora*, we are go now," he muttered tersely.

The amused smile still on her face, the woman silently nodded and stepped aside. Domingo ushered Joy through the door and down the street to their wagon.

Although the encounter had lasted mere seconds, Joy had quickly understood Domingo's actions. As the horses trotted around the plaza she timidly asked him, "Is *she* . . . one of those women?" The polished confidence of the woman had shaken Joy. Somehow she had envisioned "those kinds" of women as defeated and broken. Roxanne Cleary was undoubtedly neither.

"*That* one! She is—!" Domingo sighed in agitation. "*Señora* Joy, do you know what 'madam' is?"

"Something tells me it's not merely a French woman," Joy responded a bit tartly.

Dom laughed wryly. "*Verdad*! You are right." He sighed again but added nothing more.

"Indeed," Joy said to herself, somewhat disappointed. The woman had intrigued her but Uli would have to fill her in later.

When they returned to the lodge, delicious smells were already coming from the kitchen. Marit was determined to make an impression on their first guest. She had breads and pies cooling on the back of the stove and was just sliding a pot roast into the oven.

That afternoon Billy returned to the lodge with their guest in the "new" carriage. Joy had managed to locate and purchase a four-seat buggy that had seen better days. Mr. Wheatley mended and polished its worn seats and livery to a fare-thee-well.

Billy extended his hand to assist their guest. From the windows Joy examined her. She was, perhaps, 40 years old or thereabouts, dark-haired and handsomely dressed. The woman looked about her with interest, her eyes sparkling.

Joy opened the lodge door. "Welcome to Corinth Mountain Lodge." She smiled and extended her hand. "I'm Miss Thoresen, your hostess."

Mrs. Van der Pol took her hand. "Thank you. I'm looking forward to my stay. What is that delicious smell?" She looked about the great room. "What a lovely room! Rustic but elegantly furnished."

She followed Joy up the stairs to the room at the end of the hall. Breona stood waiting for her.

"Mrs. Van der Pol, this is Breona. She will be looking after your needs while you are here, although any of the staff would be pleased to help you."

Breona bobbed a curtsy. "May I unpack for you, ma'am?" Joy had worked with her to say it just so rather than "May I be unpackin' for you, ma'am?" Joy smiled at Breona from behind Mrs. Van der Pol's back.

"Yes, thank you." She turned to Joy. "This is quite charming! I'm particularly looking forward to seeing the views you wrote of."

"Ah!" Joy replied. "Well perhaps you would like to see one now? The small balcony just outside your door has one of my favorite views."

She opened the door and led her guest outside. The wind pulled at them, but the snow-clad mountains, with the sun just beginning to set, were changing from white to brilliant reds and oranges. Mrs. Van der Pol's hand crept up to her throat as she soaked in the grandeur before her.

"Magnificent." That was all she said for several moments until Joy involuntarily shivered. "Oh, my dear. I apologize for my thoughtlessness." They returned inside and found Breona just opening a trunk and beginning to unpack.

"I will leave you for now," Joy said smiling. "That delicious aroma you commented on when you arrived is dinner. We will serve at your convenience, of course, but the dinner rolls will be ready shortly, and I believe you will enjoy them most fresh from the oven."

Later that evening as Breona and Marit gathered in the kitchen for pie and coffee, Joy tentatively mentioned the woman she had met that day with Domingo. Marit looked clueless but Breona nodded perceptively.

"Oh yis. A 'madam' is bein' th' woman who runs a whorehouse, Miss Joy, pardon m' French. Miss Cleary? *She* ist th' chief woman as runs them two fancy houses."

Joy's mouth opened soundlessly.

Breona chuckled without humor. "It's belavin' I am thet Marit 'n' me barely missed th' honor o' knowin' Miss Cleary up close and personal loik."

Chapter 41

Mei-Xing crouched in the deep snow behind the shrubbery. She was bruised and deeply scratched. Her ankle throbbed and her ribs stabbed with every breath. She looked up and saw the knotted strand of clothes dangling from the third floor window high above her. The "rope" she had devised only reached to the bottom of the second floor windows, so she had been forced to drop the rest of the distance.

Over the pulsing pain of her ribs her heart pounded even louder. She shivered, and not just from the cold. If they caught her again, she had no illusions about what they would do to her.

She had spent seven months in Corinth, seven months in these houses. Seven months since she had arrived in Denver and had been met by a man she distrusted immediately. Seven months since Roxanne had met her at the door and shown her to an overly sumptuous room. Seven months since that same night when she had been fed a drink that had made her feel lethargic and weak, and had been bathed, dressed in satin, and "given" to an elegantly dressed man. He had taken her innocence and then praised her to Roxanne and "reserved" her for several weeks of exclusive use.

Mei-Xing's heart hardened in bitterness as she remembered. It hadn't taken her long to realize that Bao had lied to her and that, undoubtedly, this was the punishment Fang-Hua had devised for her—the retribution she felt Mei-Xing deserved for rejecting her beloved son and causing him to leave his family.

She cursed and used words she had heard often in the last seven months. She cursed and swore she would punish Fang-Hua and her toadies. Someday.

Mei-Xing had learned that the two houses had distinctly different purposes and housed girls accordingly. New girls were brought to the first house where men paid a high price for a girl's innocence, especially young girls.

The second house was proudly advertised as the "Corinth Gentleman's Club." Roxanne bragged that the club was the most exclusive of her employer's houses. Nothing in Denver compared to the Corinth Gentleman's Club, she assured "her" girls.

After Mei-Xing had been a few weeks in the first house, the man who had reserved her for his exclusive use had tired of her. Because

Mei-Xing had been educated and well brought up, what Roxanne described as "refined," the madam had decided to train her for the gentlemen's club.

"Persuaded" by repeated rapes and beatings, many of the girls working in the club had looked at their options and elected to do as they were told. They learned what Roxanne and the "quality girls" had to teach. After they mastered the skills required of them, they entertained the men who frequented the club with gracious conversation, flattery, drinks, food, and gaming, as well as intimate and . . . unusual pleasure.

The club existed outside of Denver *explicitly* for men who had "exotic" tastes. Roxanne was proud of this distinction, but Mei-Xing had learned through experience what "exotic" tastes consisted of.

Mei-Xing spat more than blood from her mouth. *You mean perversions*, she thought and spat again. The very things Uncle Wei and Auntie Fang-Hua profited from in Seattle.

No matter what the cost, she thought, *I was right to reject your son.*

Not all the women at the club had been forced into prostitution. The girls rose late in the day and talked as they had their first meal together. Savannah, a buxom blonde from the Deep South frequently declared that "being a whore beat picking cotton and growing old and haggard from birthing a dozen babies any day of the week."

Tory, a tall, "high-yeller" woman merely shrugged when asked her story. Mei-Xing admired Tory's graceful sophistication and her wide, dark eyes, even though they were often sad. Once Tory had offered the insight that she had never known a full belly until a "kindly gentleman" had taken her off the street at age 12.

Because the club was so selective, Roxanne only used "the best" girls there and only those in their "prime." As they aged or if their attitudes and skills were not exemplary, they were placed in less selective Denver bordellos.

In a very few of the women Roxanne recognized an aptitude for business and a hunger to make money. She trained those women to run new houses in the city.

Apparently business was very good.

When Roxanne had approached her about the gentlemen's club, Mei-Xing had outwardly agreed. She wasn't naïve—she had seen and heard what disobedience produced.

When she was moved to the club to begin her training they gave her the name of "Little Plum Blossom," an irony that cut Mei-Xing deeply. A dressmaker from Denver had designed and sewn a costly wardrobe for her. She was to be marketed as an exotic oriental treat, so her costumes were sewn in what these ignorant white people felt were "Chinese" style. They painted her face in a garish caricature of a geisha, uncaring or oblivious that geishas were Japanese, not Chinese. Mei-Xing certainly had not corrected their errors.

She was considered a valuable commodity for her exquisitely tiny body and her face's ivory perfection. Roxanne told her proudly how much excitement her début had generated and how much she brought per "visit."

And she had endured many visits.

She had carefully acted her part for two months. It hadn't been long enough. They had been waiting for her to make a move and had anticipated it. Two men had taken turns beating her and using her for three hours. Tory had been assigned the task of cleaning her up and nursing her through her pain. Mei-Xing had also been refused food for five days. At the end of that time she had promised Roxanne to cooperate and "be a good girl."

"You had better, my dear," Roxanne had warned severely. Her dyed red curls shook emphatically "We only allow one such mistake. You remember Betty? I believe she is servicing filthy cowboys and drunks in a lice-ridden crib off Market Street in Denver now. And why? All because she was foolish enough not to see the golden opportunity she had here. Mei-Xing, you can have years of good food, beautiful clothes, and your own comfortable room—and what do you have to do? Just be the lovely, gracious woman you are and enjoy the adoration and gifts of wealthy men."

Roxanne paused on her way out of Mei-Xing's room, concern on her face. "I hope you take my warning to heart, my dear."

And so she had cooperated. More than that, she had worked toward becoming as successful as Savannah and Delilah, the most sought-after "doves" in Corinth. She had played her part well and garnered much success until, after another three months, she felt ready to try again. Try because of what she had overheard a few days ago.

Darrow had been complaining to Roxanne about the blonde woman who had stolen two new girls right out from under his nose. He was complaining because that woman, instead of running scared as she should have, had established a small inn on the ridge. It stuck in his craw.

Mei-Xing heard him say, "I think she fancies herself as some reformer, tryin' to rescue whores and help them find Jesus. Well, if she thinks that, Morgan will fix her wagon, he surely will."

Roxanne had answered, "We've ended our 'help wanted' advertisements. And she won't be finding any girls to help from *my* houses."

That was when Mei-Xing knew she had to try again. Run and get to that blonde woman. Mei-Xing cursed under her breath as she thought of what had happened. That pig Darrow and two other men had been waiting for her—*again*. It was as though they had known she was listening and read her mind.

Roxanne let them have their way with her, but Mei-Xing had not cried. Not once. While they beat and savaged her she had drifted away to somewhere else in her mind, the place overlooking the sea where her father and mother had taken her as a girl. She could hear the waves crashing and the surf pounding on her body as the men slapped and pinched her, but it was the ocean she saw, not them. It was the sea salt she smelled, not their rank sweat and her own blood.

When it was over, Roxanne came to see her. "It's too bad, Mei-Xing, it really is. You could have had such a good life here." She shook her head sadly as she examined Mei. "Your nose is broken. Likely your looks are ruined. In any event, you are no good to us here anymore. We'll make arrangements to have you moved in a few days."

Mei-Xing hadn't waited, though. As injured as she was, they assumed her spirit as well as her body was broken. They weren't expecting her to run again. She had fooled them, though, and had dropped from her prison window, even though her body was battered and still bleeding. Now she listened carefully. Only the silence of the late night over the freshly fallen snow answered her.

The snow could be a problem. Her footprints might be tracked. Mei shuddered. It would be Wednesday morning in a few short hours. She had to get to her destination before then. Wincing, she padded slowly across the snowy lawns of the Corinth Gentleman's Club. She reached the curving drive, followed it to the avenue and, walking carefully inside a few wheel and tire prints, trudged into the darkness.

Chapter 42

Edmund O'Dell was beginning to feel like a cork on a bobbing sea and nearly as addled. He'd left Denver two months ago with nothing but wisps of leads that refused to connect to any of the missing persons cases he was working. Breezy Point had been a bust—he didn't know where Bickle had gotten his information, but it was wrong. Nothing he'd gathered linked to his cases in any meaningful way.

Following his look into Breezy Point he'd taken the train back to Omaha on one of his "whims," a niggling notion that refused to be silenced. He'd found nothing and returned to Chicago, even more frustrated.

In the meantime, additional reports from other Pinkerton agencies had filtered back to the Chicago office. Two more missing women and then—nothing. The ads that the agent in Boston had found in the newspapers of seven major cities had stopped, canceled. Hope was fading for the missing girls the agency had connected to the advertisements.

O'Dell admitted he was more than frustrated. He was angry. Whoever was behind the kidnappings had caught wind of Pinkerton's interest. Now the trail was going cold and the unscrupulous men behind the scheme were going to get away with it.

Not only that, but he couldn't escape the impression that his "strangest" missing persons case was somehow linked to the others. O'Dell had never felt an impression as strong as this, even as he admitted that no evidence even suggested, much less supported, such a claim.

A cork. On a bobbing sea. Addled. He repeated those words to the rhythm of the train he rode on as it steamed west toward Omaha. Again.

What was it about Omaha?

Three days later, O'Dell turned up the collar of his overcoat against the stinging wind. He stood in front of a newly constructed mercantile emporium that occupied most of the block. His guide, a street-wise urchin known only as Stick, provided running commentary. One of the Omaha Pinkerton men had recommended him, and Stick had been well worth the daily rate O'Dell paid him. The kid had a mind like a steel trap and was an encyclopedia for detail. For the past three days they had tramped through the city, O'Dell allowing the kid to be tour guide.

"... sawr the fire m'self, I did. You never sawr such a fire! When the winders blew out—BOOM!—you shoulda seen ever'body run! Even the firemen! An' when the place kerlapsed, first that roof blew up in the air and then straight down! Best fire I ever sawr. Couple months later, they builded this place. Kinda swank, huh?" Stick had obviously enjoyed that evening.

"Let me guess. Arson, right?" O'Dell speculated.

"Right you are, sir! How'd ya know?"

O'Dell grinned at the boy. "Fires are something of a hobby of mine."

Stick grinned back in complete admiration. "Lordy, that lady had some bad luck, I'm tellin' ya. First her husband drowns in the ocean, then somebody burns her out, and on top of that, they made her stand trial fer burnin' her own place!"

"She do it?"

"Her? Heck no. Ever'body 'round here feel kinda sorry fer her, ya know? It were a big scandal. Prac'ly ran her outta town—an after that they prove' she din't do it. Guy who did got away, though."

"Then what did she do?"

"Dunno. Nobody knows where she went. She shore were a pretty lady, too. Long, blonde hair, jest like moonlight."

Something kept niggling in the back of O'Dell's mind and he almost brushed it away ... *almost*.

"Tell me about this woman again?"

"Well, sir. She an' her husband owned this store, see. Then he went off to some big eastern cities to buy some fancy stuff for a *new* store and then got on this boat and it *sank*, ya see, an—"

The hair stood up on the back of O'Dell's neck and he shuddered. "When was this?"

Chapter 43

Joy was pulled from her sleep by a quiet knock on the attic apartment's door. She threw on a wrapper and went to the door. Breona's curious face peeped out of her room.

"It's Billy, miss," a voice whispered.

Joy opened the door a few inches. "What is it? Is everything all right?"

"You'd better come and see."

Joy and Breona dressed quickly. They could hear soft whiffles coming from Marit's room and tried not to wake her.

Downstairs in the kitchen lit by a single candle they found Billy, Mr. Wheatley and, huddled at the table, a tiny figure. Mr. Wheatley stood soberly against the wall as though alarmed; Billy looked from the girl to Joy and back, tears in his eyes.

"Billy, would you please light a lantern?"

Joy cautiously moved around the table until she could see the figure seated there. As the light flared, the face turned toward her. Joy gasped softly.

The young girl's features were swollen and bruised. One eye was closed, the other was filled with blood; her nose trickled blood that her hand mechanically swiped at. Her mouth twisted in what might have been a smile but was only a grimace.

"I'm very sorry to wake you, Miss Thoresen." The words were a whisper.

Joy sat down gingerly opposite the girl as if she might unintentionally jog her and cause her pain. "You know my name?" Joy hardly knew what to say.

"Yes. I heard them speaking of you a few days ago."

"They?"

The girl swallowed and coughed. Joy could see how much the coughing hurt her and gestured for Breona to get her a glass of water.

"At the . . . house. Roxanne . . . Miss Cleary and . . . one of the men."

At Roxanne Cleary's name, the pieces fell into place. "You have escaped from them," Joy breathed. Breona edged around the table so she could see the girl, too. As she glimpsed the girl's battered face, her hand rose involuntarily to her mouth.

"Well. So far," was all the girl answered.

Joy reached carefully for the girl's hand. It was crusted with blood and she tried to pull it back but Joy gently covered it with her own.

"We will help you," was all Joy said.

Several moments passed and then it was as if the girl released a breath she had been holding for a very long time. Her head bowed slightly and she gasped and then began to rock, backward and forward, backward and forward. The sobs were silent and then grew louder until they came as gasps and then a rasping, keening wail that echoed through the house.

The sheer anguish of the moment was too much for Billy and Mr. Wheatley. They both fled out the back door, and Joy heard the unmistakable sound of someone savagely kicking the oil barrel again and again.

Joy moved around the table, sat next to the girl, and gradually— oh! so carefully—wrapped her arms around her. "Breona," Joy whispered. "Put water on for tea and for a bath. Gather soft clothes, bandages, and a clean nightgown, please."

Over the next hour Joy and Breona gently bathed the girl and managed to spoon some tea and soup between her split and swollen lips. Marit, wandering down the back stairs into the kitchen as the sun came up, took in the scene and burst into confused tears.

Joy sent her out of the room with instructions to let Billy and Mr. Wheatley in the front doors but to send Billy immediately to get Flinty and Domingo and then the sheriff and Dave Kalbørg. He was to take one of the two shotguns. Mr. Wheatley was to have the other loaded and nearby.

Breona eased the girl into a nightgown and together Joy and Breona helped her up the stairs and into Joy's bed. "I want to give you laudanum to help you sleep," Joy whispered to the girl as she lay shaking in the bed with pain.

"No! No!" The shaking intensified and Joy saw the terror in her eyes.

"Whatever you say," Joy answered carefully. "But I want you to know something." When the girl's one open eye finally fixed on her, Joy continued. "I have sent for help. We have guns, and the sheriff will be here soon. We will *not* allow anyone to take you. Do you understand?"

The terror slowly ebbed and Joy held the girl's hand until she slid into an uneasy sleep.

Joy explained the situation to Sheriff Wyndom and David Kalbørg in the kitchen. Both men wore grave expressions, but the sheriff seemed more disturbed than David.

"Miss Thoresen, I'm concerned that you don't realize the gravity of your actions."

"My actions? Of which actions are you speaking?" Joy responded evenly. "I took in a woman who has been severely beaten. And worse."

The sheriff shuffled his feet and looked down. David became very still.

An edge crept into Joy's voice. "Let us be plain here, Sheriff, shall we? The woman upstairs in my bed was being held against her will and used as a slave. A *slave*. Slavery was abolished by law in this nation decades ago. The issue here is not *my* actions but *yours*, Sheriff. You are either the defender of law in this town or you are not."

Wyndom's head jerked up and color raced from his leathery neck into his face. He answered her, punctuating each word, his voice rising in volume. "You have no right to speak to *me* about—" but Joy shouted over him.

"I have *every* right to expect you to *do your job*! Innocent women are defiled right here in Corinth—right here in the town you are sworn to protect! And you know all about it, *Mister* Wyndom. If you do nothing to help them, you are *not* the sheriff in this town and are as guilty of their degradation as the men who kidnap and *rape* them!"

Wyndom's face went from red to white as he struggled to control his shock and anger. Finally he answered Joy carefully, "Miss Thoresen, I am one man. The real power in this town is stronger than you realize. If it becomes known that you have that woman in your lodge, I cannot guarantee your safety or that of your employees."

Joy stared daggers at the man until he looked away in shame and frustration. "Look," he muttered, "I don't know how to handle this or how to remove that woman from Corinth without Darrow and his thugs finding out. Darrow's boss, Morgan, has eyes and ears everywhere and this is a small town with only a few ways in or out. I am outmanned and outgunned."

Joy reached a hand to the sheriff's arm and, her voice much softer, answered, "That may be so. But God is on our side. And we dare not remain silent in the face of such evil."

His weathered face screwed up into a sardonic smile. "You really believe that, don't you? You know you will start a war here? And people will be hurt, their lives ruined?"

"Ruined? *Ruined*! How many young girls have been *ruined* in the past year?" Joy's words were sharp as a blade. "We are already in a war, Mister Wyndom. And people are already being hurt. We must choose whether we hide from the truth or side with the truth."

"They are already out looking for her."

"Then we must be ready to defend her."

Wyndom looked down and laughed harshly. "A couple of inexperienced young bucks, two old men, and myself. Should make for a quick battle."

"No." David spoke sharply. "Joy is right. I have shirked my responsibilities also. No more. I will stand with you, too. And so will others."

Joy suddenly thought of Uli and the children, of the church and the threats to burn it. "We need help. From outside."

Wyndom frowned. "I could call on the law in Denver . . . but I know many of them are corrupt, bought by the gambling and prostitution crime bosses. We don't know who to trust."

"I do," Joy announced suddenly. "We can bring in the Pinkertons."

"Like adding gasoline to a fire, miss," Wyndom warned.

But Joy was adamant. "David, we need to send a wire to Arnie. His Pinkerton man in Omaha will know whom to send from Denver and will know how to get them here quickly. Arnie will make sure it happens."

David nodded. "All right. I'll get that done before this gets any bigger. They may cut us off from the telegraph and the trains before long."

"Wait. Wait a moment." Joy's brow creased and she paced the kitchen deep in thought. "You say they are looking for her. They · cannot know with any certainty that she is *here*—there is no way for them to know that. What if we continue to act normally while keeping her hidden?"

Wyndom and David thought on her idea. "It might work," Wyndom admitted. "So we don't act like we're drawing up sides? We just act as usual. But we will still need outside help. This is just a delaying tactic."

David nodded in agreement. They determined the contents of the wire and he left quickly. Joy looked at the sheriff again. "We will need your leadership, Sheriff Wyndom. Sooner or later this will come out. My friends and I will stand, but we will need your guidance."

"So it's 'sheriff' again?"

She inclined her head. "A man is a man when he acts like one, isn't that so? You are the sheriff here when you act like the sheriff."

He winced. "You don't pull any punches, do you?"

"Come with me. I want you to see what they have done to this poor girl."

Joy led him up the back stairs and they quietly entered Joy's room. Breona sat beside the bed holding the girl's hand. Joy could see the young woman start and tense as Sheriff Wyndom followed her into the room.

"It's all right. He is the sheriff," Joy soothed.

Joy twisted the lamp stem until light bloomed in the room. One swollen, blood-red eye slowly gravitated toward Wyndom, who flinched as he took in her tiny, battered frame. Breona excused herself and Joy sat down beside the bed, taking the girl's hand in her own as Breona had done.

"You know my name," Joy began. The girl blinked her one open eye. "I would be honored if you would call me Joy from now on." The girl blinked again and Joy felt a slight pressure on her hand.

"Can you tell me your name?"

Joy saw the girl's cracked lips move but no sound came out. Pain creased her face.

Joy tore off a piece of clean cotton, dipped it in water, and gently swabbed the girl's lips while squeezing several drops into her mouth. She repeated this several times. Finally the girl began to whisper.

"My name is Mei-Xing."

"Mei-Xing," Joy repeated. "That is very pretty. Is that your last name, too?"

"No."

Joy thought she understood. "Do you have family?"

Mei-Xing closed her eyes.

"I understand. You don't need to tell us." Joy patted Mei's hand gently. "Sheriff Wyndom needed to see what . . . those people did to you. We don't want to tire you though. I will have Breona make some bland soup for you. Something that won't sting your mouth."

Joy got up to leave and saw panic in Mei-Xing's eyes again. "Don't worry. We won't leave you alone. And we are guarding the lodge."

Downstairs, Sheriff Wyndom gathered everyone together. "Morgan's men don't know where Mei-Xing is yet. We have decided to keep them guessing as long as possible."

He gave instructions to go about their normal routines. Flinty and Wheatley he set on the second floor, out of sight but with window views of all sides of the lodge. "We all need to have the same story if anyone comes asking questions. I want you to keep an eye out for anyone approaching the lodge. Give warning so that all of you can be prepared. And anyone who doesn't work here should stay out of sight. That means you," he nodded at Flinty, "me, Pastor Kalbørg, and anyone he brings with him."

Wyndom gestured to David. "You and I need to backtrack and try not to let anyone know we were here this morning." He pointed at Billy. "Find the girl's footsteps to the back door. Wipe them out. She was bleeding, too—get rid of any signs of blood."

An hour later Darrow and three men strode into the lodge. They found Marit placidly polishing the furniture. Joy was at the lodge registration counter busily writing responses to recent guest inquiries. Their only guest, Mrs. Van der Pol, was nodding in a comfortable parlor chair, a book in her lap.

Joy frowned, put a finger to her lips, and indicated the napping woman. She came out from behind the counter and walked out the front doors. Darrow and his men reluctantly followed her. She pulled the door snugly behind them and rounded on Darrow.

"Mr. Darrow. I heard Sheriff Wyndom warn you quite emphatically *not* to trespass on my property. I must insist that you leave immediately." Indignation flashed in her eyes, and one of Darrow's men growled at her challenge.

Darrow's eyes narrowed and he ignored her protest. "You have any unexpected visitors last night or this morning?"

Joy pulled herself up to her full height. "Visitors to our lodge send advance reservations. The only guest we have at the moment is Mrs. Van der Pol—whose rest you had better not have disturbed!"

Her mouth set in a straight line, Joy was the picture of a righteously outraged innkeeper. Darrow continued to stare at her. She stared back, lips pressed tightly together.

"We are looking for someone," he finally stated.

Joy shrugged in annoyance. "And what has that to do with us?"

"Thought you might have seen . . . someone." The staring contest continued.

"I told you. Now, before I send someone for the sheriff, I suggest you get off my veranda and off my property."

Darrow's voice dropped and he spoke very softly, "Miss Thoresen, I want to give you a word of advice. We might be dancing around at the moment, but unlike others, I see through you. If I find that you have put your oar in where it does not belong *again* . . . let's just say that this, this *lodge*, as you like to call it, well, unexpected things have been known to happen. Accidental fires, for instance."

If Darrow had expected Joy to quail at his threat, he was surprised—and taken aback at her reaction.

Flushing in rage, Joy shoved Darrow. Hard. Off-balance, he stumbled back—and off the steps of the lodge. Before he or his men could react, Joy shouted at him, "You sorry excuse for a man! You think you can scare me? I've been burned out before, you *coward*! Don't you *ever* set foot on my property again! If I see you here again, I *promise* I will shoot you myself!" She turned, let herself inside, and locked the door behind her.

Darrow picked himself up and, snarling at the assistance offered by his men, dusted the snow off his backside. Without another word he strode back toward the town.

Inside, Joy leaned her back against the locked door, her breasts heaving. Two graying heads peeked over the second floor railing. "They're headed back ter town," Flinty called softly, Wheatley beside him. The kitchen door opened. Billy and Domingo filed solemnly into the dining room where Marit stood awestruck— dusting rags hanging limply.

From the living room a cultured female voice called, "I really do think I should know what is going on, don't you?"

Chapter 44

With Flinty and Mr. Wheatley keeping watch from above and Breona staying with Mei-Xing, the rest of the household gathered in the parlor. Mrs. Van de Pol studied Joy with a keen interest.

"I should let you know that I am a light sleeper. I couldn't help but notice . . . a great deal of activity late last night. Quite early this morning, actually." She smiled. "I suppose that is why I dozed off while reading. In point of fact, I was wondering if you took on another guest in the night. An unexpected one?"

Joy met the woman's frank gaze. "I apologize, Mrs. Van der Pol, for disturbing what was supposed to be a restful stay for you. We, ah, are having some community, er, issues. Rather than continue to provide a less-than-tranquil visit for you, perhaps it would be best if we made arrangements for you to return home first thing tomorrow. I think that would be . . . safest."

The woman studied Joy for several moments and then said decidedly, "I would like a word with you, Miss Thoresen. Would you be so kind as to walk with me to that delightful overlook just down the path?"

Joy and Mrs. Van der Pol donned cloaks and hats against the chill air and set out down the path. Joy was convinced that her guest would have complaints, and rightly so. If she also complained to her influential friends in Denver, it would spell the end of Corinth Mountain Lodge before it had even well begun.

The two women stood together looking out into the vast wilderness below and beyond them, the beauty both breathtaking and humbling. Joy told herself again that she did not come here often enough. The older woman sighed in contentment.

"I cannot get enough of this. I truly hope to come again in the spring."

That was not at all what Joy had expected. "You wished to speak with me, Mrs. Van der Pol?" Joy hated to break the wonder of the moment.

"Yes." She chose her words carefully. "I am a Christian woman, Miss Thoresen. I have come to understand that you are also?" It was both a question and a statement.

"I am. I have not always followed as faithfully as I could have . . . *should* have, but I am giving my all now . . . as best I can." Her words sounded hollow and somewhat insincere to her own ears.

Mrs. Van der Pol nodded. "I believe that all of us tend to walk a winding path. Not intentionally, of course. The path Jesus sets before us is straight and narrow but like children trying to walk a chalk line, we often step off that path. What is important is that we allow him to take us by the hand and put our feet back on that path. Don't you agree?"

"That is an apt description," Joy answered.

The older woman nodded. "I wish to confide something in you, Miss Thoresen." She looked sideways at Joy who nodded in surprise.

"Of course! I would be honored."

Mrs. Van der Pol looked out into the vastness again. Her face was tinged with a certain sadness. "Miss Thoresen, while I am a follower of Jesus, my husband is not. Quite the opposite, I'm afraid. You see, I believe he attends this town's . . . entertainment on a frequent basis."

Startled at this revelation, Joy absorbed what she heard in silence.

"I discovered his deception quite by accident. He usually employs the ruse of some business dealing elsewhere when he . . . visits here. I came to Corinth because I wanted to see for myself what drew him. Of course, it is all very respectable on the outside, isn't it? And I can't very well see the inside of those two beautiful houses. Jesus talked about something similar, I believe, when he said 'clean on the outside but dead men's bones on the inside,' hmm?"

She sighed. "I also came to think and pray. About what I am to do. Is there anything I can do, Miss Thoresen?" She turned to Joy. "You took in a girl last night, did you not? Did she run away from one of those . . . houses?"

"Yes," Joy answered frankly. "She has been badly beaten. Horribly beaten."

"I want to see her."

It was said with such strength that Joy was taken aback. "For what possible purpose?"

"Because I am going to help somehow. I want to expose the deeds of darkness to the light. Even if I am to tell only of *this* incident, I will do so. And I am an influential woman, Miss Thoresen. I can be a valuable ally."

"Indeed," Joy answered. Suddenly she felt as though great avenues of possibilities had opened, even if she couldn't yet clearly envision them. And her heart lightened.

"Please call me Joy," she added, smiling.

Mrs. Van der Pol returned her smile. "And I am Emily."

Chapter 45

O'Dell had filled a notebook. He had meticulously entered everything that could be uncovered about Joy Michaels into that book. He shook his head. Where had this woman gone? What was her connection?

His one attempt to interview Arnie Thoresen, Joy Michael's cousin and attorney, had been met with unyielding refusal. The two Pinkerton agents Thoresen had hired were both down south, unable to give him an introduction. And no one else in Omaha had heard of the woman's whereabouts since the day she left the city five months past.

It was just a matter of time until he found what he needed, though. He was almost ready to approach the cousin again and force an interview. Almost.

He reached the Omaha Pinkerton office that morning and saw Stick leaning against the brick wall. The kid was hoping for another day of work, but O'Dell had exhausted his need for Stick's service.

"Hey kid."

"Mornin', Mr. O'Dell, sir!"

"Listen, I'm not going to need you today . . . I'm probably heading home." O'Dell flipped him a half-dollar. "You've been great, though."

Stick handily caught the fifty-cent piece. "If'n I find out something more for you 'bout Missus Michaels, you want I should bring it by?"

"Absolutely. If you find something, give it to Mr. Groman. Now take off—and don't spend that all in one place."

O'Dell entered the offices and went straight to the desk of Patrick Groman, head of the Omaha office. He flipped his bowler onto one of Groman's chairs and dropped into the other.

"I'm headed back to the Chicago office. Wanted to let you know and thank you for your help—especially the kid. I think I'd keep an eye on him. Couple of years, he could make a good agent."

They both turned to the sound of a small commotion in the outer office. Then Groman's door burst open and Arnie Thoresen stepped inside.

He frowned when he saw O'Dell. "I need to talk to you," he growled at Groman. "Now."

O'Dell and Arnie Thoresen descended the steps of their car in Corinth before the train had fully come to a stop. After Arnie had shown Groman the wire from David Kalbørg, Groman had summoned O'Dell into his office and told Arnie flatly that O'Dell was the man Arnie wanted with him. After Arnie had accepted an introduction to O'Dell, the two of them had caught the next train to Denver and on to Corinth.

O'Dell had picked up a lot of the information he had been looking for from Arnie during their trip. Bickle might have missed it, but not by much. It hadn't been Breezy Point—rather, an insignificant township with a grandiose name: Corinth.

Arnie and O'Dell stepped off the train in the twilight. Arnie, who knew the way, was about to gesture the direction of the lodge when three armed men leaning against the small station stood up. They scrutinized Arnie and O'Dell and began moving their way.

"Follow my lead," O'Dell whispered.

O'Dell, surprising Arnie, began walking to meet the men. "I say, any of you chaps know where a couple of thirsty blokes can buy a drink in this town?" He addressed the tallest of the three men in a perfect British accent. The men immediately relaxed.

"It's a walk of 'bout half a mile," one of them offered. "But *Charlie's* has good beer." The other two nodded.

Tipping his bowler at them, O'Dell set off in the direction indicated. Arnie followed along quickly.

"That was quite a trick," Arnie admitted.

"I have my talents. Now how do we double back?"

Several minutes later, Arnie and O'Dell, having circled around the lodge through the trees, knocked discreetly on the back door. Billy's voice boomed a challenge from beyond the door, "Who's there?"

"Arnie Thoresen. And a friend."

Billy threw open the door and welcomed them inside, checking first to see if anyone had seen them.

"Arnie!" Joy hugged her cousin with abandon. "I am so glad to see you—so relieved! Where are the Pinkerton men?" She saw a second man enter and gasped in surprise. "*You!*"

O'Dell had removed his derby hat, but Joy saw it in his hand. He bowed slightly. "Edmund O'Dell, miss. Of Pinkerton's, Chicago."

"Chicago? But we saw you in Denver—you assisted us when Darrow tried to take Marit!"

"That was indeed . . . serendipitous, miss." He could see the puzzlement on her face, but he was equally surprised—it was *her*. He was struck—again—by the woman's beauty. *Lovely* . . . The word came, unbidden, to him.

Arnie introduced O'Dell to the small group gathered in the kitchen, and then asked, "Where is Breona, Joy?"

"She is upstairs . . . with our other guest."

Joy asked Billy to fetch Breona. Then she sat Arnie and O'Dell down with coffee and began to tell them about Mei-Xing. She described Darrow's visit to the lodge looking for the girl and the precautions they had taken to remove traces of Mei-Xing's path to the lodge. "We are doing our best to act normally and go about our regular routines. It will take a few weeks for Mei-Xing to heal. Until we can spirit her out of town, we will keep her hidden on the third floor."

O'Dell stole another look at Joy Thoresen. She was gorgeous. And fearless! His heart tipped over a bit and he yanked his attention away from her.

"So you think Darrow and his crew are still looking for the girl—what did you call her?—and don't yet know she's here?"

"Mei-Xing," Breona answered. "She's a China lady. Bein' from Seattle parts."

"Why, Breona! How did you find that out?" Joy asked, surprised. "She seemed reluctant to talk about her family."

"Aye, that she is. But we got t' talkin' and she let on aboot th' seawater an' all from near where she growed up."

O'Dell frowned. "We haven't had any reports of girls taken from west of here, only east."

He shrugged and returned to his present concerns. "I agree with your approach. The longer you can keep up the pretense that all is normal, the better. As some like to say, you may have 'dodged a bullet' this time."

He thought for a moment. "Arnie and I got off the train posing as travelers. I think the men watching the siding bought our story. Perhaps I can keep up the pretense by taking lodging here and walking openly around Corinth."

He directed his next words at Joy. "Just what is your plan here, Miss Thoresen? What are you trying to accomplish in Corinth? Because whoever hired those men has a large investment in this town, a significant, money-making investment. Whoever that is, he calls the shots in this place—law or no law. If they find you are hiding this girl, they will view you as a threat to that investment. And respond accordingly."

"If other girls hear that one of their own has escaped and actually gotten away, they may be emboldened to try also. Believe me, the man who runs this 'business' will not allow that to happen—and if you are found to be involved, they may well go to war against you. You said yourself that Darrow threatened to burn you out. So just what is your plan in all this?"

O'Dell had put things into a perspective Joy hadn't seen before. What *was* her ultimate objective in Corinth? Joy tried to recall what exactly the Lord had spoken to her, the scriptures he had used, and how to put it into words. Right then it seemed a bit of a muddle in her head.

"My plan?" Joy pondered his question a few moments, her brow furrowing. "I . . . I may seem naïve to you, Mr. O'Dell, but I know that while people are often selfish and sometimes much, much worse, no one can right every wrong or hope to expunge evil from the world. It seems evident to me that the world will never run out of wrongdoing."

Joy looked earnestly at O'Dell. "I think, though—no, I *believe*—that when some good thing is placed before me to do, I can—and *should*—do at least that *one thing* to the best of my ability."

"Placed before you?" O'Dell queried.

Joy nodded slowly. "I am a Christian, Mr. O'Dell. I am not a perfect person, by any means, but I am forgiven, and that gift of forgiveness guides every choice in my life now. I believe the Lord brought me—us—to Corinth to help . . . perhaps not *every* girl but certainly the ones he puts in our path."

She explained, briefly, about meeting Breona and Marit on the train and then encountering Darrow in Denver. "You see, I know that the Lord brought us together. And then he brought *you* at just the right time to help us in that train station—and here you are again! That's quite amazing, don't you think?"

"Perhaps more than you know," O'Dell muttered to himself.

Joy, however, was still pondering his question. She could hear Grant's voice in her memory, hear him earnestly asking her,

> *". . . You see, my plan is also my dream, the vision of my future that I believe the Lord has given me. It is*

*the dream I cannot live without. So, I'm wondering if
your plan is the dream you cannot live without . . ."*

She looked up. "What is my plan here? My plan is to help as many girls as the Lord brings to us. I know he is in this, just as I know Mei-Xing came to us because she knew we would help her. I won't give her up, nor any girl who comes for help, not for anyone or anything."

She glanced around the table, a bit self-conscious at the serious expressions staring back at her. O'Dell could not keep the admiration off his face.

Joy blushed faintly. She saw the admiration . . . and something else? Was it . . . regret? She lowered her eyes. When was the last time a good man had looked at her like that? For a moment she was nonplussed—it had only been 15 months since Grant had died. Her heart was not ready to entertain another man's affections, nor did she think it ever would be.

"Thank you, Mr. O'Dell, for coming to help us again. I don't know what will happen but I know what I hope for. I *hope . . .* that a stream of young women will find their way to our doors and that we can help them find healing and a better life."

She paused and added, "I may even hope to break the back of this evil business, if only here in Corinth, but my *plan* is to help as many girls as the Lord brings me." She looked earnestly at O'Dell. "And that is not merely my intention, It has become my dream."

Chapter 46

The following day Arnie, O'Dell, and Joy met privately to discuss their next steps. O'Dell had been up since dawn checking the perimeter of the lodge.

"I didn't find any trace of Mei-Xing's path to the lodge."

Joy nodded. "Sheriff Wyndom sent Billy and Domingo out immediately to cover her tracks. The snow has melted some since that night, too."

"Still, someone has been watching the lodge. Probably the last two nights."

Joy stared at O'Dell. "We didn't know . . ."

"Your men aren't trained to see what I see. Whoever is watching keeps well into the trees and makes their way there by skirting the edges of the canyon. It's good that you haven't tried to remove Mei-Xing."

"She can't be moved. Not for several weeks. She has broken bones and is quite weak," Joy replied.

"Even if she were able to be moved, it would be a mistake. Keeping her hidden here is the best plan—for as long as it takes." O'Dell was deadly serious.

Joy nodded again. "Yes. We can do that."

"You have some good men, but you need a night man. They are watching us—and we need to be watching them. Without them knowing we are watching, of course."

"Perhaps Domingo would be willing to do that," Joy suggested.

"I'll give him direction, if you agree," O'Dell replied. "Now. About my cover story. I'll be out and about the town, having a few drinks, and making myself known. I might decide to winter in Corinth since the snow has set in. Is the hunting any good here?"

He cocked an eye at Joy. "I might let on to a few Corinth natives that a certain young innkeeper has caught my eye . . . and that I'm staying at her lodge to press my suit."

Joy, blushing furiously, stammered back. "I-I don't know how I feel about that."

"It's just plausible enough to allay suspicions. You don't already *have* a gentleman caller, do you?"

Arnie glanced at O'Dell then. He knew O'Dell already had the answer to his question.

"Certainly not," Joy replied firmly.

Arnie thought he caught a glimpse of satisfaction in O'Dell's smile.

"Then my story should hold up. For a few weeks anyway." O'Dell looked to Arnie. "You, on the other hand, are her cousin and have been here before. You and I shouldn't be acquainted—yes, we arrived together, but that, if asked, we shall say was coincidence. You should probably head back to Omaha before Darrow and his men see us together again. But not before you tell Joy what you told me on the way here. The new information the Omaha Pinkerton office gave you?"

Arnie pursed his lips. "The last time I was here I told you, Cousin, that I had Pinkerton still investigating for us. Well, you remember the insurance company you had your policy with?"

"Yes. Liberty Indemnity."

"They lost a great deal of standing in Omaha after the . . . trial." He glanced apologetically at Joy. "I apologize, Joy, but O'Dell here already knows about that."

Joy answered sharply, "I'm surprised Mr. O'Dell is willing to 'court' a woman with such a stained past."

O'Dell heard both the anger and hurt in her quick retort.

"You were cleared of all charges, were you not? You are an innocent woman who was defrauded of all she owned," O'Dell said evenly.

"Yes. Defrauded even of my reputation," she shot back.

"Joy, Joy," Arnie said soothingly. "O'Dell is a Pinkerton man. He is sworn to confidence. Now let him help us. Yes?"

"All right," Joy sighed. "What about the insurance company?"

"The community turned against them. They lost many of their policy holders and nearly went bust—*should* have gone under, in fact."

"They didn't?"

"No. Someone bought them, and at a very good price." Arnie's eye sparkled a little. "The buyer provided an infusion of capital at just the right time—and then began to market the company . . . in Denver. Where the company is now slowly recovering its footing."

He paused to let Joy digest that information. "Hubris is an interesting thing, Joy. Even the most brilliant men are, at some point, blind to their own pride."

He smiled knowingly. "We think that Shelby Franklin saw the impending fall of Liberty Indemnity and was unable to resist plucking such a bargain. In this he overestimated his 'brilliance.' The company was bought by a financial consortium. That 'consortium,' Pinkerton was able to discover, is actually owned by a man named Dean Morgan, possibly an alias for Franklin. The Pinkertons have tracked *him* to Denver and are investigating him even now."

Joy's head spun. "Dean Morgan? *Dean Morgan!*"

"What is it, Joy?" Arnie viewed his cousin's distress with concern.

She shuddered. "Flinty and Domingo told me someone named *Dean Morgan* is the man who took over Corinth—who supposedly had Judge Brown killed and now owns . . . *those houses!*" Joy couldn't think straight. "Are you saying *Dean Morgan* is Shelby Franklin?"

Arnie and O'Dell's news paled before this piece of information. The possible connection between Franklin and Corinth stunned them all. It was several moments before Arnie spoke again.

"I brought everything the investigator uncovered regarding Liberty Indemnity and this man, Dean Morgan, with me. I wanted you to see it because you have the sharpest business mind I know, Joy."

He handed a folder to her.

O'Dell met with Joy and Domingo that afternoon. "Miss Thoresen has a great deal of confidence in you, Mr. Juarez."

Domingo nodded his thanks to Joy. "*Gracias, señora.*

"I've found evidence that the lodge is being watched at night," O'Dell continued. "From the trees where the watchers have a side view of the lodge. They can see who comes and goes from both the front and back entrances. I feel it prudent for Miss Thoresen to assign a man to keep an eye on *them*. I would prefer two men at night, but one is better than none. Are you up to the job?"

Domingo's eyes flashed. "*Si*. And if you want two men, *señora*," he said, turning to Joy, "I have a cousin who would work with me."

Joy groaned inwardly at the thought of another man on her payroll. She looked to O'Dell who nodded. Well, the Lord had done a fine job of meeting their needs to date. She needed to trust him for this, too.

"Yes. Please bring him around for an interview."

Joy's head was still spinning over the possibility that Dean Morgan and Shelby Franklin were one and the same. She had spent an hour studying the packet Arnie had handed to her. The information on Dean Morgan painted a picture of a successful financier who occupied offices in a prominent area of the city. A man with no criminal history.

Although he was new to Denver, Morgan had already made inroads into Denver society—and some of Denver's distinguished citizens were already touting Morgan's investment advice to their high-society friends. However, Morgan's arrival coincided with Franklin's disappearance from Omaha *and* the purchase of Liberty Indemnity. Those two facts couldn't be mere coincidence!

Morgan apparently also had ready money because he was buying into Denver real estate and he had invested cash to prevent Liberty Indemnity's demise. Unlike Franklin or aliases he may have employed in other cities, Morgan was not keeping his investments easy to cash out. Rather, he was going through all the motions of making a name for himself by putting down roots.

Joy pondered this change in his behavior. She had never met the man and yet his actions had changed her life forever. And although she had come to this distant town in the mountains to begin again, it nearly felt as though he was dogging her steps—that she could not escape his evil influence on her life.

She had read and reread the information. Now she was overwhelmed emotionally and felt the need to pull herself away from everyone and everything to pray and think.

Late that afternoon she asked Billy to accompany her to the overlook. Leaving him up the path from the vantage point, she sat down on a bench and stared at the valleys and mountains spread before her. Finally gathering herself she began to pray.

First she just poured out her heart to the Lord, expressing her confusion and weariness but also placing her trust in his strength and guidance. For a long time afterward she waited, watching the distant peaks as the sun began its daily color show upon their snowy faces.

Then she opened her Bible and began to read aloud several psalms of worship and thanksgiving. Her heart lightened as she read the songs of praise aloud. Was there anywhere in the world more suited to those psalms?

> *They that trust in the Lord shall be as mount Zion,*
> *which cannot be removed, but abideth for ever.*

As the mountains are round about Jerusalem,
so the Lord is round about his people
from henceforth even for ever.

For the rod of the wicked
shall not rest upon the lot of the righteous;
lest the righteous put forth their hands unto iniquity.
Do good, O Lord, unto those that be good,
and to them that are upright in their hearts.

"Oh Lord," she prayed. "Make my heart upright in all I say and do. Do not allow the rod of the wicked to rule over this town, over these mountains that praise you every day. Help me, O God. I need your guidance. I trust in you, Lord—and you have said that those who trust in you will not—*cannot*—be removed. Amen, Lord. So be it."

Joy left the overlook peaceful in heart and mind.

Chapter 47

Joy wrestled with sleep during the night. She tossed and turned as a recurring dream worried her slumber.

In her dream Robertson gripped her arm and hissed, "Cooperate with us or . . . unfortunate events will unfold . . . I guarantee that if you do not accept our terms, you will regret it, *Mrs.* Michaels . . ." Then Joy heard the thud of his boot and Blackie's whimper.

Blackie, dear Blackie!

She struggled and freed herself from Robertson and then ran! As she raced to escape Robertson she ran headlong into Darrow. She smelled him, the stink of his hair and skin, and his foul breath whispered into her ear, "Put your oar in where it does not belong *again* . . . well, unexpected things have been known to happen . . . *accidental fires*, for instance."

As she fled from Darrow, a dark man, his face unseen, stepped in front of her. It was Franklin! She scrambled to run the other direction only to encounter another dark man. Morgan!

Screaming soundlessly she fled from him but was cut off by a wall of fire. It raged before her and, as she turned back, the flames blocked her escape that way, too. Above her she heard an explosive boom as the windows of her apartment burst outward and showered her with shards of glass. As the pieces sliced and pierced her, the fire caught on her body and she was burning! *Burning*!

Joy sat straight up in bed sobbing and shaking in fear. Even in her chilly room sweat dripped from her face. She stumbled to her wash basin and sponged the heat and moisture away, telling herself again and again, "It was a dream. Only a dream!"

For an hour she huddled in a chair, her lamp turned high enough for her to see the print of her Bible, though it lay unread in her lap. At last she felt calm enough to go back to bed. She was shivering with cold when she finally fell back to sleep.

Some time later she dreamed again. This time, however, her dream was peaceful. Someone walked with her down a long, beautiful path until they gazed together at the distant mountains from the overlook.

Her companion radiated comfort and protection. They continued walking, and the closer she kept to his side, the safer she felt. For what seemed a moment, she became distracted and bent to look at something along the path. As she lingered, she felt the comfort of her companion fade. Looking around she saw he was now some distance away.

"Wait for me!" she called. She hastened to catch up to him and they continued on their walk, Joy secure and at peace by his side.

As they meandered down the lovely path he spoke to her. She didn't hear the words, did not take any meaning from them, but she heard the sense of rightness of them. They reached the end of the path where a closed gate stood. Her companion reached out his hand and opened the gate. He stepped through and then turned to her.

"Did you hear my words, child?"

"Yes! Yes, they were beautiful. Thank you." Joy had never felt such contentment.

"Do you remember what I said?"

Joy mulled his question. "Nooo, not exactly. That is, I remember . . . the *sound* of your voice. I love the sound of your voice." She smiled into her companion's face. It was so dear, so noble.

"In the morning, you will still not remember what I said," he replied. "But you will remember the sound of my voice. And when the idea comes to you, you will know it is mine, because you know me and know my voice."

"Yes, sir," Joy answered.

"Do what I tell you and all will be well." He touched her gently. Then he closed the gate, and Joy was distressed that he was on one side and she on the other. She pressed her face against the slats of the gate and watched as her companion walked away. Strangely, he still felt near.

"Dear Jesus," she murmured. "I love you so." Leaning against that gate she fell asleep again and rested deeply.

Chapter 48

Joy awoke in the morning with a sense of something . . . momentous. Her two dreams were still so vividly real to her. She shuddered and put the first one from her mind but relived the second dream as she washed and dressed.

*In the morning, you will still not remember what I
said, but you will remember the sound of my voice.
And when the idea comes to you, you will know it is
mine, because you know me and know my voice.*

She glanced at the folder Arnie had given her to read. Something nibbled at the back of her mind but she could not grasp it.

Down in the kitchen Breona and Marit were already sipping hot coffee. Marit was preparing breakfast for Mrs. Van der Pol and Breona was putting together a tray for Mei-Xing. Joy helped herself to coffee and soon Billy, Mr. Wheatley, Arnie, and O'Dell were crowding into the kitchen for coffee and breakfast.

Joy took breakfast to their guest herself. Emily smiled her welcome and, at her invitation, Joy brought her own coffee to the table while Emily ate her breakfast.

"My time here is nearly gone," Emily said with a small sigh. "Randolph will return from his trip back east and I must be home when he returns."

She looked keenly at Joy. "I want you to know, though . . . that I will be praying for you. And I have a small group of Christian friends, women who can be trusted. I want to share your work with them. If you approve, that is."

Joy had, with Mei-Xing's permission, brought Emily to her and introduced them. Emily had sat with Mei-Xing for a half hour. Joy was not privy to their conversation, only that Emily had the traces of tears on her face when she came downstairs.

Joy thought for a moment. "It might be prudent not to mention my name or the name of this town." She looked at Emily. "What we are hoping to do here could be endangered."

Emily nodded her understanding. "I appreciate the delicacy of the situation." She thought for a moment and then asked, "Joy, if you are successful in helping additional girls, what would you do for them?"

"I would hope to lead them to Jesus," Joy answered simply.

"And after that? You could not, for example, continue to run this lodge if many more girls found shelter here." She smiled. "I'm thinking in the longer term—how would these girls get on in life? Where would they go from here?"

"I have wondered that myself," Joy admitted. "We have . . . friends who have helped a few to safety, but then what? I wonder where those women are and if they have found honorable employment or—" she shook her head, "have resorted to their old life because they are unprepared to live honestly in society."

"That is my point precisely, Joy," Emily replied. "And I wish that, when you come to that juncture, you would call on me. In the meantime, I and my friends will be praying for you—for your safety and success. But also for the future. I will be asking the Lord to guide me. I know that at the right time, things will be clear. To both of us."

Joy pondered Emily's words that morning. After breakfast and morning devotions she asked Billy to accompany her to the overlook again and this time stood, in the same place she had stood with the companion of her dream, and gazed toward the peaks.

Joy did not for one moment believe it to have been an ordinary dream. And she began to feel a sense of urgency. But what had he meant?

She thought again about the information Arnie had given her to read. Her analytical mind began to tick through each fact. Franklin. Liberty Indemnity. Cash infusion. Morgan. Financial advice. Personal holdings. Real estate. Corinth. Corinth investors. Corinth township. Liberty Indemnity.

"Lord, help me to hear you!" Joy prayed in frustration. She went through the facts again and, like a string of beads, they were all, in some manner, connected. Somehow! She just did not see, could not grasp. She thought again of the policy she and Grant had taken out with Liberty Indemnity in Omaha and how it had sorely let them down. She recalled Arnie's frustration and her disbelief as they had reviewed the policy—

Joy stood still, her mind whirling. *Liberty Indemnity was going broke. Then Liberty Indemnity was Franklin. Franklin was Morgan. Morgan was Corinth—no, Corinth was held by Morgan, in more ways than one . . . what if . . .*

What if . . . She began to pull on the thread of an idea. She teased it out and looked at it from several perspectives. Her eyes widened. It was more than audacious . . . it was crazy, foolhardy . . . it was . . .

She raced past Billy on the trail and flew up the two flights of stairs to her room. Pulling paper and pen from her little desk, she began to sketch out her thoughts. She again looked at the idea from several angles and clearly saw the destruction it would require. Joy put her hands to her face.

Do what I tell you and all will be well.

Oh Lord Jesus! Help me!

She refused dinner when called and remained in her room until she had completed her work. It was up to Arnie now.

Joy had no place private to meet with him other than her room. The great room was too open. Mei-Xing occupied an alcove in the little parlor in the attic apartment. Her room would have to do.

"Arnie. I need to speak with you," Joy said. Arnie saw her white face and came immediately. They cloistered themselves in her room as Joy explained.

"You have got to be joking, Joy," Arnie's face was aflame with anger and indignation. "This is monstrous!"

"Was Franklin afraid to act in Omaha, Arnie? Will he have magically changed his character because he has changed his name? *He* is the monster, Arnie, but we know him now. I am like a bothersome gnat to him at the moment. When I annoy him enough will he hesitate to swat me aside? No he will not!"

She took a calming breath. "He has, however, changed one thing, and in that one thing he has made himself vulnerable. Is it unreasonable to know your enemy and prepare for what he is known for? No, so I am preparing. And this time I *will* be prepared. This time it will be enough."

"Will you do this for me?" She stared at her cousin. She held out instructions and letters of authorization.

Reluctantly he took them from her hand.

Vikki Kestell

Chapter 49

The following morning Mrs. Van der Pol rose early to catch the train back to Denver. She had been with them only a week, but Joy would miss her. Arnie would accompany her down the mountain and then travel on to Omaha. Joy and Emily exchanged a heartfelt farewell before Billy drove her and her luggage the short distance to the train.

Arnie and Joy also had a quiet word before he left. The rest of the household, unaware of the details of Arnie's exchange with Joy, nevertheless saw the strain between them.

O'Dell watched both of them carefully but asked nothing. After Arnie left he kept an eye on Joy.

Joy worked furiously to catch up on the duties she had neglected the previous day. The lodge had a few paying guests coming over Christmas, which was only weeks away. While the lodge was empty they could prepare for Christmas and the guests.

O'Dell, in his role as British tourist, wandered the town. He swapped news and stories with the bar and store keepers, asked hunting advice from locals, and generally made himself known.

At lunchtime, Breona suggested that Mei-Xing was feeling well enough to venture downstairs. Joy agreed so Breona helped the girl navigate the stairs. As they entered the kitchen, the household greeted the girl. Her face had the mottled green and yellow hues of fading bruises. She swayed against Breona who quickly placed her in a chair at the kitchen table.

Joy firmly restricted her to the kitchen. "This room is the only downstairs room you may safely be in. It has no windows other than that high one. The great room, however, must be out of bounds for you. Not only has it several large windows, but this is a lodge, and people walk in without knocking."

As she sipped a cup of broth at the kitchen table, Mei-Xing heard Joy recount how Breona and Marit had almost been snared by the false 'help wanted' advertisements. Mei-Xing listened attentively but did not comment.

Now that Mei-Xing's face was mending, Joy could discern the great and delicate beauty beneath the bruising and swelling.

Mei-Xing did not speak unless asked something, but her eyes took in everything—eyes that dropped their gaze whenever someone looked at or spoke to her. Eyes that spoke of shame and held little hope.

Chapter 50

During devotions the following morning, Joy watched Marit with concern. Something was a little off—she was slower than usual and a bit distracted.

"Marit, are you feeling all right?" Joy finally asked. Breona, usually the perceptive one, shot Marit a penetrating look.

"I . . . I think I am," the girl confessed, "but I do feel a bit funny."

"Funny how?" Breona demanded.

"Um . . . I'm not hungry," Marit replied. "And my belly feels . . . tight. It gets tight and then it isn't."

Joy and Breona exchanged knowing glances. It was not out of the question for Marit to have her baby soon. They had, as closely as they could, estimated the end of December or first part of January. It was now nearly mid-December.

Joy answered carefully. "Well, please take it a little easy today. And let us know if anything . . . unusual happens."

Joy gathered the men together in the dining room and asked for one of them to stay near Marit during the day. Billy quickly volunteered. He wandered into the kitchen and offered to peel potatoes.

Wheatley and Domingo glanced toward Billy and Marit together in the kitchen and then looked pointedly at Joy.

"Really?" Joy was dumbfounded.

Mr. Wheatley chuckled and Domingo grinned and headed home to sleep. He would return in the late evening with his cousin, Gustavo.

At lunch time Marit complained of a backache. Her usually smooth brow crinkled into a tiny frown for a few seconds and then smoothed again. Billy observed her with wide eyes, but she seemed fine the remainder of the day.

Deep in the night Joy was awakened by a soft knocking on her door—again. "Who is it?"

"Breona, miss. It's Marit. She's a-cryin'."

Joy slipped into their common area. She glanced into the alcove where Mei-Xing slept. The girl was sitting up, wide awake. They all could hear the soft whimpering coming from Marit's room.

Breona had lit a lamp in Marit's room. By its dim light Joy saw Marit lying on her side, curled into a ball facing away from the door. Every few moments she whimpered.

"Marit?" Joy sat on the edge of the bed and touched her shoulder. Marit stirred and whimpered again. "Marit, dear. Wake up."

The girl moaned and, with some difficulty, turned toward Joy. "Oh, Miss Joy, I—" she gasped then and pulled her knees toward her chest. "Hurts."

The midwife had told Joy what to look for. "How often does it hurt, Marit?"

A few seconds later Marit struggled to sit up. "I'm not sure. I vas dreaming it hurt and . . . den you voke me."

"I, um, is the, bed still dry?"

Marit looked offended. "Yes, miss. I don't vet the bed."

Joy chuckled. "I know, dear one, I know. But when your labor begins in earnest, you may have water flow out between your legs."

Marit's eyes opened wide at this. Then she grasped her stomach and groaned.

"The midwife told us how to remake your bed. Breona, why don't we strip back the bottom sheet, lay down a rubber sheet, and cover it with towels?"

Breona nodded and hustled to the linen closet. Mei-Xing hobbled to the doorway.

"May I do something? To help?"

"Yes, I think so. I know it will be hard for you to get down the stairs by yourself, but if you can do so, would you put a large kettle of water on to heat? And perhaps make some tea. It will likely be a long night."

Joy helped Marit don socks and encouraged her to walk about their little apartment. While she did, Joy and Breona remade Marit's bed. Breona was tense and silent. As soon as they finished, she went to check on Marit.

Joy heard a quiet knock on the apartment door. When she opened it a crack, she found Billy at the top of the stairs.

"Billy! Why are you up?"

His hair was disheveled and one suspender was twisted. "Mei-Xing's makin' a racket in the kitchen. Mrs. Michaels—I mean, Miss Joy—should I go for the midwife? Is she OK?"

Joy didn't have the heart to tease him. "*Marit* is all right. She may be in labor, but it's too soon to send for the midwife."

"Mei-Xing's a-heatin' the stove and boilin' water an all. Are you sure she's all right?"

"Is Mei-Xing all right?" This time Joy did tease him. A little. Then she smiled. "Would you like me to ask Marit if you can come in for a minute?"

He flushed. "Yes, ma'am. Thank you."

A few minutes later he stepped into their apartment. Marit was sitting in a chair, her arms wrapped protectively around her middle. They looked at each other and Joy saw the relief on Billy's face.

"Are you doin' all right?" he asked awkwardly.

Marit nodded, fidgeting a little under Joy's scrutiny.

"Well. OK then. I ought to . . . Miss Joy, when you need the midwife, just call me. I'll fetch her." He looked at Marit again and backed out of the room.

"*That* one," Breona snorted and then chuckled.

Dawn came. Joy and Breona took turns staying with Marit while the other managed the morning's work—including the cooking that Marit usually handled so efficiently. The men seemed subdued that morning, but Joy had no time to think on them.

Mr. Wheatley and Billy managed their chores; Domingo and Gustavo ended their night shift and left for their homes; and O'Dell donned his derby and walked the perimeter of the lodge and then kept to his usual routine of walking about the town, carrying a shotgun he referred to as "his fowling piece," and playing tourist.

Mid-morning, Breona reported that Marit's water had broken and Joy dispatched Billy for the midwife. Dinner was a sad affair—Joy's stew was lack-luster and her biscuits slightly scorched.

All the while they waited . . . waited with the door to the stairway cracked an inch or two. Occasionally they heard faint crying from Marit. When this first happened, the men, with the exception of Billy, fled the house. Billy turned white but stayed, withdrawing into himself and staring straight at the wall.

As Joy and Mei-Xing finished cleaning the kitchen, they heard a new sound. A mewling that rose until it was the faint but unmistakable squalling of a newborn. If possible, Billy turned whiter and stared hopefully at Joy.

"Let's give them some time and then I'll go check," she said quickly. They waited 15 minutes by the clock and then Joy could wait no longer. She threw wide the door to the stairway and the ragged cries of a baby echoed down from the third floor. She ran up the two flights, arriving breathless at the attic apartment.

"A boy!" Breona announced with glee. The midwife was now cleaning the babe, who was protesting vigorously, his hands trembling and waving above his head.

"Marit?" Joy asked.

"See fer yersel'," Breona answered proudly. "A trouper, that 'un."

Sure enough, Marit looked tired but elated and glowing. Breona had a washbasin of warm water and was about to bathe Marit's sweat-soaked face.

"Let me," Joy asked. She smiled at Marit and gently sponged her face, her chest, and arms. "Feel better?"

"Yes, miss." She looked anxiously around Joy to where the midwife was wrapping the baby tightly in a swaddling blanket.

Joy moved and the woman handed the baby to Marit who cautiously took the bundle.

"Oh!" Marit gasped. "He's . . . beautiful!"

Breona and Joy grinned. "Yes," Joy agreed for both of them. "Yes, he is."

Chapter 51

Christmas was nearly upon them. The household had been distracted and delighted by the arrival of Marit's baby boy, but now they needed to focus on preparations for Christmas and their holiday guests.

Flinty, whose eyes and ears gathered more tidbits of gossip and news than most bartenders in Corinth, dropped in one morning and reported that "visitors" arriving on the train were increasing daily.

"It's th' Christmas rush, pardon m' blasphemy, miss," he offered shrewdly. "I been a-livin' here 22 years. Ever since Judge Brown built them houses a few years back, we git a spate of partiers ever' holiday season. Th' bars an' th' boardin' houses in town'll be full up till after New Year's. New Year's'll be the worst of it, too, it will."

He made an indignant sound. "No decent woman can walk th' streets of Corinth 'tween Christmas and New Year's. Disgustin' is what it is."

O'Dell raised his eyebrows. "That, Mr. Flynn, may be a blessing in disguise." He shot an amused look at Joy. "Maybe all the praying has bought us a bit more time. If Darrow and his men are busy ferrying their customers they won't have as much time to keep an eye on this place."

Joy didn't reply but *time* was exactly what she was praying for. Time for Arnie to accomplish the tasks she had given him. Time for her plans to ripen to maturity. Until then, they must purposefully keep from attracting further attention to the lodge. Mei-Xing was healing but keeping her safely out of sight was paramount at present.

When the baby was a few days old Marit began coming downstairs again to help. Joy and Breona made a comfortable little sitting area in the large pantry room where Marit could nurse in private and without having to climb two flights of stairs. But it soon became apparent that a certain corner of the kitchen was becoming everyone's favorite place to loiter.

In that corner Billy and Flinty had placed a small rocking chair and second cradle, one they had painstakingly built together. As Marit slowly resumed her cooking and baking duties, someone always found an excuse to sit near the cradle and stare at the tiny baby. Joy began shooing the men off to give Marit and the baby breathing room.

Marit seemed to be recovering nicely from her pregnancy and childbirth. Motherhood suited her, Joy mused. She noted how the girl was looking and acting less child-like and more woman-like as her figure filled out and her confidence in mothering the baby grew. She was still quiet and sweet, but her face radiated a calm strength that had been lacking when Joy had first met her on the train. Was that only a few months ago?

And gifts! So many of the women of the church treated Marit as they would a daughter. They showered her with hand-made baby blankets and gowns, diapers, and tiny sweaters, hats, and clothes.

All who first saw the baby asked his name and, universally, Marit replied that she hadn't decided on a name yet. However, after two weeks she still had not named the infant—not that suggestions were lacking. Needing to call the baby something, nearly everyone in the lodge had bestowed their own pet name on him: Breona called him "Báibín" (baby), "Little Lamb," and "Lambie"; Flinty referred to him gruffly as "Buster." Domingo, after hearing the volume of the baby's squalls, took to referring to him as "*El Jaleo*"—the racket. Mr. Wheatley, as he gently rocked the infant, cooed, "little man."

O'Dell, on the other hand, took pains not to refer to the baby in any manner and steadfastly declined to hold or even touch him. Joy noted a tinge of panic in O'Dell's expression any time the infant was too near him and she laughed openly at his discomfort.

Joy was frustrated by the baby's lack of a name. One evening as she wrote a letter at the lobby desk she complained to Breona, "Why hasn't she named that baby? What is she waiting for?"

Breona, that shrewd look on her face, pursed her lips and replied speculatively, "I'm wagerin' it's on th' boy's father she's waitin', miss."

Joy swung around and fixed Breona with a frown. "Whatever in the world do you mean?"

Breona's chin lifted in the direction of the kitchen. "*That* one, I'm thinkin'."

Joy heard the murmur of Billy and Marit's voices in the kitchen as Marit finished the dishes and Billy dried them.

"'Least I'm belaivin' she's hopin' he will take th' job. An' be givin' th' boy his name." Breona shrugged in her inimitable way. "Seems loik it'd be a prayer answered. If'n you're b'laivin' in prayer an' all."

Joy stared at the closed kitchen door.

It was Mei-Xing who began to spend most of the day near the babe while Marit worked. The bruising on her face was nearly gone. The most visible reminder of her injuries was a nose that was decidedly off-side. Not as easily seen—or healed—were the cracked and bruised ribs, the strained ankle tendons, the scabbed cuts and scratches beneath her clothes, and a heart that was destroyed.

Since she was unable to stand for long or lift much, Mei-Xing sat silently in the little chair near the cradle watching over the baby or at the nearby table cleaning vegetables and doing other easy hand work. After a few days of helping Marit in the kitchen or with the infant, Mei-Xing began to feel productive and perhaps a little needed.

She told herself not to become emotionally attached to the baby, but her heart was in such need of love that it drank in the sweet acceptance a baby offers. More than once the corner of his little blanket soaked up tears that no amount of effort could stem.

With the rest of the household, she gathered in the kitchen for devotions after breakfast each morning. The morning Bible study was now an accepted part of the daily routine. While not everyone was a believer in the Savior, they had all become engaged in the Bible reading and discussions.

Joy could hardly believe that she was leading the study herself, having only taught a girl's Sunday school class in the past. One morning it occurred to her that she was, unconsciously, emulating her father. Joy had grown up watching Jan lead young men in Bible study and had, without realizing it, begun to lead the lodge's devotions as she had seen him lead their family's and the men's studies he had led in their home.

They always ended their study in prayer, mostly with Joy asking for guidance and strength for the day. Once in a while though, someone would mention a need that the group would pray over: Domingo asked prayer for his mother's health; Flinty mentioned that his knee was causing him pain. And Billy asked for the Lord's direction in his life.

Chapter 52

Christmas was on Friday. The lodge's guests arrived two days prior. Billy, driving the lodge buggy, fetched a young couple and their small daughter from the morning train and an older couple from the afternoon train. Their guests' first sight of the great room had prompted delighted exclamations.

Joy had asked Billy and Mr. Wheatley to gather copious amounts of evergreen boughs several days before. The women had tied them together into long strands that the men hung in swags along the ceiling line around the entire room. On the mantle of the large stone fireplace they arranged pine branches in which they nested the largest pine cones they could find.

In the middle of each wall's center swag, Breona tied large red bows, their ends curling and trailing down. She then positioned the most elaborate bow she could fashion in the middle of the mantle. On the two dining tables they had created centerpieces that resembled miniature forest scenes, including Flinty's hand-carved wooden deer grazing under tiny pine trees.

Completely filling a corner of the parlor stood a 12-foot Ponderosa pine, its branches festooned with swooping strands of popcorn and red berries. On the end of each branch dangled a small, glittering star.

Flinty, at Joy's request, had cut each one from lightweight wood. The household had spent several evenings sipping cider while painting the stars a bright white and then coating them with glue and silver glitter. The stars gently twisted at the end of green thread hangers, sparkling in the light from the fireplace. And from the top of the tree gleamed the largest and brightest star of all.

"No' seen better, even in th' foine houses o' Boston," Breona had stated with satisfaction.

But the crowning piece of their decorations was a simple, even crude, manger scene. They placed the roughly carved Mary, Joseph, and empty manger amid straw strewn across a brown cloth at the foot of the tree.

Now their guests were admiring the decorations and sipping the spiced cider that Marit kept warm on the back of the great room's oil stove. The mingled aromas of cinnamon and cloves warmed the air.

Their guests' young daughter sat cross-legged before the tree staring in awe at its loveliness.

Her mother, smiling broadly, approached Joy. "Would you allow us to put a present under the tree for Molly on Christmas Eve? And, if we could do so without harming your wonderful mantle, would it be possible to hang her stocking there?"

Joy quickly agreed and asked Billy to find a way to hang Molly's stocking from the mantle. She noticed the other couple, a man and woman in their later years, nodding in appreciation.

The older woman leaned her head toward her husband and whispered, "It was a good idea to come here for Christmas, Geoff. Thank you. Thank you for getting us away from the loneliness of that empty house." She smiled nostalgically across the room at Molly, who was busily counting the stars on the tree.

With all of her guests present in the parlor, Joy announced, "As you know, tomorrow is Christmas Eve. Our household will be singing carols together here in the great room after dinner. I hope you will join us as we celebrate the Savior's birth."

And sing they did. Snow blanketed Corinth all the next day. The very air around the lodge smelled of snow. Within the warmth and serenity of the lodge, Joy, her household, and their guests gathered in the great room to sing the old carols of Christmas.

By candle- and fire-light alone, they raised their voices to sing.

O'Dell would have preferred being elsewhere—anywhere elsewhere, he insisted to himself—but he also told himself that, as a "guest" at the lodge, he needed to keep his cover story intact by participating in the holiday activities.

He didn't sing, of course, but he listened. The songs rising around him evoked emotions and memories he had thought long gone. "Strange . . ." he muttered, and for a moment clearly saw in his mind's eye . . . his mother bending over him, her eyes tender with love . . . and felt her gentle hand on his head.

"Joy to the world!" Mr. Wheatley sang, his voice raspy and thin. His heart was full of thankfulness. It wouldn't be many years—perhaps only months!—before he would see his Savior face-to-face. In the meantime, for the first time since he was a boy, he had a family, people who needed and loved him.

"The Lord is come!" Marit sang the words from her heart. Something wonderful was happening to her in this place. God was drawing near her day-by-day. As surely as the sun rose each morning, the Lord himself was making his home in her heart . . . and she was coming to grips with the immensity of his love for her. Tears started in her eyes. So much joy! How had she lived before without this joy?

As she hugged the baby in the crook of her arm, she made to wipe her eyes with her other hand. But another's finger carefully caught the tear making its way down her cheek. She looked up. Billy placed his hand over hers and gently squeezed it.

"Let earth . . . receive . . . her King!" Breona had sung those words all her life but tonight they struck her differently than they ever had. *Receive her King? Have I received the King? Is that what Miss Joy means? Is that what all the Bible blather is about?* She frowned but kept singing.

"Repeat the sounding joy, repeat the sounding joy," Joy warbled. She wasn't much of a singer, but she knew all the tunes and all the words. Were Mama and Papa singing these very songs tonight? Were they with their grandchildren at Søren and Meg's? Were Sigrün and Harold there, too? Kjell and Karl and all of their children?

Joy thought of the last Christmas she and Grant had spent together. They had been so happy, so in love.

"Repeat . . . repeat . . . the sounding joy." She was still in love with Grant and, as Mama said, would never stop loving him. But, for the first time since he had died, Joy acknowledged that it might be—*would be*—possible to be happy again. And it would be all right to be happy again.

She glanced around the room. Her heart was full this night. She looked from face to face, at her friends and her guests, each one dear in their own way. She turned to her left. O'Dell was staring back at her, something hidden but bold at the same time in his eyes. Blushing, Joy turned away.

> *We three kings of orient are*
> *Bearing gifts we traverse afar*

Mei-Xing sat by herself in the kitchen, listening to the music, and wondering. Wondering why, alone in this darkened room, hiding from those who would destroy her if they found her, she felt strangely *not* alone for the first time in—oh, so long!

She sighed, but not in despair. She was traditional Chinese and unfamiliar with these Christian customs and these Christian songs.

But she liked the one they were singing. It spoke to her, somehow. And through the kitchen's single window, high above the sink, she could see only a patch of dark sky and, framed by the window, a single star twinkling down on her.

> *Ohhh! Star of wonder, star of night*
> *Star with royal beauty bright*
> *Westward leading, still proceeding*
> *Guide us to thy Perfect Light*

Star of wonder. She felt that wonder this night. *Guide us to thy Perfect Light.* Was there a Perfect Light to be found in this world, in this life? She looked to the star casting its light on her. And she wondered.

Long after Billy, Mr. Wheatley, and their guests had gone to bed and all the lights in the lodge but the glow from the fireplace had been extinguished, Joy, Marit, and Breona broke their own sacrosanct rule. They locked the front door and carefully checked that every window curtain was tightly drawn.

O'Dell, shaking his head, watched as the women encouraged Mei-Xing to limp into the great room. They helped her to a soft chair in the parlor where she could view the glimmering tree. Marit drew a tiny wooden infant from her dress pocket and placed it tenderly in the empty manger under the branches of the tree.

Then they gathered about Mei-Xing, Joy holding her hand gently in her own, and Joy, Marit, and Breona softly sang,

> *Silent night, holy night*
> *All is calm, all is bright*
> *'Round yon virgin, mother and Child*
> *Holy Infant, so tender and mild*
> *Sleep in heavenly peace*
> *Sleep in heavenly peace*

O'Dell looked away, sensing that he was intruding on something precious. Something of which he had neither place nor part.

Chapter 53

January 1909

The lodge had no further guests booked after New Year's, and the household at the lodge eased into a more relaxed routine. Joy focused her energies on preparing advertising for the spring when they could expect more guests. She turned much of the day-to-day running of the house over to Breona's capable hands.

The second week of the month she received mail from Arnie— much looked-for mail. The envelope he sent was thick, crammed with copies of reports she had requested. More importantly was his letter telling her he had done as she requested. Carefully cushioned between pages so as not to bend or fold it, was the document—at least the initial one—she had asked for, dated for January 15. She looked at the calendar and began to count 90 days ahead.

One morning after breakfast as the group finished devotions, Billy asked, "Miss Joy, may I say a word before we get to work?"

"Of course, Billy. What is it?" Joy thought and hoped she knew what it might be. Breona pinched her leg under the table.

"Well, I, that is, Marit and me, we, um," Billy's face flamed red as everyone began to grin before he could get the words out.

"Yes?" Joy offered encouragingly.

"Gonna get married," he finally choked out.

Marit was red-faced, too, but Joy, Breona, Mei-Xing, and Mr. Wheatley began to laugh and clap happily.

"When you goin' to do it?" practical Mr. Wheatley asked.

"Actually, we need to talk to Pastor Kalbørg about that," Billy replied, grinning now himself. He held Marit's hand possessively and she smiled into his eyes. "And we have to figure out where to live."

Joy was taken aback. Where to live? Of course. They couldn't live at the lodge . . .

"Would you . . . I mean, do you intend to stay working here . . . both of you?"

They both nodded, but Billy answered. "Yes'm, if you'll keep us on. We just need a place of our own. Hopin' we can find something nearby."

Joy's thoughts were whirling. She loved the idea of them getting married, but hated the thought of their happy household breaking up.

Could she add on to the lodge? Give them a little apartment? The lot on which the lodge sat was more than large enough.

"And one more thing," Billy added shyly.

"Yes?"

He looked at Marit. She smiled and ducked her head. "We have a name for the baby. Our baby."

"William Bartholomew Evans. Junior."

Chapter 54

Dean Morgan steepled his fingers together and eyed Darrow placidly. Darrow fidgeted and did not meet Morgan's gaze. Something about the man unnerved him—as did the silent, ever-watching Asian sitting by the door *behind* Darrow. Ever since Judge Brown had vanished and this man had stepped into Brown's shoes—effortlessly, it seemed—Darrow had felt off-balance and edgy. And he sure didn't like having his back to Morgan's ice-like bodyguard.

"So a very valuable commodity, one that I particularly prized, is missing and has not as yet been recovered?"

Darrow weighed his words carefully. "Miss Cleary had already decided that the was girl to be sent down here to Bailey's. She had tried to escape and so we disciplined her but Miss Cleary said she—the girl—lacked . . . I think Miss Cleary called it 'the necessary enthusiasm' to be one of the club's special girls." He licked his lips nervously.

Morgan tsked. "Yet I understood her to be a great favorite at the club. Why, even here in Denver in an inferior house such as Bailey's I would expect her to be quite a little star. Surely we could have been more . . . persuasive? But perhaps I should be speaking to Miss Cleary about this rather than you."

His gaze hardened. "In any event, we really can't have our girls traipsing about, now can we? But perhaps more importantly, should we be permanently *damaging* such a rare and potentially valuable flower?" Morgan picked up a sheet of stationery and read aloud from it. "Miss Cleary writes, '*regrettably, the young lady's looks were ruined.*' Her nose, I believe, was broken? Is this so, Mr. Darrow?"

Darrow shivered involuntarily. No one knew when Judge Brown had left Corinth, and no one had heard from him since. The rumors only added to Darrow's unease. "Yessir, regrettably, Mr. Morgan, sir. I'm sorry to report that, ah, one of my men was, er, that is, *may* have been too *enthusiastic* . . . in that regard. And we weren't, ah, expectin' her to bolt, er, that is, *run* again . . . what in her condition . . . afterwards and all."

"I see."

Those two words hung ominously in the air until sweat began to run down Darrow's neck and back.

Finally Morgan spoke softly. "I believe, Mr. Darrow, that you have been an . . . exemplary employee and that your loyalty is not in question."

Darrow felt a wave of reprieve? relief? wash over him.

"However . . ." Here Morgan paused again and Darrow's gut clenched. "I have determined that a more . . . firm and *tasteful* management of these . . . issues is required. To this end, I have secured the services of Mr. Giles Banner. Mr. Banner, would you be so good as to come in, please?"

Darrow was momentarily confused. More tasteful management? Services? Then he saw a man step from the doorway to the left of Morgan's desk. He was slender and half a head shorter than Darrow. His eyes and hair were as black as the Chinaman's and his hair was slicked back from his face.

"Mr. Morgan?" The man nodded deferentially to Morgan and then turned to look Darrow over. Darrow felt the cold disdain of the man's appraisal.

"Ah yes. Mr. Banner, this is . . . Darrow. Mr. Darrow, as of today Mr. Banner will be assuming management of security in Corinth. I have given him my assurance that he will receive your utmost cooperation."

Darrow's eyes narrowed and shot from Banner to Morgan and back. He'd been demoted? Under this guy? As he tossed those words around in his mind he glanced again at Morgan. And froze.

"As I said, I have given him my assurance that he will receive your full cooperation. I can expect him to receive that, can I not, Mr. Darrow?"

The thinly veiled threat hovered between them, and Darrow's survival instinct kicked in. Choking on the words he nodded at Morgan and then Banner. "Yessir, Mr. Morgan, Mr. Banner."

"Good man. I will be asking Mr. Banner for regular progress reports. They will, at my request, include the state of morale among his men."

Darrow heard the slight emphasis on the words "his men." Then the Chinaman was opening the door and Darrow found himself standing outside. Cursing violently under his breath he strode away toward the station mulling over the sudden alteration in his fortunes.

Morgan motioned Banner to the front of his desk. "Mr. Banner, Corinth is a very profitable segment of my businesses. However, the situation has become a little disquieting as of late. It would be tedious and troubling if I deemed it necessary to relocate my *special club*. I trust you can set things right?"

"I can, Mr. Morgan." It was a statement without boasting or hyperbole.

"I expect you can, Mr. Banner. Please find the recalcitrant 'Little Plum Blossom' and return her to Miss Cleary. I desire a success with her, not a failure. Even with a broken nose, this will reestablish a proper tone in Corinth, don't you agree?"

"Yes sir, I do." Banner's words were devoid of emotion.

"Oh. And if certain citizens have been concealing or otherwise aiding the little flower, I would like them to be suitably corrected."

"Yes sir. You can rely on me."

Chapter 55

Shortly after the evening train arrived in Corinth that evening, Flinty pounded on the back door. Breona let him in.

"Miss Joy, I come t' tell yer som'pin." His weathered face creased in concern. "New feller in town, name o' Banner. Darrow's thugs'r all kow-towin' and Darrow's a-lookin' like he et a lemon." He glanced around knowingly. "T' big boss sent a new gun, that's what."

O'Dell and Joy exchanged worried looks.

Just before sunrise the next morning, Billy knocked on Joy's door. "Miss Joy," he hissed.

"What is it?"

"We got more company."

Joy wiped the sleep from her face and dressed hurriedly. When she entered the kitchen two women were standing nervously near the door. Billy and Mr. Wheatley stood outside their room, watching with caution. They had wisely not lit any lamps in the kitchen so it was difficult for Joy to make out their visitors' faces.

One of the figures, a girl with a deep coffee-and-cream complexion and tangled mass of dark hair shadowing her face, addressed Joy. "Please forgive me for waking you, miss. Would you be the lady who assisted Mei-Xing?"

She was scared, Joy could tell, even if she couldn't see her face clearly, and yet she was well-spoken and held herself erect with a stately grace. The other woman was excruciatingly thin, her brown hair lank and lifeless. She held her arms tightly around her middle, as if she were in pain.

Joy chose her words carefully. "I believe that if certain people knew we had assisted the girl who ran away from Miss Cleary's, it might lead to difficulties for us."

"On my soul, miss, I am no friend of theirs." She swallowed hard, her fear palpable. "We are in mortal trouble, miss, and must get off this mountain *soon* or . . ." she shuddered.

"Does this have something to do with the new boss in town? The man called Banner?"

The brown-haired girl whimpered and Joy looked at her more closely. Something certainly wasn't right with her.

The dark-haired one nodded. "He is evil itself, miss. I-I beg your pardon." Abruptly, her eyes teared and she pleaded with Joy, "Please help us! He'll kill Helen if he discovers us."

Joy was a little amazed. This young woman possessed the manner and diction of a well-bred gentlewoman.

At the name 'Helen,' Mr. Wheatley straightened. "Your name Helen?" he asked the brown-haired girl kindly.

She looked as though she hadn't heard him but finally nodded. And Joy remembered that Mr. Wheatley's sweetheart had been named Helen.

"What is your name?" Joy asked the dark-haired one.

"Tory, Miss Thoresen. Mei-Xing was a dear friend. We just want to get away . . . as she did."

Joy nodded. "She spoke of you, Tory. She said you took care of her when they assaulted her."

"Yes, miss. I did." She laughed without mirth. "We are all obliged to perform that service for another girl at some point. Then they return the favor . . . when it is our turn."

Her laugh quickly died. "It is different with Helen. It may be hard to see just now, but she was a great beauty only five weeks ago—she speaks French and even knows philosophy! But she's grown sickly and . . . hasn't been able to work."

"I overheard that man Banner tonight tell Roxanne he intends to make an example of her . . . because . . . because he said he 'needs to set a proper tone' and she's not long for this world anyway." She glanced sadly at Helen.

Joy stared in horror at Tory. "He means . . . to *kill* her?"

Tory nodded sorrowfully. "In front of the other girls! That's why we had to leave right away. Please. You have to help us, miss. We are begging you!"

Joy nodded again. "Wait here." She went quickly up the stairs and into the little alcove they had fixed for Mei-Xing. The girl was awake and anxious. She had obviously heard Billy's knock and his message.

"It's all right, Mei-Xing. You have some friends waiting for you downstairs."

They descended the stairs into the kitchen. As soon as Mei-Xing and Tory saw each other they embraced affectionately. Tory turned back and held out an arm to Helen who joined them as they held each other.

At that moment, O'Dell entered the kitchen from the great room. "What's the commotion?" He took in the scene quickly.

Joy nodded to him and asked Billy to discreetly fetch Domingo and Gustavo from their watchman duties in the lodge's stable. He stole out the back door. She looked up at the kitchen window. It was near sunrise but still dark outdoors. What if Darrow's men had seen the girls come to their back door?

"Dear Lord, please hide us," she whispered.

They waited quietly until the two night watchmen followed Billy silently into the kitchen. Domingo and Gustavo were bundled against the cold and spent a few moments pulling off their mufflers, hats, and gloves.

"Did Darrow's men see these girls come here?" Joy asked them straight out.

Domingo rubbed his arms and hands but smiled. "No, *señora*. Those *hombres* left early. They have been cheating on their lookout duties lately and leave an hour before dawn most mornings." He glanced curiously at the girls.

Joy thought hard. "What about the girls' tracks?"

O'Dell motioned to Billy and Mr. Wheatley. "Dress warm. We have work to do."

Domingo and Gustavo began to put their gear back on also. "We will help."

Joy told herself to breathe and began to relax a little. She addressed Mei-Xing and her two friends. "All right. Please sit down. We'll wait a little to put some lights on, but Mei-Xing, would you please start some coffee?"

The girl immediately busied herself to do so. In the three weeks since Christmas Mei-Xing's health had greatly improved and she was now able to get up and down the stairs without too much difficulty. She was also, of her own initiative, taking on more work about the kitchen and in the attic apartment, the only areas of the lodge where she could go.

Joy trudged back upstairs to wake Breona. It would be an early day, but they would let Marit sleep a little longer since baby Will regularly woke her in the night.

Where would she put these new girls? How would they get them out of Corinth? She didn't have the room to add more girls and hide them forever. What if Darrow or this new man *Banner* discovered them here?

Joy shuddered and then stopped halfway to the attic apartment to chastise herself. Wasn't this what the Lord had brought her to Corinth for? He would not have put those girls "in their path" if Joy and the rest of them were not ready and able to help them. Stiffening her spine and her attitude, Joy finished her climb to the attic and gently aroused Breona.

Later that day she and O'Dell found a corner in the parlor to talk. O'Dell had been walking about town as usual with his feelers out for news. The bartenders in his usual haunts always had news and bits of gossip to share.

Flinty, too, had reported back on what he had seen and heard. He had seen a sullen Darrow and three mounted men riding the trails around Corinth that led off the mountain. O'Dell had heard from a loquacious bartender that "Miss Cleary's place had a lot o' excitement goin' on." The bartender had overheard that "the new boss, Banner, slapped Miss Cleary's face" and "she's gonner hev a shiner, fer sure."

Joy envisioned Roxanne Cleary with a swollen, bruised face. She was surprised to find that, rather than exulting in the woman's pain, she was feeling sorry for her. She reminded herself to pray for the woman.

Breona and Joy discussed where to put the two girls. "'Tis seemin' plain t' me, miss. Ye and me mus' be movin' into two o' the guest rooms. Put t' two new girls in our'n beds. They'll be safest up top, I'm thinkin' an' will be havin' a bit o' breathin' room there."

Joy agreed. Breona and Joy, with help from Billy, moved their simple things into the two guest rooms closest the back stairs. Joy asked the two girls to remain in the attic apartment. Joy was worried about Helen. She *was* ill. Breona put her to bed in her room and tried to coax a little soup into her. Tory hovered nearby, concern etched on her face.

"Mr. O'Dell, can you help us get those girls off the mountain?" Joy couldn't bear the thought of Banner and his men forcibly searching the lodge and finding them. She pondered how cavalierly Banner had told Roxanne Cleary he would dispose of Helen and shivered. Darrow was bad enough—was it possible this man was worse?

O'Dell touched her arm gently and Joy jumped. She had gone off into her thoughts again.

"Miss Thoresen, if I can find a way, I will." He was looking at her "that way" again. Joy averted her eyes and simply nodded her thanks.

Chapter 56

"Uli, we can't manage the lodge and add more girls to the house," Joy mused. "If the Lord keeps sending us girls—which is, of course, exactly what we want—we won't have room for lodgers!" She chuckled ruefully. "I didn't realize there might be something called 'too much success.'"

Joy and Uli were sitting in the lodge's parlor enjoying a quiet moment. Uli stirred her coffee and nodded in agreement. "I understand that you want to help the girls to heal and then train them so they can support themselves respectably, but in honesty, Joy, I don't think Corinth is the right place for such an endeavor."

Joy had to admit that Uli was probably right. She had been pondering this problem for a while and wanted to share her heart with Uli.

"I feel the same way . . . not that I want to leave Corinth or shut down the lodge. I love this house! It is our home now. And it is a safe haven, the first place girls can escape to—those who were kidnapped and brought to Corinth and who manage to get away."

"In addition, the lodge stands against the sin in this town, even if we must tread softly and secretly for now. But, while I feel the lodge is an important step in God's plan, I know there is a larger need."

She opened her arms wide. "I don't want to be a sheltered, naïve, Christian who is blind to the pain and suffering of others— particularly women, Uli. And I feel like I am just beginning to understand how many women are *trapped* in . . . prostitution."

Joy had initially found it hard to use words like "prostitution," but had no choice but to overcome that reticence so that she could describe what they were striving against. "Mr. O'Dell tells me that every city has hundreds of . . . places where the services of girls . . . are sold."

She laughed ruefully. "I think he meant to discourage me with the vastness of the problem but it had the opposite effect." She fell silent for a long moment. "I know we cannot solve the ills of the world, but I must try to do the little part God puts before me. You know, I often stand on the overlook and gaze eastward into the distance. Lately when I do, I can almost see, in my mind's eye, *Denver!*"

"I can visualize the Market Street area, and I can almost hear the crying of women who daily sell their souls in back rooms and bordellos just to eat or because they are forced. They need Jesus, Uli! They need to be set free on both the inside and the outside. Who will take the Good News to them and break those chains?"

She saw that Uli's eyes were wide as saucers and chuckled. "I can see that I astonish you, dear Cousin."

Uli stared at her. "You have been thinking about this." It was a statement.

"Yes. And I have . . . ideas."

Uli smiled. "Of course you do. It's God's gift working in you."

Joy laughed at her. "What do you mean?"

"It's what I said. God has given you a gift for solving problems—not just solving *symptoms* but coming up with creative ways to *fix* things."

"Here David and I were thinking how wonderful we were to help one girl at a time escape. We were leaving all the hard work to others and cowering in fear that we would be found out. Who knows where those girls are now and if they were able to leave that life behind? You think beyond the immediate need, Joy; you look for *real* solutions. I see that as a gift from God."

Joy flushed with pleasure at the praise. "I don't know. It just comes to me, so perhaps . . . yes, it *must* be the Lord. I've been wondering how to help not just the girls in Corinth but others. I realize it is not just a problem here, but in many cities . . ." Her voice trailed off.

"Tell me what you are thinking, Joy."

Joy's eyes shone intently. "I'm thinking . . . of a training facility and small businesses that can support several, perhaps many, women escaping from prostitution. And a house, likely a small one at first, but later a large one, arranged like a home for *many* young women. Guided by one or two mature, godly women who can love these girls and teach them how Jesus heals all wounds. Show them how to dress and live modestly and behave in a manner on the outside that reflects what God is doing on the inside. Teach them how to cook, manage a home, and provide for themselves."

Uli nodded encouragingly.

"And the businesses. Not just one, but two or three. I still have a great deal of inventory in that warehouse in Omaha. I have a bit more money, too. Not enough for what I have in mind perhaps, but . . . Anyway, I could send for the inventory and set up a fine furnishings store with what I have. I would hire an experienced manager who can train the girls how to present themselves, to sell the furnishings, and to run the business. And then perhaps we could open a restaurant, just a small one, where the girls can cook and wait tables."

She took a breath and rushed on. "And a sewing shop. If we train some of the women as seamstresses, they can work at making clothing and doing alterations. And . . . and I can't but help hoping that some of them will find godly men who will love them as the Lord loves them, marry them, and make happy families and homes." She sighed.

"Where would you get the money to do all this, Joy?"

"I know. It is so much! But . . . wouldn't other Christian people help us? People like Emily Van der Pol. She begged me to let her help somehow. If she helped us find one or two wealthy patrons, wouldn't they want to see this work go forward and encourage their friends to help?" Joy rubbed her eyes. The enormity of the prospect was overwhelming.

She was surprised when Uli chimed in enthusiastically, "And scholarships! Some of these women would make fine teachers or nurses. If we could help them get educations."

Joy clutched Uli's hands. "Brilliant! Oh Uli, we need to pray on this and find God's leading on how to start."

"Yes. Right now."

The two women bent their heads and earnestly prayed together, taking turns lifting each idea to the Lord and asking for his guidance and provision.

Any hope of quickly removing Tory and Helen from the mountain faded as a strong storm pummeled Corinth that night. Snow buried the rails up the mountain and train service came to a standstill.

While Joy fretted, O'Dell reminded her that most of the town was buried also. "Banner and his men can't track the girls. In fact, the whole town is battened down tight. Flinty says a blizzard is 'fixin' t' fly.'"

He chuckled and tried to draw Joy out. "Seems that Flinty's bum knee lets him know when the next blizzard is setting up."

"It's not just getting them off the mountain," Joy explained. "Helen is doing very badly." She hesitated and then spoke her worry aloud. "I fear that if she doesn't see a doctor soon she may die."

O'Dell's brows creased. "I didn't realize she was that poorly."

Joy looked out a window. Snow was falling again in large, powdery flakes.

"I'm wondering . . . when the trains begin running again, would you be willing to take a short trip to Denver?"

O'Dell scrutinized Joy for a moment. "I can tell you are hatching some sort of plot, Miss Thoresen. Care to share with me?"

A week of blizzards at last tapered off. Crews running steam-powered snowplows along the rails labored for two days to clear the tracks until the trains could run again. Mid-morning O'Dell stepped off the train in Denver and held up his derby to hail a cab.

Although he was unannounced, Emily Van der Pol received him and greeted him cordially. She ordered tea and, after it arrived, she listened with growing amazement as he outlined Joy's request.

When he finished, she thought soberly for several long moments. "If I understand you correctly, this needs to be done quickly?"

O'Dell nodded. "The sooner the better."

"It is dangerous. We could fail."

He nodded again.

Finally she straightened her shoulders and answered. "Yes. I'll do it."

O'Dell returned that evening. Joy and Breona had already made preparations. They only needed to wait.

On Friday, the men Banner had assigned to watch the trains observed Mrs. Van der Pol and two of her close friends as they stepped off the afternoon train. In the winter twilight the men carefully noted three finely dressed women disembarking with their luggage. They were draped in warm wools and furs. All three women sported the most elegant hats of the season—large veiled affairs bedecked in feathers and bows.

The men watched as Billy Evans handed the women into the lodge's carriage and drove them the short distance to their accommodations.

Sunday afternoon the same men carefully observed as Billy Evans assisted Mrs. Van der Pol and her two veiled companions, one of the women leaning heavily upon another, back onto the train.

At the lodge that evening Joy dined with her two remaining guests, Viola Lind and Grace Minton. Their prayers before the meal were heartfelt.

"Thank you, Lord, for your covering grace this day," Joy prayed. Viola and Grace's 'amens' were soft but sincere.

The three women looked at each other across the table. Grace spoke. "Emily will take good care of Tory and Helen, Miss Thoresen, and we will help. Thank you for giving us guidance on how to do so."

She paused delicately. "As you know, my husband passed last year. I . . . am a woman of independent means now." She looked directly at Joy. "I want to be part of this work you propose to begin in Denver, and we know others who can also be trusted and have the means to assist."

Viola nodded in agreement, and Joy shivered, in relief but also in anticipation. She recalled the words of Isaiah and shook her head, marveling at what God was doing.

> *Sing, O barren one, thou that didst not bear;*
> *break forth into singing, and cry aloud,*
> *thou that didst not travail with child:*
> *for more are the children of the desolate*
> *than the children of the married wife,*
> *saith the LORD.*

On Tuesday morning Viola and Grace mounted the train to Denver. The men watching at the siding, a different crew than those who had watched Sunday afternoon, may have experienced some minor confusion, but they were loath to interfere with two such obviously wealthy gentlewomen.

Joy accompanied the two women to the siding and made a small show of sending them off. They intentionally passed close enough to the men for them to clearly see Grace and Viola's faces.

With Tory and Helen safely away, Joy turned her attention toward a permanent solution for Mei-Xing. Mei-Xing would never be taken for a wealthy woman up from Denver for the weekend, no matter what the disguise. She was too tiny and too Asian to escape detection. Besides . . . that option had been used and would likely not work again.

No, what they needed was a different means of getting her off the mountain. Until then, her safety, and that of all the residents of the lodge, hinged on *keeping her hidden.*

Joy and Breona moved back into their rooms. After proposing her idea to Breona, Marit, and Mei-Xing, Joy commissioned Flinty to build a hiding place for Mei-Xing in the attic, one that would elude a search should any of Morgan's men forcibly enter the lodge. He and Billy discussed a number of possibilities and decided that the alcove where she slept afforded the best location.

"We're fixin' t' build a sofa here that pulls up from th' back like a lid," Flinty explained. "At night it's a bed, see? An' durin' th' day it's a parlor sofa. But at any time, she can lift it up, scoot inside, and pull it closed."

"It don't need to be big, neither, she bein' s' tiny an' all. We'll fix a handle on th' inside. She can pull th' lid down on hersel' and shut it up tight. When th' coast is clear, she can push it open an' git out by her ownsel'."

Flinty padded the floor of the box so that it was comfortable enough, and Billy cleverly added hidden holes to let in air. Mei-Xing watched these preparations with her usual silence, but Joy noticed that the girl seemed more relaxed after trying the arrangement several times. They exchanged a glance and, for the first time Joy could recall, Mei-Xing offered her a smile.

Chapter 57

Joy was looking for one of the men to accompany her to the little grocer in the town proper. Billy and Breona were at the siding selling some of Marit's baking. Mr. Wheatley was nursing a cold and Joy did not want him to go out.

"I'll accompany you, Miss Thoresen," O'Dell offered, twirling his derby on one finger. "Besides, we should probably give the merchants of Corinth *some* indication that I am making progress in my suit for you; otherwise my excuse for lingering in Corinth will start to look a little thin, don't you think?"

Joy gave him a penetrating stare, but he merely waited, fiddling with his infernal hat. "Fine," she finally muttered.

"What? No 'thank you, Edmund'?" he pressed.

"Thank you, *Mr.* O'Dell," Joy answered loftily. He only grinned.

They stepped out into the frigid air and Joy was suddenly glad to have a brisk walk ahead of her. She had been cooped up too much lately. They set off at a good pace and Joy began to relax and warm inside her wrappings.

Half an hour later they reached the little town square and stepped onto the planked walk along the main street. Wordlessly, O'Dell reached out and took Joy's hand, tucking it under his arm. She resisted but he held fast, looking straight ahead and saying quietly, "Don't look now, but we are being watched. Act like we are a happy couple for a few minutes."

Joy glanced side-to-side nervously. O'Dell pinched her arm.

"Stop looking around. Just relax."

Joy did as he instructed and managed to look his way and smile a bit.

"Better," he grinned back.

Then Joy saw the black-haired man leaning against the wall outside the barbershop down the walk. Staring at them. Staring at her. She didn't recognize him, but obviously O'Dell did.

As they passed by O'Dell nodded calmly, "Banner."

"O'Dell," the dark, lean man replied, tipping his hat to Joy. "Ma'am."

Joy's faced flamed at the mention of Banner's name. She cast her eyes downward, refusing to acknowledge his greeting.

A few moments later they entered the grocer's, the little bell over the door signaling their entrance. The grocer, Mr. Marsh, wiped his hands on his apron and stepped behind the counter.

"Miss Thoresen, Mr. O'Dell," he greeted them. "How can I help you?" His eyes went to Joy's hand tucked in the crook of O'Dell's arm. Joy quickly removed it, her face flaming under the grocer's inquisitive gaze.

She gave her list to him and then turned in curiosity when she heard whimpering behind the counter. Mr. Marsh paused in filling her bag and chuckled.

"My Bessie gave me a new litter of pups a few weeks back. Would you like to see?"

Joy did. She missed Blackie terribly at times. She crossed behind the counter and looked under it. In a wooden crate a black dog with a single white patch at her throat lay on her side. She was nursing six chubby puppies. They wriggled and squeaked as they pushed against her to encourage her milk to come down.

"Pick one up if you like," Mr. Marsh said.

As she bent over, the mother eyed Joy. While not all shepherd, it was obvious the mother had shepherd blood. Joy gently rubbed the dog's head and spoke reassuringly before selecting a fat little ball of slicked-down fur. The pup, like his mother, was more black than white; nevertheless he had several white markings, the most notable the patch that covered one side of his face.

"Aren't you beautiful?" Joy crooned. The puppy nuzzled and squirmed against her neck, rooting for a nipple. As though suddenly tuckered out, he sighed, stilled in her hands, and fell asleep under the curve of her jaw. Joy recalled the warm comfort of Blackie resting his head on her hand, both of them needing each other's closeness. Her eyes misted over at the memory. After a few minutes she returned the puppy to his mother and turned resolutely away.

O'Dell, pretending to look over the grocer's limited selection of cigars, had watched Joy pick up and hold the puppy. He had not missed the vulnerability and sadness momentarily steal over her.

On their walk back to the lodge Joy ventured, "So that was Banner, the new 'boss' in town? You two seemed to know each other."

"I made a *point* of making myself known to him almost immediately, Miss Thoresen. I believe I heard you call it 'hiding in plain sight.' We've had a few drinks in the same bar and just this week I told him a long story about a stag I shot in the forests of upper New York State. A *very* long story."

Joy stopped and looked hard at him. O'Dell chuckled and his laugh sounded a bit wicked.

Switching to his British voice he quipped, "I'm a jolly good story teller, Miss Thoresen. On that occasion I took a rather perverse pleasure in acting at being half drunk and then peppering the tale with the most inane and boring details I could concoct."

He laughed aloud and returned to his normal accent. "Banner squirmed for ten minutes. Wanted to escape in the worst way, but I had a hold on his coat sleeve, the slimy bas—"

He stopped. "My apologies. I only meant to say that I rather enjoyed twisting his tail for a few minutes."

Joy stared at him again for a long moment and then, on her own, took his arm and they continued walking.

"I think I might have enjoyed watching him twist too," was all she answered.

Vikki Kestell

Chapter 58

January crawled to a close and February turned to nasty weather with a will. During the month Corinth was often snowed in; after each storm they would be deprived of train and mail service until the plows came through and crews dug out the cuts where the blizzards had packed in the snow. The foul weather significantly reduced the number of visitors to Corinth and reduced movement about town.

Perhaps because of the weather, the night watchers, as stealthily as they had appeared, also disappeared. For those at the lodge it provided a sense of security that, while perhaps not permanent, allowed the household to relax for a time.

Joy, sitting at the lobby desk, looked at the calendar and, for the hundredth time, counted days. Days until all would be in order—if her plan were ever needed. She looked about her and sorrowed a bit. Would everything they had built here be the sacrifice that was required?

She carefully penciled a light "x" on April 15.

One day, mid-month, O'Dell ventured out-of-doors even though he had to break trail through freshly formed drifts. Joy happened to see him go, but must have been upstairs when he returned. Later that afternoon when she came down the back stairs into the kitchen, she was greeted with smug and knowing looks from Marit and Breona.

Then she heard it. A quivering little whimper. Coming from the pantry. And then Breona chortled. She *chortled*!

Joy shot her a sharp look and threw open the pantry door. There, in a small crate, huddled on a pile of rags—the puppy from the grocer's! Lounging on a straight-back chair next to the box, feet stretched before him, sat Edmund O'Dell.

He tipped his derby down over one eye and drawled, "I've been sitting here ever so long, Miss Thoresen. I believe the little guy is getting hungry. And the fact is that I detest dog hair," he added in a dry tone, "particularly on this suit."

Joy looked from him to the box again. "I don't understand."

"I was remiss," he replied archly.

"I beg your pardon?"

"Not at all—I am asking *your* pardon. I completely neglected to give you your Christmas gift."

"My what?" Joy was staring at the whimpering puppy. He was *so* much bigger than when she had first seen him just a few weeks ago! He was a pudgy butterball covered in curling black and white fur.

O'Dell stood and flicked an imaginary speck of lint from his sleeve. "Merry Christmas, Miss Thoresen, albeit two months late."

With that he picked up the chair and left the pantry. Joy turned to say something to him, but the puppy, believing he was being abandoned, began crying in earnest.

Joy scooped him up into her arms and he began to wiggle and push until he found the warmth between her breasts. She stared down at the pup, who was snuffling her and pushing to get near her face. She slowly smiled.

She told herself just how much bother the pup would be until house broken, how much work and attention he would entail, and— oh!—how Breona would fuss! Even as she sternly listed all the perfectly valid reasons not to accept the pup—foremost because O'Dell would assume that her acceptance of his gift constituted permission to advance his suit—she refused to be deterred.

"I want you," she whispered onto the top of his furry head. "I haven't had anything that is *mine* to love in such a long time . . ."

The puppy sneezed. Joy laughed and he sneezed again. "Bless you!" she whispered. "Bless you, Little Blackie."

Chapter 59

It was finally March and yet another blizzard shut down the trains and confined the population of Corinth to their homes. After three days, Joy was happy to hear the prolonged whistle of an engine as it made its way into town early that morning. She glanced out a second-floor window toward the siding and saw the train easing to a stop, black smoke pouring from the engine's stack.

Several minutes later, she heard knocking at the kitchen door and the muffled sounds of voices. Curious, she came down into the kitchen—

"Arnie!" She flew into his arms, delighted to see her cousin. He held her tightly but was quiet. When she pulled back and saw his face, her heart clenched with dread.

"W-what is it?" She was afraid to ask the question that terrified her most.

"I've come to take you home, Joy," Arnie said. The creases around his eyes were etched in sadness.

"Papa? Is it Papa? Is-is he . . ." She could not choke out the words.

"No, not yet. The Lord willing, we'll get you home before . . . before he . . ." Arnie couldn't finish his sentence. "Your mama hasn't been able to get word to you, so I said I would come and find a way. I didn't want you alone on the train anyway . . . not with Darrow and that bunch about . . ."

He stopped. "We need to go as soon as possible, Joy. They told me the train can't go farther up the mountain yet, so they will turn the engine around and take the train back down to Denver in just a little while. I have asked them to wait for us."

"Uli! Uli will want to . . . she will need to come!" A sob caught in Joy's throat.

"I'll have Billy tell her and David to catch the train in the morning. But we need to go *now*, Joy."

Her mind was whirling. She had to pack, she had to give directions for while she was gone—someone would have to watch after Blackie. She was oblivious to those around her as she tried to organize her racing thoughts. She came back to herself when someone placed a hand on her arm.

"We'll take care of everything." It was O'Dell. He bid her look at him. "You are not to worry, Joy. Everyone knows their job, and I will look out for the lodge's safety. Just pack your bags and go to your mother." His eyes held her steadily and Joy allowed herself to believe him.

"Thank you. Yes." She turned to go upstairs but turned quickly back. "But what abou—"

"I will take care of Blackie," O'Dell said, knowing immediately what her concern was.

Joy stammered her thanks and hurried up the stairs. She didn't see the dark look Arnie bent on O'Dell as soon as her back was turned. O'Dell just shrugged at Arnie's challenge and went to find Billy and Mr. Wheatley.

Less than an hour later Joy and Arnie were on their way down the mountain, and Joy was praying she would reach her beloved Papa before his spirit flew away.

Chapter 60

It took Joy and Arnie a day and a half to reach RiverBend. Kjell and his son Nathan were at the station waiting for them. They had been there in the morning when the early train came in and had returned for the afternoon train, in hopes that Arnie had reached Joy and had brought her home.

"He's still hanging on, Joy. We knew he would not let go until he had seen you." Kjell had tears in his eyes; Joy knew that Arnie, Kjell, and their siblings would feel her papa's passing as deeply as she and Søren would.

When they finally pulled up outside Jan and Rose's little house, Joy saw numerous wagons and buggies in the yard. Relatives and close friends congregated in tight knots on the porch around the outside of the house. Several hands lifted in silent greeting.

They wouldn't all be there unless . . . Joy thought frantically. The tiny hope that it was all a mistake began to flicker.

Rose opened the front door and flew down the steps to her daughter. They embraced and Joy begged Rose, "Please tell me he is still here, Mama! Please say he will be all right soon!"

Rose just gripped Joy tighter, willing herself not to break down. "Come inside, Joy. Papa needs you," was all she could manage.

The first people Joy saw in the living room were Pastor and Mrs. Medford. Behind them were Søren and Meg and several of their children. Meg, red-eyed, nodded at Joy.

Søren pulled Joy into his arms. "I'm so glad Arnie brought you, Joy. Papa has been holding on, believing you would come." He hugged her tightly and then whispered in her ear. "Be strong, Little Sister. He isn't as you remember him. He is very weak. Just let him know you are here."

With that he gently led her into her parents' room.

The room was bathed in the soft glow of lamp light. Joy could see her papa's figure under the covers but . . . he was so still and so strangely small! She crept to the edge of the bed and sat down on a chair beside the bed. She sought and found his rough hand and held it in her own. It was cooler to the touch than it should have been and she could not stem the tears that began to course down her face.

"Papa? Papa, it's Joy. I'm here, Papa!" She slid to her knees on the floor, her forehead on their joined hands, her tears bathing them.

She felt a gentle pressure and lifted her face, saw his eyes blinking, looking straight ahead, searching for her. Standing, she leaned over where he could see her.

"Here I am, Papa."

"My . . . my Joy Again . . ."

"Yes, Papa!"

"Joy, my Joy . . . I b . . . I b . . ." He took a ragged breath and tried again. "I b-bless . . . I bless you and . . . your chil . . .dren . . . my daugh . . . ter." He struggled to take another breath. "Your chil . . . dren. The Lord will . . . give you . . ."

The door opened and Rose and Søren entered the room. As Rose crossed to the other side of the bed, Jan's eyes tried to follow her. She climbed on the bed, knelt near him so he could see her, and took his other hand.

She smiled for him and saw his blue, blue eyes brighten with love. His lips moved and she leaned toward them to catch his words.

"My little Rose."

"Yes, Jan!"

Then he closed his eyes and sighed . . .

Chapter 61

The morning dawned cold but still. As the sun rose, it revealed a fresh jacket of frost coating the fields as far as the eye could see. Sunlight reflected off the frost, and Joy closed her eyes against the brilliance of a million glittering, shimmering diamonds.

Down the road, beginning at the Thoresen family cemetery, past the Thoresen houses, barns, and cornfields, over the creek, and beyond Jan and Rose's farm, the line of mourners stretched. They arrived in wagons, buggies, and motor cars and stood quietly beside their vehicles.

Six young men carried Jan from his home that morning. The bearers were some of the men of the community whom Jan had taught and mentored from their teen years into godly manhood. They bore Jan's simple coffin from the house in which he and Rose had lived and loved to the bridge that stretched over the creek.

At the bridge they surrendered their precious burden to Jan's six oldest grandsons and great-nephews. Down the road, past the lined mourners they marched, holding themselves gravely erect, most with tears dropping off their trembling young chins.

Finally, at the gate to the Thoresen homestead, they yielded this honor to the men with whom Jan had shared the closest bonds: Søren, Karl, Kjell, Arnie, Jacob Medford, and Brian McKennie.

Rose and Joy followed closely behind the procession, accompanied by Sigrün, Uli, Meg, Anna, Kjell and Karl's wives, Fiona McKennie, Vera Medford, and dozens of grandchildren, grand-nieces and -nephews, and their families.

As the family passed, the mourners lining the road fell in behind them. Joy cast a look back. She realized that every family for miles around was probably present or represented. Her heart swelled with pride and gratitude.

At the entrance of the Thoresen cemetery they paused. The bearers entered and the family followed. The rest of the swelling crowd gathered around the iron fence that bounded the Thoresen plot.

Joy swallowed when she saw the mound of earth heaped at the head of an empty grave. She and Rose drew near and gratefully sank down on chairs that had been provided. While they waited for everyone to settle, Joy held her mama's hand and looked at the headstones next to where her father would be buried.

To the left: *Elli Katrin Thoresen*

Papa's first wife.

To the right: *Kristen Maria Thoresen*

Papa's first daughter.

Her papa's body would rest there until Jesus called him at the last trumpet. Rose and Søren and Joy had read that passage together from 1 Corinthians 15 the night before.

> *Behold, I shew you a mystery;*
> *We shall not all sleep, but we shall all be changed,*
> *In a moment, in the twinkling of an eye,*
> *at the last trump: for the trumpet shall sound,*
> *and the dead shall be raised incorruptible,*
> *and we shall be changed.*
> *For this corruptible must put on incorruption,*
> *and this mortal must put on immortality.*

We shall be changed, Joy pondered. *And this mortal must put on immortality.*

With a start, Joy realized that there was no place for Mama near Papa! Where would she be buried? Then, at the thought of someday also losing her mother, Joy quickly pushed those thoughts away.

She sought out other headstones nearby: Aunt Amalie, beside her husband, Karl. Several tiny graves: a daughter Søren and Meg had lost in her first year and the two infants Karl and his wife had lost in childbirth.

What had Papa meant when he said "I bless your children. The Lord will give?" Joy did not understand. She wiped a tear from her cheek. Rose turned to her and squeezed her hand.

"I love you, dear daughter," was all she said.

"I love you, Mama," she returned.

Jacob Medford began to read from the Bible.

> *Jesus said unto her,*
> *I am the resurrection, and the life:*
> *he that believeth in me,*
> *though he were dead, yet shall he live:*
> *And whosoever liveth and believeth in me*
> *shall never die. Believest thou this?*
> *She saith unto him,*

> *Yea, Lord: I believe that thou art the Christ,*
> *the Son of God,*
> *which should come into the world.*

The Christ! The Son of God! Thank you, Lord, for the hope of the resurrection, Joy prayed, rejoicing even in her sorrow.

Joy had a sudden thought. *I wonder if Papa and Grant can see each other?* Then she thought, *They are both waiting for us . . . safe in Jesus. I'm so glad!*

Pastor Medford finished his message and prayed, his voice cracking a little, "Now Lord, we ask you to receive your servant, Jan."

He looked around at the family and the mourners and, with tears streaming down his face, declared in a strong, loud voice, "Jan Thoresen, enter thou into the joy of thy Lord!"

Chapter 62

Everyone had gone at last and Joy and Rose were alone. The house seemed . . . bare, soulless . . . without Papa. Joy wondered how her mama would ever be able to sleep in their bed again without Papa. She couldn't help but remember the long nights without Grant.

Mother and daughter sat close together before the fire and Rose began to ask Joy about Corinth, the lodge, and the girls they had helped escape. She asked about Joy and Uli's hopes to establish something larger and more effective in Denver. She listened carefully as Joy described the ideas she and Uli had discussed.

"We will need a home, perhaps two, with enough bedrooms to accommodate the girls as they leave their old lives. It will be difficult for them to envision a hopeful future—not just to escape those who kept them in bondage, but to also escape the memories and the shame."

"I will seek some mature women who know God's Word and who can mother these girls, lead them in Bible study, and help them to see themselves the way God sees them when Jesus covers not just our sin but our shame also."

"And businesses. The girls will need new skills and honest employment if they are to truly leave their old lives. We will certainly open the fine furnishings shop first. Then perhaps a small café, a sewing school, and dress and millinery shops, places of training first and then gainful employment. Uli has suggested that we could even solicit scholarships to send those with aptitude and desire to business school, nursing programs, even teaching . . ."

"In even the most basic of decisions these women may require gentle encouragement and support. After all, choice is something that was taken from them entirely. It is a freedom they have not exercised in some time."

She finally stopped and looked at Rose. "So much to do, Mama. I know how to run a business, and I believe we can turn profits on every one of our ventures, but even with a profit, we will need to raise more money than I have. The need is very great. Mrs. Van der Pol and her friends, like Grace Minton, will certainly assist us, but it will be a large work, so much more than I can afford and manage on my own. And . . . we will face terrible opposition from some corners."

"Come spring in Corinth I hope to find a way to communicate with the girls in the houses. That may be the most dangerous part. We know this 'Dean Morgan' and his hired thugs may retaliate if they find us out." Her expression darkened. "If God would grant me this, I would hope to see those houses where such evil is practiced closed down forever."

"So there are significant risks . . . and not merely to the money you have invested." Rose searched her daughter's face.

Joy leaned forward and whispered, "Yes, so we must be careful but also prepared. Not to strike back, for that is not God's way. But as Jesus said, we must be 'wise as serpents and harmless as doves.'"

She took a deep breath and made the decision to confide in her mother. Trembling, she revealed the dream she'd had and the intricate plan she felt the Lord had led her to formulate.

"Are you sure, Joy?" Rose stared soberly at her daughter. "All those details . . . things I don't readily follow . . . and the expense of it. Money you surely need elsewhere?"

Joy bowed her head for a moment. "No, Mama, I can't be *sure,* so I have prepared in the manner I have described to you. But I *believe* the Lord led me to do so. Standing for those defenseless women in Corinth poses great risk and our only defense is the Lord . . . so is the cost of obedience too much? Mustn't I obey him if I feel he has given me guidance?"

Rose took Joy's hand and squeezed it firmly. "Yes, yes you must! I know what it is to hear the Lord tell me to do something daring and dangerous. I am proud—and I know that Papa is proud—that you are careful to obey the Lord, Joy."

Joy looked into the fire. "I can think of no greater honor than to help these girls reclaim their lives and their futures."

She paused. "Mama, you and Papa gave me a legacy of faith—a heritage I am proud to own. Both of you passed it to me as your daughter and to Søren as your son. I have no children of my own . . . yet I am now the holder of that legacy. My faith in the Lord stirs me to pass that great gift on, to give that heritage to spiritual daughters since I have none of my own. I feel that I must, that I *must* give to these girls the hope I have found."

"I almost feel . . ." Her voice tapered off.

Rose leaned toward her. "Yes? What is it, Joy?"

Joy laughed self-consciously. "You may think I'm over-spiritualizing this."

"Try me," Rose smiled back.

"Well." Joy was silent a long moment. "I feel very strongly, Mama. I feel that everything I have gone through, everything I lost, and the things I had to endure and overcome prepared me for a great work for God. A work I can give my all to." She spoke softly, almost in a whisper.

"I have lived through a fiery trial and, by God's grace, have survived. Through that fire, I have tested God and found him faithful, but he has tested me, too—tested my trust in him. I have come full circle, into something that is no longer only yours and Papa's, but my very own."

"I mean, I knew Jesus *before* but now I have found him anew, in a more complete and 'adult' way, perhaps. Now I have my own confidence in him. And in knowing him so dearly, so intimately, I feel that I have received a call on my life. One that I would never have heard, let alone answered . . . before."

She looked at her mother, tears shimmering in her eyes. "I am called to give my life to this work, Mama. No matter what it costs, I must follow this through."

Rose nodded. "I bear witness to that call on you, Joy. And, if you will have me, I will join you. I will come and help mother these young women."

Joy sat up in shock. "Mama! How can you? This is your home— you could never leave this place where you and Papa lived together—where he is buried!"

Shaking her head, Rose declared softly, "Joy, your papa isn't here anymore. I don't want to be alone in this house with only memories. I have fulfilled my purpose here. Now I must follow where my Lord leads me, just as you must."

She smiled wryly. "Joy, you perhaps do not know . . . that I have a little money. My first husband left me well off. Your papa and I have lived simply all these years and the money has only grown. That money will be yours one day—shouldn't we invest it where it will produce eternal dividends?"

"But Mama, you must think ahead. Now that Papa is gone . . . you must not risk so much!"

Rose looked back from her own tears. "Ah, Joy. I suppose it is possible I could lose some or all of my substance, but what is that, in comparison with the legacy we can both hand down to these young women? No, I have had quite a bit of time this last year to pray on where and how I would live after Papa went to heaven. I have only been waiting for the Lord to bring the circumstances to light."

She straightened resolutely. "I will help you buy the homes we need and start the businesses to employ our girls, Joy. What I have is not enough to do all, but God will provide what is lacking."

They clasped hands and Rose vowed, "I am with you, Joy. I am with you heart and soul."

Chapter 63

Joy was still in RiverBend helping her mother sort through her things and make the difficult choices of what to keep and what to give away. Rose had made her mind up to accompany Joy when she returned to Corinth.

In Corinth at the lodge, things were running smoothly enough. On Sunday morning the household dressed and left for church as usual, all except Mei-Xing, of course, and O'Dell. O'Dell, who did not attend church and who usually stayed at the lodge on Sunday mornings, was feeling a bit stifled with the extra responsibility. What he wanted today was some fresh air and breathing room.

He had so perfected his British persona in Corinth that the townspeople had taken him for granted—which is just what he had intended. He carried his shotgun and could be seen bringing back game to the lodge on a daily basis. It was the perfect cover.

As the churchgoers left, he sent Mei-Xing to the third floor and grabbed his shotgun. Blackie whined and scratched at the door so he attached a leash and set out for a walk to clear his head and give the puppy some leash training.

The three men hiding within the trees near the lodge waited until he was out of earshot to try the lodge's back door. It was locked as expected, but one of them gave a nod. The reinforced frame splintered under the repeated impact of a heavy boot.

Once inside, Banner sent Darrow and another man upstairs to search the bedrooms. He remained downstairs and sauntered through the kitchen into the great room. He examined with interest the furnishings and looked for any tell-tale sign that Morgan's flighty "Little Plum Blossom" or the two other girls, Tory and Helen, were hiding or had been hidden within the lodge.

Mei-Xing heard the crash as the kitchen door broke under Darrow's boot. She froze momentarily. Then treading softly to the apartment's door she opened it a crack and heard the clomping of boots marching up the stairs.

With a shudder, she closed the door quietly and scanned the apartment's little sitting room. She had been sipping a hot cup of tea—she dumped it quickly into a house plant near Joy's window. Taking the warm cup with her she pulled open the sofa hiding place and crawled inside. As she tugged the lid closed she heard the two men open the door of the apartment.

"Looks like the women live up here," one man said. He kicked open Marit's door. "Got a baby bed in this 'un."

The other man only grunted and she heard him enter first Breona's and then Joy's room. "One room for each of the three women. No extra beds."

She recognized Darrow's voice immediately and began to tremble. Clamping her hand over her mouth she stilled the whimper that threatened to spill from her. At that moment she felt the lid move above her!

Darrow slouched on the built-in sofa and stared around the apartment looking for clues. All the rooms on the second floor were empty and perfectly arranged, except for the one that the English gent used. The rest were obviously waiting for guests. He snorted. *Like they would have guests this time of year, what with the blizzards and several feet of snow!*

He studied the apartment and tried to figure where they would hide the little China doll . . . because he knew in his very bones that they *were* hiding her. Either that or they had somehow used magic to spirit her off the blasted mountain!

"Toss those beds in there, Bob."

He heard the other man overturning the mattresses and pulling the bedsteads away from the walls. For good measure, Bob pulled out drawers and dumped their contents and opened the wardrobes and pulled the clothes from them, dropping them on the floor and then walking on them.

"Nuthin', Mr. Darrow."

Darrow's eyes narrowed. The only upside to this failure was that Morgan wasn't going to skin *him* with that . . . *look*, that calm yet menacing *look*. No, *Banner* would be on the hot seat for that one.

"Let's go." He and the other man stomped back down the stairs. They stopped again on the second floor and deliberately tossed the beds as they had on the third floor. Most of the wardrobes and dressers were empty, but Darrow had Bob pull out the drawers and drop them on the floor anyway.

When O'Dell returned from his walk—carrying the puppy who had run out of steam an hour ago—the kitchen door was standing ajar, dangling at an odd angle, one bent hinge ripped from the splintered frame. Choking on curses of self-recrimination and worry, he set the dog down outside and cocked the shotgun he carried.

Blackie, anxious to be inside, pushed at his legs. O'Dell, not unkindly, used his foot to firmly hold him back. He shot a cursory look around the kitchen then opened the pantry and nudged the pup inside. The great room seemed undisturbed.

With trepidation he mounted the stairs, stopping on the second floor landing to listen carefully. He heard nothing but the creaking and popping of the house in the cold air.

Silent as a cat, he crept up the stairs to the attic apartment. Here he found destruction—broken chairs and vases, a potted plant and its soil strewn across the carpet. The three bedrooms, wrecked.

Standing in the middle of the sitting room he whispered, "Mei-Xing! It's O'Dell."

Nothing.

A cold hand gripped his heart.

He was about to open the hiding spot himself when the lid slowly rose. He yanked it open and lifted her out and then put an arm about her shaking shoulders. "It's all right, little one. They're gone."

Mei-Xing looked around at the destruction and then up at O'Dell with brimming eyes. "It was Darrow. And two other men." She bowed her head. "This is my fault. All I do is bring ruin wherever I go."

O'Dell emphatically shook his head. "No, you're wrong. This is *my* fault. I allowed myself to become complacent and I broke my own rule. I left you alone."

He held her at arm's length and glared fiercely into her face. "It is *not* your fault that those . . . men are evil. Joy is right. We can't fix the evil in this world—we can only fight it when it is in front of us."

As Mei-Xing sobbed on his chest, O'Dell ran his hand through his hair in frustration. "By God, I am near ready to go to war over this little town."

When the others returned from church O'Dell met them and gave them the sobering news, not sparing the blame for his own actions. "This is my fault and my responsibility. I apologize to all of you, but particularly to Mei-Xing for the fright this gave her. Breona and Marit, I am so sorry about your rooms and your things."

He had already re-hinged and closed the kitchen door to keep the cold out, although it would no longer latch or lock. It was obvious that both the door and the frame would need to be replaced.

"I let my guard down," O'Dell said through gritted teeth.

"Looks like we all did," Billy answered gravely. "We started thinking they weren't watching us no more. Well, they are."

Flinty just set his lips together firmly in a way that said he agreed with O'Dell—the blame lay with him. But the old man did not utter a word of recrimination. He and Wheatley set out for his shop to gather what they needed to remake the door.

Breona and Marit went upstairs to survey the damage and there they found Mei-Xing, humming softly, tidying up. She had swept up the broken pottery and potting soil, placed all the drawers back in the dressers, and remade the beds. Not knowing how Breona and Marit wanted their clothes refolded and placed in the drawers or hung in the wardrobes she had simply gathered them and laid them on the beds. In Joy's room, Mei-Xing was carefully doing for Joy what she was not present to do for herself.

Breona remarked to Marit. "Let's be givin' Mei a hand. I'm not wantin' Miss Joy to be coomin' home t' this on top o' all her grievin'."

Chapter 64

Rose Brownlee Thoresen was leaving RiverBend, perhaps for the last time. She had kept that thought from intruding as she and Joy sorted her household and she made herself choose what to keep and what to give away. Søren's youngest son, Jon, and his fiancée would be marrying in the fall. Rose had offered the house for them to live in and they had gratefully accepted.

Rose and Joy wrapped and boxed up a few treasures Rose would store in the attic, packed Rose's trunks, and waited that morning for Søren to take them to the train. But when they were in the wagon, Rose looked back and, with great gulping sobs began to truly say goodbye. Joy held her mother's hand tightly and she and Søren resolutely set their faces forward, allowing Rose the dignity of her grief.

In Denver, Emily Van der Pol met them and took them to her home. They were to spend two nights with her so that they could meet with the small group of women Emily had assembled. She assured Joy that the women were honor-bound to keep her confidences.

"I want to let you know that we sent Tory and Helen to dear and trusted friends in Philadelphia." Emily told them. "Sadly, Helen passed away not long after they arrived."

Joy and Rose received her announcement soberly. The news was not unexpected to Joy, and she knew Tory would grieve for her friend. "And Tory?"

"She is settling in. We have found a place for her with two older women, sisters, both widows and well off. They have apprenticed Tory—with her approval, of course—with one of the finest clothiers in their city. A personal friend of theirs, I might add. Tory, with her strong sense of style and elegance, may do well there."

The following afternoon Joy and Rose accompanied Emily to Grace Minton's home where they took lunch with seven distinguished-looking women. After lunch, Joy shared about the work they were doing in Corinth and the ideas she and Uli had formed. When she finished she answered questions. Then Joy asked Rose to address the group.

Rose engaged frankly with the women, some her age, but most a few years younger. "As you have no doubt already noted, my daughter is very committed to helping women escape from prostitution, a life of . . . shall we call it what it often is? A life of slavery. A life in which a woman's body is not her own but is subject to the whims and debasing acts of any man with money."

"For many of these women, prostitution was a 'choice' between starvation and daily bread, homelessness and the very roof over their head. I have often thought *there but for the grace of God go I.*" She smiled, but her smile was pained.

"We are here today to talk about the practical aspects of funding a home where a few of these women can find refuge, forgiveness, and hope for the future. Joy has provided you with the details, and I . . . I have committed to using my own funds to buy such a house."

As the eight women heard this, they looked on Rose with new respect.

"My purpose today is to challenge your group. Will you do no less than I?" She looked at each of them in turn. "I know that some of you are blessed as I am to have your own money. Perhaps, for some of you, your husband holds the purse strings, which makes helping our work financially a bit more difficult. However, what I propose is this: Every dollar *we* raise toward these endeavors you, as a group, will challenge yourselves to match."

Several of the women began to whisper together; one or two asked additional questions. For a few minutes the group lapsed into silence and then Grace spoke.

"Mrs. Thoresen, Miss Thoresen, would you be so kind as to excuse us for a few minutes? We would like to discuss this and pray over your proposal. Perhaps you would enjoy seeing our small collection of paintings in the library?"

Joy and Rose went to the library to wait. After 30 minutes a maid brought them tea. Another 30 minutes went by before Emily came into the room, smiling.

"Would you please rejoin us?"

When they returned to the parlor, Joy could not help but notice the smiling accord of the women waiting for them. Grace spoke for the little group.

"We have been praying for months—ever since Emily called on us to help safely remove Tory and Helen from Corinth." She laughed a little. "I will admit that was more excitement than I perhaps wish to experience on a regular basis, but . . ." and here her face crumpled and she struggled for composure. "When we realized what we had saved them from, it has been our fervent prayer that the Lord would show us how to enter more fully into this work. You have provided that guidance today."

She looked around the room to approving nods and turned back to Rose and Joy. "We accept your challenge."

That evening Emily, Rose, and Joy had just finished dinner and were discussing in what areas of the city to look for a house when the door to the parlor opened and a gentleman with graying hair entered. As the three of them stood to greet him Joy noticed how flushed Emily became.

"Ah, there you are, my dear. I apologize; I did not realize we had guests," the man greeted her affably. And then he caught sight of Joy and halted as though thunderstruck.

She, too, froze for a moment but stared directly into his disquieted eyes. She knew him. He was the man who had so brazenly looked her over and tipped his hat to her at the little Corinth station. She remembered him—and she knew that he recognized her.

Emily made awkward introductions. "I believed you would be out of town one more night, Randolph. My friends are on their way in the morning, but we have had . . . a delightful visit."

Mumbling hurried pleasantries, Emily's husband retreated from the room. Emily took a deep breath, and Joy and Rose glimpsed the pain Emily usually managed with such dignity, that of an unfaithful marriage. She turned to them.

"Randolph was not really himself just now. He seemed quite . . . undone, particularly when meeting you, Joy." She looked down, red with shame. "Perhaps you have encountered him before?"

Joy nodded. "I'm sorry, Emily. I have. And I am certain he recognized me . . . from Corinth."

Emily shook her head in regret. "I had not anticipated that he would be home early. Well, I have always placed my many problems in the Lord's hands, especially those concerning Randolph. I must trust that my God is orchestrating things to his good pleasure." She sighed and looked at Joy and Rose frankly. "Sooner or later he will know what I have undertaken in partnership with you."

She added somewhat to herself, "Sooner or later there will be a confrontation and all the lies will be laid bare. God grant me the strength on that day to do what I must."

Chapter 65

April 1909

Joy and Rose boarded the narrow-gauge D&RGW to Corinth the following morning. As they headed toward the mountains Rose exulted over the views. Joy never tired of the splendor rising before them. For a long time they watched in companionable silence as the train chugged toward the mountains and then began its climb into them.

Joy and Rose arrived late afternoon in Corinth. While spring was making inroads upon the prairies and even around Denver City, Corinth lagged behind. They bundled themselves against the chill before leaving the train and found Billy and Marit selling breads and hot coffee to their fellow travelers.

Marit embraced Joy and shyly greeted Rose. Billy, who had met Rose many times in Omaha, smiled at her with affection. "I'm mighty sorry for your loss, Mrs. Thoresen," he added softly.

Rose nodded her thanks, and then Billy offered, "Shall I run back to the lodge and get the buggy?"

"Just the wagon, Billy. Mother has a number of trunks, and we are both accustomed to riding in a wagon." She turned back to Marit. "How is little Will? I have missed him! And Breona? Mr. Wheatley? Is he well? Oh, how I've missed all of you."

She longed for Little Blackie and his affections. Perhaps she would even be pleased to see O'Dell again.

Several days later, sometime after midnight, Mr. Wheatley awoke to a soft knocking at the back door. He roused Billy and they stepped into the kitchen and opened the newly repaired door a crack. Two figures huddled on the doorstep in the dark.

"Miss Joy?" Joy awoke with a start, slightly disoriented. It took her a moment to recall where she was. She was back in her room in the lodge in Corinth. Breona, Marit, baby Will, and Mei-Xing were in the apartment with her. Joy had installed Rose in one of the guest rooms on the second floor. Little Blackie, snuggled against her feet, raised his head toward the door.

Then she heard the knocking again. "Miss Joy?" It was Billy.

Feeling that she was reliving other nights, Joy walked into their little sitting room and saw Mei-Xing's wide-awake eyes watching her. Joy cracked the door.

"It's happened again, miss. Some girls are downstairs in the kitchen."

When Joy entered the kitchen she found the girls standing by the back door. One looked ready to bolt at the first sign of trouble. They were both shaking with cold and covered in only the flimsiest of dresses.

"Hello," she greeted them softly. "Would you like something warm to drink?"

The nervous one studied her. Finally she nodded.

"Billy, please find some blankets? I will stoke up the fire. Our guests are very cold."

As Joy was adding fuel to the stove, Rose entered the kitchen. She took in the situation immediately. "Please. Come rest yourselves at the table, girls." She held out an arm and gestured them further into the room.

Both of the girls were incredibly young, perhaps only 13 or 14 years old. While their clothes were made of expensive fabrics cut in recent fashions, the girls' bosoms scarcely filled out the low-cut bodices. Their faces were garishly painted. One girl's hair was dirty blonde; the other's was a plain brown, both pinned up in a style beyond their years. They looked like children playing dress-up in their mother's closet.

As they sat down Rose gently patted the blonde on the shoulder. The girl yelped in pain and swatted Rose's hand aside.

"I'm so sorry," Rose apologized. "I-I didn't know . . . are you hurt?"

"It's nuthin'," the girl shot back defiantly. She sent a concerned glance at the brown-haired girl who sat in a stupor, shivering and glassy-eyed.

Joy set mugs of tea before both of them. The blonde wrapped her hands around the warm mug and blew into the cup, anxious to sip on it. The other girl stared straight ahead, oblivious to her surroundings. After a moment, the blonde took the other girl's hands and gently placed them around the mug.

Joy sat down across from the blonde girl. "I'm Joy. This is my mother, Rose. What is your name?" Rose came around to Joy's side of the table and sat down next to her."

The young woman examined Joy for several minutes. "They call me Ruby."

"It's nice to meet you, Ruby," Joy replied. "What is your friend's name?

Ruby's hardness cracked a little. "Beth. She's not . . . in a good way."

"I can see that," Joy answered carefully. "What can we do to help her?"

Ruby looked down and when she looked back up, her eyes flashed with a wild, angry light. "Give me a gun. Give me a gun so I can *shoot* that son of a bi—" She bit off the curse words and then snarled, "That *monster*, Banner."

Joy sat back in her chair in shock. Billy and Mr. Wheatley shifted uneasily where they were standing near the door.

"You would like to . . . shoot Banner?"

"Jest try me!" Ruby shouted. Her eyes were almost frantic.

Joy waited until Ruby calmed a little. "Can you tell me why, Ruby?" She steeled herself to hear what Ruby had to say and she saw her mama, eyes wide, clutch the edge of the table.

"What he done to *her*, fer starters." She spat out the words, pointing at Beth and, as suddenly as her anger had flared, it died away. She whispered sadly, "What he done to me . . . and others."

Joy didn't know what to say or do. She turned to Rose, who shook her head wordlessly.

Oh Lord, please tell me what to do! Joy prayed silently. She looked at Billy and Mr. Wheatley. Billy gestured outside and Joy nodded. They slid out the door. He and Mr. Wheatley would hide out in the stable until it was light enough to cover the girls' tracks.

"Can you . . . can you tell me what Banner did to you, Ruby?" Joy kept her voice as calm and soft as she could manage.

"Wouldn't ya rather see?" Ruby yanked the bodice of her dress from her shoulder. Her shoulder and arm were covered with bite marks, most of them horribly swollen and bruised, at least two oozing blood where the bites had broken the skin.

Rose gasped and put both of her hands to her mouth. Joy, dreading and sensing something this awful, had willed herself not to flinch. If Beth were as badly abused, it would explain why she was traumatized.

She looked Ruby in the face for a long moment. "I'm glad you and Beth came to us, Ruby, and I'm so sorry you've been ill-treated.

Would you allow us to draw you a hot bath and find you some warm, comfortable clothes?"

Ruby looked stunned by the offer of simple kindness. Joy continued. "We have some salve that will help with the pain. Then we'll tuck you into bed so that you can get a good rest. Tomorrow we will figure out how to help you get off this mountain."

Joy crawled into her bed again just after sunrise but could not sleep. How had Ruby known to come to the lodge for sanctuary? Should they bring in Sheriff Wyndom and show him the girls' wounds? Ruby had . . . *fire*. She was a survivor, but . . . Beth was locked in a world of her own for now.

When Joy did see Ruby and Beth late in the morning, Beth was still sleeping so soundly Joy wondered if she would ever wake. Ruby, though, was up and prowling about, needing to know the "lay of the land" and where the doors were. Just in case.

After she had eaten hungrily she looked directly at Joy. "Can you get us to somewheres better'n Corinth? I grewed up in these mountains . . . sure like t' get far away."

Joy studied her for a moment. "There may be a way." She took a breath and then asked, "Would it be all right with you if I asked you some questions? If you would rather not answer, that is fine."

The girl, pale and childish-looking now that her face was washed of the paint she had worn, just shrugged.

"Some of the . . . working girls . . . here in Corinth . . ." Joy fidgeted trying to find the words.

"What about 'em?"

"Some of them were lured to Denver by newspaper ads for honest work, and then they were abducted." Joy just said it straight out, but Ruby only nodded, not shocked.

"Heared som'thin' 'bout that," she admitted.

"That isn't how you . . . started working?" Joy reddened.

Ruby's sardonic laugh echoed through the kitchen. "Mebbe not the 'zact same way." She rocked her chair on its back legs and then let it drop with a bang. "M'stepfather. He was always bashin' me 'round. When m' mam died, he started lookin' at me wrong, too. Said I's 'evil' fer temptin' him. One day he bashes me on th' head an' I wakes up in Miz Cleary's house. Guess he sold me there."

Joy's mouth opened but she could not speak. She thought of her papa and the great care he had taken for her life, for her safety, happiness, and nurture.

Ruby had talked on, oblivious to Joy's discomfiture. "—Not to the club, o'course. Th' girls gotta be extry special fer that. You know. R'fined an' s'phisticated-like."

Ruby had told her, with a touch of pride, "I grewed up in these mountains—know all them trails. 'Stead a headin' down on foot an' freezin' t' death, I tore off a piece o' Beth's dress and snagged it up on a bush back b'hind the station where one o' the trails starts. Then we hot-footed it over here." She laughed. "Bet that old fool Darrow will be runnin' down thet trail t'day."

Ruby hugged herself. "We been at th' house six months, I guess. They only keeps new girls there 'bout that long. When one's 'bout played out an' they're ready t' ship her off t' Denver, that's when they let . . . Banner hev 'er."

"And he . . . they let him do whatever he wants?"

Ruby just gave Joy a dark, knowing sneer.

O'Dell interviewed Ruby also. He showed her some sketches sent from the Boston Pinkerton office. The sketches were of five missing women who had answered ads and then disappeared when they arrived in Denver. The lead agent had compiled the sketches using descriptions or photographs provided by family members.

Ruby studied each one carefully. "That 'un looks a bit like Cookie. That's what they call her, but I think she said her real name was Gretchen. No, Gretl, like 'Hansel and Gretl.'"

O'Dell grinned but it wasn't a pleasant grin. "Gretl Plüff. She went missing 18 months ago. You said you've been at the house six months and that is how long they usually keep the girls there?"

"Yes sir." Ruby answered O'Dell carefully, intimidated by his wolf-like grin. "But they kept her on t' cook, see? Cookie. She's a better cook than a whore."

O'Dell and Joy exchanged looks. O'Dell's face was implacable; Joy was near tears.

Later that evening Joy asked Ruby the question that had kept her awake. "How did you know to come here? How did you know we would help?"

The girl pursed her lips. "Guess it don't make no difference. Heard that pig Banner and his lap dog Darrow talkin' 'bout you. You, 'specially, miss. Said they knew you helped those high-dollar girls. Jest couldn't figure how." She laughed harshly. "Banner's got it bad 'bout you, lady."

Joy shivered. They weren't fooling Banner after all.

Well, that changes things, she thought. *That . . . and the date . . .* Joy sought out the calendar on the kitchen wall. *April 14.*

Joy nodded. "We're going to take you off this mountain. Soon. Within the week."

"In front o' Banner's men?"

"Yes. Right out in the open." Joy shivered, but set her mind resolutely.

This time it was Ruby who trembled. "You'll take care o' Beth?"

"Yes. And you, too."

"'Cause she cain't take what he done t' her again." She wrapped her arms around herself. "Not sure I can neither."

The following day, in the late morning, Joy called a meeting with O'Dell and her staff. She didn't mince words.

"I sent Arnie and Anna a wire this morning and am waiting for their reply. I have asked them to take in Ruby and Beth. As soon as they can meet us in Denver, we will take the girls down on the train."

"And you plan on hiding them how?" O'Dell was irritated and worried.

"That's the thing, Mr. O'Dell. I don't plan to hide them. Sheriff Wyndom and I will escort them to Denver. I will ask Domingo and Gustavo to set up here at the lodge while we are gone."

The resentment and anger toward Banner and men like him smoldered in her eyes. "Ruby is 14 years old. Beth is 13. They have been beaten, bitten, starved, and savaged."

She took a deep breath. "We don't hide any longer."

She looked around the room and saw the slowly nodding heads. It was Breona, her feisty Irish friend, still stubbornly resisting God's gift of salvation, who answered firmly: "Amen t' that."

O'Dell, however, stomped off in disgust. Joy was refusing to allow him to come on the train with them. "Can't you see? It is more important for you to maintain your guise as a guest here and protect the lodge while we are gone."

O'Dell did see, but he didn't like it. He chewed the stump of a cigar and pondered when he needed to call in reinforcements and how long it would take them to mobilize.

He would send immediate updates to Parsons in Chicago and Groman in Omaha, but would have to call on the Denver office for men when the time came. He scribbled out the wire's contents and walked it over to be sent.

After the meeting, Billy and Joy took the lodge's buggy to the sheriff's office. She met briefly with him and later that day he paid a visit to the lodge.

Beth and Ruby were staying in the room next to Rose. Beth had finally awakened and eaten a little. Rose stayed with the girls at all times, hoping to draw Beth out of the stupor she so quickly lapsed into.

Mei-Xing helped Rose with the girls, too. For some reason, she was drawn to Rose and Joy found them talking earnestly several evenings. Once Joy saw Rose lay her hand on Mei-Xing's forehead and caress the girl tenderly. Mei-Xing had closed her eyes, tears running down her face as Rose simply loved on her.

Joy explained to Ruby and Beth that the sheriff would come and talk to them. She asked Ruby if she minded showing him the bite marks on her arms and shoulders. Ruby shrugged.

When Wyndom arrived, he was accompanied by a young man wearing a deputy badge. Joy nodded to both of them. "Ruby and Beth are both children. Ruby will show you some of what Banner did to her two nights ago."

When they returned downstairs from meeting with the girls, Wyndom was gray and sober. Joy lost no time pressing her advantage. "This is your opportunity, *Sheriff* Wyndom, to do the right thing. I am taking those girls down to Denver in a few days. I expect you to provide an escort."

Wyndom sighed in defeat. "You win, Miss Thoresen. I'll do it." He turned to the young deputy. "Just so you know, Luke here is my nephew, outta St. Louis. Corinth can't afford any deputies, but I am permitted to deputize volunteers. He's backing me up on a volunteer basis."

"I'm glad you are here, Luke," Joy said with sincerity.

"Yes'm. Thank you. Banner's men have been up and down the back trails searchin' for those girls. I heard they found a piece of one of the girl's dresses snagged up on a bush." His eyes twinkled. "Heard they ain't had any luck, though."

The corners of Wyndom's mouth turned down. "It's not tomorrow or when we take those girls down the mountain I'm worried about. We'll only be gone maybe eight hours. It's what happens after you poke that snake with a stick that has me concerned."

Joy nodded. But she knew they could not turn aside.

Chapter 66

At their usual morning devotions Rose asked Joy, "Have you studied the new birth yet, Joy?"

Joy stared at Rose for a long moment. "I haven't, Mama! I don't know why I haven't thought to do so." With all the responsibilities that preoccupied her mind, she *did* know, and gratefully turned the morning study over to her mother.

Rose smiled at the faces around the table. "I think it is wonderful that this house commences each day with prayer and study in God's word. But just as every journey has a beginning, a starting point, each person's spiritual journey also must have a beginning, a starting point."

"You see, the Bible tells us that even as we are physically born, we must also be spiritually born. Jesus called it being 'born again.' He said until we are born again we cannot see his kingdom—*but*, after we are born again we become not just part of his kingdom but part of his family also."

"If you have been struggling to understand the things in the Bible, I venture to say it is because you have not yet experienced that spiritual birth. I remember how much I wanted to know God and to know about him, and how hard it was—until I received that spiritual birth."

Attentive eyes watched Rose and she warmed to her message. Breona's brow was furrowed deeply as she listened. Mei-Xing sat impassive, eyes cast down.

Rose continued, "The most precious thing about this new birth is that it is free. Jesus offers it to anyone who desires it. And, oh! What a great thing it is! Let me read you something about it." Rose opened her Bible and began to read aloud:

> *Therefore if any man be in Christ,*
> *he is a new creature: old things are passed away;*
> *behold, all things are become new*
> *For he hath made him to be sin for us,*
> *who knew no sin;*
> *that we might be made*
> *the righteousness of God in him*

Rose looked at each person around the table again. "Let me tell you in plain language what this passage says. First, it says, 'if anyone, man or woman, *be in Christ.*' To 'be in Christ' is to enter his kingdom and his family. Second it says, if you *are* in Christ, you are *a new creature.*"

Rose looked down for a moment. "Third, it tells us *old things are passed away; behold, all things are become new.* Please hear what God is saying to us, to all of us. If we bring our lives to Jesus, our sad, broken, even ruined lives, he tells us that we become *new* creatures. Not only that, but our old lives pass away. All things—*all things*—become new in him."

She looked intimately at each person around the table. "We get to start over, brand new, clean, forgiven, and fresh. All Jesus asks is that we confess him as the Lord of our lives. It is as simple as this," and Rose read aloud:

> *. . . if thou shalt confess with thy mouth the Lord Jesus,*
> *and shalt believe in thine heart*
> *that God hath raised him from the dead,*
> *thou shalt be saved.*
> *For with the heart man believeth unto righteousness;*
> *and with the mouth confession is made unto salvation.*
> *For the scripture saith,*
> *Whosoever believeth on him shall not be ashamed*

"Shame is a horrible thing to live with. Sometimes shame comes from what *we* have chosen to do. Sometimes it comes from what others have done to us. But Jesus tells us *whoever believes on him*—Jesus—*shall not be ashamed.*"

Joy watched in awe as hungry hearts received the simple words Rose spoke. *Thank you, Lord, for bringing my Mama to help! O God, you knew my limitations and brought her to fill up what I lack and what we so desperately need.*

Heads bowed and hearts prayed. Tears flowed. And so did forgiveness and grace.

Chapter 67

Like a spring wound tighter and tighter, the tension heightened over the next five days. Then Joy received the anticipated wire: *Arriving Denver Wednesday.*

Tomorrow.

Joy surveyed sober faces around the dinner table that evening. "Sheriff Wyndom and I will take Ruby and Beth to Denver tomorrow. Mr. Wheatley, I would like you to drive us to the train in the buggy. Billy, I would like you to accompany us onto the train. I will have you buy a ticket, but as soon as the train moves past the platform, please step off and come straight back."

Beth gripped Rose's hand. Ruby stoically studied her plate. Mei-Xing, as usual, remained quiet but looked a question at Joy.

Joy felt for the young woman. "Mei-Xing, from what Tory told us, Banner and Darrow's employer considers you to be a much more valuable 'commodity,' and your, er, departure still has them very incensed. Since they searched the house, they think you are already safely away. I wouldn't want to show them otherwise."

She gave the girl a sorrowful smile. "We are, as Sheriff Wyndom called it, 'poking the snake with a stick.' We don't know what will happen tomorrow, but I have a strong sense that you are actually safer here for now."

Mei-Xing seemed to accept Joy's answer with more peace than Joy expected. "It's all right, Miss Thoresen. I . . . I like it here. With all of you." She looked at Rose who took her hand and held it. "I have nowhere else to go," she added softly.

The following morning Joy, Ruby, and Beth climbed into the lodge's small covered buggy. They took no luggage. Billy had already walked to the siding and purchased two tickets to Denver. Flinty joined him and purchased a single ticket. Then they sauntered back to Flinty's smithy to wait for the buggy to arrive.

The usual two watchers at the siding had grown to three and were immediately alert. As Mr. Wheatley pulled the buggy up to the siding, Sheriff Wyndom and his nephew Luke were just purchasing two tickets.

Five minutes still remained before the train was scheduled to depart. Joy and the girls would wait, concealed in the buggy, until the conductor signaled the train's imminent departure. Five minutes later the man stepped out onto the siding, puzzled that five ticket holders had not boarded nor were nearby to board.

Wyndom nodded toward the buggy, strode up to the siding, and handed two tickets to the conductors. Billy walked up just then and handed him three. Both men headed over to the buggy where Joy, Ruby, and Beth were climbing down. Joy saw one of the watchers nudge another and then the three of them jumped to their feet.

"Back off, boys," Wyndom's rifle was out and pointed in their direction. Luke mirrored his uncle's stance. Billy hustled the three women onto the train.

As the sheriff turned to board the train he roughly addressed the shocked conductor. "If you know what's good for you, you'll get this train moving. Now."

Wyndom stood between two cars, rifle still pointed at the watchers, while Luke began backing away.

The train sent out its shrill wail and eased away from the Corinth siding. Luke and Mr. Wheatley with the buggy hustled back to the lodge. Down the track and out of sight, Billy Evans dropped off the train's last car and quickly made his way back to the lodge also.

Chapter 68

Joy and Sheriff Wyndom returned late that afternoon—accompanied by Arnie Thoresen.

Marit put together a celebration dinner of sorts, and Wyndom and Luke joined them. Rose gave Arnie a long and heartfelt embrace before demanding to know why he was not with Anna and the girls on the way back to Omaha.

"Brought one of Groman's Pinkerton men with me," Arnie explained. "He's seeing they get back safely. Groman sent his latest report with me." He handed Joy a thick envelope. "And I also brought this, Cousin Joy."

Joy eyed the second envelope with relief. "Thank you, Arnie."

"I knew you would want it as soon as it was available."

Arnie turned to O'Dell and Wyndom. "Will this escapade push Banner to move against us?"

"Us, Arnie?" Joy asked.

"I'm here and I'm not going anywhere until this is resolved. Groman is willing to send men, but why don't we get the Denver office involved instead?" Arnie directed this question to O'Dell.

"It's time," O'Dell agreed. "You have all of the evidence the Omaha office has dug up on Morgan and we have Ruby's identification of Gretl Plüff. I suggest you and I head down the mountain tomorrow, meet with Beau Bickle, and get some reinforcements up here, pronto."

He eyed Wyndom and Luke. "I don't think Banner will wait long to hit back. That man has a short fuse."

Wyndom nodded in agreement. "If you're headed down tomorrow, we'll make a point of walking the lodge perimeter all day. You've got some good men here, but a show of force is a nice deterrent." He chuckled shrewdly.

That evening O'Dell and Arnie Thoresen walked the property line around the lodge. The new moon provided little light for their reconnaissance.

As they cautiously made their way through the trees, Arnie remarked, "O'Dell, I like you. You're a good man to have around right now and I want you to know I appreciate you."

Arnie's statement was patently an overture to something else. O'Dell stopped and faced him. "Thanks, I think. Is there something you're working your way up to?"

Arnie nodded. "Can't help but notice how you look at my cousin."

O'Dell blew out a frustrated breath. "I've tried not to, believe me."

"She's a good woman, O'Dell, but she has been through a lot, probably more than you know. I don't want to see her hurt again and . . ." Arnie's words trailed off.

"And I'm not the kind of man she should be with?" O'Dell asked. Arnie detected a hint of anger in his question.

"As I said, you are a good man, O'Dell. But you've heard Joy say she is a Christian. I haven't heard you say the same."

O'Dell was quiet several moments. "Well, you're right. I'm not much of a Christian. Haven't been to church since I was a kid."

"O'Dell, church is important, but church isn't really what we mean. For a Bible-believing person, being a Christian is much more than a church affiliation or attending church—it is a relationship with God through Jesus. It's a living, daily, walk with him."

O'Dell sighed. "It means so much?" he finally asked.

Arnie prayed for the right words. "Yes, it does. Jesus is the foundation of our lives—of Joy's life. He is the one who led her here. You heard what she said about her plans, her dream? She is not talking about a social program to help girls—she's talking about Jesus helping them, changing and healing them on the inside so that they can walk free from the life they were either forced into or chose willingly."

O'Dell stood in silence.

Arnie soldiered on. "You said that I thought you weren't the kind of man she should be with. I want you to know that perfect behavior isn't my concern. I think, given your line of work, that you would understand how 'good' people make mistakes or can sometimes get caught up in unsavory or disreputable events. Even though Joy is a Christian, she is not perfect. You don't know everything about her, but she would be the first person to tell you so."

"I may know more than you think," O'Dell said quietly. He indicated the benches near the overlook and they sat down. O'Dell rested his shotgun across his lap and slid a cigar from his breast pocket. As he lit it and puffed on it to make it draw, he stared out into the dark valley.

Finally he spoke, "Arnie, if it is all right with you, I'd like to tell you a story."

Arnie glanced at O'Dell. "All right. I'm listening."

He waited until O'Dell spoke again.

"I've been with Pinkerton for 12 years. Started out in Chicago and it's still my home office. As I came up through the Pinkerton ranks, my bosses noticed that I had a mind and an aptitude for a certain line of investigation. Turns out that I am pretty good at solving kidnapping and missing persons cases."

"After a few years with the agency, those were the only cases Pinkerton assigned to me. Other Pinkerton offices began calling on me to advise on their missing persons cases, especially the high-profile ones where leads had gone cold."

Arnie looked at O'Dell with new-found respect. "That's a valuable and honorable service, O'Dell, finding lost people."

O'Dell smiled crookedly. "Yeah, well, the cases I get called on these days are the toughest ones. Sadly, on most of those I don't have the luxury of giving good news to the client." He looked off into the distance. "Maybe nine out of ten cases I work don't end well."

Arnie frowned as he took that in and he and O'Dell sat in companionable silence for several more minutes. "It must be difficult to give bad news to people."

"It is. Rips your heart out, to tell you the truth. You might wonder why I keep doing it, but it's that *one time*, the one case where the police or other Pinkerton agents have given up, maybe the family has given up hope, too. It's that one case where, against the odds, I find a child that's been abducted or a daughter who has gone missing . . . and I can give good news to a family. I guess that's what keeps me doing this."

He puffed furiously for a minute. "Anyway, I said I wanted to tell you a story."

Arnie nodded. "I'd like to hear it."

"All right, then. Starting about two years ago, Pinkerton offices in the east began receiving requests to find young girls who had disappeared. It was a small number, but one of our agents noticed a possible pattern to the disappearances. The missing women were typically poor immigrants. What the women who disappeared had in common was that they answered a same or similar advertisement to come work in Denver, Colorado."

Arnie sat up. "That's what Uli and David and their 'underground' network had discovered, too. The two girls they spirited away told them how they had been tricked."

"Yes. Being fairly new to America and without means to support themselves, you can understand that the women who answered the ads were desperate for work. The reports we received were that the missing girls had been untruthful with their prospective employers. They had told them that they had no family because the employer seemed to indicate that an applicant without family ties back east was more likely to be hired."

"We interviewed one girl who answered such an advertisement. She arrived in Denver, realized the danger, and managed to escape from the man sent to pick her up. She ran to a church and the folks there helped her get back to her sister in Boston—her only remaining family. She reported her experience to the police. They didn't expend much effort on a poor immigrant woman's report, but they did pass the girl off to us. The Pinkerton Agency was working on four disappearances in three separate states."

"Like I said, one of our agents saw the pattern and cross checked the cases against how long the ads had been running. That's when we realized that *many* girls had probably gone missing. However, without families to report their disappearances, we could only guess at the number. It was those few women who had a friend or family member who sought us out."

"Anyway, I was sent to Boston to interview the girl I just spoke of, and while I was there I met a man who was also looking for someone." O'Dell took a breath and let it out slowly. "This . . . is the part of the story I want you to hear."

"He walked into the Boston Pinkerton office one morning. At first blush, the Boston office added him into the small group of clients in our other case. But, upon deeper investigation, it turns out that his is an entirely separate missing persons case."

"Who is he looking for?" Arnie asked.

"He, too, is looking for a woman."

"What woman?"

"That's the problem. He doesn't know."

Arnie snorted. "What?"

O'Dell drew on his cigar. "Now let me tell you *his* story."

"He calls himself Branch. His first memories were as he recovered from a severe brain fever. He has absolutely no memories from before this. He woke up one morning and knew nothing about his life."

"However, when he sleeps, he dreams, and his dreams are always about a woman, the same woman. He sees her but cannot remember her name."

Arnie interrupted, "What does this woman look like? Young, old? Coloring?"

"She is young, with long, flowing hair. He says that she calls to him, 'Branch, Branch' and he tries to call back to her or go to her—but he cannot remember her name. And then he wakes up."

Arnie stared at the red glow of O'Dell's cigar. "You said he recovered from a brain fever. Surely you know where? Someone must know him there?"

"Yes, well, it's more complicated than that. You see, he awoke in a little fishing hamlet. I interviewed the crew from a whaler out of that village. They say they plucked him from the sea one morning. He was barely alive—his arm was tangled in a life preserver—and he had been in the frigid water for hours. They took him aboard and back to their village where they treated his wounds. He battled a fever and lingered half-way between life and death for several weeks. When he recovered, he had no memories. None."

Arnie grew very still. "You said you wanted to tell *me* this man's story."

"Yes."

"You must have felt . . . there was some reason for telling me."

O'Dell sighed. "Yes, I believe so."

Arnie tried to swallow; his throat had gone dry. "Where is this little fishing town, O'Dell?"

"On a small island off the southeastern tip of Nova Scotia. It is a remote place, and the people there are simple folks, not much in touch with the rest of the world. Often not up with current events."

Arnie shuddered. His eyes misted over. "O'Dell, when did this happen? When did those fishermen find this man in the water?"

O'Dell sighed again. "A year ago last fall."

"And he has been looking for this woman ever since . . ."

"Yes."

Arnie wiped his hand across his face and was quiet for a long moment. Finally he asked, "Where is this man . . . Branch . . . right now?"

"He was in Chicago last I saw him."

Arnie rested his shaggy head in his hand for a long moment. Finally he spoke and his voice was grave. "Not a word to my cousin, O'Dell. Not a word." He stood up. "I need to see this man myself."

O'Dell put out his cigar. "I know. The Chicago office knows where I am. I'll send word to them to send him out to Denver."

Arnie touched the other man on his shoulder. "I'm sorry, friend. I realize now what you have been struggling with."

O'Dell nodded but said nothing. The glow of his cigar burned silently in the dark.

Chapter 69

O'Dell and Arnie left in the morning. Joy expected to see the sheriff and his deputy soon afterwards, but they did not appear. Growing concerned, she had Billy ask Flinty if he could come and keep watch from the second floor with Mr. Wheatley.

Around three o'clock, Mark, the son of one of David's deacons, tapped on the door. Breona let him in and he asked for Joy.

"Miss Joy, we got some trouble. Pastor sent me over t' let you know 'bout it."

"What is it?" Rose came up behind Joy and they both held their breath.

"We're told the sheriff an' his nephew were ambushed last night on their way home. Group o' men with clubs. He an' his nephew managed t' get away but they couldn't get back t' the sheriff's house, so they went t' the pastor's place."

"Are they all right?" Joy began to feel light-headed.

"Sheriff got busted up pretty good," the boy replied soberly. "Miz Kalbørg, she's doctorin' both of 'em. We're keeping it real quiet so no one knows where they are."

So Banner and his men hadn't waited to strike back, and Wyndom and Luke were injured and hiding at David and Uli's. Joy's hand went to her throat.

O'Dell and Arnie stepped off the train and O'Dell set the pace, Arnie close behind him. Several blocks later they entered the Denver Pinkerton office.

"Bickle!" O'Dell forged his way to Beau Bickle's office. "Things are breaking open on our kidnapped girls case."

He introduced Arnie and quickly outlined the events of the last week. "Two very young girls, Ruby and Beth, found their way to the lodge belonging to Arnie's cousin and asked for help. Not in Breezy Point, but a little town west of here—Corinth."

"Arnie's cousin, Joy Thoresen, and the sheriff brought them down from Corinth yesterday and then put them on a train out of the state. Before they left, one of them positively identified Gretl Plüff. She is a girl who has been missing from Boston for 18 months. She is still being held in Corinth. Additionally, Miss Thoresen has two young women with her who answered the ads and narrowly escaped being kidnapped when they arrived here in Denver."

O'Dell took a deep breath. "Finally, she is hiding an especially 'valuable' girl who escaped from the 'gentlemen's club' in Corinth—that said club is owned by *Dean Morgan*. You must have heard of him here in town. The gang of thugs that manages security for Morgan has been looking hard for that girl."

"They broke into and vandalized the lodge Miss Thoresen owns a few weeks ago. Although they didn't find the young lady, they now know with certainty that we helped two of 'their' girls escape from Corinth. Things are coming to a head, so Arnie's cousin is asking Pinkerton to provide security."

Bickle looked unblinking at O'Dell. "Could I have a word with you, Ed? In private?"

With a sinking feeling, O'Dell managed to answer affably, "Sure, Beau. Say, Arnie, would you mind waiting in the lobby for me?" He opened the door for Arnie and as he turned his back to Bickle, managed to whisper, "Watch out," before closing the door behind him.

"You know, Ed, I tried to be a friend when you were here last, tried to steer you away from trouble. Now I'm not sure how to handle you." Bickle managed to sound a little remorseful.

"McParland know you're on the take, Beau?" O'Dell kept his tone neutral even as he seethed inside.

"I told you. He's away, and Siringo retired last year. So I'm in charge."

"They paying you well?"

"Well enough. And it's not as though I'm breaking the law— they have enough cops and politicians on the take here for that. I'm just . . . overlooking a few things when they cross my desk."

"That explains a lot. Like how we could never intercept anyone at the mail boxes. Like that wild-goose chase you sent me on to Breezy Point."

Bickle nodded. "You need to understand, Ed. Denver is still a young city, a little wild and rough around the edges. Still sorting things out, so to speak. People make their fortunes in a town like this. Why, the convention this past summer brought 50,000 visitors to Denver, mostly men, many of whom needed some entertainment."

Bickle cocked his head to the side. "The question is, Ed, are you willing to make a little extra under the table? Or are you determined to make the biggest mistake of your life?"

O'Dell snorted in derision. "You need to ask?"

"Well, I'm sorry, I truly am, Ed." Bickle lifted the revolver he held from where he had held it under his desk. "Let's take a little walk, shall we?"

"You sure you want to do that?" Every finger of O'Dell's hands wanted to wrap themselves around Bickle's throat.

"Got to. Now let's move."

O'Dell turned around and Bickle placed the barrel of the gun in the middle of his lower back. "Just open the door and walk, Ed. And don't make a fuss."

They stepped through the door. O'Dell, keeping his head straight forward, still caught a glimpse of gray suit coat on his right as Arnie's arm came down on Bickle's head. O'Dell heard a satisfying crunch and Bickle sank to the floor. Arnie held an old-fashioned six-shooter by the barrel.

"You know how to use that?" O'Dell asked.

"Only as a club. It's not even loaded," Arnie replied ruefully.

O'Dell laughed and then snatched up Bickle's gun. The two of them hauled the felled Pinkerton man back into his office. O'Dell threw open a closet and they stuffed him inside, locking his office door behind them. They left quickly.

"We don't have much time. Need to get a wire off to Groman letting him know the situation. Then we need to get back on that train to Corinth before Bickle wakes up and alerts those in local law enforcement who are dirty."

Recognizing how outgunned they would be in Corinth, O'Dell put as much information into the messages as he could while still trying to keep the text cryptic. Wanting to ensure that someone tracked down McParland, he copied the wire to both the Omaha and the Chicago office. Then he and Arnie caught the afternoon D&RGW out of Union Station.

The household at the lodge gathered around to hear what O'Dell had to report. After Joy finished telling O'Dell and Arnie about Sheriff Wyndom and his nephew, O'Dell related his and Arnie's recent experiences, including the disturbing news about Bickle and the Denver Pinkerton office.

"I don't know how many agents—if any—besides Bickle are dirty. What we do know is that the crime bosses in Denver have very good cover politically and with the police. We got a wire off to the Omaha and Chicago offices and can expect them to begin cleaning house but . . ." he looked around the kitchen table. "It's not going to be fast and it's not going to be pretty."

That evening O'Dell stood hidden within the tree line watching and waiting. He did not hear the man approach until he spoke out of the shadows.

"Mr. O'Dell."

O'Dell recognized the voice immediately. "What are you doing here?" he hissed.

"Your office told me you were here. I couldn't stay away. You should know . . . I have to find her."

O'Dell sighed in frustration and defeat. "I told you that I might have a lead, nothing definite."

The man nodded and wiped his forehead with his left arm. His other arm hung uselessly by his side. "Can you tell me anything at all?"

O'Dell, knowing that things in Corinth were reaching a boiling point, was not pleased by the complication. "I may have found her . . ."

The man's excitement was palpable. "Can you point her out to me? If I saw her, it might help!"

O'Dell thought about the promise he'd made to Arnie. "Soon. I will arrange something, but it needs to wait a few days."

The man nodded again. "All right. Thank you."

"Look. You need to stay out of sight. Things may get rough here soon."

"I can do that. You can count on me."

Despite the man's lost memories, O'Dell couldn't remember knowing a man with more innate dignity. "I know I can, Branch."

He turned to face the man, but he had melted back into the shadows and was gone.

O'Dell sighed and went back to watching.

Chapter 70

Joy was dreaming.

In her dream she smelled smoke and she twisted away from it and from the memories that came flooding in with it. In her dream she came upon the ashes of their business in Omaha, and began choking on the wet, cloying haze rising from them. She saw Billy poking at them with a stick. He turned to her, shouting, but she could not make out the words.

She awoke to chaos. Billy was in the apartment shouting that the house was afire.

Her nightmare was real.

Blackie nearly tripped her as she pulled clothes about her and grabbed her shoes. She rushed to the door and then stopped, turned back, and grabbed the leather satchel on her desk. She raced down the stairs with Mei-Xing and Breona just ahead of her and stopped in a panic on the second floor.

Mama!

But O'Dell was hustling Rose out of her room and waving at Joy to keep moving. By the time they reached the bottom floor, the kitchen was filled with smoke. Billy already had Will, Marit, and the others out the back door.

Gasping and coughing, they ran around to the front of the lodge only to find the great room engulfed, burning like a pyre. The flames quickly ate their way through the seasoned beams into the second floor. Joy and the rest of the household backed away hopelessly as the heat from the flames increased. Joy already knew what would happen . . . the fire would race upward until it burst through the roof. Then the lodge, in a mighty inferno, would collapse on itself.

"Heard the windows break in the front," Billy was shouting to Arnie and O'Dell. "Got up and saw the drapes and walls already on fire."

"Likely someone tossed torches and jars of kerosene through the windows," O'Dell seethed.

Joy stared at her home—not only her home, but Breona's, Billy's, Marit's, and Mr. Wheatley's—watched helplessly as the home they had built together burned down. She carefully clutched the leather satchel she had carried away with her. Dear Lord! What if she had left it to burn!

She felt Rose's arms reach around her waist and Joy leaned into her for a long moment. Then she straightened and checked again that each person was present and safe. Mr. Wheatley held a blanket around Mei-Xing and thought to pull it over her head to somewhat hide her.

Joy suddenly blanched. Where was Blackie? He had been with her in her room . . . had he followed her outside?

"Blackie!" The flames had turned the night about the lodge into flickering day. She broke away from her mother and raced around the yard, feeling the first fingers of panic twist themselves on her heart. Not Blackie . . . not again—please Lord!

"Blackie! Come!"

Out of the gloomy depths of the trees near the road Joy saw a shadow move toward them. It stopped, just beyond the ring of light cast by the fire. A man. He stayed there, not moving, watching them . . . watching her. Under one arm a small shadow struggled.

"Blackie!" Joy screamed. The man raised his chin just a bit as though listening. And then he bent over and released the wriggling shadow. It raced toward Joy, breaking into the light, streaking toward her. Blackie!

She bent and he jumped into her arms. Joy squeezed him hard, crying in relief. She looked back toward the man in the shadows . . . he was studying her, his head slightly cocked as if he were thinking hard.

Then he moved his hand across his face, a gesture like brushing the hair out of his eyes. And something inside Joy leapt and then froze. She didn't know why, couldn't explain the sudden anxiety that filled her . . . but she could not draw a breath, could not move. And then her legs failed her and she fell to the ground.

"Joy!" O'Dell tried to help her to her feet but she had no strength. Her vision dimmed. Her mother and friends gathered around her while behind them the fire intensified.

Flinty arrived just then, his face a mask of worry and fear. He found them all together in the front of the lodge. "Thank the Lord!" he muttered over and over, even while mourning the loss of the house he had built for his bride so many years ago. "Thank the Lord!"

Joy was finally able to draw a breath and stand. Still shaking, she peered into the trees to see again the man who had been standing in the shadows with Blackie in his arms . . . no, not arms, but one arm only. His other arm had hung at his side . . . motionless?

She caught only the suggestion of a shadow fading into the tree line. And then along the road, near where the man had been watching, other figures emerged from the darkness and advanced toward them . . . a small group of men brandishing cudgels and clubs.

At their head marched Banner; near his side strode Darrow, slapping his club on his open hand in thirsty anticipation. The gang formed a threatening barrier that backed Joy and the rest against the burning lodge.

O'Dell withdrew his revolver and made sure Banner and his men saw it. He saw Arnie shielding Rose and Joy and spied the old six-shooter in his hand.

"You have bullets in that gun now?" O'Dell asked, half joking.

"Yup."

Near Banner Joy made out one of the Corinth town council men, Ernest Fletcher. Banner gestured to him and he stepped forward, glanced at a paper clutched in his hand, and cleared his throat.

"Joy Thoresen!" he shouted.

Arnie held her fast. Fletcher shouted her name again.

"What d'you want with her?" Arnie shouted back.

Fletcher peered behind Arnie and saw Joy. He pointed at her. "Joy Thoresen! I have a warrant for your arrest. Step forward to be taken into custody."

Joy gasped but Arnie clutched her arm tightly.

O'Dell growled fiercely. "On what charges?"

Fletcher consulted the paper he held and shouted back. "Arson. Endangering the property and disturbing the peace of the Town of Corinth. And attempted murder."

Rose moaned behind Joy and sagged against Arnie. In a spontaneous, protective gesture, the lodge's household encircled Joy. Arnie, O'Dell, and Billy formed an outer ring with the women toward the center. Mr. Wheatley handed Mei-Xing over to Breona and faced the mob with the other men.

The mood of Banner's men was turning ugly; the only things preventing them from forcibly taking Joy were O'Dell's revolver and Arnie's pistol. And then three of Banner's men revealed guns.

Joy saw the standoff and, in an instant of clarity, realized . . .

People I love will likely die this night if I do nothing.

Joy closed her eyes and prayed earnestly the words she had heard Emily whisper only weeks before, *God grant me the strength on that day to do what I must.*

Abruptly she shoved the satchel into her mama's arms, slid outside the protective circle, and began walking toward Banner. Behind her O'Dell cursed and called her back. She kept walking.

Banner sauntered toward her, an open smirk of satisfaction playing on his face. "I think you and I will finally have a meeting of the minds, Miss Thoresen," he gloated.

"You are behind all of this, Banner," she said loud enough to be heard over the roar of the flames. "*You* set this fire—and are only trying to place the blame on me. But everyone knows you're a liar. *And* a sadist. Tell me—do your men know that you enjoy abusing and violating *little girls?*"

Banner's face tightened. With no warning, he drove the end of his cudgel into Joy's side. She heard a faint crunching and then the pain engulfed her, bending her double and sending her to her knees, retching.

O'Dell and Arnie lunged toward her but Banner's men, guns out, blocked them. Banner dragged Joy up and signaled two of his men to take her. When she pulled against Banner, he slapped her face with an open palm.

Joy's head was ringing. She could hear O'Dell and Arnie shouting but was being dragged away.

And then someone fired a shot.

Oh God! She steeled herself for the chaos and killing to follow but instead a silence dropped on the scene. Sheriff Wyndom's voice boomed out of the darkness.

"All you men holding firearms . . . drop 'em. *Now.*"

For a moment no one moved. Then in the silence was heard the ominous click of a hammer locking into place. Pistols began to drop to the ground. O'Dell and Arnie held theirs on Banner until Wyndom's voice ordered, "You too, O'Dell. Thoresen."

Duane Wyndom and three men wearing deputy badges walked out of the shadows into the light of the burning house. Wyndom moved painfully with the aid of a crutch, but his gun hand was steady.

"Now drop the clubs. All of them."

He ordered two of the men to pick up the dropped weapons. He and Luke kept their guns trained on Banner and his gang.

Banner's eyes glittered with animosity. "Seems I underestimated you, Wyndom."

"Seems you did, Banner."

"See here, Sheriff," Fletcher remonstrated. "You have no business interfering in this arrest!"

"Wrong, Fletcher," Wyndom replied. "I am the law here. Arrests go through me."

"This is a duly sworn warrant!" Fletcher insisted. "And we have been appointed to serve it."

"Oh? By whom?" Wyndom demanded. "Mighty convenient you showin' up with an arson warrant and all . . . This place hasn't even stopped burning yet. Mighty *timely*, indeed."

Fletcher waffled for a moment. "Judge Morgan," he finally conceded.

"*Judge* Morgan? So he's a judge now?" Wyndom laughed harshly. "Even more interesting."

"The, er, council appointed him judge last evening," Fletcher answered.

"Even if the warrant is good, I would be the one to serve it. A judge has no legal standing to circumvent a standing law man."

"They, uh, that is *we* assumed, er—*believed*—you were, er, out of commission, Sheriff," Fletcher looked to Banner for help.

"You *assumed* wrong." Wyndom motioned with his gun. "Get moving."

"Where are we going?" Fletcher asked nervously.

"Town square. Now move along."

Chapter 71

News of the fire had wakened and turned out most of the town's citizenry. Those who rushed to the lodge to help fight the fire arrived too late but witnessed the tail-end of the confrontation between Banner's men, the lodge's residents, and the sheriff.

Joy could hear the bells of David Kalbørg's church pealing, and more townspeople were gathering as the two groups, Joy's household and Banner's gang of thugs, approached the little plaza. Reports that Wyndom was bringing them into town at gunpoint were stirring speculation and concern.

The band of refugees from the lodge was ill-dressed, disheveled, and smoke-stained. Rose and Arnie supported Joy as they marched ahead of Wyndom and his men. Her side stabbed her viciously with every breath and she feared her ribs were broken. She was worried, too, that Banner, Darrow, or one of their men would look closely at the blanket-clad figure huddled under Mr. Wheatley's wing. So far no one had recognized Mei-Xing. Billy carried little Will, Marit and Breona stayed close beside him, and O'Dell brought up the rear of their straggling troop.

Banner and his disarmed men grudgingly obeyed Wyndom's commands but glared with menace in his direction. In the grassy area of the town square, Wyndom stepped up onto the monument's pedestal where he could be seen. He was about to speak when the crowd to his left began to murmur and then parted.

Dean Morgan walked through the wide berth they gave him.

Joy had never laid eyes on the man but she had no doubt as to his identity. Everything about him spoke of the power he seemed to wield so effortlessly: the superior manner in which he held himself, the confidence of his demeanor, the exquisite cut of his suit. And the bodyguard whose icy manner cleared the way for his employer.

"Sheriff. Glad to see you up and about." Morgan smiled mildly. "Perhaps, though, you are a bit 'out of the loop,' on this issue. Mr. Fletcher?"

"I, uh, *did* tell the sheriff that we had a warrant and that you had authorized us to arrest Miss Thoresen." Fletcher swallowed hard. "He, uh, refused to allow us to take her into custody."

"I see. Hmm. Sheriff Wyndom, I must ask you to stand down and let this warrant be served."

Murmurs arose from the citizens gathered in the plaza. Most knew Joy. She saw David and Uli elbowing their way through the throng, saw their anxious faces looking for her and the others.

"Settle down, everyone, settle down." Fletcher was in his element now. The crowd in the town square quieted to hear what was next.

Obeying a nod from Morgan, Fletcher called loudly. "Joy Thoresen, I, uh, *we* arrest you for arson and . . . and . . . um, attempted murder." He hadn't read from his paper this time and fumbled his words, his delivery falling a bit flat.

Joy concentrated on breathing; for a moment the pain in her side was so intense she could not find the strength to inhale. She had to push aside everything else, even the sound of Marit sobbing softly behind her.

Concentrate, Joy, she ordered herself. *Do not falter now.* She grasped the satchel Rose still carried. She knew she had to respond perfectly—as a follower of Jesus, she could not take vengeance on this man. Whatever the consequences of this night, they had to be of his own making.

"Actually, Mr. Fletcher, I believe the people of Corinth should hear what I have to say. After that, perhaps they will arrest *Mr. Morgan*, and not me, for arson and attempted murder."

If the plaza had been quiet before this, it was now breathless. Not a soul made a sound. Except Morgan. He snorted in amused derision.

Fletcher glanced nervously at Morgan for direction. The stare Morgan turned on him, rather than embolden him, froze him in place.

Banner, backed by three of Morgan's men, moved toward Joy. "*Miss* Thoresen. No one is being arrested except you. And we will add the charge of public slander against Mr. Morgan to the other charges." He looked around, daring anyone to challenge him. "The good people of Corinth are witnesses to that slander."

Joy raised her voice and shouted. "I believe the good people of Corinth will want to know why their city's treasury and their personal investments have been wiped out."

The crowd in the plaza murmured and several men called out, "What is she talking about?" "What does that mean?"

Her friends and family watched her with wide, startled eyes. Breona was still and watchful, the way she always was when danger raised its head. Even Marit stopped weeping and stared at her open-mouthed.

Morgan flushed but controlled himself. "It means absolutely nothing, of course. I assure you, the city's funds and your investments are safely held by my company. This is merely more slander."

"Is it, Mr. Morgan?" Joy's voice echoed high and clear across the plaza. She closed her eyes briefly against the pain and then forced herself to stand taller.

"Why would I burn my own lodge? Even though it wasn't making a profit just yet, it was paid for. And it is . . . *was* my home. Why would I burn my own home? I am, however, well insured." She unsnapped the satchel and pulled out a document. "I hold my policy in my hand." She held it up for all to see.

"And that is likely your motive, Miss Thoresen," Morgan sneered. He called out to the sheriff, "Sheriff Wyndom, I demand that you do your duty and assist in taking this woman into custody. The issue of her insurance has no bearing on the charges against her."

"But it does." Joy lifted up the policy for all to see. "You should know that I am fully insured up to $100,000 against flood, wind, theft, vandalism, and *fire*. I am even insured," she paused momentarily, "Against arson. The arson coverage came into effect just eight days ago—April 15."

"I paid an exorbitant premium to *double indemnify* against arson. To be clear, I had to wait 90 days for the coverage to come into effect, but now that it has, I am insured for $200,000 in the case of arson."

The crowd gasped at the large amount.

She turned in a complete circle, holding up the policy, until she was again facing Morgan. "The company with whom I hold this policy is Liberty Indemnity out of Omaha."

Morgan looked like he was thinking hard. His brows pulled together into a dark line.

"You forget that I grew up in Nebraska, Mr. Morgan. You forget that I lived in Omaha, have family there—and have been burned out once before. I learned a bit about fire insurance through that experience. I also have . . . connections in Omaha and a community there that esteems me and knows I was once *wrongly* accused of arson. Liberty Indemnity was willing, even eager, to double indemnify my property against arson based on our . . . history."

She stared hard at Morgan. He had started to flush.

She called out to the crowd again, "Liberty Indemnity." She faced Morgan. "You are familiar with this company, are you not, Mr. Morgan?"

Joy's eyes locked on Morgan and then slid over to where Marit, Breona, and Mei-Xing were watching. The many months of work, worry, and prayer, most of her savings—and the futures of these young women God had allowed her to snatch from the snare of the enemy! All were on the line.

It all came down to this moment. Would her tremendous risk pay off or would she fail, and fail these women, her sisters?

She coughed and bit back a whimper as pain knifed through her side and into her lungs. Drawing another ragged breath she cried out, "Liberty Indemnity. A wholly owned subsidiary of Morgan Investment Holdings. Isn't that true, Mr. Morgan?"

Speculation and confusion rippled through the townspeople. A Corinth business man, Seth Ryan, called out, "I still don't understand! What does that mean?"

"What it means, Mr. Ryan, is this: *Liberty Indemnity* owes me $200,000. Where will that money come from? Liberty Indemnity had a very bad year last year, enabling Mr. Morgan here to pick it up at a bargain price."

"However, according to my very reliable sources in Omaha, Liberty Indemnity is still recovering—and will be unable to pay the claim on its own. Its parent company, *Morgan Investment Holdings*, is its banker, its guarantor. Is that correct, Mr. Morgan? It means Morgan Investment Holdings will pay me. Am I right, Mr. Morgan?"

"And I'm wondering—*as should you all*," Joy addressed the people standing in the dark around her and then faced Morgan again, "What impact my claim will have on your company, Mr. Morgan. · How will it affect the City of Corinth and the people standing here who have invested their life savings with Morgan Investment Holdings? Does your company have $200,000 in ready, available funds, Mr. Morgan?"

She turned her back on him and spoke to the crowd. "The answer is *no*. Morgan Investment Holdings does *not* have that money. How do I know this? I know because I have been having him investigated for the past four months. I know because I am a business woman. And I understand what he has been doing."

She walked slowly around the edge of the shocked and silent crowd, looking into every face. She knew that everything hung on her making them see and understand.

"I know that Mr. Morgan is *greedy*. He is sinking his fingers into as many pies as possible as quickly as possible—here and in Denver. Why? *Power*. He wants it—he craves it. In his drive for power he is overextended—operating on a very thin margin." She paused and said slowly, "In plain language, that means he is cash-poor."

A few heads were starting to nod.

"Liberty Indemnity cannot pay my claim, so its parent company, Morgan Investment Holdings, must pay. But in order to pay *my* claim, Morgan Investment Holdings will have to sell many of the investments and properties it has only recently purchased."

"*Your* investments. Corinth's investments."

She turned back to Morgan.

"It's not a good idea to sell what you have only recently bought, is it, Mr. Morgan? You would likely have to sell at a loss, and you would lose a significant amount of invested principal. Why, after you paid me, if the City of Corinth or these good people wanted their money, Morgan Investment Holdings would be broke. Wouldn't it, Mr. Morgan?"

Angry shouts erupted across the plaza as people began to comprehend.

Morgan shouted over them, "Calm down, calm down! This is utter fabrication on this woman's part. Your investments are perfectly safe with me—she is a liar and is attempting to bring down this town! Sheriff, put an end to this immediately!" Morgan spoke to Sheriff Wyndom but gestured to Banner's men and they advanced on Joy.

Sheriff Wyndom, though, pulled his gun and pointed it in the air. Its sharp report stopped the men in their tracks. The crowd again went silent.

"I am the law in this town. No one—and I mean *no one*—lays a hand on this woman."

He turned toward Morgan and spoke bluntly, "Morgan, I invested everything I have with you before I knew better. I want to hear the rest of what Miss Thoresen has to say."

Morgan started to speak, but Sheriff Wyndom waved him off with the pistol in his hand.

"Miss Thoresen," he called, "I think the people of Corinth want to hear this again. We might not be quite clear about what you are telling us."

A chorus of shouts affirmed him.

Joy, faintness creeping over her, struggled to gather her fuzzy thoughts. "It is very simple, really. I have an arson clause with Liberty Indemnity for $200,000. They can't pay. Mr. Morgan's company owns Liberty Indemnity. So his company owes me $200,000." She paused, her eyes wandering around the plaza, a shadow beginning to slide down on her vision.

Gathering herself with tremendous effort, she concluded, "The only way Morgan Investments doesn't go under, taking the city's and all of your money with it, is if *the arsonist*, the man who *ordered* my property torched, is found and convicted."

Unsteady on her feet now, Joy looked over to Morgan. "It's called *subrogation*. Liberty Indemnity could go after the *personal* assets of the arsonist to pay for the claim. You have bought quite a few properties in Denver recently, have you not, Mr. Morgan? Personal purchases. All cash. All free and clear?"

The collective eyes of Corinth turned on Dean Morgan. That single action told Joy all she needed to know. They knew in their hearts Morgan had burned her out. The tide was beginning to turn.

"But you should also know, good people of Corinth . . . this is not the first time Mr. Morgan has burned someone out. This is not the first time, is it, Mr. Morgan?"

"Or should I call you Mr. *Franklin*?"

Few people in the crowd understood the significance of that name, but for those few it brought great satisfaction. Arnie's grin was ferocious. He had never been prouder of Joy. Then O'Dell yanked on his sleeve.

"Watch out—they're making a break for it!"

Banner, Darrow, and a few of the more intelligent of Banner's men were sensing a sea change in the assembly of townsfolk. They were backing away, attempting to melt into the crowd.

But a further commotion outside the town square brought Banner and Darrow to a halt. The sounds of scuffling and fighting erupted on the other side of the crowd and then,

"Halt!"

Voices in the dark announced, "U.S. Marshals! And deputized agents of the Pinkerton Agency! We have this area surrounded. Don't anyone move!"

Joy wavered on her feet. Morgan, with an uncommon fury in his eyes, hissed, "We're not done, by God. I will make you wish you hadn't been born, *Mrs. Michaels!*"

He shouted some instructions in Chinese to his ever-present bodyguard, who launched himself toward the ragged group from the lodge. He grabbed Rose and, bending her neck unnaturally, held her that way, the threat obvious. He and Morgan began to back out of the crowd.

And then, standing small and alone between Morgan and his escape, was tiny Mei-Xing. She pulled the thin blanket away from her and let it drop to the ground. She stared at the man holding Rose.

"Su-Chong." Her words ached. Her tiny hands clutched at her heart. "Su-Chong Chen!"

Morgan's Chinese bodyguard stopped. He stared in disbelief. "Mei-Xing . . . ?"

"What are you waiting for?" Morgan roared. He stood as close to his bodyguard and Rose as he could, knowing that anyone who fired at him risked hitting the woman.

But Su-Chong could not move. "Mei-Xing! How? I went back to make it right with you, to leave my father's business and take you away to start a new life. *They said you were dead.* That you killed yourself."

Mei-Xing bowed her head slightly. "Your mother told you this?"

"I—yes. She showed me your note."

"Your mother has always been very clever, Su-Chong. And very vindictive. When I rejected you and then you left, she hated me."

"She would never hurt you!" But Mei-Xing could see that he did not believe his own words.

"She lied, Su-Chong. And you must ask yourself how I came to be here. Like this." Mei-Xing stared intently into his eyes, willing him to understand what she was telling him.

They stared at each other for a long moment until Mei-Xing gestured toward Rose. "This woman has loved me like a daughter. She has given me hope that I can live again . . . without shame. Please do not hurt her."

Su-Chong glanced down and saw the woman whose life he threatened. Rose gazed unblinking at him, pain in her eyes but also calmness.

Morgan grabbed him roughly. "Go! Get me out of here! Go, you fool!"

Instead, Su-Chong looked from Mei-Xing to Morgan wonderingly. "Is this woman the 'Little Plum Blossom'? Is *she* the woman who escaped from your high-class whorehouse?"

Su-Chong saw the truth on Morgan's face. He dropped Rose and grabbed Morgan by the throat. His fingers squeezed mercilessly and Morgan's eyes bulged—and then Mei-Xing's delicate fingers were touching his arm, her eyes begging him.

O'Dell, Groman, and Groman's men pulled Mei-Xing back and wrestled Su-Chong and Morgan to the ground. Su-Chong did not resist and he said nothing. He only stared sadly at Mei-Xing as they handcuffed him and Morgan and dragged them away.

Rose, rubbing her neck, drew close to Mei-Xing. They watched together as the marshals and the Pinkertons rounded up Banner's remaining men. Rose tentatively put a hand on Mei-Xing's shoulder and the girl collapsed in Rose's arms, sobbing.

Chapter 72

David Kalbørg stepped up onto the monument's base and addressed his town's citizens. "For too long I have been afraid to speak out about the evil practiced in this town. No more. Tonight the men who run this town burned my cousin's home. Those same men may have ruined some of you financially. And it would serve you well if they have. No man can be a friend of such unrighteousness and be a friend of God's."

"But those things pale in comparison to the wicked practices that are celebrated every night in *those two houses*." David pointed down the street toward the two mansions.

"Burn 'em!" one man shouted. "Burn them like they burned Miss Thoresen's place!"

"No!" David's voice roared above the crowd. Then he whispered, and the crowd quieted to catch his words. "That is not God's way."

He sighed deeply. "Our Lord said this: 'I have come to set the captives free.' Inside those houses are young girls and women, some of whom were kidnapped and forced into a degrading life. They are slaves. Let us tend to them."

He stepped down and then asked, "I am going to open the doors of those houses and take those girls out of there. Who will take them in?"

Rose stepped forward, her arm still around Mei-Xing. "Pastor, I have a suggestion. The lodge is gone, and we—" she pointed at the members of Joy's household, "are all refugees at the moment."

She turned to the people. "It will be daylight soon. Help us to clean those houses. Rid them of every wicked thing within their doors. Scrub the houses and their furnishings from top to bottom. We will move into the houses temporarily and speak to each woman about what she would like to do. If she has family, we can help to reunite her with them. If not, they may remain with us, or they are free to go."

Rose said more and others joined in, some asking questions. Joy heard the discussion and understood part of it, but her mind was no longer functioning well. She sagged onto a bench, the pain of just breathing more than she could bear. Breona, Marit, and Uli emerged from the shadows.

"Joy." She heard her cousin as though from a distance. "Joy, I'm to take you, Marit, and Will to our home. We need to see to your injuries."

Uli's face was somewhere in the haze in front of her. Trying to look at it made Joy dizzy and she closed her eyes against the nausea. "I can't climb up into the wagon, Uli. Hurts . . . to move." The shocks of the night's events coupled with the cold night air were taking their toll. Her teeth began to chatter.

"I'll take Marit and Will and then bring bandages to strap your ribs."

Breona sat on the bench next to her. "I'll be stayin' w' ye, miss." She scooted as close to Joy as she could and gently wrapped her arms about her, trying to warm her.

"Thank you, Breona," Joy managed. "Dear friend."

"Shhh now."

Joy leaned against Breona's sturdy little body. The girl was quiet a moment and then whispered softly, "'Tis home I'd be takin' ye . . . if . . ." She swallowed a little sob.

Joy knew what she meant. Their beautiful lodge, their happy home. The only real security and family Breona had ever known.

Ashes.

It was the sacrifice required to confront the hidden wickedness within Corinth. The sacrifice was a painful one.

"As long as you wish it, Breona, you will have a home with us," Joy whispered. "We'll begin again. We will move to Denver, and you will be with us. We can't do it without you."

Breona began to shake with silent sobs. Joy found her rough little hand and they wept together.

The bench they sat on faced east where a soft glow was slowly lightening the horizon. It would be daylight in an hour.

Breona had fallen into an exhausted sleep against Joy's shoulder. Joy heard the sound of a wagon approaching and then the murmur of voices coming near.

"That was quite an oration, Cousin," Arnie whispered near her ear. "Your closing arguments were top-notch. I might need to take you on as a partner."

Joy, her eyes still closed, managed to smile. Dear Arnie would be forever teasing her.

"Come on, we need to get you and Breona back to David and Uli's."

Joy felt Uli's warmth kneeling beside her. "Arnie and I are going to wind these bandages tightly about your chest, Joy. We don't want you to move until that is done."

Breona woke with a start and wiped her face. "I can be helpin', Miz Kalbørg." Working together, Uli and Breona strapped the winding cloths snuggly about Joy's broken ribs.

With a jolt Joy remembered. "Blackie!" A dull stab of pain accompanied her cry, but the strapping had eased it considerably. "Arnie, do you know where Blackie is?"

She could make out Arnie's doubt in the early morning light. "He was with us at the lodge before we walked here."

Arnie began to call for the pup. He ran along the storefronts whistling for him but returned without him.

"He will turn up, Joy," he reassured her.

Then Joy saw him. Not Blackie, but the man in the shadows. He stepped out from the trees near City Hall. Instinctively, Joy knew he held her puppy. And that same sense of . . . dread? wrapped icy fingers around her heart. Not dread for her dog, but something more momentous.

"Blackie! Come!"

The figure walked slowly toward them. Joy heard Blackie's happy yips answering her back, but it was the shadowy specter she stared at. Her heart pounded in her throat. What was it? She needed the man to come out of the dark; she needed to see his face.

Arnie came close to Joy and she heard a sharp gasp from him. The man was closer now. Joy could see his features, still indistinct in the pre-dawn, but becoming clearer.

He stopped several yards away, stood without speaking. Something . . . something was rising up in Joy that she could not explain, could not define. Something both awesome and terrifying! Oh why did this man not speak?

"Your dog's name is Blackie?" The man's first words were tentative. Puzzled. And that *something* inside of Joy thudded wildly in her chest. She could not breathe.

"Come closer, mister," Arnie invited. "You are welcome here." His invitation was gentle, encouraging.

The man hesitated. Arnie spoke to him again. "I think you once had a dog named Blackie."

The man's demeanor perked up. "I did! I . . . I think you are right." He buried his face in Blackie's fur and the puppy licked him.

"This isn't him, though, is it? Blackie was an old dog. *Good old dog.*"

Joy sobbed in unbelief and began stumbling toward the man. She had to look into his face!

And then Joy could see brown hair within the gray . . . curling about his face, a face scarred on one side as if it had been scraped raw . . . She stared, heart hammering, at the man who stared back at her.

"It's you," he said wonderingly. "I've been looking for you for ever so long . . . I . . ."

Rusty as it was, Joy knew that voice. And then she saw his eyes.

Such lovely hazel eyes.

"Grant!"

Postscript

Joy on This Mountain ends on a wonderful note, but it also leaves many unanswered questions—what becomes of Joy? Where does the work she has undertaken lead her and Rose? What of Jan's last words to Joy? And what becomes of Breona, Mei-Xing, Marit, Billy, O'Dell, and so many others?

I don't know what to say about these questions except that this book was not their story, but Joy's story—yet only up to this place and time. We may never know what happens afterwards . . . but I am believing that someday we will!

Vikki

Defeating Human Trafficking in This Generation

I know that we Americans feel that we ended human slavery in the 1800s. Unfortunately, slavery world-wide—and in America—continues. Today more than 27 million individuals are held in slavery and more than 10 percent of those (2.7 million) are victims of sex trafficking, mostly women and children.

The situations of sex trafficking presented in this book are fictitious. Sadly, the methods described are not. Young women, in particular those who have little opportunity in their own community, are lured by the offers of good jobs into forced prostitution. This happened here in America during the period of this book and *happens still*.

If you have a heart to help those who have been ensnared by human trafficking, please seek information and ways to combat this wickedness. Below are some helpful resources.

http://www.christinecaine.com/
http://www.thea21campaign.org/
http://www.caritas.org/Resources/Coatnet/Coatnet.html
http://wellspringinternational.org/projects/

Name Pronunciation Guide

Amalie	Ah´-ma-lee
Báibín	Baw-been (baby)
Fang-Hua	Faang Hwah (Fragrant Flower)
Jan	Yahn
Kjell	Chell
Mei-Xing	Mey-Shing (Beautiful Star)
Sigrün	Sig´-run
Søren	Soor-ren
Thoresen	Tor´-eh-sen
Uli	Yoo-lee

About the Author

Vikki Kestell is a writer and Bible teacher. She holds a Ph.D. in Organizational Learning and Instructional Technologies from the University of New Mexico and has more than 20 years of experience as a program manager and writing/communication professional in government, academia, semiconductor manufacturing, nonprofit organizations, and health care.

Dr. Kestell belongs to Tramway Community Church in Albuquerque, New Mexico, where she teaches an evening Bible study for working women. She and her husband Conrad Smith make their home in Albuquerque. Visit her website, **www.vikkikestell.com,** or on **Facebook** at www.facebook.com/TheWritingOfVikkiKestell.

Made in the USA
Lexington, KY
19 April 2013